W9-BQX-839

## TITLES BY BRENDA JOYCE

## NOVELLAS BY BRENDA JOYCE

AVAILABLE FROM
ST. MARTIN'S PAPERBACKS

# DEADLY
# CARESS

BRENDA JOYCE

St. Martin's Paperbacks

DEADLY CARESS

ISBN: 0-312-98943-1

Printed in the United States of America

St. Martin's Paperbacks edition / April 2003

St. Martin's Paperbacks are published by St. Martin's Press, 175 Fifth
Avenue, New York, NY 10010.

10 9 8 7 6 5 4 3 2 1

# CHAPTER ONE

FRANCESCA CAHILL PRIDED HERSELF on her common sense, her steady character, and her intellect. In fact, throughout the city she was considered a bluestocking and a reformer but also an eccentric. This was all much to her formidable mother's dismay. Mrs. Julia Van Wyck Cahill, one of society's leading matrons, wanted nothing more than to see her daughter successfully wed. Francesca, however, had other plans. Because recently, she had become rather infamous as the city's most successful amateur sleuth. It meant she often had quite a bit of explaining to do.

And today, Francesca had received the most stunning proposal of marriage from the city's most eligible (and most notorious) bachelor, Calder Hart. How happy Julia would be should she learn of his desire to marry her. Francesca was terrified of Julia and Hart conspiring against her. After all, not only did she have no wish to marry, but she was in love with another man.

Tomorrow she would call on Hart and set him straight. How she dreaded the encounter, knowing that it would be an unpleasant one.

If only she were fifty and fat, she thought, starting grimly from the salon. She promptly bumped into her father in the hall. "Papa?"

Andrew Cahill was a benign man in appearance, rather stout, of medium height, and to look at him one would never guess that he was one of the city's millionaires. He had made his fortune in meatpacking in Chicago, moving his family east when Francesca was a child—she was now a woman of twenty. Francesca was well aware that she was the apple of his eye, and not because her sister and brother were older than she was. While she did not take after Andrew in appearance, as she resembled Julia, being blond and blue-eyed, she resembled him in character. Andrew was an avid reformer, as politically and socially involved as any one of the Mellons or the Astors. There was only one man whom she admired more—Rick Bragg, the city's newly appointed police commissioner.

Now, distraught and worried, she prayed that her distress did not show, as her father knew her too well and would demand to know what was bothering her so. Worse, she sensed he was looking for her and he did not look pleased, oh no.

"You have a telephone call, Francesca. It is Rick Bragg," Andrew said without smiling, his tone grim.

She stiffened with surprise. It was late and hardly the time for a social call—worse, Bragg would be furious if he ever learned of Calder Hart's proposal. Calder Hart and Rick Bragg were half brothers—and theirs was a tense, uneasy relationship. She knew why her father sounded disapproving—Rick Bragg was a very unhappily married man. Her parents did not like their friendship. She thanked her father, changed direction, and hurried into the library, a room paneled in wood with stained-glass windows and beamed ceilings. The receiver was off the hook, on his desk. She lifted it to her ear. "Bragg?" She had to smile breathlessly, his image coming instantly to mind—handsome, golden, resolved.

He was one of the most charismatic men she had ever met and, more important, the most noble-minded. If anyone could reform the city's terribly corrupt police force, it was he. Unfortunately, the political pressure he was under now to do so was vast.

"There has been another act of vandalism, Francesca," he said without preamble.

She clutched the receiver, forgetting her personal dilemma instantly. Last week the studio of her friend Sarah Channing had been ravaged and nearly destroyed. The case had been temporarily shelved, however, as Sarah had not been hurt. "Not another art studio?" Francesca gasped.

"Yes, and it has been thoroughly destroyed, in a similar manner to Sarah's studio, but in a more extreme way. It gets worse," Bragg added tersely.

"How can it be worse?" she whispered, already sensing what was to come.

"The artist was a young woman, just a few years older than Sarah."

Her heart lurched. *"Was?"*

There was a pause. "She has been murdered," he said. "Francesca, I need you."

Francesca forgot to breathe. Her heart leaped with excitement and a thrill she knew too well. "Where are you?"

"At headquarters."

"I'll be right there," she said, and she hung up the telephone, stunned anew. A killer was on the loose—another case was at hand. But this time the artist had been murdered. Francesca was suddenly afraid. Sarah's life might very well be in danger, too.

Francesca rushed from the library, determined not to alert anyone to the fact that she was about to enter another criminal investigation—one with Bragg at her side. Her family was well aware of her sudden penchant for sleuthing, as she had been a feature in the press several times, unfortunately. Neither her mother nor her father approved. And while Francesca was rather adept at wrapping her father about her little finger, Julia was a formidable opponent indeed. Francesca wished to avoid her now at all costs, for otherwise she would never get out of the house at this hour, and there was no possible way she could bypass the scene of this terrible new crime.

As she hurried upstairs, past a hallway lined with several paintings, an image of Calder Hart reared itself in her mind—darkly handsome, dangerously arrogant. Even the sudden happenstance of a new crime could not quite keep her mind off the personal matters confronting her. And following his image came an equally compelling one of Bragg. She shivered. How had her life ever come to this impasse?

She hadn't meant to fall in love with him. But it had been impossible not to do so, with them working so closely together. And he despised his wife, who had left him four years ago, who roamed Europe while he paid her bills, collecting lovers. More dread filled Francesca. But Leigh Anne was no longer in Europe. She had returned to the city, and she had made her intentions clear. She wanted her marriage back—intact.

Francesca knew she must not dwell on Bragg and his wife now. She quickly rushed into the bedroom of a large guest suite where Maggie Kennedy's four children lay sleeping on two large beds. Maggie was a seamstress and Francesca had suggested that she and her family stay with the Cahills for a while, since Francesca's most recent case had put them in harm's way. Her eldest boy, Joel, was a cutpurse, but he had become indispensable to Francesca in her investigative work, as he knew the worst wards of the city intimately. She quickly roused him. "Joel!"

"Miz Cahill?" he murmured, brushing long black bangs out of his dark eyes.

"There has been another murder," Francesca whispered in his ear. "The commissioner just called. Meet me in the hall."

And Joel was instantly awake. Their gazes met. Then he nodded, leaping out of bed as Francesca quickly left. A few moments later, she and Joel, both bundled up in their heavy winter overcoats, were slipping from the kitchen's back door, so as to avoid the doorman in the front hall. Outside, the night was inky blue, with a million glittering stars—and it was frigidly cold. Snow-clad lawns encircled the mansion, and a graveled drive led to a pair of wrought-iron gates, closed now, which let out on Fifth Avenue. The gaslights there lit up not just the avenue itself but Central Park on its other side. Carriages and broughams crowded the street, with one black motorcar in its midst. But as it was a weekday night, the traffic was moving quite swiftly. Francesca had just seen a horse and hansom. "Let's run. There's a cab!" she cried.

Joel grinned at her as they raced up the slick, snow-covered driveway. "Looks like we're in business again," he said happily.

Francesca raised her hand. "Cabbie! Cabbie!" she cried. The driver of the hansom saw her, yanked hard on his horse's reins, the animal and cab veering abruptly toward the curb. The driver in the following carriage cursed, slamming on his brakes to avoid a collision, the two bays in the traces rearing in order to stop.

Panting, Francesca reached the hansom. "Yes, Joel, we most certainly are in business once again," she said, and smiled.

But it was a grim smile, as murder was always a deadly affair.

The murder had taken place at 202 East 10th Street, which was just off Third Avenue. As Francesca and Joel climbed down from the hansom, the El thundered by overhead. She winced, as the noise was deafening, the train even causing the street beneath her feet to shake. But once the Elevated had passed, leaving a cloud of thick smoke in the otherwise cool, clean air, she surveyed the scene.

The buildings lining 10th Street had once, in years gone by, been extremely fashionable single-family brick homes.

Francesca recognized their style as being Georgian—they had undoubtedly been constructed at the turn of the previous century. Three and four stories high, they had been converted into apartments. One gaslight illuminated the entire block, and poorly. Frozen snow, black with dirt and other refuse, covered the sidewalk. Patches of black ice gleamed here and there.

Several roundsmen in their blue serge uniforms, carrying heavy nightsticks and in their leather helmets, had congregated outside Number 202. A police wagon was parked there as well, and behind it was Bragg's snow-dusted black Daimler. Several ragged young boys had gathered about the Daimler, pointing at it, while ignoring the cold looks sent their way by the policemen. Francesca did not like the look of the boys—they were all young adolescents, on the verge of manhood, with sullen and calculating expressions. A very drunken old lady, carrying her beer in a bucket, was sitting on an adjacent door stoop, apparently engrossed in the evening's entertainment. Every now and then she cackled at the policemen; then she began muttering to herself.

"Mugheads," Joel growled beneath his breath.

Francesca had been about to cross over the short distance to the sidewalk; instead, she froze. "Joel?"

He shot her a look. "You seen 'em before. Looks like their turf been growin' a bit. Either that, or they're on the road."

Francesca glanced in the direction of the four boys, all bundled up in torn wool coats, with rags on their hands and dirty wool caps on their heads. "Yes, I have. Wasn't that on Avenue C and Fourth?" If she recalled correctly, she had been investigating the Cross Murders at the time.

"Dunno, but yeah, that's about the right hood," Joel said.

The gang was certainly out of its home turf. "Do they usually wander about so far from their usual location?" she asked.

"Not really. C'mon. Let's get outta here." Joel tugged on her hand.

Francesca realized that the four boys had seen them.

They were all still now, and staring at her and Joel as if they might be fresh meat for their dinner plates. She inhaled for courage, took Joel's arm, and they crossed to the sidewalk. The roundsmen stood between them and the Mugheads now.

"Excuse me, miss." An officer moved to bar their way. "There is a police investigation under way. No one is allowed inside, not unless you happen to live there."

Francesca smiled. "I am a personal friend of the commissioner. He has asked for my assistance on this case. Which apartment is he in?"

The officer, a young man hardly older than she, blinked. And then a very familiar face appeared behind him—a face dominated by beefy red cheeks and thick gray sideburns. Inspector Newman's eyes met hers. "Let her go in, Wallace. Good evening, Miss Cahill. C'mish is expecting you. He's in Apartment Seven."

"Good evening, Inspector," Francesca said with a slight professional smile. "Thank you. Come, Joel."

As she went past the wide-eyed Wallace, she heard him exclaim, "Hey, she's the lady who got the Cross Murderer!"

"That's right, and she works closely with the commissioner," Newman replied, respect in his tone.

Francesca could not help being pleased. But she had worked very hard to earn the respect of the few men who worked directly with Rick Bragg.

"Hey." A lanky youth who was almost six feet tall barred her way. His eyes were shockingly blue, and red hair curled out from under his wool cap. "What *business* could a lady have here?"

Francesca tensed with some fear but stiffened her spine and her shoulders. "I don't believe that is your affair. Please step aside." She could feel Joel bristling beside her.

"Just about anything that happens around here is my *affair*," the redheaded boy said, mimicking her genteel vowels.

"Bugger off, Reid," Joel growled.

Reid laughed. "Like you can tell me what to do?"

"Please," Francesca began, but it was too late. Joel stepped aggressively forward—a diminutive four-foot-ten and perhaps a hundred pounds—and Reid stuck out his foot. Joel went facedown in the dirty snow. Reid laughed raucously.

"That was uncalled for," Francesca said, trying to control her anger. And she looked the redheaded miscreant right in the eye.

"Oh, yeah? Well, get this. We ain't in no fancy ballroom, Miz Cahill," he spat with sudden anger. "You don't belong here. Go home."

He knew of her—somehow. Francesca reached down to help Joel up. She did not think this boy read the newspapers. So how did he know her name? "Let's go, Joel," she said, laying a restraining hand on his shoulder. She knew he wanted to attack the bigger boy. She had little doubt he would be quickly humiliated—and even hurt—should he try.

"You stay out of our way," Joel snarled.

Reid laughed again. "Isn't it past your bedtime, asswipe?"

Joel started for him. A knife appeared in Reid's hand. But at that exact same time, Francesca yanked Joel backward by the collar of his torn overcoat. "I would put that away, if I were you," she said softly. And, from the corner of her eye, she recognized the man who had just appeared on the doorstep of Number 202.

He was tall and broad-shouldered. The gaslight illuminated him, revealing sun-streaked hair, a bronzed complexion, and a tan greatcoat. He was handsome in an unusual way. Indian blood ran in his veins. And he was already striding purposefully toward them.

Her heart sped. She could not help smiling. They had agreed to remain friends, to fight the attraction that had formed, but dear God, could they really do so? Francesca had never fallen in love before. She knew she would never do so again.

Reid looked over his shoulder, saw Rick Bragg, and

tucked the knife away. Whistling for his three friends, he hurried across the street, weaving in and out of the several carriages passing by. Bragg paused beside Francesca and Joel, for one moment staring after Reid with hard, unwavering eyes. Then he turned to her and their gazes met and held.

And her heart skipped wildly. So much had happened and so quickly. . . . She did not ever want to hurt this man. She simply cared too much.

"Are you all right?" he asked, his amber gaze softening.

She smiled then, as always, no matter the circumstance she found herself in, glad to see him. In the course of four difficult and confusing investigations, he had become her best friend and perhaps even an anchor for her. "Of course. I am hardly afraid of one delinquent boy." The exaggeration was a slight one, but she so enjoyed seeing respect and admiration in Rick Bragg's eyes when he looked at her.

"He has a record a mile long. And he's fifteen going on sixteen, which makes him a young and dangerous man. When he was Joel's age, he was also a kid."

Francesca knew by now that *kid* meant a "child cutpurse." Before she could comment, Joel said, "He's mean an' smart. An' he buzzed molls. Still does, from time to time."

Francesca blinked. Bragg said, "He preys upon the ladies, Francesca, so watch your purse the next time he is about."

"I can take him," Joel declared, two bright spots marring his pale cheeks.

Bragg raised a brow. "He's twice your size, Kennedy. I'd think twice about such an act of folly if I were you."

Joel spat into the street, precariously close to Bragg's feet. Fortunately, the spittle missed his shiny polished shoes.

"Joel," Francesca said in reprimand.

"We got a murder to solve or what?" Joel said angrily. He slipped past Bragg and hurried toward the front door of the building.

Francesca and Bragg watched him. He was not willing to give up his hatred of anyone associated with the police.

But then, he had been in trouble with the police for most of his young life. He was a pickpocket with his own criminal record. She tugged on Bragg's sleeve. "You are so patient with him. Thank you."

"Do I have a choice? When my favorite sleuth has made him her assistant?" A smile was in his tone.

She smiled and he smiled back. And in that single moment, the past few hours—and weeks—disappeared. In that single instant, his terribly beautiful wife did not exist, and neither did Calder Hart, his dangerously provocative half brother. In that instant, the moment when Leigh Anne had faced Francesca and demanded she stay away from Bragg had never happened—as if she had not returned from her four-year absence in Europe in order to reclaim her marriage, as if she had not confronted Francesca to discourage her and Bragg's friendship and to warn her away. Leigh Anne had, in fact, shaken Francesca's confidence thoroughly. For she had insisted that she shared a bond with her husband that Francesca could never sever.

Francesca had to pinch herself to remind her that the past few hours, days, and weeks did exist, very much so. That Leigh Anne had returned to the city and that she was Bragg's legal spouse. That Calder Hart, in what had to be a moment of madness, had told her that he intended to marry her. She shivered, feeling very much as if she were wedged between a rock and a hard place. But at least now she was on familiar footing—a crime had been committed, she and Bragg had a case to solve, and once again they would be working together.

Bragg took her arm, guiding her across the icy street. "What happened?" she asked as they entered the building.

"I have spoken to one neighbor, Louis Bennett, in Number Five," Bragg said, pausing inside a pleasant entry hall with a single chair, a table on the wall, a mirror above that. A small chandelier light burned above their heads. Joel had plopped down on the chair, swinging his thin legs. "Number Five happens to be across the hall from Number Seven, where Melinda Neville was murdered. He had come in at half past seven, saw her door open, called out, and did not receive an answer. So he peeked inside. And then he saw the vandalism—and her body. He immediately ran outside and flagged down a roundsman."

So the victim's name was Melinda Neville. Francesca paused to study the heavy wood door they had just come through, which was painted a dark green. The lock was brass. It required a key. There was no dead bolt on the inside, for the obvious reason that too many people shared the house. "Is this door always locked?"

"Yes. But when Bennett came in, it was unlocked," Bragg said. "I don't think it is surprising that the murderer would flee without locking it behind him."

"Of course not. Did Bennett see or hear anything at all? Anybody?" she asked.

"No. But he is extremely upset now, and I suspect he went into shock when he realized that Miss Neville was dead," Bragg said quietly.

A wide staircase was just ahead of them. That was typical of Georgian homes. Bragg said, "There are three apartments downstairs and four on the next floor, three more above."

Francesca nodded and started for the stairs, Bragg joining her and Joel leaping up. "Perhaps our killer is a tenant here," she said.

"Perhaps. But there are ways to pick a lock, as you know. In fact, wait one moment. Joel?"

Joel faced him. "What?"

"Do me a favor, will you? See if you can open that door from the outside if I lock it from within."

Joel narrowed his gaze at him. "I ain't no bedchamber sneak," he finally said.

"I know you are no burglar," Bragg said, appearing very slightly annoyed. But then, it was growing late and it had been a very long day and he and the child had never quite come to friendly terms.

Joel turned and went outside. Bragg locked the door and glanced at Francesca. A moment passed, and then they heard something being inserted into the lock. Francesca tensed.

Joel picked at the lock from the outside without result for several minutes, and then they heard him run off. Francesca sighed and said, "I do not think he is quite done."

"Nor do I," Bragg said, his golden eyes on hers. They exchanged smiles. A moment later the lock clicked behind them and Joel pushed through the door, grinning in triumph. "Not so hard," he announced with glee and pride.

"Well done," Francesca applauded, ruffling his thick hair.

Joel pulled away, blushing and proud, and handed Bragg a set of keys.

Bragg looked at him. "And where did you get those?"

Joel laughed. "Took 'em right out of the pocket of Inspector Newman," he said.

Francesca bit her lip to suppress her laughter. "Shall we go up?" she asked.

Bragg nodded. Francesca led the way, Joel on her heels. Number Seven was on her right at the top of the stairs. The corridor there was about twenty feet long. A faded blue runner was on the floor, and a wall sconce was between the two pairs of apartments on each side of the hall. The lighting was dim even though it was electric. Number Four faced Number Seven. Bennett's apartment, Number Five, was adjacent to Number Four.

The door to Number Seven was open. Lights had been turned on within. A uniformed roundsman stood outside the door, clearly to keep any inquisitive civilians away, and he nodded at Bragg while glancing curiously at Francesca. Inside, another detective in plainclothes was on his knees, searching beneath a faded sofa for any possible clues.

Francesca smiled at the officer and stepped inside a small salon that had been turned into an artist's studio. Two windows on one side of the room, which overlooked 10th Street, undoubtedly provided wonderful light for the artist to work in. Instantly Francesca saw Miss Neville lying on her side, her face turned away, about midway across the room. And from this distance, Miss Neville appeared to be untouched. There was no blood, and one arm was out-flung. She could have been asleep.

But of course, she was not.

Francesca inhaled. She would never get used to death, much less a death that had been inflicted in violence and brutality upon an innocent human being.

She scanned the room, shivering, as it was cold within the flat. Miss Neville had two chairs and a low table facing the sofa at its opposite end, beyond where she now lay. She had clearly been using the sitting arrangement as her salon. Both of those chairs were overturned now, as was a vase of freshly cut flowers. Red roses lay scattered about the upside-down chairs.

Francesca turned to the closer side of the room. Facing the room's two windows a few feet from the door where Francesca stood was an easel, which was also upside-down and upon the floor. A canvas lay there, facedown, alongside a palette and a dozen variously sized brushes, all of which looked to have been thrown roughly down. Paint had been dumped and thrown, splashed and splattered, almost everywhere. The back of the canvas was dripping shades of blue, purple, red, and black, and similarly violent hues dotted the room's pale green walls, the sofa, the floor, and the once pleasant beige-and-red Oriental rug. Just beyond the seating area was an open doorway; inside was a small bedroom, as impossibly neat as the studio Francesca stood in was not. "Have you searched her bedroom?"

"Yes. I found a single unopened letter, dated a year ago, addressed to Miss Neville at a flat in Paris. It was from a Thomas Neville."

"Her husband?" Her eyes widened, as here was a distinct lead.

He had to smile. "He was her brother. I opened and read the letter. The return address is here in the city. My plan is to interview him first thing in the morning."

"Shall we meet at, say, nine?" Francesca asked quickly.

Bragg smiled. "He may not be there, Francesca. I hate for you to waste your time. Besides, don't you have classes tomorrow?"

Francesca was pursuing a higher education and she had

secretly enrolled at Barnard College last fall. "I will be at your office at nine," she said firmly. She had missed so many classes that another one would not matter.

"Good," he returned as swiftly.

Francesca could not help it then. It felt good to be at his side, working on another investigation, one that they must solve, as murder was now the name of the game. Her gaze returned to the scene of the brutal crime.

One canvas remained standing against another wall, a landscape done in watercolors, but angry splotches of red and black marred its otherwise tepid pastel-hued surface. Francesca did not find the landscape at all impressive, although it was well executed.

"How'd she get it?" Joel asked bluntly. "Ain't no blood."

"She was strangled," Bragg said.

Francesca inhaled, rather dreading the evaluation she must make of the victim. "So the killer must be a man."

"I would think so. I doubt another woman could have strangled her. There are numerous bruises on her throat and neck, indicating a very forceful grip."

Francesca nodded grimly. Miss Neville would wait another moment, as she was hardly going anywhere. Francesca turned to stare at one of the room's paint-splashed walls.

For upon it, not far from the upright watercolor, amid the splatters of dark paint, was a single letter, hastily painted there in black. The letter seemed to be a *B*.

Francesca started and faced Bragg. Their gazes locked. "Bragg? Did you notice that letter upon the wall?" As the wall had been marred with so much paint in so many dark and disturbing colors, the crude letter was not glaring or overly obvious.

"Yes."

Their gazes held. Her brother, Evan, had recently and reluctantly become engaged to Sarah Channing, an engagement planned by their families. Sarah was a rather shy young woman and not at all Evan's type of lady—Francesca knew he preferred beautiful, flamboyant women. Sarah was more than retiring; she did not care at all for society or its social whirl. In fact, she was a passionate and even brilliant artist. Less than a week ago, her art studio had been attacked in a shockingly similar manner. There were no suspects. One difference, however, between the instances of vandalism now and then was that there had been an incomplete letter painted in blood red on Sarah's wall. At the time, Francesca and Bragg had thought it might be an *F*.

"Bragg? What do you make of the letter *B* on the wall over there?"

He inhaled. "It is not painted in red, it is complete, and it is not an *F*."

They stared at each other. Finally Francesca said, "That is definitely a *B*."

"Yes, it is. We shall have to go back to Sarah's and see if the *F* we thought we saw was actually the beginnings of a capital *B*. This letter *B* is a capital." Sarah's studio had been left untouched since the vandalism, as the case remained an open one. Bragg strongly felt that crime scenes should remain untainted; he worried about his detectives missing clues on the first go-round. Francesca thought his investigative technique brilliantly original.

"What message does the vandal—the killer—intend?"

"I have no idea, Francesca," Bragg said softly. "Not yet."

Suddenly Francesca stilled—chilled. "We are a team now, and most of the city knows it."

"What are you getting at?"

"First an *F,* and now a *B,*" she murmured.

He understood and started. "You think the killer is toying with you and me?"

Francesca shrugged. "I don't know. How could I? We haven't even begun to investigate. But the notion did occur to me, unfortunately." And fortunately, she had quickly recovered her composure. For it was not a foregone conclusion that the letter *F* had been painted on Sarah Channing's wall.

"Well, I do hope you are wrong, because that would indicate a very maddened killer, Francesca."

Francesca nodded, but her senses all felt heightened now,

for this was what she did best, as she had so recently discovered. "Bragg? There is one more difference, obviously,
between the Neville and Channing Incidents."

And it was a huge difference indeed. Sarah had discovered the crime at five-fifteen in the morning and had lived
to speak of it. That is, she had not seen or encountered the
vandal, and there had not been a murder.

"Yes, as Sarah lives and Miss Neville does not," Bragg
said, clearly thinking in the same vein as she.

"Is Sarah in danger?" Francesca asked slowly, with
dread. She had become quite fond of Sarah since meeting
her.

Bragg hesitated. "I simply don't know, Francesca," he
finally said.

Francesca inhaled and faced Miss Neville again. There
was no more avoiding what she must do. But Bragg touched
her elbow, a gesture of restraint. She met his gaze. "I'm
fine."

"It isn't pleasant," he warned.

"Death is never pleasant." She walked slowly across the
room, avoiding the patches of paint, aware of Bragg following her.

Miss Neville's face was turned away from her, which was
fine. Francesca looked first at her gray suit. Splotches of
angry paint had been cast upon her, too. It made Francesca
angry, for she imagined the killer throwing paint upon his
dead victim. "He murdered her before he vandalized the
studio," she said.

"Not necessarily. She might have surprised him in his act
of destruction and become rather paint-splattered as a result."

Francesca simply did not think so. She felt that Miss
Neville had been dead when the murderer had begun to tar-
nish her with paint. And while the fitted suit was not a
custom-made one, it was of a good quality, and it indicated
that Miss Neville was a gentlewoman. Francesca glanced at
her shoes—they were black-and-white kid with fancy heels
and they had cost a few dollars. The petticoat frothing about

the unevenly turned hem of the gray skirt was French lace. Francesca was perplexed.

Miss Neville lived frugally, but she dressed well. In fact, there were two rings on the fingers of her outstretched hand, and one of them was a sapphire flanked by two small diamonds. She wore it on her left index finger—had she been engaged? Married?

The other ring was a simple silver band flecked with tiny red stones. Francesca assumed the stones to be garnets.

Francesca allowed her gaze to move up Miss Neville's still form—she had a very fine figure, a small waist and a voluptuous bosom—and finally to her neck. She saw marks that were turning black-and-blue upon her throat, both on the front of her neck and on the back. Whoever had done this, he had been a strong man, probably with large hands. Her gaze moved higher. Miss Neville's hair was a pretty, bright chestnut, although severely drawn back into a chignon. A dove gray hat was pinned to her head and the skin of her right cheek was fair and flawless.

Francesca walked around her to the other side, so Miss Neville was facing her now. She sank down to her knees, looked at her stunning and very familiar face—and she cried out.

"Francesca?" Bragg reached for her.

Francesca allowed him to pull her up, simply too stunned to speak.

"What is it?" Bragg demanded.

Francesca gulped down air. "That . . . she isn't Miss Neville . . . Bragg! That . . . she is Grace Conway!" Francesca stammered, still reeling.

"What?"

"Grace Conway . . . the actress . . . I met her once . . . Bragg! She is my brother's mistress!"

# CHAPTER TWO

BRAGG PULLED HER ASIDE. "That is Grace Conway?"

"I am certain!" Francesca cried, beginning to shake. Her mind sped and raced. Her brother, Evan, was handsome, charming, and, until recently, quite the catch. That is, until recently, he had been their father's sole male heir. But the other day he had been disowned, due to his refusal to go through with his engagement to Sarah Channing, whom he neither loved nor liked. He had been forced into the engagement in the first place, with Andrew refusing to pay his gambling debts otherwise. He and Andrew had had the worst row, with Evan announcing that he was quitting the company and moving out. Unfortunately, the next day he had been badly beaten in what he claimed to have been a barroom brawl.

Evan had been involved with the beautiful actress for some time, and Francesca had run into them once on Broadway. Miss Conway was not a woman one would ever forget. She was beautiful and she had a presence about her that drew all attention. This was, most definitely, her.

"This is Melinda Neville's apartment. Miss Conway has no personal papers or calling cards on her. Wait here, Francesca," Bragg said firmly, and he hadn't even finished speaking before he was through the flat's front door.

Francesca had to sit down, but there was nowhere to do so other than the sofa, and somehow the entire room felt terribly tainted now. She did not want to touch anything. How could this be happening?

"I seen her once, in Vaudeville!" Joel cried in a hushed whisper. "With me mom and Paddy and Matt. It is her, isn't it? God's arse! Someone done stiffed Grace Conway!"

It was hard to breathe. Poor Evan! Of course, he hadn't been that involved with Grace Conway in these last few weeks, as he had recently become rather smitten with Sarah's cousin the widowed countess Bartolla Benevente. Maybe Grace wasn't even his mistress anymore. Francesca hugged herself, and she couldn't help hoping their affair was over before Grace's death. And poor Miss Conway! She closed her eyes. First Sarah Channing, Evan's fiancée, and now his mistress.

Bragg returned with a big, burly man with heavy sideburns and a beard. He was middle-aged and extremely distressed. "Please, Mr. Bennett, this is extremely important. You must take a close look at the victim."

"I don't know if I can." Mr. Bennett was on the verge of tears.

"Of course you can," Bragg said gently, keeping a firm grip on the heavyset gentleman and leading him around to where Francesca had so recently been standing.

Bennett cried out, "Good God! That's not Miss Neville! That is our neighbor, Miss Conway! She lives across the hall in Number Four!" he exclaimed.

"Thank you," Bragg said gravely. "Do you have any idea of when Miss Neville will return?"

Bennett shook his head, his loose jowls flapping.

"You may go," Bragg said, and Bennett almost ran from the apartment as if he might be the killer's next target.

Francesca stood up. "Perhaps Miss Conway saw the door open, as did Mr. Bennett. Perhaps she surprised the assailant, who then murdered her."

"Those are my first thoughts, exactly." Bragg was grim. His face was hard. He was reflective now. "Your brother's fiancée had her studio vandalized a week ago. Yesterday your brother was in a serious brawl. How is he, by the way?"

"He is in pain, on laudanum, and in bed. He has a concussion, two broken ribs, a fractured wrist, and, as of last night, a black eye." Francesca was afraid. She knew where Bragg led. "First Miss Channing, then Evan's injuries, and now Miss Conway. Bragg, Evan does not brawl."

"He said he was in a barroom brawl, did he not?"

"I haven't been able to speak to him, but I don't believe it."

"I don't believe it, either, as his injuries are too vicious. As if someone intended to hurt him—or kill him."

Francesca sat back down again. She knew Evan had not been in a fistfight. He was not that kind of man. Someone had attacked him. She was even more afraid. "Somehow this is all connected, is it not? This must be about Evan—as he is the key here between Sarah and Miss Conway."

"I am beginning to think so," Bragg said.

"That would make the fact that Miss Conway was murdered in an artist's studio a coincidence. But how can it be coincidental to what happened to Sarah? The killer here has vandalized Miss Neville's studio exactly as he did Sarah's. And if Grace Conway surprised the assailant, then he did not intend to murder her and Evan is *not* involved."

"We must focus on the facts which we do have and not leap to possible conclusions," Bragg said firmly. "Fact: this studio was vandalized in the same manner as Miss Channing's studio. Fact two: Evan is the connection between Miss Conway and Sarah Channing." He became more thoughtful and added, "Fact three: Miss Neville is the artist here."

"Then this does not make any sense at all!" Francesca cried with real worry.

Bragg took her arm. "Since when has any case made sense until its very end?" he asked quietly.

She leaned against him, gazing up into his eyes. Being with him always gave her strength. In this case, as Evan might somehow be involved, it also gave her hope. And if she did not recover her composure, she would never help solve this case! "Evan owes a tremendous sum of money, Bragg. He is far too fond of gambling. The whole argument with my father began because of his debts, which Papa will no longer pay. In fact, Papa basically blackmailed Evan into his engagement."

"You have already told me, Francesca," Bragg said with a kind expression. "He owes a terrific sum, does he not? I can't help wondering if the so-called brawl was the act of a very angry creditor."

Francesca swallowed. "I have already wondered that myself." She inhaled hard. "I fear I must leap to possible conclusions! Perhaps there is some coincidence here. What if the brawl Evan has claimed to be in has nothing to do with Miss Conway's murder and the vandalism both here and at Sarah's? Perhaps an odd killer is on the loose, and after the city's female artists. If Miss Conway surprised him, her murder might have been unpremeditated and it might have nothing to do with my brother at all."

"If that is so, then Miss Neville was the target," Bragg said.

They stared at each other as the ramifications of this new development dawned upon them both. Bragg whirled. Francesca followed him to the door. The patrolman still stood outside it, but Newman was coming up the stairs, huffing and puffing as he did so. "Newman," Bragg snapped.

The chubby inspector hurried forward. "Sir?"

"The victim is the stage actress Grace Conway, a neighbor of Miss Neville's."

Newman's eyes widened. "I seen her once, at the Majes-

tic Theatre! She had the voice of an angel, she did, not to
mention the face—"

"We must find Miss Neville," Bragg cut him off. "It is
entirely possible that Miss Conway surprised the killer and
that he is after Miss Neville as we speak."

Newman nodded grimly. "I'll get right on it, sir. Maybe
she's at that Thomas Neville's place or he knows where she
is. I can take Hickey and try to speak with him tonight."

"I wish to interrogate him myself. We'll go together, but
after we look at Miss Conway's flat. Keep two men here,
however, in case Miss Neville returns. And if she does, under no circumstances may she be allowed to reside in her
apartment. Bring her to headquarters and notify me."

Newman nodded and took off.

Francesca started toward Grace Conway's apartment.
Bragg took her arm, detaining her. "Francesca, it's late," he
said firmly.

She stiffened with surprise. "I am searching Miss Conway's apartment with you—and going to interview Thomas
Neville as well."

"Your mother will strangle *me*," Bragg said.

That was probably true. Julia was not very pleased with
Rick Bragg. The fact that he and Francesca continued to be
so close and to work so closely together displeased Julia no
end. And even had Bragg not been married, she would have
minded their relationship, as she was determined that Francesca marry into a certain amount of wealth and position.
Civil servants had very modest incomes. Francesca found
Julia's matrimonial judgment appalling. "Mama is abed by
now. I doubt she has discovered my absence. I refuse to
leave now, Bragg, and that is that."

He smiled. "You remain the most stubborn woman I have
ever met," he said, too fondly. Then his smile vanished. "We
shall compromise. Let us search Miss Conway's flat, and
then I shall take you home. Tomorrow, first thing, I shall
update you on anything Thomas Neville has said." He took
her arm.

The gesture was now a painfully familiar and intimate

one. Francesca met his gaze, warmed by it. How right it felt to be working side by side in an active investigation once again. She quickly considered his advice, thinking about what might happen if she was met at the door by Julia when she got home. She smiled and then sighed. "Very well. You are right. And I can only pray that Miss Neville is at the address on the letters from Thomas Neville."

"I am hoping so as well." Their gazes met in an understanding of how much they needed this lead. "But the last letter was written last year. He may very well have moved."

He reached for the doorknob to Number Four. "Joel? We may need—" He stopped. The door swung open beneath his hand.

Francesca started, her gaze flying to his. Behind them, Joel said, "Looks like someone got here first, now don't it?"

Francesca hesitated while Bragg opened the door fully, revealing a dark room. He stepped inside, a gun appearing in his hand. Francesca followed him, drawing her own small derringer out of her purse. New tension filled her. It did not take a great stretch of imagination to think that maybe the killer was hiding in Grace Conway's flat.

Bragg crossed the room swiftly to the closest gas lamp, which he illuminated with a match. And a small, cheerful salon became instantly illuminated. Francesca looked past the wine-colored damask sofa, several green-and-burgundy-striped chairs, a dining table that seated six, and saw two adjoining rooms. One was a small kitchen; the other door was closed. It was obviously to Miss Conway's bedroom.

Bragg moved to the open doorway of the kitchen, glancing inside. He then went to the closed bedroom door, opening it. He stepped in, and Francesca saw the room flood with light. She relaxed as Bragg came back out. "It's empty," he said.

Francesca smiled and put away her pistol. She glanced curiously around. Grace Conway had certainly put some money into her furnishings—the fabrics on each chair and pillow had been chosen with care, the Persian carpet that she now stood on appeared to be expensive, and a very small ornate crystal chandelier was over the dining room table. A large silver candelabra was in its center.

Francesca found the apartment to be in extremely good taste. Had Evan paid for the furnishings? Had he paid for the flat? She felt ill then, dreading the moment when she must inform him of what had passed.

Bragg was rummaging through the drawers of an elegant secretaire, which sat in the far corner of the room adjacent to double-sized windows with stiff brocade draperies. He sat down at the desk.

She came over, unable to resist a curious glance into Miss Conway's bedroom and flushing as she espied a four-poster bed with a rose-and-white floral coverlet and matching canopy. "Your brother has been keeping this flat," Bragg said flatly.

Her heart sank. Then, "I am hardly surprised."

Bragg shifted in the chair, turning it to face her. "She has several love letters here."

"From Evan?"

"From Evan."

"Well, she was his mistress."

Bragg regarded her closely. "I do not want this in the newspapers, Francesca."

She bit her lip and found herself moving closer to him. "If Evan is involved, it is in a peripheral way. You know that." Her gaze held his, seeking comfort and reassurance.

"I do know that," he said softly. "But I also know that men have been getting rid of unwanted mistresses since the beginning of time. A reporter like Arthur Kurland would have a field day with this, and that is what worries me."

Francesca didn't move, and mere inches separated them. "I know," she whispered, in despair. "I have been haunted by what the public will say and think if this ever comes to light! So many know Evan does not care for Sarah at all! The world knows it was an arranged match. First Sarah's studio, now Miss Conway. It doesn't look good, does it?"

He stood swiftly, and before she could move, she was on her feet and loosely in his arms. "We both know your brother is not a madman, and we both know the only person he is enraged with is your father. We will keep this quiet, Francesca, to spare your brother any unpleasantness. I will meet you tomorrow at your house," he added.

Her skirts engulfed his legs. She gripped his arms. "Evan is not involved. We both know that!"

"We both know that he is not a murderer," he said quietly.

She stared into his solemn eyes. He would always be the most steadfast man she knew. In a hurricane of events, he would never fail her. She knew what he was thinking now, as she so often did. They knew Evan was not a killer, but others might not be convinced.

"You may tell Evan about Miss Conway, but do not interrogate him," Bragg added.

Suddenly she was bitter and she pulled away. "Is that what you shall do? Interrogate him?"

"Frankly, yes," he said. "I must operate under the assumption that somehow your brother is involved." And seeing her unhappy and grim expression, he added, "But if we are lucky, Miss Conway's murder will turn out to be a disturbing coincidence and nothing more."

Francesca stepped away from him, distressed and trying to remain composed. For the first time since she had become a sleuth, she wished she did not have a case to solve.

No, she corrected silently, she wished she did not have *this* case to solve.


They had reached the Cahill mansion, Number 810 Fifth Avenue, which lay between 61st and 62d Streets, just two blocks uptown from the Metropolitan Club. Bragg's Daimler purred in the drive in front of the house; Francesca sat shivering in the front seat beside him, tired now, as it was well after midnight, but certain she would never sleep. Joel was wedged in the small space behind their seats. It had taken less than fifteen minutes to motor uptown, as there was no traffic at this time of night. They had found no more clues at Miss Conway's, although she had kept a small box filled with cards, notes, and letters from her adoring fans. To search out and interview each and every fan would take years. And Bragg had sent two roundsmen to the Channing residence just in case their killer wished to strike again, just in case he meant for Sarah to be a mortal target.

Although it was very late and she had become exhausted, Francesca wanted a moment or two alone with him. Moments alone were now rare. Had his wife remained in Europe, that would not be the case. And even though they remained separated, Francesca was determined to do the right thing, which meant their relationship would be limited to the partnership that had been formed by circumstance as an investigative team.

She hadn't meant to fall in love with him. In fact, when they had met, she had not been aware of men in any romantic way and had thought the whole notion of searching for true love quite comical. She had been rather smug, in fact, watching other young ladies throw themselves at handsome eligible men. But then she had been struck by Cupid's unerring arrow, for she had fallen in love with Rick Bragg at first sight, even before they had engaged in an engrossing political debate. Francesca felt rather certain she wouldn't have been able to control her feelings even if she had known he had a wife. She had never before met a man like him. Not only was he handsome and intelligent; he was as passionate about social and political reform as she was. Until she had realized he was married, she had dreamed of having his children, of campaigning at his side for cause after cause, of sharing his life.

For Rick Bragg had a political destiny awaiting him. Before he had arrived in New York to take up his new appointment, he had been an impoverished lawyer in Washington, where his clients had been the poor, the falsely accused, the indigent, and the insane. There was talk now of how he would one day run for the Senate. It was his dream to carry on his reforms on a national scale. And it was Francesca's dream for him, as well.

Francesca knew she was the other woman, no matter how much he still despised his wife. As her sister had so bluntly pointed out, Francesca endangered his future, his reputation, his life. Leigh Anne had every right, while she, Francesca, had none. Francesca had decided that not only would she and Bragg remain strictly friends, but she would support him in his each and every quest. And no matter how hard it was, she would not interfere in his marriage. She would support it instead.

But it was so much easier to want to do the right thing than to actually give up one's dreams.

"What you waitin' fer?" Joel grumbled, interrupting her brooding. "It's colder than a bunch of stiffs back here!"

Francesca glanced at Joel. "Why don't you go inside? I will be in shortly."

"Oh. I get it. You lovebirds want to be alone." Joel snickered and climbed over the side of the car, starting for the house.

"Good night, Joel!" Bragg called after him.

Joel shrugged and disappeared into the house. Francesca steeled herself against any desire and faced Bragg.

He was studying her. His gaze drifted to her mouth. "It's almost as if fate keeps throwing us together," he finally said. He smiled a little then. "I never expected another case." As they both knew, it was not his job to investigate crimes. But when the crime was of personal interest or had a vast public effect, he had the habit of stepping into the fray.

"Of course it is fate which does so," Francesca said, believing it with all of her heart. But was it also fate to have him married and unavailable? What kind of master plan was that!

"You remain a romantic, hopeful and hopeless," he said with a smile.

"I am not as romantic as I once was," she said softly.

His smile vanished; Francesca wished she had not opened up Pandora's box. He studied her but did not reach for her hand, as he would have once done easily and without hesitation. "I am the one who has made you unhappy," he said quietly. "You were happy before we met."

"It isn't your fault!" she exclaimed. "Bragg, I feel quite certain that even if I had known about Leigh Anne when we met, I would have fallen in love with you anyway. Anyway, what does it matter now? Yes, I am not happy. Leigh Anne is here and she wants you back. And she has every right, which means you and I must be friends and nothing more. This is a huge adjustment to make for both of us, but we will, in time, succeed," she said, hoping she spoke the truth. His friendship was the most important thing to her now.

Instantly his face tightened. "I refuse to discuss her now."

She stiffened. His reaction to the mere mention of his wife hurt her now. It was always this way. The subject immediately made him angry. But then, he had hated Leigh Anne for years—for four years, to be exact. But he had been wildly in love with her up until the day she had walked out on him and their marriage.

He had turned his face away. Francesca stared at his profile, which she adored—he had a perfectly straight nose, a firm chin, and his eyebrows were darker than his tawny hair. The pang in her breast remained. Francesca no longer felt certain that it was only hatred that he felt for Leigh Anne. His emotions seemed very complicated when it came to his shockingly beautiful and oh-so-petite wife.

"You know how I feel and where I stand," he added darkly. But he now stared up at the stars overhead and not at her.

Francesca looked away, her hands clasped loosely in her lap. If only that were the case. She no longer knew with any certainty what his feelings were. She did not doubt that he loved her, but she also knew he still, oddly, even hatefully, loved his wife. And while he had declared that he would divorce her, Francesca refused to allow it, as it would destroy his political future, and that was far more important than their own personal happiness. She sighed, the sound heavy, staring away, into the night. "Working together will certainly be a test of our resolve," she murmured.

"Yes, it will. I am very tempted to hand this case over to my inspectors and stay out of it completely."

Francesca heard herself gasp—in real dismay. For if they did not have this—their wonderful teamwork, a partnership that had already brought four criminals to justice—then they had so little! "Bragg," she began.

He lifted a hand, forestalling her. His expression was resigned. "Your brother is involved, Francesca. Or so it seems. I cannot allow Newman and a few others to oversee this investigation. Because of my feelings for you." He stared, his golden eyes intense. "I do not want you hurt," he added softly.

That stopped her. She did not, could not, move. She was warmed from head to toe and deep inside—she knew he would always protect her, never mind that she could protect herself.

His gaze had drifted to her mouth. Francesca found herself tensing, even as her own regard automatically found his lips. He had awakened the real woman inside her with his kisses. She now knew what passion was—what it meant—how strong and compelling it was. A part of her yearned for one last kiss. But Leigh Anne had been in her own home, and she was a flesh-and-blood woman now. She was no longer the horrid wife who lived abroad—she was no longer an abstraction. Francesca simply could not become the other woman.

He did not remove his gaze from her face. It became searching. "What did Hart want earlier this evening? I know he called on you. You know I do not trust him! Or was it Julia who invited him over? Does she still think to match the two of you up?" He was grim and hard now.

Francesca forgot all about his wife. She stiffened in alarm—he must never learn that Hart had decided she was the woman he must eventually wed! The half brothers were rivals. Jealousy, enmity, and distrust ran deep, never mind that when their mother had died, Rathe Bragg had taken both boys into his home and his heart, as Calder's father had wanted nothing to do with him.

There was no mistaking the heat and jealousy behind Bragg's calm tone, now, and it glittered in his eyes. Francesca laid a hand on his forearm, which was strong and hard, even through his wool greatcoat. She realized that she was trembling. Leave it to Hart to once again overturn the boat! Everything that man did was unpredictable, shocking. She was grateful that his half brother was as dependable and reliable—and predictable—as he was not.

And it seemed like days ago that Hart had come calling, but it had only been earlier that evening. *Rick is right. My intentions are not platonic ones.*

Francesca had thought that he meant to seduce her—after all, he seduced every other attractive woman who crossed his path. *What?*

*I intend to marry you.* He gave her a strange look. *I intend to make you my wife.*

Francesca realized she was filled with a new and rigid tension now. It was hard to be reassuring when she herself was not reassured. "It doesn't matter what Julia wants, or what Hart wants." She forced her tone to be light just as she forced Hart's dark, sardonic image away—no easy task. "Remember? I gave my heart to you—forever." Her tone was odd and she cleared it. Hart now loomed between them as Leigh Anne had done so recently. "No matter what happens, Bragg, no matter what happens, even with Leigh Anne, you will always have my heart," she whispered, meaning her every word. "And I will support you in your quest for reform forever, Bragg. In whatever way I must."

Their gazes locked. Bragg finally tore his gaze away, gripping the steering wheel, his hands gloved. She felt certain that his knuckles were white. "You make this very difficult," he finally said. "I do not deserve such loyalty. Francesca, I have been thinking about you all night, even with the new murder on our hands. Until I have resolved my marital affairs, I will be the best friend that you have ever had, but I will not, ever, lose control as I did the other night."

His words somehow hurt. They signaled the end of romance and the beginning of a new road that they must somehow travel. She was very, very grateful that they had not consummated their love before Leigh Anne's arrival in the city—and his control had been far greater than her own. "It was my fault," she said truthfully. "I threw myself at you."

He did not rebut. "It is over with, and not too much harm was done," he said, glancing sidelong at her, as if he regretted the encounter, too.

And how could she not? She shifted uncomfortably. She felt guilty for that interlude, as well as ashamed. Calder Hart instantly intruded upon her thoughts again, his impossibly dark and handsome face mocking her, them. *There will not be any happy endings, my dear. You may trust me on that.*

Francesca certainly believed him now. But he had warned her for some time that the love she felt for his brother would soon blow up in her face. She had refused to heed his warnings.

*It is Bragg you want for a husband, but it is me that you want in your bed.*

She felt her cheeks' heat flame. She wished, desperately, that she could forget Hart's damnable words. And this was certainly not the time to recall that particularly arrogant statement.

"The last thing I wish for you to do is become martyr over my cause," Bragg said firmly, cutting into her dismal thoughts.

Francesca managed to jerk herself solidly back to the present. "I am hardly a martyr, Bragg." She rubbed her temples.

"Are you all right?" he asked quickly.

"I'm fine," she lied.

Francesca let him open her car door for her and assist her to her feet. They started slowly up the walk. At the door, he paused, finally taking her gloved hands in his. Her heart tightened.

"Francesca, my personal future is now hard to predict. I've said this before—I would never ask you to wait for me.

And I've said this before as well—stay away from Hart. He will break your heart if you do not."

Francesca stiffened impossibly, tugging free. "We are only friends," she said. "As I have said before, his friendship is very important to me, no matter how insufferable he can be."

"He is pursuing you," Bragg said, his eyes suddenly flashing. "It is so terribly obvious! And I know he would love nothing more than to steal you away from me."

"You are so wrong. That is the one thing he would never do, not out of malice or envy or lust," Francesca said. She knew Hart would never take his rivalry with Bragg so far. He would never use her to get at Bragg. Nor did she add, *I am not yours, so how can he steal me away?*

Bragg stared. "Anyone but Hart, Francesca. Should you come to me and tell me that you were in love with Mr. Wiley, I would give you my blessing."

"Would you?" she asked doubtfully, as he referred to a suitor foisted upon her once by her mother.

"Yes, I would. It would hurt terribly, but I would do my best to want what is right for you, as you have done in thinking that you should support my marriage in order to further my career."

She stared at him and he stared back. Finally she said, "I had better go in."

It was as if he hadn't heard her. "Anyone, Francesca, anyone but my selfish, no-good, disreputable brother."

She nodded brusquely and said good night.

# CHAPTER
# THREE

"MISS CAHILL! THIS IS a delightful surprise." Alfred beamed at her.

Francesca stood bundled up in her fur-lined cashmere coat, her hands in a muff, trembling. Her shivers had little to do with the cold. She had not been able to sleep at all last night, and not simply because of the predicament her brother might find himself in. She had worried about Evan's connection to Grace Conway's death and the vandalism of Sarah Channing's studio, but she had also been haunted by Calder Hart. His shocking marriage proposal kept replaying itself in her mind as she tossed and turned restlessly for hours on end. She had spent most of the night dreading the encounter now about to take place. Hart was opinionated and difficult. She intended to firmly let him down. She prayed, however, that the conversation she must now have with him would not become a confrontation, and hoped he would see the folly of his thinking and they would both wind up chuckling over the entire affair.

But nothing ever went the way one hoped with Calder Hart.

She managed to smile at his butler, Alfred, a slim, short bald man with merry yet respectful eyes. Here, at least, she had an ally. Most of what she knew about Hart's private life—like the fact that he at times dismissed the entire staff and would wander alone around his mansion, staring at his paintings and sculptures—she had gleaned from Alfred. What she liked the most about the Englishman, however, was not the fact that he had violated Hart's trust by revealing that kind of information to her, but the fact that he seemed genuinely fond and caring of his rather eccentric and often difficult employer. "Good morning," she began, rather grimly.

"Do come in; I can see you are freezing," Alfred said, ushering her swiftly inside and closing the door behind him. Hart's mansion—which was several times the size of her own home—was ten blocks uptown and also on Fifth Avenue. His property seemed to take up an entire block, as nothing else was built upon it other than his five-bedroom guest cottage, tennis courts and stables, and a very attractive gazebo. But then, he was very flamboyant with his wealth. Francesca knew it had to do with the fact that he had grown up on the Lower East Side with his half brother in extremely impoverished conditions, until their mother, Lily, had died. Now he flaunted his wealth, not caring what society thought. Calder Hart's father had not bothered to come to take in his own bastard son when Lily had died, but Rathe and Grace Bragg had come at Lily's dying request to take in both boys. How dramatically their lives had changed when the Braggs had arrived and the boys had moved from the run-down tenement in a crime-ridden neighborhood of the Bowery to the Georgian mansions of Washington, D.C., where Rathe had been in Grover Cleveland's administration. But Hart, being Hart, had run away six years later at the age of sixteen, apparently to look for his biological father. Francesca knew that had not gone well. He had then gone to Princeton for one year, only to drop out. Now he was the owner of several shipping companies and one insurance firm, not to mention one of the world's foremost collections of art. And he had achieved his wealth and success without any help from his foster family.

Francesca suspected most of Hart's current behavior—his lack of respect for societal norms and mores, his outspokenness, his womanizing—was molded by his troubled childhood.

Francesca followed Alfred through the huge entry hall, where artworks hung on the walls and sculptures lined them. She thought about the irony of the fact that every mother of a young lady Julia knew wished to ensnare Hart for her daughter, just as Julia did. He was the most eligible bachelor in the city, never mind his notoriety, his outspokenness, and the parade of lovers he was always on the town with. How green with envy those other mothers would now be. While Francesca had never been the target of his advances—he had always been the perfect gentleman around her, never mind his reputation—somehow this notion that he must marry her was far worse than a mere attempt at seduction. She was desperately afraid—and she was as afraid to comprehend why.

*He was the most dangerously attractive man she had ever met. He was wealthy, powerful, fascinating. But any woman who dared to love him would wind up in shreds.*

"Mr. Hart should be downstairs in a moment, Miss Cahill," Alfred said cheerfully, breaking into her desperate thoughts. Francesca knew her smile was a frozen one. In fact, she was beginning to perspire—which was the epitome of unladylike behavior. He led the way past an erotic sculpture of a beautiful young woman holding a pigeon. "He has been up since five, working in the library. Will you be staying for breakfast?"

Francesca was realizing that she was perspiring, a very unladylike action, as Alfred spoke. Breakfast? Who could eat at a time like this? She felt as if she had just been tossed by the Romans into the Colosseum where an underfed and savage lion did wait. She wished the encounter with Hart were over.

At that moment, Alfred paused beside the two wide open doors to the breakfast room and Francesca crashed into his back. "Oh! I am so sorry!" she cried, righting herself. Then her gaze veered past Alfred, and with dismay she saw an extremely familiar face at Hart's long and gleaming oak breakfast table. For one moment, as the man slowly rose to his feet—he had been sipping coffee—she thought with real dismay that it was Bragg.

And it was a Bragg, but not the police commissioner. It was his younger brother, Rourke, a medical student from Philadelphia.

"I shall tell Mr. Hart that you are here," Alfred said pleasantly.

As she wished to speak with Hart privately, this wouldn't work, oh no. Francesca felt a surge of sheer panic. She liked Rourke, but he was too astute and he had already seen too much. He sauntered toward her now as Alfred left before she could utter a protest. "Good morning," he said amiably, with a genuine smile. He looked almost exactly like his brother, except that his hair was browner than gold and his strong face was a bit squarer, his chin cleft.

"Hello, Rourke." She fidgeted nervously.

"Are you all right?" He eyed her closely, clad in a dark brown suit. "And it is awfully early for a social call, isn't it?"

She lifted her chin. "I have an urgent matter to discuss with your brother," she stated firmly.

"Do you ever rest, Francesca? You were nearly killed on your previous case. I would think you would sleep in this morning," Rourke said mildly.

"Your family makes it terribly difficult to lead a normal life," Francesca said tartly.

Rourke laughed. "I happen to agree with you. Come, do sit down. Coffee?"

But Francesca did not move. "No, thank you." Rapidly she shifted mental gears. "How is Sarah, Rourke?"

Rourke paused in the act of filling a porcelain coffee cup from the sideboard. "I had intended to call upon her a bit later in the morning," he said.

Rourke was in his third year in medical school in Philadelphia. He had come to town, joining his parents and sister and a few cousins, a few days ago. Sarah had been suffering greatly since the attack upon her studio, and Rourke had seen her through a fainting spell that had turned into a serious fever. That, however, was past. "I must call upon her, too. Will it be all right? Can I ask her a few questions?"

Rourke did not reply.

But Francesca had already become rigid. She didn't have to turn around to know that Calder Hart stood somewhere behind her. Her heart began a series of amazing somersaults.

He said, "This is a wonderful surprise," in that impossibly seductive murmur he so often adopted around her.

She slowly turned.

He leaned against one of the open doors, devastatingly dark and dangerously handsome. A slight pleased smile was on his face, but sheer speculation was reflected in his nearly black eyes. He was wearing only a crisp white shirt with his black trousers. While his shirtsleeves were down and sapphire cuff links winked from them, the top three buttons of his shirt were undone, revealing a deep hollow between his collarbones and some dark, interesting skin.

He was the same height as his half brother, Rick Bragg. But Hart was far more solidly built. Francesca had been in his arms several times, platonically, of course. He had the musculature of a weight lifter or a boxer.

"Yet oddly, I am not really surprised to see you this morning, Francesca," he said in the same bedroom murmur.

It instantly brought to mind images of him looming over her in a big brass bed. "Good morning," she chirped like a foolish and silly bird.

He flashed a grin at her. Then, not taking his gaze from her, not even for an instant, he said, "Good morning, Rourke," to his foster brother.

Rourke murmured a greeting but faced Francesca. "Can

it not wait?" he asked. "Sarah needs a few more days to rest. I prefer her not to become agitated."

It was so hard to look away from Hart's mesmerizing stare. Her heart was skipping uncontrollably, and her knees were betraying her, too, for they had become terribly weak. She somehow turned to Rourke. "There has been a murder," she managed. "I must speak with Sarah as soon as possible."

Rourke stiffened. "A murder? But how does this affect Miss Channing?" he demanded, eyes wide.

Hart spoke before she could answer. "No, the real question is, Francesca, how does this affect you?" he said grimly, gripping her elbow and turning her back around.

His touch made her breathless. But she had finally admitted to herself the other day that she was as fatally attracted to him as all women were—he had merely to enter a room to leave her undone. Now he was no longer in the same good humor as a moment ago. "I am sorry, Calder, but I did not dial up another murder for my own entertainment."

He stared into her eyes. Then, "Might I assume you wish a private conversation with me?"

She nodded, eagerly and in relief.

But Rourke gripped her hand now. "Francesca, how does the murder involve Sarah?"

She met his gaze and saw his concern. "A woman was murdered in an artist's studio, Rourke. And the killer destroyed her studio very much as he did Sarah's."

Rourke paled. "Is Sarah in danger?"

Francesca touched him. "I don't know. Last night, Bragg sent two roundsmen to the Channing home, as a precaution."

Rourke nodded grimly.

Hart purred, but not quite pleasantly, "After you, Francesca."

She darted a glance at him as she hurried past his tall, strong body and saw the heat smoldering in his eyes. But whether he was angry now because she had so quickly become involved in another case, or because he was astute enough to know that last night she had been with his half brother, she did not know. "The library?" she asked in the hall.

Instead of answering her, he crossed the front hall, pushed open the door to a huge salon the size of a poor man's entire flat, and waited for her to precede him in. Francesca did so, trying not to panic. She must stay calm or she would never succeed in letting Hart down. If only they were still discussing the case. There she was on firm ground, and he was a link to the inner sanctums of the city's art world. But she had not come to discuss the investigation with him, and there was no more avoiding what had to be done.

He closed one teak door behind them. "Is Sarah Channing in danger?"

She faced him, keeping twenty feet between them now. And she softened—he wasn't heartless, which she already knew, and moments like this proved it. Concern was reflected by his dark, intent eyes. "We really don't know."

His arms were folded over his broad chest. His biceps bulged against the soft but expensive white cotton of his shirt. *"We."*

"I meant that I hardly know, as the investigation has just begun! Hart, this is not why I have come."

"I know why you have come, my dear," he said flatly. "I have been expecting you, but not quite this early."

"You have?"

He launched himself off the door, approaching. His strides were long but coiled. Francesca stood her ground, no easy task. "So you and Rick are off on another investigation," he said softly—dangerously.

She nodded. "You know this is what I do."

"I know that. It is one of the many attributes you possess which make you so unique. How often do you wish to put yourself in danger—to face death?" He was openly angry now, as her life seemed to be constantly in danger these days. "What the hell is wrong with my brother?" he exclaimed. "His wife has returned and he still gallivants about with you!"

She stiffened. "He is my friend—just as you are. And nothing more!" she said hotly.

That halted him in his tracks. "Do not patronize me."

She bit her lip. "There is no other recourse, now."

"So that is your most recent conclusion?" His gaze was searching.

She had the sudden urge to cry. But she must not. "How could there be any other conclusion?" she whispered forlornly.

"Poor Francesca," he suddenly murmured, and before she knew it, he had taken another stride and was cupping her face in his two large hands. She stilled, but not on the inside. Inside, her heart beat madly, her breath escaped, her knees buckled, and her loins filled. Their gazes locked.

His eyes weren't really black. They were the darkest shade of brown imaginable, with navy blue flecks. "In a way, I am so sorry for you."

His kindness would make the tears fall. "Please, do not be kind now, Hart. Be anything but! Mock me!"

He smiled a little and his hands seemed to tighten on her face. Francesca felt her heart lurch with excitement, and she looked at his mouth, so close to her own. They had never kissed. Not even once. The most notorious womanizer in the city had chosen to treat her with the utmost respect. Now, finally, after all this time, he was going to kiss her!

Francesca could not wait.

Her body shifted toward him of its own volition. Her thighs touched his. Her breasts, encased in too many layers of clothing to count, brushed the cotton of his shirt. Her nipples pebbled and hurt. It became impossible to breathe, anticipation consuming her.

He stroked her cheek and released her. Then he walked oh-so-casually away, as if he had not felt the beast that had risen up yet again between them.

She could only stare, stunned. He had said he intended to marry her. What was wrong with him? Why hadn't he kissed her?

He turned, sitting on the thickly rolled arm of a gold

velvet sofa, looking impossibly relaxed. But he wasn't wearing a jacket, and his posture caused the fabric of his trousers to strain across his hips, and Francesca saw that he was aroused. Her heart thundered in response.

But why should she be surprised? He had said he wanted her. He had told her so to her face.

But he was so calm, so cool, so controlled. If he were Bragg, right now she would be in his arms and *on* that sofa.

"You are staring," he said softly.

She flushed and looked up, with guilt.

His smile was tender and amused. "I can think about you, my dear, and become excited. You should hardly be surprised."

"I . . . I'm not . . . exactly," she stammered. "Hart, how can you be so controlled?"

"Experience, I suppose. And then there is determination. I told you I will not ruin you, Francesca. The day I take you to bed is the day we are married." He smiled at her as if it were a foregone conclusion.

And her bubble burst. "Then it shall never happen," she said angrily.

He laughed at her. "Here we go! The moment I have so been waiting for. I shall enjoy this drama, I am certain."

She wanted to strike him. But she had done so once, and the consequences had not been pleasant. She clasped her own trembling hands so she would not do anything so foolish again. "That is why I have come this morning. I can't marry you, Hart. I can't marry anyone, not ever," she added in haste. And she meant it. She could not marry him because she was in love with Rick Bragg. Besides, the fatal attraction that she felt for him was hardly love.

His expression did not change. But he stood up, reminding her again of a lion, that is, a dangerous predator in no rush, one absolutely sure of attaining a hearty meal. "I see. You intend to martyr yourself upon my brother's marriage and political future?" Both brows lifted.

And Bragg had called her a martyr, too. "No!" she cried. "That is not it!"

"So now you lie. To me—or to yourself?" He started toward her.

She became still, even though she wanted to back away. "I am not lying to you."

"Yes, you are," he said softly, dangerously, slowly circling her now. "Because we both know you have decided that Rick is the one true love of your dreams. We both know Leigh Anne has come back and you cannot triumph over her." He circled her again. She didn't dare move. "If you did not know my brother, I do believe I would have you accepting an old-fashioned marriage proposal at my feet within a week."

"How arrogant! How insufferable!" she said, seething.

He grinned, pleased. "I do believe you are not the first woman to call me such. Darling, I do not want to fight." He circled her wrist with his hand.

She froze.

His grip on her wrist remained, but now he compromised it, and he lifted her hand to his lips. He kissed it.

That foolish little caress of his mouth made her go hot.

He lifted his eyes and his own gaze told her that he knew. "I never want to fight with you, my dear. I can think of far better ways to spend our time." His mouth curved.

He was thinking of taking her to bed. She just knew it. And he was mesmerizing—she had to blink hard and shake her head in order to break his spell. For now was not the time to have an image of herself in a wedding dress, being pushed down onto his bed. "I just can't," Francesca whispered breathlessly—desperately. "Please, Hart. And you are not a marrying man. You told me so! Several times, in fact!"

He let her go. "All rakes have their day."

She didn't believe him. "That is what Mama said."

"Julia is a fine, strong, and clever woman. I like her, by the way."

"Oh no," Francesca said, in more despair. She could see it now, Hart and Julia, allied against her. For Julia had made it clear that Hart was the suitor of her choice. "Why, Hart?

Why? I mean, there are those who will think you are doing this because . . ." She faltered.

He grew still and watchful. "Because?"

She wet her lips. "Because of Rick. Because you hate Rick and want to take away anything he wants or loves."

"You know better than that."

She was ashamed then. "Yes, I do. But I still do not understand!" she cried.

"I have grown exceedingly fond of our friendship, Francesca. I have grown exceedingly fond of you."

"But . . . that is not love," she finally returned.

He sighed. "If you expect me to fall on my knees and confess undying devotion . . . I will. But I do not believe in love, and that has not changed. I admire you. I want you. I enjoyed every single moment we have shared. Well"—he shook his head and almost laughed—"except for the ones when you turned some of my hair gray. I desire more of your friendship, more of your companionship. I desire you in my bed. Isn't that enough?"

She squared her shoulders. "No. It isn't enough, Calder, not at all."

"Impossible woman," he said fondly. "If I told you that I loved you, would it change your mind?"

She stared, undone. In fact, she was so shaken that she could not even think.

He sighed. "Francesca, the one thing I will never do is lie to you. I really do think *love* is a synonym for *lust*. I think it is a convenient justification, in today's society, to leap into bed with the person one desires. How many happy marriages are there? Name one," he added in a soft challenge.

Now she wanted to cry. But it had nothing to do with Rick Bragg and everything to do with Calder Hart. Her mind raced. "Mama and Papa are happy," she finally said, after a pause that might have been a full minute. She did not want to recall their vicious argument the other day, an argument during which her benevolent father had walked out on Julia.

They had been fighting over Evan's gambling debts and reluctance to marry Sarah Channing.

Hart raised a brow. "Sunday night, before dinner, you told me that they were at odds," he said.

She grimaced in more despair. "They are not fighting now. They love one another, Hart; they do."

He shrugged. "I prefer not to mold your thoughts. You are free to believe as you choose. I only expect that same graciousness from you."

She stared at him. "Of course I am free to think as I choose," she said, thinking about how her mother would argue that point, and then adding the concept of an entire society determining what one could, or should, and should not do. "I can't marry you. I am not marrying you. I am sorry, Hart, but that is my final answer."

He stared.

The urge to cry vanished. She tensed, not liking his far too speculative and watchful regard. "Hart?" She sensed he was about to pounce.

He began to smile. "Francesca, you may protest, rationalize, fantasize, until you are old and gray—I will not change my mind."

She stiffened even more. "Then we are at an impasse, you and I."

"I doubt it." He started toward her. She did not move. But he didn't touch her, instead, he paused beside her, close enough that she could smell his cologne, and breathed, "I always get what I want, my dear."

She was about to refute that, but he moved behind her and said, "Whether the object of my desire is a painting. . . ." And his breath feathered her nape. "Or a sculpture." He moved beside her. "Or a lucrative shipping contract." He paused in front of her, tucking a tendril of hair behind her ear, his fingers grazing her skin. "Or a woman," he finished.

She had become paralyzed. It was rather how she imagined it felt to be caught in a spider's sticky, fatal web. The terrible part was, she believed him. She knew this man could move a mountain should he decide to do so. "No, Hart. Not this time," she finally said.

He looked at her and stared, unsmiling, no longer amused, confident, and very, very intense.

She wet her lips. "Because if you insist upon this course of action, you shall lose our friendship." The words had popped out of their own accord.

His eyes widened. In that moment, as she saw the rush of anger, she knew she had gone too far. "You threaten *me?*" he demanded.

She leapt backward, away from any proximity with him. "No!"

"Oh ho, I know a threat when I hear one!" he cried, closing in on her.

She backed up, hit a chair, and fell into it.

He loomed over her and placed both hands on either arm, imprisoning her there. "Do not ever threaten me, Francesca," he warned.

"It wasn't a threat. But you are placing me in a terrible position!"

"And to think I thought you valued our friendship as much as I do," he said harshly.

And she saw the hurt in his eyes. "I do!" she cried desperately. "It was so foolish of me to say such a thing! Hart! I didn't mean it!" And it was she who now reached up to cup his face in her own hands. "Hart! I didn't mean it!"

He shook her off. "Never threaten me, my dear. And know this: I am a very willfull man. And I am also a very patient one. If you think it through, you will realize that we should do very well together—and that I am offering you a way out of the miserable mess you have made for yourself." He straightened and gestured at the door, a demand that she leave. "It has been an entertaining morning, but I am afraid I have a full agenda today. Good day, Francesca."

She somehow got to her feet, unaided. "Hart—" She hated ending their conversation this way. In fact, she simply could not. She needed to have him smile at her, even if it was smug, and call her "my dear."

"Good day." He was firm. "Alfred! Show Miss Cahill out." And after Alfred appeared, opening one of the two teak doors, Hart strode out with long, hard strides, the anger still etched upon his face, although it was fading now.

Francesca hugged herself. Why did they always come to odds? The answer was obvious. Because he was more than stubborn and he felt he was always right.

But she had stupidly threatened to end their friendship. How could she have said such a thing when she hadn't meant it? What if he remained so angry that he ended their friendship? Real fear paralyzed her then.

In such a short time, his friendship had become irresistible to her.

"Oh, dear. Miss Cahill, here." Alfred handed her a freshly laundered handkerchief.

Francesca took it and dabbed at her eyes. "He is so very angry with me," she whispered, and it struck her then how unbearable this impasse was. She needed Hart, as oddly as it seemed, as a dear and a staunch friend. But he clearly was not going to come around to her way of thinking. Dear God, he still intended to marry her. What should she do?

She closed her eyes. Marrying Hart would be like throwing oneself in front of a runaway locomotive. It would be suicide.

She looked at Alfred. "I think I must go after him," she said hoarsely.

"There, there, Miss Cahill, no harm has been done," Alfred said kindly.

"I am afraid you are wrong," Francesca said.

"Mr. Hart cannot stay angry with you for very long, Miss Cahill," Alfred returned, smiling as if he knew something she did not. "I do promise you that."

Francesca looked at him through rising tears, panic, and confusion. "He wants to marry me, Alfred."

"I know." Alfred beamed. "He told me so last night."

# CHAPTER
# FOUR

FRANCESCA HAD JUST HANDED off her coat and was about to dash down the hall, in order to then amble into the breakfast room as if she had just come downstairs for the first time that morning. But her father chose that moment to appear in the entry hall, carrying the *Herald*. His eyes widened with surprise when he saw her. "Francesca? Where have you been at this early hour?"

She looked at him with a bright smile, her mind racing. He would hardly believe her if she told him that she had been out for an early-morning stroll, as it was freezing outside. "Good morning, Papa," she said, noting that he looked tired and not at all like his usual self. "Is Evan awake? And how is he this morning?"

"You did not answer my question," Andrew said, coming forward. He was of medium height, a bit portly, but with a kind face and even kinder eyes. He did not appear to be the king of a meatpacking empire. However, he was the smartest man Francesca knew. His kind expression hid a razor-sharp mind, his easygoing attitude a character with determination and willpower.

Francesca sighed. "I had some personal business to attend to, Papa. Could we not leave it at that?"

Andrew reached her side. "Please do not tell me that you have been out and about this morning with Rick Bragg."

"No, I have not," she said honestly.

That softened him. "I am glad to hear it. Although I fear you are still carrying a torch for that man."

"Papa, you admire and respect him as much as I; he is your good friend. Would you truly blame me if he did keep a piece of my heart forever?" she asked simply.

He patted her arm. "No, I would not, not when you put it that way. But a piece of your heart is something we can all live with—it is something you can live with, too, in time. What other personal business could you have possibly had at this early hour?"

He disliked Calder Hart—he had said that he did not trust him and that he did not like his casual womanizing ways. Francesca smiled. "I am twenty, Papa. Surely I can keep some of my affairs to myself?"

He sighed, kissed her cheek, and said, "I am going down to the office, but only for an hour or two. Evan is up, and he seems a bit better this morning. Your mother is with him." Now worry was reflected in his eyes, and with it, Francesca saw guilt.

She hugged him, hard. She adored her father and she always would. "This is not your fault! The row you both had is not why Evan has been so badly injured! Do not blame yourself!"

He nodded at her grimly, clearly continuing to feel responsible for the plight his son was now in, and accepted his coat from a servant. "Have a good morning, Papa," Francesca offered.

"I shall try," he said.

She did not watch him go. She already knew that Bragg was not yet present, as neither a coach nor his motorcar was outside in the drive, and the doorman had not said he was waiting for her. Francesca hurried upstairs and to Evan's room.

His door was open. Maggie Kennedy was seated on the bed at his side, apparently reading the newspaper to him. The pretty seamstress, who remained at the Cahill home recuperating from a knife wound, had proven herself to be an angel of mercy where Evan was concerned. Francesca hesitated in surprise, for Julia was also present. She had pulled up a heavily upholstered chair and sat close by the bed.

Julia Van Wyck Cahill remained a beautiful woman, and Francesca had often been told that she looked so much like her mother. She had a small oval face, high cheekbones, a slim and pretty nose, and thick, waving blond hair. Francesca's complexion was tinged with gold and apricot and her hair was the color of rich honey, unlike the fairer complexions and lighter hair that her mother and sister shared. The Cahill women were universally acclaimed to be beauties. Francesca thought her mother and sister were great beauties, but she herself was too serious and too intellectual to ever be put in that category. She hardly minded. She had more important issues to deal with every day.

Julia never left her rooms before noon. Francesca knew that she got up around nine but took care of household affairs in the privacy of her suite before coming out. But Julia adored her son. Francesca doubted she had left his side all night. Now Maggie stopped reading and everyone glanced at Francesca.

"Good morning," she said, too brightly. Her gaze was on Evan, who was propped up against numerous pillows, the eye he had almost lost bandaged like a pirate's, the skin around the patch a vicious purple, green, and blue. His lower lip was cut and swollen, and his left wrist was in a cast. But he seemed to smile at her.

"Ow," he then said, scowling. "God, I cannot even grin!"

Julia stood, unsmiling. "Good morning, Francesca. Are you just getting up?"

At least her mother did not know that she had been out.

But she didn't want to lie now. "Mama, is everything all right?" she asked cautiously, noting now that in spite of her mother's perfect ensemble, a dark gray double-breasted suit in pebbled cheviot, trimmed with antique moiré and silk braid, she looked terrible indeed. Circles of fatigue marred her complexion, and grim lines had formed around her mouth, pulling it downward. Her Van Wyck blue eyes were hazy with worry and grief.

"I could not sleep. I tossed and turned all night. I checked on Evan a dozen times. But he is better today, thank God," Julia said.

Francesca went to her and took her into her arms. She held her as if she were the mother and Julia the child— something she had never done before. "It will be all right. Evan is on the mend," she said, glancing past her mother at Evan and Maggie.

Hurt and with a black patch over his left eye, Evan still was dashingly handsome. The pretty redhead was offering him a sip of water, holding it to his mouth while supporting his head with one hand. Evan smiled and then grimaced at her. "Thank you, Mrs. Kennedy. You really do not have to play nursemaid; I am quite fine this morning."

"Hush," she murmured, setting the glass down on his bedside table and standing. "You are not well yet." She smiled softly at him, but like Julia, her expression was filled with worry.

Evan gazed up at her. "You have been too kind. Do you always treat barroom brawlers so graciously?"

She smiled more naturally now. "Never, as I do not approve of fisticuffs, Mr. Cahill." She softened even more. "But you and your family have been nothing but kind to me and my children. It is the least that I can do."

Evan smiled again and then grunted in pain.

"I shall leave you all alone," Maggie said softly, and she swished past them in her little fitted navy suit, which she undoubtedly had made for herself. A mercerized lawn shirt-waist peeked out from behind her suit jacket, starkly white, and the color was wonderful on her. Since coming into the

Cahill home, Maggie had seemed to age in reverse until she looked her actual age, which was mid- to late twenties. When Francesca had first met her she had been so worn with the ordeal of her life that she could have been twenty or fifty—it had been impossible to tell.

Francesca wondered once again about her brother. He was a gentleman. Yes, he had kept an actress for a mistress, but he had not a lewd bone in his body—she knew he would never carry on with a housemaid. Maggie was hardly a housemaid, but she was a seamstress—during the day she worked at the Moe Levy Factory. Their social circles did not conjoin or overlap. It was as simple as that.

And currently Evan was smitten with Bartolla Benevente, a strikingly seductive and widowed countess.

But Maggie seemed rather drawn to Francesca's brother. She worried now. Evan was kind and charming, it was his nature, and maybe she had better advise him to be a bit more cautious in his responses to the pretty redhead. Francesca liked Maggie very much and did not want her casually hurt.

"Thank you for reading me the newspaper, Mrs. Kennedy!" Evan called softly after her.

Maggie paused at the door. "It was my pleasure, Mr. Cahill." She smiled at everyone, ducked her head, and left.

Julia now sat at Evan's hip. She took his right hand in her own but did not speak.

"I am fine, Mother," Evan said, smiling now without a grunt of pain in spite of his cut lower lip.

"You are not fine. And you are a gentleman who does not brawl, much less in saloons," Julia said flatly, with distress.

"I have made another grave mistake. Due, undoubtedly, to my fatally flawed character," Evan said.

"Evan, don't," Francesca said, knowing he mocked what Andrew seemed to think of him.

"Is that not what Father is saying?" Evan demanded with a flash of anger. "And all because I will no longer jump through his hoops and be his lackey."

"Evan, you must speak more respectfully of your father," Julia said, remaining distraught.

"I am sorry, Mother." He meant it and patted her hand.

"Your father has been up all night as well. We both regret everything! You must change your mind about leaving the house. I will make sure your engagement to Miss Channing is off."

"It is off, because I decided so," Evan said evenly. "Let's talk about this unpleasant subject another time."

Julia was still. "Surely you do not think to still move out?" she finally said, eyes wide.

"As soon as I am able. I am sorry, Mother, but this isn't simply about Sarah. It is about my entire life up-to-date. And it is about Father." He was firm.

And Francesca was so proud of him. She had never realized how difficult it had been to be Andrew's only son. She stepped forward. "Mama? Evan isn't going anywhere for some time, as he has quite a bit of recuperating to do. Might I speak with him privately? I haven't had the chance to do so since, the . . . er . . . brawl."

Julia nodded, tears shimmering in her eyes. Francesca went into shock, as her mother was the strongest woman she knew and simply did not cry. Instantly Francesca took her hands. "Everything will be fine!" she exclaimed.

"Will it? Andrew is still angry with me, Evan is leaving his house—and he is lucky to be alive. Connie and Neil remain at odds, with Connie dejected." Neil Montrose was a titled Englishman, whom Francesca's sister Connie had married four years ago. Recently he had been unfaithful, and Connie had learned of it. "And you are in love with a married man, never mind that his wife has returned to town to prevent a sordid affair! Will everything be all right, Francesca?" Julia demanded with some anger now.

Francesca could only stare in shock. She must never underestimate her mother again. Julia knew everything that went on in town—and in this house. Francesca finally said, "I am not having a sordid affair."

"Well, praise be for some common sense at last," Julia snapped, and she walked out.

Francesca did not move, and then she met Evan's unwavering and speculative stare. She turned and closed the bedroom door, then went swiftly to his side. She sat down on the bed. "Are you better today?"

"Much, actually. Through the haze of pain and laudanum, I heard Doctor Finney tell Mother yesterday that I am young and strong and that I'd be up on my feet in a few days. Yesterday I did not believe it, but today I rather think he might be right."

"I am glad," Francesca said, patting his hand.

He eyed her. "So you have given up your love affair with the commissioner?"

She sighed. "I love him. I always will. But it was the most terrible experience of my life to actually meet his wife, Evan. Until then, I think I didn't really believe she existed. When she was tucked away in Europe—where she had a number of lovers, I might add—she seemed so distant, almost unreal. But she is real. She exists. And not only is she terribly beautiful; she is determined to reclaim her marriage. I am filled with guilt for loving the man who is her husband. Yet I cannot change my feelings. But I can change my behavior, and I have. We will remain friends, but nothing more."

He took her hand. "I think you believe every word you have just spoken, but I know you, Fran. You are a creature of impulse, and sometimes, sadly, your judgment is lacking. I am worried about you."

She instantly recalled her suspicion, shared by Bragg, that an angry creditor had done this to Evan. And she also recalled the reason they must speak. "And I am worried about you. Evan? What really happened?"

He looked away. "I was drunk. I got into a fight. And that's the gist of it."

"You're lying."

His gaze slammed to hers with heat. "I don't like the accusation, Fran."

"I am your sister! I love you! I want to help, Evan. And I can. The one thing I am good at is helping others and you know it! Is this about the money you owe?"

Their gazes locked. He did not look away. "Yes."

"Oh, God." Francesca stood. She stared down at him in fright. "Did they mean to kill you?"

"No. He wants his money, Francesca. This was a warning." He was grim now.

Francesca stared. "Who, Evan? Who wants his money?" Evan looked away, clearly refusing to answer.

"And if you do not pay up?" Francesca had to know what might happen. She knew her brother's debt totaled almost $200,000.

"Then I suppose I will wind up far worse."

"Worse? How much worse could it get?" she cried.

He just looked at her now.

Of course it could get worse before he died—he could lose his legs, his arms, his mind. "Evan, we must go to Papa. He will pay off this brute! He would never allow you to remain in such danger."

"No."

"Evan!"

But her brother was furious now. "He dared to blackmail me into marrying Sarah Channing by refusing to pay my debts! I am finished with him, Francesca. I would rather die than beg the cash from him now."

"You fool! For if you continue on this course you will die!" she shouted.

"Keep your voice down," he advised.

Francesca stared. And she saw the resolution in his eyes. "You will not yield on this, will you?"

"No, Francesca. I am quitting the company, my engagement is over, and I am moving out. And I will find a way to raise something to begin to pay off LeFarge."

"LeFarge? That is his name?" she asked quickly.

He groaned. "Stay out of this, Francesca."

But she filed that bit of important information away.

"How much money do you need, right now, to stave off this man?"

"What?" He struggled to straighten as he sat.

"I will help you raise the money, Evan. And I promise you, I will not go to Papa."

He stared. "Fifty thousand would be a good gesture."

She had known the sum would be vast; still, she reeled. How on earth would she raise $50,000—and instantly? Who did she know who had such an amount of money on hand?

"I know. It is a vast sum." Evan was glum.

It was as if electric lightbulbs went off inside her brain. "Fran?"

She sat down. Calder Hart was extremely wealthy. In fact, he had written her a check for $5,000 for one of her charities without even thinking about it. But did she dare ask him to loan her such a sum?

When he refused to back down on the subject of their marriage?

She wet her lips. "I can get the money, Evan. I am certain."

He gazed at her, amazed, and then he shook his head, beginning to smile. He winced instead. "Ow! Only you, Fran, could pull such a rabbit out of your hat."

Her heart beat hard now in anticipation of the vast favor that she must ask. But other matters now demanded her attention. She stared at him, hating having to tell him about his mistress. But know he must, and there was simply no avoiding it.

"Why are you so grim? Fran . . . what is wrong?"

She inhaled and took his hand, clasping it hard. "Evan, something terrible has happened and there is no easy way to tell you."

She saw his mind race. He leaned forward, grimacing. "Bartolla?"

She now winced. "No, Bartolla is fine." So that was where his heart now lay. "There has been a murder, Evan," she said.

His eyes widened. "Not . . . Sarah?!" he cried.

"No, not Sarah. Although the murder took place in a studio that was vandalized very much as hers was."

He was confused. "I don't understand. I do not know another artist. How does this affect me?"

"Grace Conway was murdered. Evan, I am so sorry."

What little color Evan had drained from his face. Francesca held his hand and at first did not hear the knock on his bedroom door. He stared blindly at her. "How can this be?" he finally managed. And she saw tears rising up in his vivid blue eyes.

"Evan, we don't know. The investigation had only just begun," Francesca said gently.

He touched his head, looking away from her. "She was such a wonderful woman. She was full of life . . . and she was funny! Was . . . I can't believe I am saying *was*."

This time, Francesca started when the knock sounded on his door yet again. "I was in shock when I realized it was she," Francesca said hastily. She leaped up and rushed to the door, only to find her mother standing there with Bragg.

Julia was too polite to scowl; still Francesca recognized her grim reluctance now. Francesca's gaze met Bragg's. While she did not smile, her heart quickened with pleasure. "Good morning," she said. "I have just broken the news."

"Good morning," he returned, his gaze lingering upon her for one more moment before moving past her, to her brother.

"What news? What is going on that I do not know about?" Julia asked firmly.

Bragg turned to her. "As I said, I must speak with your son on official police business, Mrs. Cahill."

Julia stared with concern. "This is not about his injuries?"

"No, it is not. Grace Conway was found murdered yesterday evening."

Julia's expression did not change.

"Mama," Francesca said softly, taking her hand. "Miss Conway was Evan's mistress."

Julia started and jerked her palm from Francesca's grasp. "I hardly think so!"

Francesca exchanged a silent look with Bragg. From the bed, Evan said, "It is true. She was my mistress, Mother." His tone was hoarse.

Francesca gave up and ran to his side. "What can I get you?"

"Nothing." He clasped his chest with his right hand. "How this hurts. She was so full of life . . ." he trailed off. Then, angrily, "No one deserved to live more!"

Bragg faced Julia. "I'd like a few words alone with Evan, please. Perhaps he can be useful in this investigation," he said.

Julia finally nodded, wary now. "And Francesca?"

Before Bragg could reply, Francesca piped up briskly, "She was found in an artist's studio, Mama, one vandalized as Sarah's was. So you see, the cases seem to be connected. I am afraid I am working on Miss Conway's murder with the police."

Julia made a harsh sound, and Francesca did not like the look in her eye. It seemed to say, *Not for very long you're not.* Julia left the room, but not before saying, "I expect to be apprised of this terrible affair before you leave my home, Commissioner."

Bragg nodded.

When they were alone, he approached Evan. The tip of his nose had turned red. A tear stained his cheek. Bragg said, softly, "I am very sorry, Evan."

Evan glared at him. "I want to know who did this! And I want to know why!" he cried angrily.

"We intend to find the killer, Evan," Francesca interjected.

He glared at her now. "You should not be involved and you know it!"

"But I am involved," Francesca said quietly. "Because you are my brother and Sarah is my friend."

Evan stared, and then his gaze shot to Bragg. "Is Sarah in danger? And what do you mean, Gracie was found in an artist's studio? Was it Sarah's?"

"No," Bragg said, keeping his tone gentle. "She was

found in the apartment directly across the hall from her own, Number Seven, which belongs to Melinda Neville. Do you know Miss Neville, Evan?"

"No. But I have seen her about from time to time. Gracie was in Miss Neville's apartment when she was murdered? I did not even know Miss Neville was an artist," he said, in clear anguish. He suddenly covered his face with his hands.

"Apparently she was. As she has yet to return to her apartment, could you give us a description?" Bragg asked.

Francesca looked at him. "She hasn't returned?"

"No." They exchanged a significant glance.

"Did you locate Thomas Neville?" she then asked, after a moment of reflection.

"No. He vacated the address on the letter six months ago. However, I expect to have learned his forwarding address from the landlord, whom Detective Hickey is on his way to see even as we speak."

Francesca nodded. "I read his letter, Bragg. He was fairly ordinary. Apparently Miss Neville spent a year in Paris. He wished to know when she was coming home when he wrote it." She shrugged.

Bragg met her gaze. "I find it odd that she kept the letter and never read it."

Francesca was surprised. "The letter was sealed when you found it?"

He nodded.

"That's easy," Francesca said quickly. "She probably tossed it in the drawer of her bureau and forgot about it. Still, I cannot get a feeling of what their relationship was really like."

"I think he missed her." Bragg faced Evan. "Evan? A description of Miss Neville would be very helpful."

He let out a harsh breath and stared up at the ceiling. "She was small, boyish. A severe expression, short dark hair, big dark eyes. That is all I recall," he said woodenly.

"Can you think of anyone who might wish to harm either Miss Neville or Miss Conway?" Bragg asked.

"Absolutely not!" he cried. "I mean, I know nothing

about Miss Neville, but as for Gracie, those who knew her loved her! She was amusing—she made everyone laugh! After dinner she loved to sing—and everyone loved her to do so! And she was kind, Bragg. She did not have a mean bone in her body. Well," he amended, and stopped.

"Well what?" Francesca asked quickly.

"She was extremely upset with my engagement to Sarah, no matter how I explained that I did not love, like, or find Sarah in the least bit attractive. We fought a few times over that particular subject, but I really do not want to think about those times now." Tears filled his eyes. "I would rather think of all the good times we shared. We were together for almost a year and a half," he added.

"So you met when? And when did you begin keeping her?"

"We met the summer before last. I began keeping her right after the Fourth of July." He smiled, as if recalling a particularly pleasant memory. Then he looked at Bragg. "How in hell would Grace and Sarah be connected? I don't understand any of this," he said.

Francesca clasped his shoulder while Bragg said, "Unfortunately, you are the only connection here, thus far."

"What?" he gasped. And then he paled. "You are right. Two women close to me—well, Sarah was not close, but one would think so, in the light of our engagement. . . . Oh, God! Is this somehow my fault?"

"It is not your fault," Francesca said firmly.

He cast wild eyes at Bragg. "Did LeFarge do this? And if so, why . . . when he has already done this to me?"

"LeFarge?" Bragg asked. "Is this the man to whom you owe money?"

"Yes." He was grim and he fell silent.

"Do you wish to press charges?" Bragg asked.

"Absolutely not, for then I should undoubtedly wind up dead!" Evan exclaimed.

Bragg glanced at Francesca, who pleaded with him silently now to back off. She could not tell him that she was

going to Hart to borrow enough money to appease LeFarge.
He would be very angry indeed.

Bragg faced Evan. "Other than LeFarge, who are your
enemies?"

"I have no enemies," he said.

"Are you sure you cannot think of someone who might
be so angry with you that he would taunt you in this way—
by striking at those women dear to you?"

"No! Is that what you are thinking? That some madman
who hates me is striking at women I care for? For if that is
so, then Bartolla is in danger, as are Fran and Connie!" He
now paled.

Francesca faced Bragg. "Before Miss Conway was strangled, just after Sarah's studio was vandalized, I wondered
if the vandal were a young woman jilted by Evan and perhaps so maddened with jealousy and rage that she had struck
out at Sarah. But now that theory must be dismissed."

"I agree," Bragg said. "The killer is a man. I cannot
imagine a woman being able to strangle another woman,
Francesca. Not with the force and strength used to asphyx-
iate Miss Conway."

Evan cried out. He covered his face with his hands, his
shoulders shaking. A muffled sob escaped.

Francesca rushed to sit protectively beside him. She
looked at Bragg. "We are overtaxing him. He is injured and
in grief."

Bragg nodded. "We can continue this another time.
Hopefully something will occur to Evan, a name or face of
someone who was after Miss Conway, or someone who has
been loitering about her flat."

Evan did not respond. He lay back more deeply against
his pillows, dropping his hands. Tears stained his cheeks.
"You must find the bastard who did this!"

Francesca fussed with the pillows. "We will," she vowed.

"If only we had not fought so bitterly last week," he said
hoarsely, in more anguish.

Francesca stiffened with dread.

"You fought?" Bragg asked. "With Miss Conway?"

Evan nodded, clearly briefly at a loss for speech. Then he said, "The last time I saw her, she would not even speak to me."

Francesca wanted to tell him not to say anything else. She was getting a very bad feeling indeed. She leaned close, murmuring, "Evan. No."

But Bragg said, "What was the nature of your argument?"

Evan was grim. "I ended our affair. You see, I am rather taken with someone else, and it wasn't fair to Gracie to continue on as if nothing had changed, when I was no longer in love with her."

Francesca was in despair.

Bragg said, "And she was angry with the breakup?"

"Furious. She cried, she threw things, and she cried again. It was extremely difficult and unpleasant," he added.

Francesca could no longer stand it. "Don't say anything else!" she cried, leaping to her feet.

He blinked at her. "Why ever not? It's the truth, Fran!"

"Because someone might think you decided to get rid of your unwanted mistress, Evan!"

He understood and blanched.

Francesca faced Bragg with hands on her hips. "Which we both know he would never do," she said defensively.

"You and I do know that," Bragg said. "But the world does not."

"Bragg, Evan was attacked by LaFarge's thugs on Monday afternoon. Grace Conway was murdered Tuesday evening. So let the world leap to erroneous conclusions if it will!"

Bragg said slowly, "Actually, the coroner has stated that Miss Conway has been dead for some time."

At first she didn't understand. "What?"

"In case you did not notice, Miss Neville's apartment was frigidly cold."

For a moment she couldn't speak. Then, "When does he think Miss Conway was murdered?"

"Twenty-four to thirty-six hours before her body was found by Mr. Bennett."

Her mind raced. "Bennett found her at half past seven on Tuesday night."

"That's correct," Bragg said, and they stared at each other.

It was Evan who spoke up from the bed. "Which means I could have murdered her before I was attacked on Monday afternoon."

Bragg turned. "Yes. Miss Conway was apparently murdered sometime between Monday morning and Monday night."

# CHAPTER FIVE

THERE HAD BEEN A time when it had been easy to get up in the morning, to bathe, eat a slice of toast, take some tea, dress. It felt like it had been years ago, the life of another, different woman. Now, her morning routine had become a vast, tiring chore, one difficult to accomplish and complete. As Connie started downstairs in the home that had been a wedding present from her father, she was stunned to realize that it had only been a month ago that she had been a happily married woman. Now, the hurt she carried with her night and day continued to weigh her down and remind her that she should have never trusted Neil.

He was the last person she would have ever dreamed would hurt her.

Neil. His handsome face filled her mind, but his turquoise eyes were accusing. Panicked, she shoved his image aside. He was the traitor to their marriage, he was the one who had lied and committed adultery, and she was the one suffering now.

Connie did not know what to do. Other women would look graciously the other way, pretend all was well, and continue on as if nothing dire had happened. That was her mother's advice. Connie knew she must continue on, somehow, yet she knew she simply wasn't strong enough to do so. And that left her in a terrible dilemma, because *divorce* was simply not a part of her vocabulary.

She continued downstairs, clad in a dusky blue skirt that she had never liked, clasping the smooth wood banister. Their home was a magnificent one, just around the block from her parents' mansion, on Madison Avenue and 62d Street. It had four stories, vaulted ceilings, marble fireplaces, and two guest suites. It had been built during the year of their engagement, an engagement that had happened within weeks of their first meeting and Neil's whirlwind courtship. Connie no longer knew what to think of her memories. Once, she had treasured each and every one. Once, she had known that Neil had fallen in love with her just as she had with him. Now, she wondered. Their marriage was a typical one; he was an impoverished British lord, she a wealthy American heiress. Perhaps he had never loved her at all. Perhaps he had married her for her money and she had been so foolish as to think his gallantry was love.

Connie brushed several tears aside as she crossed the ground floor. She felt fairly certain that she had a luncheon that day, but she intended to cancel it. She knew she must continue on with her girlfriends and the wives of Neil's associates—she knew it as surely as if Julia had insisted she do so. But how could she? The whole city knew of Neil's affair. She simply could not smile over grilled sea bass at the Hotel Astor, and pretend that nothing was wrong. And she was tired of the almost gleeful looks on the other ladies' faces. Fran had once told Connie that her marriage was the envy of society; she had already known that quite a few of her friends adored her husband. She knew that if, God forbid, anything had ever happened to her, Neil would not remain a bachelor for long.

She heard the girls then. Charlotte was laughing and Lucinda was howling in protest. Connie smiled. Her heart warmed. And for one moment, as she listened to the girls, she forgot about Neil, and the pain of his betrayal faded; for one instant, she was Connie Cahill Montrose again, a vibrant, beautiful happy woman with a perfect husband, a perfect marriage, a perfect life.

Connie hurried into the family room, a small, cozy parlor where she often read to the girls while Neil listened and browsed through a newspaper.

Her two daughters, the one three and precocious, the other just eight months old, were both on the floor. Charlotte was playing with her dolls and mercilessly teasing the howling Lucinda. Mrs. Partridge, their nanny, was scolding Charlotte, but she was ignoring the tall governess. She was as stubborn as her Aunt Fran.

"Charlotte, that isn't fair," Connie said swiftly, hurrying forward. "You must share your dolls with your sister." She knelt beside them both.

Charlotte leaped up to wrap her arms tightly around Connie's neck. "Mommy, Mommy! Mommy, Mommy!" she cried.

Connie hugged her back and thought, aghast, *Dear God, in my grief I have been neglecting my daughters!* It was one thing to cancel luncheons and teas, to beg off evening affairs, to avoid her husband, and quite another to have become careless with her own children, whom she treasured more than life itself. "Darling, you are squeezing every drop of air from my lungs; I can hardly breathe," she said gently.

Charlotte released her. "How beautiful you look!" she cried, as if surprised. "How pretty your dress is! Mommy, you aren't sick anymore? Daddy said you were sick. He said we must allow you to sleep, that we must be very quiet. That we mustn't disturb you!"

Connie bit her lip, filled with guilt and moved to tears. The pain returned—she could imagine Neil softly telling the girls how to behave for their mother's sake. He would have Charlotte on his lap, explaining very seriously what she must and must not do. Then he would address Lucinda as if she understood his every word, which of course she did not. But Lucinda would have gurgled happily anyway. Both girls adored their father.

How had it come to this? Their life had been so perfect, once!

"Mommy? Don't cry," Charlotte whispered, tugging at her skirts.

Connie sat fully down on the floor, Charlotte crawling quickly onto her lap. "Darling, I am not crying; I merely have dust in my eye." She smiled brightly. "What shall we do today, sweetheart?"

"Will you take us to the park, then? Or can we go shopping? Can you buy me a new doll? Or a bonnet with a red ribbon?" Charlotte asked eagerly.

Connie laughed and it felt good. Although Charlotte resembled Connie exactly, with her perfect oval face, fine features, and bright blue eyes, and she was platinum blond, a shade or two lighter than her mother, she was so much like Francesca in character. Charlotte's nature was a demanding and curious one. It had never ceased to amaze Connie that she had such a bold and clever daughter.

"I will take both of you shopping," Connie decided, as it was too cold to play in the park. The idea of dressing up the girls and taking them to Lord & Taylor became distinctly appealing. However, the evening that loomed ahead worried her—they always had plans; they always went out. Recently Connie had been begging off with a migraine. "Mrs. Partridge? Do you have any idea what plans my husband has made for this evening?"

"I think he said something about a birthday ball," the nanny responded, smiling at her. And Connie realized she saw relief in the governess's eyes.

Connie stood, dismayed. A ball was an endless affair. She did not want to go—she had no intention of going—Neil could attend without her. He had been attending most functions these days alone. The birthday must be Letitia Hardwick's. Letitia was a good friend, and once upon a time Connie had adored balls. Now she paused. Letitia was a very sultry brunette who frankly admired Neil. She had told Connie many times how lucky she was to be married to such a man. Letitia's husband was older, unattractive, and severe. Connie was suddenly afraid.

She was afraid that Letitia would try to seduce Neil behind her back.

She told herself not to be absurd. Letitia was her friend. On the other hand, her only real friend was Fran, and Connie suspected but did not know for a fact that Letitia already had had several affairs.

"Connie," Neil said from behind her, surprise in his tone.

She stiffened. All of the joy she had been feeling vanished. There was dread and dismay, but there was also hope.

She turned and intended to smile, but her frozen facial muscles would not respond. Yet her heart quickened treacherously. She would always find him handsome. No one was more attractive than he.

But he was not noble. He had only pretended to be.

Neil was smiling at her, but his expression was strained and there was worry and anxiety in his gaze. "You look wonderful," he said.

"Good morning," Connie said evenly. "I hadn't realized you were home."

Disappointment covered his features. She stiffened, because she knew him so well and she knew her cold manner was hurting him. But this was what he deserved. Wasn't it? "This is a wonderful surprise," he said huskily. "How glad I am to see you. Are you feeling better?" he asked. He had shoved his hands in the pockets of his dark trousers, as if he did not know what to do with them.

"Actually, I do feel better." She smiled grimly, fortifying herself against him.

"That is wonderful," he said, clearly meaning it. He smiled at her, but uncertainly. "Did you have breakfast yet? Can I order you some toast and tea?"

"I'm not hungry," Connie said flatly. And she looked her husband in the eye, daring him to dispute her.

A silence fell.

"Mommy, we had pancakes this morning! They were so delicious!" Charlotte cried, tugging on Connie's hand but glancing anxiously back and forth between her parents.

Connie bit her lip, realizing that her daughter was fully aware of the tension between her and Neil. She bent down. "You know what, darling? I would love some of Cook's pancakes—with maple syrup, too."

"I'll tell Cook to make you a fine breakfast, Lady Montrose," Mrs. Partridge said with a smile.

"Thank you," Neil told her.

Charlotte now ran to Neil. "Daddy will have a second breakfast with you, Mommy," she announced.

Connie tensed. "I'm sure your father has business affairs to attend to."

Charlotte's expression became mulish. "No, he doesn't. He's having breakfast with you. Isn't that right, Daddy?" She turned and gave her father an amazingly significant look for a child of three.

Connie could hardly believe it, but her little daughter was playing matchmaker.

"We will all keep your mother company while she dines," Neil said firmly. Then his turquoise gaze found Connie's.

Their eyes held.

Connie felt herself flush and she looked away first.

"I have missed you, Connie," Neil said quietly.

She started, dismayed, and if the children hadn't been present, she would have run away. Instead, she faced him with a brittle smile. "I've hardly been away, Neil."

"They miss you, too," he said, referring to the girls.

She could hardly breathe. "Don't do this."

"Don't do what? Tell you the truth? That I love you and I miss you?" he asked, his brilliant gaze intense.

Connie stared, her hands clenched. How dare he talk about the truth when he had lied to her! In fact, she wanted him out of the house!

But there was another part of her that wanted her marriage back. That wanted Neil back.

Neil's resolute expression crumbled. "I see I am talking to a brick wall," he said, turning away.

"Mommy isn't a brick wall," Charlotte said in confusion. "Mommy still loves you, Daddy. I know it!"

Neil whirled, aghast.

Connie was as stricken. She raced to her daughter. "Of course I love your father," she cried, and although the words were reflexive, she closed her eyes, horrified. Because she had spoken the truth.

Somehow, impossibly, she still loved her husband. In spite of what he had done.

*But hadn't she been the one to chase him into the arms of another woman?*

Connie knew the rules of a good marriage. They had been instilled within her as a part of her education while she was growing up. It was the wife who always admitted that she was wrong, whether it was the truth or not. It was the wife who always gracefully took the blame, if there was blame to be had. Wives did not argue with their spouses. If one's husband wished to tell you that he had just climbed Mount Rainier, one must agree—cheerfully. Wives were elegant, genteel, well dressed, and well coiffed. And a wife never refused her husband's sexual advances.

But Connie had done just that.

She had made it clear to Neil after Lucinda's birth that she did not want him to touch her. She had made it clear that she did not want to share her favors. She found lovemaking shameful. Or rather, she was ashamed of what happened to her in bed. No one had to tell her that ladies simply did not behave like whores, as she certainly did.

Charlotte raced to Neil, beaming. "See? I told you, Daddy. You don't have to be so sad anymore."

Connie clasped her hand over her mouth to hide a gasp.

In return, Neil gave her a very angry look, one that said, *This is what you are doing to the children!* But ever the gentleman, at least on the surface, he said, strained, "May I take you and the girls for a carriage ride in Central Park? It is a beautiful day."

"I am taking them shopping," Connie said. "I promised Charlotte."

He kept his face rigid, but she knew him so well, and she saw more hurt and disappointment in his eyes. "Very well," he said softly. "I see that I am intruding. That was not my intention. I think it is a grand idea, a day of shopping for the ladies." He smiled down at Charlotte.

"But you can come, too, Daddy," Charlotte said. "We can all go, *together*."

Connie could not bear the idea. "Charlotte, your father has appointments to keep. It shall be a day just for us ladies. We shall have so much fun! Perhaps, as the weather is clement, we shall do the Ladies' Mile."

Charlotte pouted, looking displeased.

Neil said, without any emotion, "Your mother is right. I do have many business affairs to attend to. I will see you all later." With that, he swept Charlotte up for a hug, kissed Lucinda warmly, and strode out, not sparing Connie a single backward glance.

She stared after him, stunned.

And she was afraid. For it occurred to her that she was about to really lose her husband.


The Channing residence was on the West Side, commonly referred to as "Dakota" by Manhattan's residents, as it was so far away from everything and everyone. Sarah's mother, Abigail Channing, had been widowed for the past few years, and she had built herself a huge and grotesquely ornate mansion with her dead husband's money. Ignoring the many gargoyles glaring at her and Bragg, Francesca paused on the front stone steps. A tall, round tower reminiscent of medieval times graced each corner of the house.

Bragg spoke briefly to the uniformed roundsman standing on the paved walk not far from the front door. "Any trouble at all last night or this morning?"

"No, sir," the young man said nervously. He smiled at Bragg.

Bragg did not notice. "Anyone suspicious lurking about? Any odd visitors or deliveries?"

"Not a single visitor, Commissioner, sir." The blond man almost saluted Bragg now as he spoke.

Francesca bit back a smile and saw Newman huffing and puffing as he raced up the stone path toward them, having just alighted from a cab. She banged the door knocker twice. "You have instilled the fear of God in them," she murmured.

"I doubt that, but there will be another round of demotions next week." He smiled at her.

Francesca was surprised. "Why?" He had already demoted 300 wardsmen, reassigning many detectives to foot patrol. By breaking up unit after unit, he had hoped to stop the graft, corruption, and bribery rampant in the force.

"There have been rumors of a series of shakedowns in Germantown. I suspect a showdown with Tammany Hall is imminent."

Francesca did not like the sound of that, and her heart lurched with fear. It had been a miracle, really, that Seth Low, a Citizen's Union candidate, had won the mayor's office from the Democrats and Tammany Hall. In spite of being opposed by the likes of Odell and Platt, Tammany Hall was an extremely powerful political force—that is, they lured German factory workers to the polls with outright bribes of beer and cash. Bragg was but one man. She did not want to see him take on such a huge and significant battle, not alone.

Understanding her completely, he said softly, "I will be fine, Francesca."

She breathed hard. "I do hope so."

Newman reached them, breathlessly greeting them both. "Sir? We got a lead on Miss Conway. Apparently a week ago—Bennett thinks it was the Monday or Tuesday before last—she had a huge row with a man. He could hear her shouting and all kinds of objects being thrown around her flat." Bragg avoided Francesca completely while she was grim and resigned. It had obviously been a terrible row, she thought.

Bragg hesitated. "Do we know who that man was?"

Newman was grim. He flushed, darting a glance at Francesca. "Er, seems she had a lover. Might have been someone, er, named, er, Evan, er, Cahill."

Bragg sighed. Francesca clasped Newman's arm, deciding to take him off the hook. "I know she was my brother's mistress, Inspector, and I also know that he broke up with her last week. But he is not a murderer. He would never do such a thing."

Newman was grim. "I got to tell the c'mish the facts, Miz Cahill. I am sorry," he added.

"Let's keep this quiet, Newman," Bragg said. "As I do not want the newsmen of this city getting their hands on this and blowing it all out of proportion. It will only make finding the real killer that much harder."

"Yes, sir. Didn't tell a soul. Except Hickey was with me, of course, when we interviewed Mr. Bennett again."

Francesca quickly spoke up. "Please press upon Detective Hickey the need for discretion."

"He's discreet. You don't need to worry about him. C'mish, sir? We found three art galleries in a ten-block radius from the scene. Hickey an' me are going to start interviews when they open. Seems likely she might be known in a gallery close to her home."

"Good work," Bragg said with a smile, clasping Newman upon the shoulder. He seemed more than pleased—had he been four-legged and shaggy, he would have rolled over.

They turned to the business at hand. Francesca knocked again. A servant opened the door a moment later and ushered them in. "Any leads on the whereabouts of Thomas Neville?" Bragg asked over his shoulder. The manservant asked them to wait, hurrying off to find either Mrs. Channing or Sarah.

"No, sir. We been havin' trouble finding his old landlord, sir. George Holiday seems to be in a bit o' debt and on the run from the banks. But we'll catch up with him sooner or later."

"This will slow down our investigation," Bragg murmured to Francesca.

She agreed wholeheartedly.

His words were barely spoken when Abigail Channing came pitter-pattering toward them in her low-heeled slippers and a huge burgundy velvet gown. She wore rubies to complement the dramatic gown, more suitable for evening than for day. But she was a very wealthy widow. "Commissioner! Francesca! What a wonderful surprise," she cried in her breathy, childish voice. Her delight was childish as well. Francesca knew, however, that she meant no harm.

"Hello, Mrs. Channing." Francesca smiled somewhat fondly at her.

The strawberry blonde quickly gestured them to enter a huge, exotically furnished salon—every time Francesca entered the room she expected the bear rug on the floor, complete with a head and fangs, to leap up at her—and offered them refreshments.

Bragg declined. "Mrs. Channing, we are still investigating the incident in Sarah's studio last week. We do need to speak with your daughter," he said.

"How is Sarah?" Francesca added.

"She is much better," Mrs. Channing said. "She was up and about quite early this morning. That Rourke Bragg is a wonderful doctor!" She beamed. "And so handsome, too!"

Francesca decided not to correct her, though Rourke was not quite a legitimate doctor yet. When she had gone to get Sarah, Francesca said to Bragg, "There is something I have been thinking about."

He smiled. His amber eyes were soft and warm. "Do tell."

She smiled back, her heart stirring at the look he was giving her. "The roses in Miss Neville's apartment. They were fully opened. One or two were dying. That would make me conclude that they had been bought a day or two before. Two days before seems more likely, which would make it the day of Miss Conway's murder. Someone brought Miss Neville flowers, Bragg. She has an admirer."

"Unless the vase was empty, and Miss Conway was carrying the roses when she was murdered," he said. "And it should not surprise me if the flowers had been hers, considering the box of admiring mail we found in her flat."

He had a point. "Bragg, I am bothered now. Could Miss Neville be in hiding? It has occurred to me that perhaps she saw Miss Conway murdered—and that she knows the killer's identity."

"Francesca, we do not know that she is in hiding or that she saw anything. Perhaps she came home before the murder and then went out again." But his expression told her he did not believe his last theory.

"Then where is she? Why hasn't she come home? Is she with a lover? Surely one of her neighbors might know if she has that kind of friend." A new thought struck her. "We should go round to the art galleries until we find someone who knows her!"

"I have already put that task on Newman's list. He'll start with the galleries on Broadway, closest to her flat, and work his way out from there."

Francesca now wondered if Hart knew of Miss Neville.

"What is it?"

She hesitated, aware of her cheek warming.

"Francesca?"

"I should speak with Hart. As he knows just about everyone in the art world, he might prove very useful to us in this investigation."

Bragg didn't appear thrilled. "Yes, *I* should speak with Calder," he said. "And I intend to do so before the day is out."

Francesca decided to drop the subject. Of course, sooner or later she had to speak with Calder on behalf of her brother and she could easily kill two birds with one stone. Now, however, was not the time to think of Calder Hart.

*I always get what I want . . . whether the object of my desire is a painting . . . a sculpture. Or a lucrative shipping contract. . . . Or a woman.*

She shivered, his face implanted there in her mind, dark

skin, high cheekbones, dark eyes, and flashing white teeth. The problem was, he wasn't merely arrogant, for she believed his every word.

But this time, of course, he was in for a big surprise.

"What is distracting you, Francesca?" Bragg asked, taking her arm. "Is it Evan?"

She started. "I am very afraid for him," she breathed, then realized she had lied to Bragg, in a way, for her worries had been about Hart in that moment and not about her brother.

"I am going to pay a call on Andrew LeFarge and make my position very clear," Bragg said softly, steel resolution in his eyes. "If he should be so foolish as to harm a single hair on your brother's head again, he will have this city's entire police force after him."

She melted. Hart disappeared from her mind. "You would threaten him, using your position as commissioner to do so, for me?"

"Yes."

Their gazes locked. This was why she loved Rick Bragg—he was always there for her no matter what.

And then Sarah and her mother appeared on the threshold of the salon. Instantly Francesca rushed forward to embrace the petite brunette. Sarah looked much better than she had the other day. The color had returned to her cheeks, light to her dark eyes. She had taken all of her wonderful waist-length Pre-Raphaelite curls and coiled her hair into a severe bun, which detracted from her small, fine features. As always, she was wearing an ensemble that did not suit her at all—this one was a dark green suit and it made her look sallow. Black silk braid crisscrossed her short fitted jacket and excessively flounced skirts. A cream-colored shirtwaist was beneath. Lace frothed from the collar and cuffs. Francesca knew that Sarah was oblivious to her appearance and to fashion in general, and she knew also that Mrs. Channing ordered her daughter's clothes. While Francesca applauded disinterest in fashion in general, almost every time she first saw Sarah, she winced. Sarah was small and delicate and the gowns she wore simply overpowered her. Francesca wondered now if she might convince her sister to take Sarah shopping, as Connie had the most elegant taste in clothes.

Sarah smiled now. "This is a wonderful surprise, Francesca," she said softly. "Hello, Commissioner. How are you?"

"Very well," he said with a smile. "I see you have recovered from your recent bout with fever?"

"Yes, I am doing quite well," Sarah said evenly. "The next time you see your brother, do give him my thanks."

"He stayed up with her all night when she was feverish!" Mrs. Channing exclaimed. "I thought poor Sarah might expire, she was so ill! He ordered me to my rooms, saying he would manage everything and that I should not distress myself. And lo and behold, when I got up that next morning, Sarah was well on her way to recovery." Abigail Channing beamed. She then sighed, dramatically. "If only I were ten years younger. You do know, Commissioner, that the two of you look wonderfully alike. How old is Rourke?"

Francesca hid a smile. Ten years would not do it, oh no.

Bragg said, amused, "He is twenty-two or -three, I think. May we speak with Sarah alone, Mrs. Channing? This is official police business."

Mrs. Channing's face fell. Her expression became distinctly worried now. "Oh, I do hope we have seen the last of that, that ruffian who so upset my daughter and who dared to come into our home and destroy her studio! Not that I am not a bit pleased that Sarah has finally taken some time away from her art, but really, I should not like such an event to occur again."

Francesca took Mrs. Channing's arm and guided her to the door. "It is unlikely he would return, Mrs. Channing," she said soothingly. "But he does need to be brought to justice, do you not agree?"

"Oh, yes! Wholeheartedly! And it is so wonderful of the commissioner to be taking such an interest in our tiny little case." She beamed from the other side of the threshold now.

"It is my pleasure," Bragg said gallantly.

As Francesca began to close the door, Abigail waved.

"Oh! Commissioner! Might you and your wife be inclined to dine with us one evening? I am so looking forward to meeting her."

Francesca's heart lurched. So word had traveled, and swiftly, but how? Leigh Anne had only arrived in the city yesterday, and then Francesca corrected herself. No, she had learned of Leigh Anne's arrival yesterday but did not really know how long she had been in town. Who had spread the news of her advent? Francesca wondered if it had been her own mother. Now Francesca resolved not to think about the dramatic meeting she had had when Leigh Anne had come to call on her in her own home. But finally coming face-to-face with Bragg's wife had been so unpleasant and so adversarial that Francesca doubted she would ever forget the meeting.

Bragg managed a polite smile. "I am extremely immersed in police affairs, but hopefully, we shall have the opportunity to do so, and soon."

Francesca shut the door on a pleased Mrs. Channing and turned to regard Bragg. She knew there was little else he could have said in response to such an invitation; still, she was disturbed, dismayed, and even jealous.

Sarah interrupted her thoughts. "Has something happened? Something has happened, hasn't it—for the two of you to be here on such an insignificant matter!"

She was distressed. Francesca rushed to her, but not before sending Bragg a warning glance. "We would like to take a second look at your studio, Sarah. And ask you a few more questions."

Sarah shrugged free. "Francesca, I have already told you everything. I discovered my studio at five-fifteen in the morning in a shambles. Someone brutalized all that I hold dear in this world. And we still have not a clue as to why. I am haunted by that question!" she cried.

Bragg approached. Calmly he said, "Could you come with us?"

Sarah nodded, appearing extremely grim. Francesca slid

her arm around her. "Sarah? Perhaps another look at your studio will jog your mind a bit."

"Perhaps," Sarah said. "But has something else happened?"

Francesca and Bragg exchanged a swift look. Francesca quickly decided that as Sarah was far stronger than she looked and extremely intelligent—not to mention that her life might be in danger—she should know the truth. Apparently, Bragg had reached the same conclusion, for softly, he said, "Did you know another female artist, Miss Melinda Neville?"

Sarah shook her head, her brown eyes dark with intensity. "No."

"Her studio was vandalized in a very similar manner to yours," he said.

Sarah stared at him. "What does this mean?"

"There is more," Francesca said gently, taking her arm very firmly. But as she did, Sarah cried out, as if in pain.

"Are you all right?"

She nodded, but it was a moment before she could speak. "I bruised my arm. It is very sore—and quite purple, I might add."

Francesca now recalled Rourke's comment, as he had seen the bruise, perhaps when he had examined Sarah when she was ill.

"What is it that you are afraid to tell me?" Sarah asked.

Francesca hesitated, glancing at Bragg. He nodded at her. She said, "A woman was found murdered in Miss Neville's studio, Sarah."

Sarah turned white. She quickly sat down on the closest object of furniture, the edge of a plush green sofa. "Oh, God. Miss Neville?"

"No, it was an actress, Grace Conway."

Sarah was bewildered. "I don't understand."

"Nor do we," Francesca said with what she hoped was a reassuring smile.

Sarah stared, and after a pause, asked directly, "Am I in danger?"

Francesca hesitated.

Bragg said, "I don't know. But for safety's sake, I am leaving two police officers here, one outside and one just inside the front door."

Sarah nodded, appearing flustered, breathless, and anxious all at once. "Was this actress's murder an accident, perhaps?"

"Perhaps," Bragg said. "Shall we?" He gestured at the door.

Sarah stood, and she and Francesca followed Bragg out. Francesca hadn't expected Sarah to know about Miss Conway's involvement with Evan and was relieved that she did not. And even though she knew that Sarah's engagement would be ended, and soon, by her brother, to both his and Sarah's relief, at that moment they were still officially affianced, and Sarah had to be told about Evan's injuries. As they went down the hall, Francesca said, "I don't want you to worry, but Monday afternoon Evan was in a bit of a brawl."

Sarah halted while Bragg swung open the door to her studio and went inside. "A brawl?"

"Yes," Francesca said, having no intention of telling her about Evan's debts. "He was a bit smashed up, and he is in bed, but he will be fine in no time."

"Oh! Poor Evan! I shall have to call on him immediately, of course." She stared at Francesca.

"I am sure he should like that," Francesca said, knowing it hardly mattered to him.

"I will do so this afternoon, of course," Sarah said firmly. Then her expression changed, becoming worried, and she looked past Francesca and at the open doorway of her studio. "I wonder if I will ever want to paint again," she murmured, more to herself than Francesca.

"Of course you shall!" Francesca cried, meaning it. "You are too brilliant to ever stop doing what consumes you, Sarah!"

Sarah's smile was wan. She shivered and did not move forward.

Francesca did. She paused on the threshold of the studio, which was filled with midday light. Nothing had been touched. And the room remained a scene of carnage and wreckage, with paint splashed everywhere, canvases overturned, and one canvas mutilated. That canvas was a portrait of the stunning countess Bartolla Benevente, Sarah's cousin.

Francesca saw everything in a glance and looked straight at the wall. There, amidst splatters of red and black paint was a crude letter. It looked like this: $F$

Francesca stared. The letter could be a $B$, an $F$, an $E$, or perhaps even a $K$. It was not necessarily an $F$.

"Francesca," Sarah whispered.

Francesca turned and saw that Sarah's face was pinched with tension and fright. She left the studio, joining her in the hall. "What, dear?"

"I have such a pounding headache," Sarah whispered, clasping her hands over her ears.

"Maybe you should go upstairs and lie down," Francesca suggested.

Sarah shook her head, dropping her hands to her sides. "I can't. I am afraid I might fall asleep," she said.

Francesca could not understand what that comment meant.

"I have been having the oddest nightmares! There is paint everywhere, and when I turn to run away, I run right into a man. And the moment I do, he grabs my arm, and then I wake up, screaming." She stared at Francesca now.

Francesca stared back, highly alerted now to a possibility that had not yet been considered. "And this is a dream? Can you see the man's face? Do you know who this man is?" she cried.

"That's just it," Sarah whispered. "The moment he grabs my arm, I look at him, but then I am awake, and I am looking at my bedroom," she said. "Francesca? It feels so real. It feels like déjà vu."

When Francesca did not speak, Sarah added, "It feels as if it really happened."

• • •

Only one other apartment was occupied by any tenants at Number 202 East 10th Street. That apartment was Number Two on the ground floor. Francesca and Bragg were greeted by a matronly woman with a grim expression and unsmiling eyes. Peering at them through the slightly cracked door, she said, "Yes?"

"Mrs. Holmes?" Bragg smiled.

"I don't want to buy anything," she said, closing the door abruptly.

Francesca lifted her brows as Bragg knocked again. "I am afraid I am an officer with the police and I am here on official business," he said to the closed wooden door.

This time the door was opened by a young woman a few years older than Francesca. Francesca gazed into a pair of soft and worried brown eyes, framed by auburn hair that was tightly drawn back from her face. The woman opened the door fully. "I am Catherine Holmes. I beg your pardon; my mother doesn't care for unexpected callers," she said softly.

"We are sorry to intrude, but we must ask a few questions," Francesca said with a slight and equally soft smile.

Catherine Holmes met her gaze, nodded, and let them into a modestly furnished flat. Her gaze returned to Bragg. "I've seen your caricature in the newspapers. You are the police commissioner."

"Yes, and this is Miss Cahill," he said.

Remaining anxious, Catherine Holmes offered them a seat in the small parlor, clasping her hands repeatedly in her apron, which she wore over a dark serge skirt. "Is this about poor Miss Conway?" she whispered.

"I am afraid so," Bragg remarked.

"She was very pleasant—and very beautiful," Catherine Holmes said, perching on a chair. "I cannot think of who would wish to do such a terrible thing." Tears filled her eyes.

Francesca leaned forward to touch her hand. "Were you friends?"

Catherine Holmes shook her head. "No. But we did pass from time to time in the entry hall. For an actress, she was a very nice lady."

Francesca hesitated. "Did you also see her male friend from time to time?"

Catherine Holmes blinked, straightening. "Yes," she said slowly. "He was here often. I couldn't help but notice him, as he was so handsome."

Francesca thought that the cat might get out of the bag rather quickly, should the press ever interview the neighbors about Grace Conway. Evan would undoubtedly be identified almost immediately. Which meant they must find the killer even more quickly, to spare her brother any more pain.

"Can you think of anyone odd who has been lurking about Miss Conway?" Bragg asked.

Catherine Holmes shook her head again. "She had only the one visitor, the gentleman. She really didn't stay in very much—she was almost never home."

Francesca blinked at her.

"I am always home," Catherine Holmes said quite ruefully. "I take care of Mother. And our parlor window opens onto Tenth Street."

Francesca got up and walked behind the sitting area to the window. She pulled apart the draperies and had a perfect view of the entrance to the building. She whirled. "Are you certain you did not see anybody unusual leaving or entering this building on Monday?"

Catherine Holmes seemed pale. "You did not ask me that, but the answer is no. I hardly sit and watch the front door of the building all day long."

Francesca glanced at the rocking chair set by the window. Someone certainly liked sitting there and watching the world go by. "Does your mother sit here?"

"Once in a while. She has gout and arthritis and she prefers to remain in bed." Catherine Holmes stood up. She seemed more anxious than ever. She would have been a pretty woman had her expression been less worried, somber, and severe.

Francesca wondered if she was hiding something. She would bet her last nickel that poor Catherine Holmes, trapped in a dismal apartment with her scowling, ill mother, would sit at the window and watch the passersby, yearning for another life and another world.

Bragg stood. "Did you know Miss Neville, Miss Holmes?"

"No. She moved in a month or so ago and kept to herself. But I know she is an artist and that she had just come from Paris. Her brother told me so."

Francesca froze. "Thomas?"

Catherine Holmes nodded. "Yes. He comes to see her every day, or so it seems." She hesitated. "Although I haven't seen him since poor Miss Conway was murdered."

Francesca and Bragg shared a glance. "Do you know where we can find Thomas Neville?" Bragg asked oh-so-calmly.

"No, I don't. He was very talkative, but he never mentioned where he lives." She looked from Bragg to Francesca and back again. "What is this about?"

"We have been trying to locate him," Bragg said.

"When did you last see and speak with Miss Neville?" Francesca had to cry. "And was she a friend of Miss Conway's?"

"I don't see how they could be friends when she had only just moved in," Catherine Holmes said. "But I last saw her Monday night."

Francesca trembled. "Monday night?" Grace Conway could have been murdered on Monday night!

Catherine Holmes looked wary now. "Yes. She had forgotten her keys. I happened to be coming in myself, and I let her in. It was six P.M. I know, because I had promised Mother I would be back by six at the very latest."

"That is very helpful," Bragg said, clearly tamping down his own enthusiasm now.

While Francesca wanted to jump up and down. "And

then what happened? Did you see her go out again?"

"No, I did not." Catherine Holmes was stiff now. "I had to make supper and put Mother to bed. I have no idea if she went out again or not, but that is the last time I saw her."

"Thank you very much, Miss Holmes," Bragg said, taking her hand.

She seemed surprised by the gentlemanly gesture. She flushed.

"Thank you," Francesca added, grinning. She grabbed Bragg's arm and practically dragged him into the hall. "Do you know what this means?" she cried.

He smiled. "I think so."

"Miss Neville returned in the approximate window of time in which Miss Conway was murdered. Do you think she found her body . . . and then ran away? Or perhaps she even saw the murder!" she cried, her excitement rising with this last and hopeful thought.

"Or perhaps the murderer saw her as well," Bragg said.

Francesca's elation vanished. "You're right. This is not necessarily good news. I am worried about her, Bragg."

"Then that makes two of us," he replied.

# CHAPTER
# SIX

WEDNESDAY, FEBRUARY 19, 1902—2:00 P.M.

"I SIMPLY CANNOT BELIEVE what has befallen Evan, Julia," Bartolla Benevente said. She and Sarah were following Julia upstairs in the Cahill mansion. As always, Bartolla was resplendently dressed, in a sapphire ensemble, and she was wearing the jewels to match her slim little jacket and skirt. But now she was pale in spite of the rouge on her cheeks. She had reacted badly when she heard of Evan's accident.

"I can only thank God he is getting better every day," Julia said, her expression drawn. "Thank you so much for calling, Countess. Sarah, dear, and how are you?"

Sarah flushed with guilt. Bartolla, her cousin, was going on and on, with genuine concern, about Evan's welfare. While she had not said a single commiserating word—and he was her fiancé. Not that she did not care. Of course she cared. He was the man chosen to be her husband—never mind that she wished, desperately, that she might remain unwed. And he was nice enough. He had always behaved courteously toward her, and Sarah knew he was very disappointed that she had been chosen to be his bride. Not that she blamed him. She was skinny and plain and entirely obsessed with her painting. Men never looked at her the way that they looked at her cousin or Francesca. "I am fine, Mrs. Cahill," she murmured.

Bartolla took her arm possessively. "Sarah has completely recovered from that odd bout with fever that she had. I, of course, am anxiously awaiting news from the police and Miss Cahill as to whom the culprit was who dared invade our home and wreak such havoc on Sarah's studio. Sarah has been so very brave."

Sarah gave Bartolla a small smile. She was as anxious to know who had violated her beloved art studio and wished her cousin would not sing her praises. She had been nourishing the tiniest kernel of hope, deep within herself, that something or someone would interfere with her wedding and that she might remain a single young lady somehow.

Yet she knew her hopes to be utterly foolish.

"Yes, Sarah is very brave. This is so terrible, first Sarah's studio, and now this assault upon my son." Julia was so grim, and Sarah had the odd feeling that she knew more than she was letting on.

"I have come to know your son a bit," Bartolla commented as they swept up the corridor. "It is simply so surprising that he would find himself in a barroom brawl." The countess smiled at Julia, but her stare was penetrating.

"Boys will be boys," Julia murmured, not meeting Bartolla's regard. They all paused at Evan's door, which was ever so slightly ajar.

Sarah stood behind both women. She was barely five feet tall, while Bartolla was perhaps five-foot-seven and Julia somewhere in between them both. So at first Sarah could not see into the bedroom at all.

"Well, well," Bartolla murmured. "Who is that?"

"Mrs. Kennedy is still with us," Julia said. "And she has been a savior, really."

"I can see that," Bartolla said, her tone odd.

Sarah found her curiosity piqued. She was no fool—she

had seen the sparks flying between Evan and her cousin. If the truth be known, she wished them well—once she had even come to the hopeful conclusion that maybe they could run off together, leaving her alone, a spinster with her freedom. Of course, neither one would ever betray her in such a manner. Now she edged between the two taller women and saw a surprising sight.

Mrs. Kennedy, the seamstress who had made an amazing red ball gown for Francesca, sat on the bed by Evan's hip. They were engaged in a quiet and casual conversation, but there was something so intimate about the scene that even Sarah felt a moment of surprise. It was like walking in on two very old and dear friends—or on a husband and his wife.

Maggie laughed. Evan was smiling, but even so, he looked dreadful, with his face black-and-blue and a black patch over his eye.

"Evan? Your fiancée is here with the Countess Benevente," Julia said.

Maggie leaped hastily to her feet. She faced them, eyes downcast, two bright pink spots on her face.

"Hello, Evan!" Bartolla cried, sailing into the room. She ignored the seamstress, treating her as if she were a piece of the room's furniture. "We just heard about your terrible accident, and we are so distressed!"

"Bartolla!" Evan sat up straighter, surprised, and then he was smiling. Sarah felt a pang, watching their gazes meet and hold. There was no doubt that they were genuinely fond of each other. She despaired. Perhaps she should be the one to run away.

The idea was not without merit.

"Sarah, hello," Evan said.

Sarah started, realizing that Mrs. Kennedy had fled and that Julia was leaving the three of them alone. She managed a smile. "Evan, I just heard, and I am so sorry," she said softly. "How badly are you hurt?" she asked worriedly. And to think that she had been absorbed in the trauma of what had happened to her silly studio. It was only a room.

She could paint Bartolla's portrait again. The walls could be cleaned, new canvases and paints bought. What had been wrong with her?

"I shall be as good as new in no time," he said as Bartolla sat down on the bed, exactly where Maggie Kennedy had been seated.

"What can I get you?" she asked.

"A sip of water?" he asked, smiling at her.

Bartolla found the glass of water on his bedstand. She leaned forward, exposing quite a bit of cleavage, as her jacket was low-cut and she wore only a lace chemise beneath. Evan's gaze dropped, then quickly lifted. Sarah turned away, walking to the window.

She didn't care. She didn't care that Evan was smitten with her cousin, as well he should be. Bartolla was gorgeous, vivacious, clever, kind. She was everything a woman should be.

Sarah paused before the window and stared down at the back lawns, which were blanketed in snow. She hugged herself, felt a patch of paint, and realized she had a spot of purple on her green skirt. Looking down, she found several blotches, and she sighed. Her stomach turned.

It was only a studio. It was only a room. So what if one canvas had been destroyed? Nothing else had happened. There was no reason for her to feel so ill every time she thought about it. Or was there?

She closed her eyes, vaguely aware of Evan and Bartolla in quiet conversation behind her. Her stomach felt violently ill now, and in the shadows of her mind there was a threat. Lurking in the black fog, somewhere, was something terrible, or someone.

She shivered and suddenly felt eyes upon her.

*In the shadows there was a man. A terrible, terrible man.*

The sensation of being watched increased. Sarah had begun to shake when her arm was seized from behind. She cried out, whirling, and came face-to-face with wide topaz eyes and a hank of dusty blond-brown hair falling directly into them.

"Miss Channing?"

Sarah pulled away. Her vision cleared, and she came face-to-face with Rourke Bragg.

"Are you all right?" he asked, his amber eyes unwavering upon hers.

She did not like the way he stared. And she liked even less the fact that when she had been terribly ill and afraid, he had decided to be her doctor. Why, he wasn't even a doctor—he was only a medical student. And she realized his hand remained on her wrist. She pulled away. "I am fine. Good day, Mr. Bragg."

He eyed her as if he did not believe her, then smiled, but it did not reach his eyes. "You seem so sad," he said.

"I am hardly sad," she snapped. Not that it was his business!

"No?" He gestured with his head toward the couple on the bed, darkness coming to his eyes. "You truly have every reason to be angry, not sad."

She knew what he meant. She shrugged. "I don't care. She is beautiful. He should be marrying her."

Rourke shook his head with disbelief. "I can't believe you mean that."

He was annoying her again. "I do," she said tartly. "And what do you really care about my feelings, Mr. Bragg?"

He stiffened. "I happen to be in the healing profession. It is my nature to care. It is why I shall one day become a doctor."

She felt terrible for being so rude. "I'm sorry. I don't know what overcame me . . ." She trailed off. She knew why he made her so uncomfortable. She felt very certain he had seen her skinny body unclothed when she was feverish, and she didn't like it, not one bit. But she was too embarrassed to ask if the vague recollections she had of being ill and naked in his arms were true.

"How is that bruise?" he asked.

"Better." She turned toward Evan and Bartolla. They had their heads together and Evan was chuckling over some misadventure being related by the countess.

"He is a fool," Rourke said. "I feel sorry for him."

Sarah had no idea what he meant. She squared her shoulders. "I think he is kind and gallant. Unlike most men." She gave him a significant look.

Rourke laughed, hard. "I am not insulted," he said, still chuckling. "You know, appearances are truly deceiving, are they not? You are not a timid little mouse at all. One day, your forward manner will get you into trouble, my girl."

So now he was insulting her? "I am not your girl," she snapped.

"You do not have to tell me that!" he returned as swiftly.

That gave her pause. He was rather good-looking, in that golden Bragg way—if one was in the habit of admiring men, which she was not. Then she gave it up. She was an artist, and while she preferred painting women and children, she had an artist's eye and the man confronting her was simply gorgeous. He had those uniquely high cheekbones, inherited from some Indian ancestor, a straight, strong nose, a cleft chin, not to mention intriguing dimples. He was tall, six feet or so, with very broad shoulders and very slim hips. Undoubtedly he had a lady he was seriously courting back in Philadelphia—which was fine with her. More than fine, in fact.

It was an oddly comforting notion.

"You are undressing me with your big brown eyes," he said, a soft, soft murmur.

She jumped. "I beg your pardon!" But even as she spoke, she knew she had been taking a very personal inventory of his lean thighs and she felt heat growing in her cheeks. "I was doing no such thing!"

"And this brings to mind a question I would like to ask you," he said firmly.

Sarah nodded, desperate to get their encounter over with, desperate to leave the room.

"Hart mentioned something to me about a casual supper this Friday night. We are going to an opening of a gallery first. He thought you might wish to join us," Rourke said, his usually mobile face quite expressionless.

Her heart leaped. Calder Hart was a world-famous collector of art, and he had recently commissioned Francesca Cahill's portrait from her. That commission might give her some renown in the art world. Sarah could think of nothing more enjoyable—or frightening—than an evening spent in his company, discussing art. She wondered if he might give her a viewing of his own extensive collection at some point in the evening. She prayed it would be so. She opened her mouth to reply and could not get a single word out.

Rourke laughed, clasping her shoulder with a large, strong palm. "I take it that is a yes?"

Feeling like a fool, Sarah nodded. And finally, she got the words out. "Oh yes. An evening with Mr. Hart. Oh, yes indeed, I would not miss it for the world!"

His expression odd, Rourke said, "Good. I'll pick you up at five."

"What do we do about Miss Neville now?" Francesca asked seriously. They had paused on 10th Street, not far from the front door of Number 202.

"We continue to follow any leads which come our way. If she is alive, we will find her. If not, we will find her body."

"What a grim thought." Francesca shivered. Her mind continued to analyze each twist and turn of their new case. "I think Sarah confronted our killer, Bragg."

He started. "Did she say something? And if she has seen him, why hasn't she said so?"

"She is having nightmares about the vandalism, and in each and every dream she finally faces a man whom she cannot see."

Bragg's eagerness vanished. He shook his head. "Francesca, that hardly means she witnessed anything. She remains distressed enough to be having nightmares."

"I have a very strong feeling," she said. And then she sighed. She had an errand she must do, one she very much regretted.

"What's wrong?" he asked quickly.

"I am going uptown to Barnard to cancel my enrollment there," she said softly. How the very notion hurt, but she had concluded that there was no other choice. She had gone to great pains to enroll secretly—so her mother might never know. She had been so certain she could attain her AB degree. It had been a goal of hers for years.

"Francesca, you must not drop out!" Bragg exclaimed.

"I fear I have no choice," she said, meeting his wide, concerned eyes. "I have no time to study. I missed an entire week of classes due to my burned hand. Now we are hot on the trail of another killer. I fear a life of crime-solving is far too busy to include the pursuit of a higher education."

"Francesca, I know how much your studies mean to you, and I am firmly against your letting them go. Could you not speak with the dean and see if you could continue on a part-time basis?"

She hesitated. "I thought about it. But, Bragg, there is so little time!"

"Of course, you must do what you think is best," he said, clearly not supporting her decision.

"Well, I shall see what the dean says. She rather liked me . . . initially."

"Perhaps she will suggest the solution I have posed," he said easily. Then he faced her more seriously. "I have several meetings I must attend, but I do hope to speak with LeFarge later this afternoon."

Andrew LeFarge—the owner of several gambling halls— the man to whom Evan owed a small fortune. She grabbed his sleeve. "I must come with you."

"Absolutely not!"

"Why? Because he almost killed my brother?" There was simply no possibility that she would not go with him to speak with LeFarge. "He may be our murderer!"

"Yes, he may. But even if he is not, he is a very dangerous man. He lives outside of the law. I don't want him even taking a single glance at you, Francesca. Why don't you visit the several galleries Newman and Hickey found?

That would be incredibly helpful, especially if you found someone who knew Miss Neville."

It was simply unacceptable that she could not interview Andrew LeFarge. "You are trying to distract me! The galleries can wait until tomorrow." Her mind raced. "I have the time now. Perhaps I will interview him alone."

He threw his hands in the air. "Fine! But that is blackmail, Francesca, and you know it."

She smiled happily. "It did work."

"I will pick you up at five," he said.


They were ushered into a stately mansion by a British servant. Francesca was more than surprised as the man took Bragg's card, placed it on a silver tray, and hurried away to give it to his employer. Removing her coat, Francesca glanced around the elegant hall. Oak floors gleamed underfoot, and several pleasant paintings graced the wood-paneled walls. Through an arched entryway she saw another reception hall, this one decorated in red and gold with a magnificent chandelier. Other doors leading off the entry were firmly closed.

"This man appears to be a gentleman," she whispered.

"His reputation precedes him and he is not welcome in polite circles," Bragg remarked. "He is also a huge supporter of Tammany, Francesca."

"Does all of his wealth come from indebted gentlemen?"

"He has three 'saloons' in the city. If he has other investments, we do not know about them," Bragg said as the servant returned, another gentleman with him.

LeFarge was short and husky and he had donned a blue velvet smoking jacket over his white shirt and evening trousers. Matching velvet slippers monogrammed in gold with the initials *ALF* were upon his rather small feet. He had a large nose, fathomless dark eyes, heavy black brows, and a warm, slightly amused smile on his face. "Commissioner Bragg!" he cried effusively. "What a delight, my good man."

Bragg nodded politely. "Good evening, Mr. LeFarge. I am afraid I am here on police business."

"Really?" LeFarge blinked innocently, then smiled warmly at Francesca, extending his hand. "What a lovely lady! Miss . . . ?"

This man was responsible for having her brother beaten almost to death. Francesca did not extend her hand. "My name is Cahill," she said softly as the anger began to build within her in wave after frightening wave. "Miss Francesca Cahill."

"I should have guessed," he said, dropping his hand but continuing to smile. "The infamous lady investigator! Do, please, come in. I am dressing for an affair, but I can give you both a few moments."

He turned away, reaching for a pair of heavy rosewood doors. His portrait was on the wall on the left, and in it he was in a military uniform that appeared to be nineteenth-century and French. The pose was also Napoleonic. Francesca halted before the portrait, not at all amused. In it, LeFarge did resemble Bonaparte.

Bragg instantly took her arm, his gaze locking with hers, a warning there. Francesca had begun to shake. But she understood, and she nodded. She must control herself.

He nodded in return and they followed their host into a magnificent salon.

"Can I offer you refreshments?" LeFarge asked, gesturing at a red velvet settee flanked by a pair of darker red damask chairs. "A scotch, Commissioner? A sherry for the lady?"

"We will be brief," Bragg said.

Francesca realized she had folded her arms tightly across her chest. She sat down stiffly on the edge of one damask chair as LeFarge poured himself a scotch from a crystal decanter on a bar cart. He lifted the glass at them both, smiling. "To our city's finest police officer and its finest amateur sleuth."

Francesca trembled. The words were there, on the tip of her tongue: *Did you kill Grace Conway? Did you assault Sarah Channing? Did you think to get at my brother for his debts in this way?* But she said nothing—she simply stared.

And over the rim of his glass, he stared back at her, his eyes turning black.

She shivered, certain that a threat was there.

"Can you recount to me where you were Monday morning?" Bragg asked.

LeFarge looked surprised. "I was here in my library until noon. I spend every morning going over my business affairs," he said.

"And then you went out?"

LeFarge seemed amused, and he sipped from his drink. "I had lunch with Harold Levy and Jacob Cohen at the Waldorf Astoria, my good sir. Our luncheon was at one. It went an hour or two. Might I ask why you are posing these particular questions?"

Bragg smiled grimly. "A friend of Evan Cahill's was murdered on Monday, Mr. LeFarge."

He seemed shocked. "Is it anyone I know? And how is Evan handling it? Oh, do send him my regards!" he cried.

Francesca stood up—she had had enough.

"Francesca," Bragg warned.

She knew she had lost all of her control. She did not care. "Do not dare to pretend that you are a friend of my brother's!" she cried.

"But I am. I see him frequently, several times a week, if not more. He is a constant guest in my saloons. I am very sorry a friend of your brother's has been killed." He seemed compassionate.

"Miss Conway was murdered," she said rigidly.

Bragg took her arm.

LeFarge set his glass down. "Not Grace Conway, the lovely actress?" He seemed genuinely stunned.

"Unfortunately, Miss Conway has been murdered," Bragg confirmed.

"And you think I had something to do with it?" He laughed. "Commissioner, you are barking up the wrong tree! My business is money—not murder!"

"Where did you go after your luncheon with the gentlemen Levy and Cohen?"

"To the Royal," he said. "I was there all evening, and you may ask anyone." He continued to smile and then finished his scotch.

"How well did you know Grace Conway?" Francesca asked coldly.

He faced her. "Not well. But she came in with your brother quite often. I had actually hoped to entice her to supper, should she ever tire of Evan. I am so sorry she is dead."

Francesca stared, not believing a single word he said.

He raised both brows and met her stare, his gaze unwavering and steady. Then he said, "Do give Evan my regrets."

Francesca turned and walked out.

But not before she heard Bragg say, "Evan Cahill is a personal friend of mine, LeFarge. I am extremely concerned for his welfare. He himself has recently had an *accident*. But then, I think you know that?"

"No! I hadn't heard! Is he all right?" LeFarge gasped.

"He is fine. And I intend for him to stay that way. In fact, should anything befall him again, I will make certain that the responsible party never sees the light of day again. That is, I shall toss him in the cooler in the basement of headquarters and throw away the key."

LeFarge chuckled. "How melodramatic you are, my good man. I can hardly imagine you violating the letter of the law that you are sworn to uphold. Commissioner, I have to go. But would you meet me for a drink, say tomorrow evening? I think we can continue this discussion then."

"I'm afraid I have other plans," Bragg said.

Francesca was waiting on the other side of the doorway. She watched LeFarge shrug, clearly unperturbed. "And that, my good man, is your loss." He saluted them both with his now empty glass.

Francesca and Bragg walked out.

# CHAPTER
# SEVEN

Rick Bragg stood with his arms folded across his chest, in his shirtsleeves, gazing out the window of his office. Below, Mulberry Street remained a land of hoodlums and cheats. Even now, with several police officers loitering within his view, not far from his double-parked roadster, he watched a cutpurse strip the wallet from a gentleman who was on his way to headquarters. Farther down the block, a brawl was imminent, as two louts, both clearly drunken, were shouting and about to engage in punches and blows.

The brownstone across the street was where the city's newsmen loitered, awaiting scoops for their respective newspapers. He could clearly see into the window of one apartment, where several reporters were sipping coffee and standing about gossiping. He recognized one of them as Arthur Kurland from the *Sun*. The newsman had proven himself an adversary, perhaps even a dangerous one. However, Kurland might prove very useful where LeFarge was concerned. Bragg hoped to learn whatever he could about the gambling hall owner from the newsman.

Several drays were slowly passing by, as was a hansom. But most of the traffic below Bragg was on foot. He saw the entire familiar scene, yet in a way he also saw none of it. He was thoroughly preoccupied.

There were no new leads on the Conway Murder, and because of the possible involvement of Francesca's brother, Bragg was extremely concerned. Had Evan not been the connection between Grace Conway and Sarah Channing, he would not have involved himself in the case at all, as his job was to manage the entire police department, not to undertake the investigation of a single crime.

Had Grace Conway's murder been a brutal accident? Or was Sarah Channing lucky to be alive?

Were they dealing with a vandal . . . or a killer . . . or both?

At all costs, he did not want Francesca hurt by any of this, which meant he must protect her brother no matter what transpired.

Suddenly he started. A hansom had stopped on the block below his window and Francesca was alighting from the cab. He smiled instantly—she always brought a smile to his face—and then he felt his smile vanish. Francesca was an amazing woman—there was no woman he respected or admired more. He had never meant to become so terribly fond of her. He hadn't meant to fall in love, not with her or any other woman—he hadn't thought it possible, actually. For as much as he had cared for the few women he had been with since his separation, when Leigh Anne had left him, something within him had died.

And then he had met Francesca. As beautiful as she was, it wasn't her looks that had attracted him—it was her wit, her intellect, her humor. One conversation—which had turned into a political debate—and he had found himself ensnared.

He watched her cross the sidewalk, disappearing from his view, and was aware that she would be in his office in a moment. He was pleased about it, no matter that he should not be. Then he thought about his wife. He turned away from the window, closed his eyes, and sighed.

She felt like an iron collar about his neck.

Yet he knew if he could somehow grip that iron shackle, he could tear it off and be free.

Wide, innocent-looking emerald green eyes assailed his memory. But there was nothing innocent about her!

His telephone rang. Bragg's desk was a terrible clutter of papers, files, and folders. The telephone was on the desk's edge, and as he lifted the receiver from the hook, the rest of the telephone clattered to the floor along with several files. "Rick! I am terribly remiss; there is something I forgot to ask you yesterday when we spoke," Seth Low, the city's mayor, said tersely, without formality.

"Good morning, sir," Bragg said quickly. He had spent late yesterday afternoon in a meeting with the mayor, who, while indicating just how pleased he was with Bragg's current efforts to reform and revamp the police department, was exceedingly anxious now about Bragg's enforcement of the Blue Laws, which kept the saloons closed on Sundays. Bragg was torn. He was the kind of man who believed that one must follow the letter of the law without exception, yet he knew that in doing so he might cost Seth Low his chances of reelection in the next two years. Low had politely asked him to reconsider his position. "What can I do for you?"

The mayor was not renowned for his warmth. He got to the point. "I have a box at the opera tonight. I'd like you to join us with your wife," the mayor said.

Bragg froze.

"Rick? You there?"

He felt himself smile stiffly. "Yes, sir, I am. You do know that we are somewhat separated?" He could have kicked himself. *Somewhat separated?* Their separation was irreconcilable; of that there was no doubt.

"Of course I know! You were very clear on that point when we discussed your appointment as the city's police commissioner two months ago. But she is back now. I meant to tell you that you must reconsider your separation. We have enough trouble, and we don't need anything personal landing on our overheaped plates."

How much clearer could the mayor be? Bragg was grim. "Of course we shall attend, sir. It would be a pleasure." But in spite of the professionalism upon which he prided himself, he was furious. He could envision nothing more distasteful than escorting Leigh Anne to any function for an entire evening. But more important, she was attaining what she really wanted—status as his wife.

"Good. Think about a reconciliation, Rick. Even if just for the rest of your term. A public announcement would do. Now. What is this I have heard about Grace Conway having been murdered?"

Bragg stiffened. So the news was already out? "She was found strangled Tuesday evening, sir. The murder took place sometime Monday, between that morning and that night."

"Strangled? What does this mean? Don't tell me the city has another madman on its hands?"

"I wouldn't leap to conclusions, and I am personally working on the investigation with several of my finest inspectors," Bragg said.

"Keep me posted," Low said. "We will have a cocktail at six at the mansion. See you then." He hung up.

Bragg inhaled, his thoughts racing right to his wife, whom he had not seen since Tuesday. Reconcile? He had practically been given an order. He had no intention of reconciling, not ever.

But if the mayor wanted Leigh Anne at the opera, so be it. The real question was, how could he contain his anger during the course of an interminable evening? He reminded himself that this was his political duty. And then another voice from deep within told him that it was his marital duty as well.

"Good morning," a cheerful voice came from the doorway.

He started, his gaze meeting Francesca's. Inside, he instantly softened and warmed.

Her smile faded. "Is everything all right?" Her blue eyes, the color of cornflowers, were worried.

He sighed. "Come in. Shut the door behind you." He bent and retrieved his telephone, hanging up the receiver.

Francesca came forward. "You seem tense."

"The mayor knows about Miss Conway. Word is out, and it will only make our job harder," he said grimly.

She grimaced. "She was more famous than I suspected. I am not surprised the word has gotten out. I imagine quite a few policemen have been gossiping about her death."

"Someone from the Department is talking too freely," Bragg agreed. Then he softened. "How did it go with the dean?" He knew Francesca had gone to Barnard that morning, instead of the previous afternoon, as last evening she had told him it was the very first item on the next day's agenda.

Francesca smiled. "She doesn't want me to drop out entirely—and she admires my work as a sleuth! So I am staying on, but part-time, as you suggested. I have dropped all my courses this semester but two. I was at class this morning," she added happily.

"I am very pleased for you, Francesca," he said, meaning it and clasping her hand on impulse.

They looked at each other. Francesca no longer smiled, but neither did he. He removed his hand, as did she. "Why are you really worried?" she asked softly.

He almost sighed. This woman could see into his soul, or so it sometimes seemed. But he would not bring up his damnable wife now. "I am inundated with police affairs. Low wishes me to back off of enforcement of the Blue Laws."

Francesca's clear blue eyes widened. He felt as if he had lied to her, which, in a way, by omission, he had. He hated it. "How can you leave the saloons open on Sundays? Half of the city is expecting you to bring a new morality to it."

He did smile. "And you are in that half, of course."

"Yes, I am." She smiled back at him.

"I think I will let a week or so go by without doing

anything and see if that might make the recent efforts I have made these past few weeks seem less threatening."

Francesca nodded. "And is there anything new on the investigation? I was thinking we might begin with the three galleries Newman mentioned today, if you are not too busy. I also wish to return to the scene of the crime. Surely we have missed a clue that might lead us to Miss Neville's current location. I am haunted by the notion." She smiled, but seriously and more to herself than to him.

Her sincerity was simply adorable. He had never met anyone with such a pure heart of gold. His heart quickened, and images flashed in his mind from the night they had spent together on the Albany train. Images of Francesca with her hair down, her cheeks flushed, her eyes glazing over.

He offered her a seat before his desk, which she took, while he cleared his throat and his mind. "Hickey and Newman interviewed Levy last night. They are, I hope, interviewing Cohen this morning. Apparently LeFarge did have lunch from one to three Monday at the Waldorf Astoria," he said.

"What kind of business did Mr. Levy have with LeFarge?"

"He is an importer of silk and other expensive fabrics. Apparently LeFarge wishes to redecorate his gambling halls and the meeting was one of legitimate business concerns."

Francesca didn't believe it. "And that morning?"

Bragg shrugged. "His butler, Keebler, claims he was in his library. But we can hardly trust the statement of his paid manservant."

"Too bad we can't put him on the witness stand with his hand on a Bible," Francesca remarked dryly.

"It may come to that." He had to smile.

"Do you think LeFarge is our killer?" she asked, her expression and tone terse.

"I honestly don't know, but the man is as smooth as a river stone and as slippery as a snake. The attack upon Sarah's studio could have been a threat which your brother missed."

"But why murder Miss Conway at the same time he attacked Evan?"

"Perhaps it was a double threat—or a mistake."

"LeFarge is clearly without the slightest morals," she said darkly. Then, "I apologize for being so utterly unprofessional yesterday, Bragg."

He laid his hand on her slim shoulder. "I understand. You don't have to apologize."

She smiled up at him.

And as he stared at her he quickly recalled what it was like to take her in his arms. Francesca was the most honest and open woman he had ever known—and it was one of the reasons he cared for her so. She did not have a sly or calculating bone in her body—unlike his abhorrent wife. No two women could be more different.

It was never easy being alone with Francesca. There was always an attraction, a passion, pulsing between them. Sometimes it felt like a powerful magnet. How many times had he been so very close to giving up on his self-control and making love to her? Somehow, he had done what was right in the end.

And her passion was explosive. He knew that now.

"Bragg?" she asked warily, as if sensing the new and unwanted direction of his thoughts.

He turned them off, with an effort. "I doubt we will learn much from his staff at the Royal," he said, turning away.

"No, but we could learn quite a bit from his customers there."

"That is an effort I will make alone, Francesca," he warned quickly, facing her. "The Royal is no place for any lady, and especially not for you. You would be recognized by dozens of gentlemen there, and your reputation would never recover. Do not even think of setting one foot inside that door!"

She stood. Her eyes flashed. "You coddle me. I would hardly be in any danger by entering a fancy gambling hall, and I think my reputation is already in shambles, as the entire city knows I prefer being a sleuth to a bride."

He sighed. "I want you to stay away from LeFarge. He worries me. He is a dangerous man, never mind his false smile and pretense at surprise."

"I know that. Look at what he has done to my brother!" Francesca cried.

He went to her and touched her chin. "But Evan is on the mend, and LeFarge has been warned."

Francesca nodded grimly. Her eyes had grown moist.

He almost pulled her close, into his embrace, but he knew better—he knew the gesture meant to comfort would quickly turn into a kiss. Instead, he let her go. "I cannot go either to a gallery or back to the scene now, as I have some work to do before a luncheon engagement. You are free to enter the flat at any time, Francesca. The warsdman posted there will let you in."

"Then I will take Joel and do some sleuthing on my own," she said huskily. "He is waiting outside." She stood, her eyes unwavering upon him.

Bragg stared back. "I suppose the little cutpurse will hate me for all time."

"He will come around," she said quietly as he helped her on with her coat. He walked her to the door and said, "Be careful. If anything new develops, please come to me first before chasing a lead that could be dangerous."

She finally grinned at him, both tawny brows lifted. "I am hardly a china doll."

"It is that very attitude which keeps me awake at nights!" he exclaimed. That and his unrequited desire, he thought grimly. And a future that was looking darker and darker by the moment.

"I promise to exercise caution and good judgment," she said with a smile.

He doubted it. "I'll see you later," he said.

She hesitated, pressed her lips to his cheek, and quickly spun about and left.

Bragg stared after her until she had disappeared from view. He realized he was smiling once more. But Francesca was the woman who could always put a smile in his heart as well as upon his face.

He had never felt that way about Leigh Anne.

The smile disappeared. He would have to send her a note about the upcoming evening. The tension that had vanished instantly riddled him again. He could think of nothing less pleasant or more distasteful than escorting his wife to the opera that night.

The sooner he convinced her to return to Boston, where her father was ill and perhaps dying, or to Europe, where she kept a string of lovers, the better.

But yesterday had got away from him and he had never found the time to call on her in order to discuss the impossibility of the present being maintained in this way. Or had he avoided what would become an extremely unpleasant confrontation?

"Rick?"

Bragg started, not having heard his chief of police, Brendan Farr, come to the door, which he had left wide open. The constant pinging of the telegraph and the intermittent ringing of telephones had become familiar and pleasant sounds to him, music to his ears, so to speak. "Come in, Brendan," he said with a brief smile. He was glad to be distracted from his personal life.

Brendan Farr was six-foot-four, broad-shouldered and leonine, with a head of iron gray hair and similarly colored eyes. After quite a debate, Bragg had promoted him from inspector to his current position. He had felt that Farr's loyalty to him for such a promotion would outweigh the man's previous history of disloyalty, self-service, and corruption. The one thing Farr was, was clever. He should know which side his bread was buttered on, but Bragg had begun to regret his choice. During an investigation last week, Farr had engaged in some questionable actions, and Bragg wasn't sure if he was loyal or not.

"Everything all right, Rick?" Farr asked, taking the chair in front of Bragg's heavily cluttered desk as Bragg gestured for him to do so.

Bragg sat down opposite him. "Just the usual preoccupations." He smiled.

"You seem worried," Farr commented. "If anything is troubling you, I would be more than glad to help."

"Low has asked me to cease the Sunday saloon closings," Bragg said, leaning back in his cane-backed chair. "But the Moral Right demands it."

Farr lifted two bushy brows. "I will support whatever choice you make. You are caught, though, between a rock and a hard place."

How true that was. "I expect no less," Bragg said noncommittally. Then, switching the topic and aware that Farr had not given him a single clue as to what he was really thinking, he said, "So what may I help you with?"

Farr leaned forward. "I just learned that we have a murder investigation on our hands. I would appreciate it if you would tell me when a high-profile woman has been strangled, Rick. I was an admirer of Miss Conway's."

Bragg knew he should not be surprised that Farr had somehow learned of an investigation taking place at headquarters; after all, if the mayor knew, so did half the political world. Not one to underestimate his chief of police, Bragg tensed. How much did he know? And could he trust Farr or not? "I have assigned Newman and Hickey to handle the preliminary investigation," he said blandly.

"Yes. I spoke with them both at length, last night," Farr said. He was grim but gave no clue as to whether he knew of Evan Cahill's involvement with the actress. "She was so beautiful. I saw her once at the Empire Theater. It was a show I will never forget."

"She had many admirers, apparently. We found a great deal of fan mail in her apartment."

"Care to fill me in?"

"Well, it all seems to begin with the vandalism of Sarah Channing's studio on Friday, February fourteenth," Bragg said. "Miss Conway was found strangled Tuesday evening by her neighbor Louis Bennett. She was in an apartment belonging to Melinda Neville, an artist, and her studio was also vandalized. Miss Conway lived across the hall from Miss Neville."

"Yes, I have learned all of this from Inspector Hickey," Farr said. "And there are no leads as to where Miss Neville is now?"

"Another neighbor saw her return home Monday at six P.M.," Bragg said. "She did not have her keys, and Miss Holmes let her in. She has not been seen since. And the coroner has determined that Miss Conway died sometime on Monday." Bragg shrugged.

"Perplexing," Farr murmured. "Well, at least the press has not got wind of it. Miss Conway was a bit of a celebrity, and the moment a newsman learns of her murder, it will be headlines. Which will surely make our jobs more difficult."

"Yes, I agree."

Farr stood. "If you need anything from me, let me know."

Bragg also stood. "Brendan? There is one other aspect of the case which I think you should know about," he said. It was always better to make an adversary think he was one's ally until there was no other choice.

Farr raised his heavy brows and waited.

"Until recently, Miss Conway was the mistress of Evan Cahill."

Farr didn't blink. And then recognition showed in his eyes. "Miss Cahill's brother? The gentleman engaged to Miss Channing?"

"Yes. I am keeping it quiet, as I am not sure yet if he is somehow involved."

Farr started. "You don't think—"

"No." Bragg cut him off. "Evan is not capable of murder. But the newsmen of this town would love nothing more than to speculate upon his involvement, and out of respect for his family, I do not wish to make this information public."

"I understand," Farr said, not batting an eye.

Which worried Bragg. Because Farr knew how closely he and Francesca worked together, and Bragg felt certain that he disapproved, but whether it was of Bragg's friendship with Francesca or her involvement in police affairs he could not be sure. "Thank you," Bragg said in dismissal.

"Keep me posted," Farr returned. He turned and halted in his tracks.

Bragg looked up and froze. In fact, he forgot to breathe. Leigh Anne stood in the doorway.

Their gazes met, locked.

She was ethereal in her beauty, a tiny woman with fair and flawless skin, a perfect little body with a waist small enough for a man to span with his hands, and with sultry emerald green eyes that always seemed to whisper bedroom thoughts. Her hair was thick and long and raven black. She wore it neatly pinned up now beneath a smart black hat. She wore a suit trimmed in mink, that matched her eyes exactly. She smiled at them both. "Rick. I hope you do not mind?"

His heart beat then, hard and fast. But he knew what she intended. She intended to make their marriage public now by coming to his place of business. And by doing so, she had him by the balls. He had to acknowledge her, introduce her. It was another way of weasling back into his life.

He glanced at Farr and saw that he was, like all men, instantly bewitched. "Why would I mind?" Bragg asked with a cold smile. "Brendan, I do not believe you have met my wife."

When Farr was gone, the door closed solidly behind him, Bragg turned and faced his wife, leaning against it. She smiled uncertainly at him. He knew it was an act meant to throw him off-guard. But she had already succeeded in her clever plans. She had won this round.

"Rick? I had somehow thought you might call on me. It seems like we have so much to discuss." Her emerald eyes never left his face.

He felt defensive. "I am extremely busy, Leigh Anne."

"I know. I have been reading all the newspapers. The city adores you. You are their hero, Rick," she said softly, her eyes shining now.

"I am nobody's hero," he ground out.

"You are the knight in shining armor meant to bring the villains in the police department to their knees."

"Is that why you have come? To congratulate me on six successful weeks in office?" he asked sarcastically.

"Is there a chance that we might have one decent and civil conversation?" she retorted.

He felt guilty then. "I am sorry. I am tired and over-worked, not to mention preoccupied." He did not move from where he stood against the door.

She hadn't moved, though, either. "I hope some of your preoccupation is over me."

"It is not," he lied.

Her face fell. She turned away from him. He could not see if her expression changed, as he suspected it did. He watched her from behind as she gazed around the office. If only she had become old and ugly in the past few years. The thought was not a charitable one, but it was an honest one. Instead, she remained as petite as ever, although her small hips seemed more curved and womanly now.

She walked over to the mantel where he kept a dozen family photographs. When she had finished studying them, she faced him with a smile. "I understand that Rathe and Grace are in town," she said, referring to his father and stepmother.

"Is this why you have come down to my office? To discuss my family?"

Her smile faded. "Will you always be so hateful and so angry with me?"

He itched to lay his hands on her slim white throat. He itched to squeeze the very breath from her. Instead, he shoved them in his pockets, trembling and appalled. "We had an agreement, you and I. You were to remain in Europe, and I was to provide handsomely for you. I upheld my part of the bargain; you have broken yours."

Her mouth tightened. It was the color of rosebuds. "I beg your pardon. My father lies at death's door. Of course I would come home. And it was not a part of your bargain that you would take a mistress and flaunt her about an entire city."

He stiffened. "Francesca is the last person I care to discuss with you. But she is not my mistress. I love her too much to treat her with such disrespect."

Leigh Anne's eyes widened.

"Have you forgotten the man that I am?" he demanded.

She shook her head. "She led me to believe that she was your lover, Rick. And no, I know the man you are. Honest to a fault. There is no one more virtuous. I just wish, still and foolishly, that your honesty had extended to our marriage as well, that it had extended to me as it does to everyone else."

He exploded. He reached her in two strides, grabbed her small shoulders, unintentionally lifting her off her feet. And in holding her, he was reminded that she was not fragile, and that appearances were deceiving. "You dare to accuse me of dishonesty where you are concerned?" He saw red.

She clung to him. "You are hurting me!" But her eyes darkened, becoming almost black.

He became oddly paralyzed, with her suspended in the air, her skirts enveloping his thighs. Their gazes locked. He could not help but notice her lips were parted and that small breaths escaped them. *When he made love to her, her eyes would turn black with heat, but the moment she climaxed they would turn smoke green.* He set her down instantly.

She did not back away. Breathlessly she said, "I refuse to retract how I feel and what I believe."

She had told him that he had broken every single promise he had made to her. She had expected a life in a mansion, a life with servants and teas, balls and soirées. Instead, he had turned down a position with Washington's most prestigious law firm, opening up his own practice to serve the city's poor. Instead of buying a mansion not far from his parents' home, they had let a small, run-down flat just a stone's throw from the city's rat-infested tenements and knife-wielding gangs. "I do not want to rehash the past," he said tightly.

"But I do," she returned as firmly.

"Good God! Is that why you have come? I am sorry, Leigh Anne, sorry that after we were married I could not go through with our plans! I am truly sorry! But nothing will change the decision I made four years ago—just like nothing will change the fact that you left me, without a word of warning."

"I warned you. I tried to tell you again and again how unhappy I was—but it was a bit difficult getting through to you, now wasn't it?" Her eyes darkened, but no longer with excitement and desire. "I mean, you left for that shabby practice of yours at dawn, and when you came home, somewhere around midnight, even if I was awake, you were asleep on your feet. Oh, except for your ability to make love to me! You were always too tired to talk about us and our future—but never too tired to make love!" Tears filled her eyes.

If he allowed himself to feel guilty, she would win. "Very well. I refused to listen, and I used you selfishly."

She sighed and laid her delicate palm, encased in a fine kidskin glove, on his arm. He flinched. But oddly, he did not shake her off. "You hardly used me, Rick. That is not what I said or meant, and you know it."

*There had been so many heated nights and mornings....*

"I never turned you away, because I wanted to be with you as much as you wanted to be with me," she added frankly, allowing her hand to finally drop from his arm.

The gesture was a caress of sorts. He stiffened, aroused inexplicably, and he paced away. He reminded himself that he hadn't been with a woman since he had arrived in New York, about to accept a politically important appointment. It had been almost two months, during which he had been tormented by his desire for Francesca. But he knew he was fooling himself.

Leigh Anne had always had the ability to arouse him with a mere look, a single word, a soft breath.

"Leigh Anne." He cleared his voice. "I have a dozen things I must get through today. What is it that you want?"

"You know what I want."

He whirled.

But she wasn't playing the seductress now. Her look was direct and steady and resolved.

"Refreshen my memory," he managed.

"I want to resume our lives, Rick."

"Why? Why now?" he demanded, even though he already knew. Now that he was in a position of prominence and power in New York City, and perhaps on his way to the U.S. Senate, she intended to be his wife again. For she knew he could offer her a life of glamour and prestige now and, if all went well, eventually one of wealth and power, too. This had nothing to do with love and everything to do with avarice. His wife remained a selfish, calculating bitch.

She smiled grimly. "When we were separated, I carried the oddest notion with me. It was that I would always be the one woman you loved, and that there would never be anyone else. That notion was, somehow, comforting. It was my anchor."

He could not imagine her speaking truthfully now, and he could not imagine where she was leading.

She sighed. "Rumors of your love for Miss Cahill reached me in Boston, Rick. I was stunned, I told myself the rumors were wrong, but I could not put what I had heard aside. In fact, I was distressed, extremely so."

He did not believe her. He wanted to laugh in a disparaging manner, but somehow he did not.

"And I decided to come to New York to find out for myself if the rumors were true. And the moment I saw the two of you together, when you were coming out of Grand Central Station, I knew I could not allow you to love another woman. I was jealous. I am jealous. Erroneously, I had thought I would always be the only one capable of holding your heart. The only one who really had your heart. Well, that is apparently not the case. But we are still married, and I will fight for my rights as your wife."

"A pretty speech," he said coldly. "I am almost moved to applaud."

"Rick! I am speaking to you from the heart!"

"Then so shall I. I love Francesca Cahill, and I want a divorce."

She stared, her mouth trembling, more beautiful than ever, appearing fragile, vulnerable, hurt.

"So the impasse remains," he said, aware of being cruel.

She inhaled, hard. "Not necessarily," she said.

He stiffened, sensing a devious blow. "No? You want a marriage; I want a divorce. Surely you do not have a way out of this dilemma?"

"I do." She wet her lips, the tip of her tongue small and pink and very moist and flitting nervously about.

He stared.

"Allow me to resume my place in your life as your wife for one year, and if, after that time has passed—a time in which we share all that every husband and wife shares—if you still wish for a divorce, I shall give it to you."

He was stunned. "No! Absolutely not!" Was she insane? Did she think he could tolerate her in his life, his home, his bed, for an entire year? What clever ploy was this? He strode to the door, flinging it open. "Good day, Leigh Anne."

She did not move. "Very well. Then we shall make it six months."

He started, staring again.

She wet her lips nervously another time. "Rick, I will put it in writing. Six months of marriage, and if you still feel this way, you shall have your divorce. With your connections, that means in seven months or so you would be a free man—free to wed Miss Cahill, if that is what you really want."

His heart beat hard, urgently. For one moment he saw Francesca in his mind, but he could not think about her now. He felt as if his entire life were at stake. In seven months he might be free of this witch. All he had to do was accept this amazing bargain. Of course, he would have his lawyer draw up a contract. He did not trust his beautiful little wife for a moment.

While she, clearly, believed he would change his mind after the prearranged time. But of course, he would not.

"Rick? This is fair. It gives us a chance to find out if we should really part ways, or if we should honor the vows we once made and stay together instead."

Her words were another blow. When he had made his marriage vows, he had intended to keep them forever. He was the kind of man who married only once and forever. Very cautiously he said, "Six months as man and wife. Six months and not a single day more."

"Yes." Her face was pinched with tension now. It only made her more beautiful.

It was hard to think clearly—he sensed a fatal trap. But in seven or eight months he would be free, finally. All he had to do was keep a clear mind and remind himself of the liar and adulteress that she really was.

And how hard would that be? He had been aware of those facts for four long, painful years.

He smiled.

She tensed, her eyes widening.

"I'll do it," he said.

# CHAPTER
# EIGHT

MAGGIE KENNEDY PAUSED NERVOUSLY before the open door to Evan's bedroom. She was wearing her best ensemble, a pin-striped gray jacket and a matching skirt. The white shirtwaist beneath had lace detail at the collar, where she had pinned a pretty cameo, one that had belonged to her mother. Maggie only owned two hats—as she could not make them herself—and a jaunty black affair with a satin ribbon was pinned atop her head. She had carefully pulled her shoulder-length Irish red hair into a chignon, but a few wisps escaped around her face. When her mother had given her the cameo, she had also given her tiny pearl ear bobs, and Maggie wore those as well. Her only other jewelry was her plain, unadorned wedding band. But on its inside Joe had engraved: "Joe Kennedy, Forever Yours."

Was he laughing at her now? She could see him so clearly, as if it had not been five years since he had died. He had been short and brawny, but he'd had the face of an angel—their eldest, Joel, took after him exactly. No, he probably wasn't laughing; he was looking at her sternly, although there was that twinkle in his eye. And he was chiding her for her foolish ways.

*Now what could you be thinkin', Mrs. Kennedy? To carry on with a gentleman? I know you be missin' me, but a gentleman? You might as well hope to land on the moon! Ah, Maggie, darlin', how I wish I was with ye now. . . .*

Tears filled her eyes. She would always miss her husband, and he was always right. In a way, since he had died, he had become an angel sitting upon her shoulder, guiding her in the difficult task of raising four children alone.

"Be brave," he whispered now, his black eyes soft and fond. "Tell the gent good-bye an' begone with you an' the children."

Silently she told him not to rush her. Maggie glanced inside Evan's bedroom and saw that he was sleeping. Her heart skipped, lurched. Maybe it was better this way, she thought, oddly miserable. She knew that this was the perfect opportunity to sneak away.

An image of the stunningly elegant and beautiful countess filled Maggie's mind. Sitting there on Evan's bed regaling him with anecdotes of her life in castles in Europe, a life filled with duchesses and dukes, her hand stroking his shoulder, his cheek, his hair. And Evan had not minded, not that any man would. He had laughed at her stories, but when she touched him his laughter had died.

Maggie hadn't meant to spy or eavesdrop. But when his fiancée had excused herself for a moment, leaving the room, Maggie, who had been pacing in her own bedroom, the door wide open, had crept out into the hall. The handsome doctor had left a bit earlier, and she knew very well that Evan and the beautiful countess were alone.

The door had been left ajar. Maggie had glanced in, only to find the countess leaning over Evan, her milky white bosom almost falling from the jacket she wore, her mouth on his.

Evan had not pushed her away. The kiss had been long and, from Maggie's perspective, quite intimate.

Maggie didn't blame him. She knew his upcoming marriage was an arranged one, and she would have to be deaf and blind not to know that he did not want to marry his fiancée.

"Foolish gel," Joe whispered in her ear now. "What do ye think to do? Wind up on yer back with yer skirts up over yer head? I know it's been a long spell, my girl, but we both know that isn't you."

Maggie wiped her eyes. It had been five years since she had lain in her husband's arms, breathless and glowing from their lovemaking. And she did not want to be a passing fancy, a lightskirt, a trollop, a whore. She was never going to be in a man's arms again, and she was never going to be held and loved the way Joe had held and loved her.

She would not say good-bye. She turned to go, trying not to recall a vivid image from the other day, when Evan had returned home with her three little ones, Paddy and Mat and Lizzie. They had all been bundled up in coats and hats, scarves and gloves—her children clearly in new garments Evan had bought for them. And they had all been laughing, shrieking, screaming. Lizzie had been on top of Evan Cahill's shoulders, beaming. As everyone was covered with snow and a huge grinning snowman now graced the front yard of the Cahill home, Maggie suspected quite a frenetic snow fight had just taken place. She had looked at the four of them and had, somehow, felt another piece of her heart warm over.

"Maggie! Mrs. Kennedy!"

She froze at the sound of his voice, and slowly she turned.

He smiled at her. "Did you wish to speak with me? I must have dozed off."

She wet her lips, reluctant now to enter the room. And even with black-and-blue mottling his face, even with the black patch worn to protect one eye, he remained one of the handsomest men she had ever seen, almost as handsome as Joe.

"Mrs. Kennedy?" His smile faded a little. "Do come in.

Is something wrong? Are you going somewhere?" His gaze drifted over her small body.

Maggie nodded, forced a smile, and entered the room. "How are you today?" she asked softly.

He looked now at the purse and gloves she carried. "You did not come to visit this morning. I had to ask a housemaid to read yesterday's news to me."

Maggie had brought him a breakfast tray yesterday, along with the *Herald*. She felt that her small, odd smile had become frozen in place. "I fear we must be leaving, Mr. Cahill," she said.

He started, his smile vanishing, and he jerked to sit upright. As he did, he uttered a soft groan. Maggie wanted to run over to him and help him into a comfortable position, as Joe had once had broken ribs and she knew just how painful the injury was. But she gripped her bag and gloves and did not move.

"Leaving?" he gasped, pale now. "What do you mean? Surely you do not mean that you and the children are moving back to your home?"

She nodded. *Ye have been a fool, Mrs. Kennedy. Stayin' so long in this fancy home, as if it were where ye belong. Ye don't belong here and ye never will. An' ye never should have let the children get so fond of the fancy gentleman in the bed.* Maggie swallowed. Joe was never so cruel. But he was being cruel now.

"Have I done something to offend you, Mrs. Kennedy?" Evan asked seriously, appearing extremely upset.

"Of course not," she said quickly. "You have been nothing but kind and generous, as has your entire family. But there is simply no valid reason for us to remain here. Our home is downtown."

He stared. "I think I have offended you, but I cannot think of how." He grimaced then. "I see no reason for you to leave. The house is a large one. Mother doesn't mind. She said it herself, I heard her, she thinks of you as a saving grace, and she is most appreciative of all that you have done to help me through my injuries."

Maggie knew that. Julia—whom she found to be the most elegant and intimidating woman she had ever met, bar none—had actually thanked her herself. "I am no longer ill, Mr. Cahill. It is time for us to leave."

He did not speak for a moment. Maggie wasn't used to seeing him unsmiling and so grim. Then, "Of course. You must make sure that Jenkins or another coachman sees you and the children safely home."

Once again, he was so terribly kind. "We will take the Elevated," she said.

"Absolutely not." He reached for the bell by his bed and rang it. "Jenkins will drive you home. I insist."

Maggie nodded as a housemaid appeared and received Evan's instructions. When she had fled to order a coach brought around, Evan smiled grimly at Maggie. "It has been a pleasure getting to know your children, Mrs. Kennedy." He hesitated, flushed. "May I be bold?"

Her heart skipped with absurd hope. "Yes."

"I will miss them."

She stared, felt moisture gathering quickly in her eyes, and refused to listen to Joe chide her now. "They will miss you, Mr. Cahill," she said.

He hesitated again. "May I take them curling sometime soon? We had a rousing time last week, sledding and ice-skating, but we did not curl."

She nodded, incapable of speech. He was referring to the popular game of sliding kettle-like objects across the ice.

He glanced away and then back at her. "And you should be most welcome to join us," he added tersely.

She meant to smile, but it felt like a grimace. "I doubt I shall have the time," she said.

"Of course."

"Good day, Mr. Cahill. I do hope you feel better soon."

"Good day, Mrs. Kennedy. I . . . I wish you great luck in your future endeavors."

She smiled without looking at him and fled.

THURSDAY, FEBRUARY 20, 1902—1:00 P.M.

The first gallery was around the corner on Fourth Avenue. Francesca climbed out of a hansom with Joel, facing an old limestone building with a set of deep steps leading to the scarred and closed front door. Had the sign, GALLERY HOELTZ, not been hanging above the front door, she would not have found it. As it was, the windows on either side of the entrance were too high and narrow to see inside.

She smiled cheerfully at Joel. "Shall we?"

He smiled back, but he seemed a bit glum. "Sure."

As they started up the stone steps, she asked, "Is anything wrong?"

Joel sighed. "We're goin' home today, Miz Cahill."

Francesca started, finding the front door locked. "I had no idea! Maggie never said a word!"

Joe shrugged. Then, "She's awful upset. Can't think why."

Francesca stared at him, for an instant recalling Maggie's laughter and her brother's smile, but then the front door was opened by a short dapper man with a goatee. "May I help you?" he asked, looking Francesca over, with obvious approval—perhaps thinking of her as a potential client—and then noting Joel, with similar disapproval.

"Yes. Are you the gallery owner?"

"Yes, I am. We usually see clients by appointment," he said firmly.

"I am Francesca Cahill," Francesca said, handing him her calling card. It read:

> Francesca Cahill
> Crime-Solver Extraordinaire
> No. 810 Fifth Avenue, New York City
> All Cases Accepted No Crime Too Small

He studied it for a moment, then regarded her grimly. "Very odd. So you wish to speak to me or view my collection? I have some fine upcoming artists on hand," he said.

Francesca knew which way the wind did blow. "Actually, I must do both."

He began to open the door more fully, then glanced at Joel. "The boy?"

"He's my assistant," she said.

The man grunted, his dour humor not changing, and let them both inside.

The front hall was narrow and dark. They followed him up a steep staircase, at the top of which light was pouring onto the landing. A moment later they had entered a sunny room that had clearly once been an entry hall. The door had been removed to the two adjoining rooms, which had once been a salon and dining room. Paintings were hanging on every visible space, while others were stacked up against the walls, on the floor. Here and there a sculpture rested. Francesca took it all in with a glance.

She smiled at Hoeltz. "We are trying to locate a young artist by the name of Melinda Neville," she said. "Miss Melinda Neville."

He said, "Is this a jest?"

Francesca started. "No, it is not."

He said, "Follow me."

Francesca and Joel exchanged glances and followed him through the far room. He paused before a pair of portraits done in a classical and stoic manner. In one, a lady and her daughter were posed in ball gowns, seated together on a gold velvet settee. Francesca recognized them both. "I know these women," she said. "That older lady is a friend of my mother's, but I do not recall her name."

Hoeltz smiled. "That is Mrs. Louise Greeley and her daughter Cynthia."

Francesca took another glance at the tall, attractive woman, whose set expression and determined eyes reminded her, in a way, of her own determined mother. Her daughter, who was perhaps Francesca's age, if not a bit younger, was quite plump but also pretty, with a soft, full face, orange-red hair, and freckles scattered upon her pert nose. The daughter looked unhappy—miserably so.

Then Francesca looked at the portrait beside it. A young black-haired man of twenty or so stood in a very rigid pose. Had he not been in a dark suit, Francesca might have guessed him to be a young military officer. His eyes were as dark as his hair, his nose long, his mouth set firmly in a tight line. He might have been attractive if he were smiling, but as he was not, he looked far too serious and far too severe. Francesca knew she would not like him if they ever met. And the pose, with his hand upon one hip and his severe expression, was terribly familiar. Had she seen this work of art before?

Suddenly a notion struck her, hard. Had the artist who had done LeFarge's portrait also done this one? The works seemed terribly similar to her uneducated eye.

"And who is this?" she asked finally.

"Thomas Neville," Hoeltz answered.

Francesca gasped. "Miss Neville's brother?"

"Yes, Melinda's brother. And now I must ask, why are you trying to find her?"

She blinked. Hoeltz had referred to Miss Neville in a manner indicating that they were good friends. "The police wish to interview her, as do I," she said softly.

He started. His dour look disappeared. He was wide-eyed now. "Why?"

"The actress Grace Conway was found murdered in Miss Neville's flat," she said.

He turned white. "They were friends," he said, looking as if he might faint at any moment.

Francesca gripped his arm to keep him upright. "May I assume you were Miss Neville's friend as well?"

He looked at her with the same wide, stunned black eyes, and he laughed. The laughter was not a happy sound—it was, instead, rather hysterical. "Friends? We are hardly friends!" he cried.

Francesca waited.

"She is my mistress," he said.

. . .

Bragg had chosen the Fifth Avenue Hotel for their lunch. Hart strode down a dark, rather dreary corridor, the wall paneled in wood and covered with the portraits of some of the city's most famous and infamous men from the century before. Dark, unwavering eyes stared down at him as he passed. His curiosity was piqued. He hardly had a social relationship with his half brother, so why the invitation to dine?

It quickly crossed his mind that, other than the Bragg family, the only thing they had in common was Francesca. Clearly she would be the subject of their luncheon. Did Rick wish to warn him away from her yet again? He could not help but be amused. He was not the kind of man who took orders from anyone. And he could not help imagining his half brother's reaction should he tell him of his intention to marry the lady in question.

The dining room was extremely crowded, as the hotel did a busy luncheon; table after table was occupied by gentlemen. The room was a sea of dark suits and sideburns. Hart paused on the threshold, instantly espying his half brother seated at the room's most coveted table, facing out upon everyone. His mouth quirked. Was Rick enjoying his newfound power? Somehow, Hart knew the answer was no, and it was a shame. But then, Rick was just too noble to enjoy the perks of his position.

"Mr. Hart, sir!" The maître d' rushed over to him, fawning and obsequious. "It's so wonderful to see you, sir. It has been at least six months!"

"Good afternoon, Henry. I see my party has arrived. I can find my way, thank you."

But Henry rushed forward, leading him through the linen-clad tables, saying, "The commissioner just arrived. Perhaps not a minute before yourself, sir."

Hart wasn't really listening. He was nodding at the various gentlemen he passed, all of whom he knew, for one reason or another. A few men he purposefully made eye contact with. He had slept with their wives at one time or another and would not evince the least bit of guilt or regret. After all, he hadn't been the first lover in their beds, and he wouldn't be the last.

Which was why he had always preferred married women. Those who were already unfaithful, that is. They understood the game and would make no demands. But now his life was going to change.

He knew he would never be bored with Francesca, and he also knew that if she ever married someone else, he would lose her friendship. No husband would tolerate her being his friend, and with just cause. And it was this last certainty that compelled him to proceed. Her friendship had become as vital to his being as the very air he breathed. And it did not matter that she did not "love" him.

He refused to contemplate the fact that she thought that she "loved" Rick.

Bragg stood when Hart reached the table. He was not in a good mood, as he was scowling, an unusual expression for him. Hart instantly wondered what Francesca had done to cause his irritation. He smiled then, to himself. She had the worst penchant for putting herself in danger, all in the good cause of helping some needy soul. But the trials and tribulations of a relationship with Francesca Cahill were surely worth it. In any case, as he had put his neck on the chopping block, he would soon find out. He sat down. "My, we are dour today."

"Good day, Calder," Rick said with a terse nod.

Hart decided this would be an amusing luncheon after all, and he lolled a bit in his chair. A bottle of red wine was being placed on the table. "Château Lafite? At a luncheon? Are we celebrating?" He knew that was not the case.

"I am sure you are pleased that I am out of sorts today, but no, we are not celebrating. I have a migraine," he said, nodding at the waiter to open the wine.

"Is she giving you a run for your money? She can be a bit of trouble, I suppose. What has she done now that I don't know?"

"She is hardly giving me a run for my money." Rick grimaced. "But she has given me this migraine. She dared to come down to the office this morning," he added.

Hart was confused. After all, Francesca was frequently at headquarters. "Odd, I thought you enjoyed having her downtown."

"What the hell are you talking about?" Rick said savagely. "The last thing I need is Leigh Anne appearing at my place of business."

Hart's eyes widened when he realized that they were not discussing the same woman. "I was referring to Francesca," he said mildly, enjoying himself now more than ever. Oh, ho! So his brother was out of sorts because of his gorgeous little wife. He should have known. Nothing had changed, now had it?

Bragg was tasting the wine, and he choked. "Francesca?" he asked. Then, setting the glass down, "Why are you staring at me as if I have grown two heads?"

"Apparently she is not the woman on your mind," Hart said, flashing his teeth in a bare imitation of a smile. "Don't you think you have hurt her enough?"

"You may mind your own affairs where Francesca and I are concerned," Bragg said flatly. He turned to the waiter. "The wine is very good."

Their glasses were filled. Hart made no move to pick up his menu. "I really meant it. Your friendship with Francesca is putting her in a terrible position and you know it."

"Don't you ever think to be her defender," Bragg snapped. "That role hardly suits your black heart. We are both struggling to do what is right. Neither one of us expected Leigh Anne to appear in our lives."

"So what did you intend? To take a young, untried, and innocent woman as your mistress?"

"No," he said slowly, "that is not what I intended and you know it. Nor did I intend to fall in love with her. But it happened, and now we are both suffering for it."

In a way, Hart felt sorry for his brother, too, but as Rick had always gotten the respect and accolades, he refused to entertain such compassion now. Let Rick sleep in his own untidy bed. "How long will Leigh Anne be staying?" He couldn't wait to hear the answer.

Bragg looked at him, positively suffused with anger. "Six months."

His curiosity escalated wildly. "How odd that you do not send her away."

Bragg set his wineglass down. "You know, I did not come here to discuss my wife—or Francesca. I came here to discuss a case."

Hart hardly wanted to talk police business, although he did wish to know what Francesca and Rick were working on. "Well, that is a new twist." He did not touch his wine. "What dastardly crime has been committed now?"

Bragg drummed his long fingers on the table. "Grace Conway, the actress, was found strangled in an artist's studio. The studio was vandalized exactly as was Sarah Channing's," he said.

Hart was at attention now. "You do not pull any punches," he said, stunned. "But Grace was Evan's mistress!" And his mind raced. First an assault upon Sarah's studio and now this, the murder of Grace Conway. And Evan Cahill was the single man involved with them both.

"You knew Miss Conway?" Bragg asked sharply.

"Yes, I do—I did. In fact, two years ago we had an affair. She was a wonderful woman," Hart said grimly, the fact of her death just sinking in. But he was also thinking about Francesca. How could he help her brother now? For surely he was, somehow, involved. "I don't like this," he said abruptly. "How is Evan Cahill involved?"

"We don't know. Do you know of an artist named Melinda Neville? A Miss Melinda Neville?"

"No, I have never heard the name."

"Miss Conway was in her studio when she was murdered. The two women were neighbors," Bragg said. "And now, Miss Neville seems to have disappeared."

"I can find out if anyone is handling her work," Hart said. "Shall I ask around the various galleries which I frequent?"

"I would appreciate it. We are concerned that Miss Neville may have been the killer's target."

"How is Francesca taking this?"

Bragg looked him in the eye. "She is managing very well. We both wish to keep the fact that Miss Conway was Evan's mistress out of the news journals."

"A good idea," Hart said.

The waiter approached. "Would you gentlemen like to order?"

"A moment, please," Bragg said. The waiter left. "Any idea why someone would start violating various art studios? Ones belonging to young women?"

"No. But I shall certainly think about it."

"Any odd characters in the art world these days?"

Hart grinned. "Most of its denizens are odd, Rick."

Rick accepted that, and he began to spin his menu around with his fingertips. Hart felt the moment that his brother's thoughts veered from the criminal investigation. A set expression closed his face. It was an expression Hart had seen many times, four years ago, when Leigh Anne had run off to Europe.

He finally sighed. As much as he disliked his brother, they did share a drop or two of blood. "Care for some advice?"

"From you? If this is about my personal life, I don't think so."

He leaned forward. "Get her out of your system once and for all. Fuck her brains out. And send her away. If you wish, I shall give you a tidy sum with which to pay her off. A single large one-time payment and the two of you are done." He was disappointed with himself for being so benevolent with his impossibly virtuous brother. He would much prefer to gloat over the impasse Rick now found himself in. Nor did he really wish for Bragg to be running about the city with no wife in sight. Still, should that day come, it did not change the fact of his marriage. Leigh Anne would never give him a divorce and Francesca was too hot-blooded to wait for years and years for her supposed knight in shining armor.

Bragg leaned back in his chair, his amber gaze unwavering. "I seem to recall that you do not give a damn about my life, so why the sudden advice to sleep with my wife, and why the hell the offer to loan me enough money to pay her off?"

Hart hesitated. "Even you do not deserve the pain of such a viper."

"Really? I think there is more to your offer than meets the eye, Calder; I am just not sure what is really on your mind." He leaned forward, tension knotting his neck and shoulders. "Let me guess why you are so generous with your advice. If I follow it, you shall be free to pursue and seduce Francesca yourself and then, should I send Leigh Anne away, I will be deeply, impossibly in your debt!" He stared, grimacing. "You are the last person I wish to owe my life to. I would never be able to pay you back; therefore, my answer is no, thank you."

"I shall do as I choose with Francesca whether you are screwing Leigh Anne or not. And you are a fool," Hart said coldly. "Why this city thinks so highly of you I shall never know. But know this—I am not making such an offer again."

"That is fine with me. As I have no intention of ever being a puppet on your strings," Bragg said calmly.

Hart was furious with himself now. And he felt like a small boy who had offered a cookie to his dog, only to have his hand bitten. "How melodramatic. Here's a thought—by refusing my offer you will become reconciled with Leigh Anne and led around by your nose hairs for the rest of your life. You shall be a puppet on her strings!"

"Funny how you did not deny your intent to seduce Francesca," Bragg returned coldly.

"If I denied it, would you believe me?" He decided he had had enough. Besides, he wasn't hungry, anyway.

"No."

They stared at each other. "I will kill you if you hurt

her," Bragg said. "She is not for you. Stick to Daisy and the likes of her, Hart," he warned.

Hart grinned. "I was thinking the same thing. I will kill you if you hurt her. Oh, wait! It's too late. You have already hurt her, haven't you?"

Bragg started. "This simply amazes me, that you think you could ever be her hero!" Bragg leaned forward, lowering his voice. "It is me whom she loves. Not you. She could never love a blackguard. You may wish to protect her from me, but she needs protecting from you. I am getting a divorce, Hart. And while I would never ask Francesca to wait for me, if she is free when I become free, I am marrying her," he said flatly.

Hart stared. The room had become still and silent around him. His heart felt as if it had stopped. And was that icy fear he had just felt coiling around his guts? "No," he said slowly, harshly. "You are not."

"I doubt you can predict the future, or have you become psychic?" Bragg mocked.

"But I *can* predict the future," Hart said, standing and tossing his linen napkin down. "You see, by the time you obtain your divorce, Francesca will no longer be free."

Bragg also stood. "What does that mean?"

"It means she will be married to me," he said.

# CHAPTER
# NINE

FRANCESCA AND JOEL SMILED at the officer standing outside Melinda Neville's apartment. He instantly moved to bar their way. "Miss Neville?" he asked quickly.

Francesca continued to smile at him, handing him her calling card. "No, I am afraid I am not Miss Neville," she said with false cheer. She felt terrible for Bertrand Hoeltz, who had not seen Melinda since Monday morning when they had taken a *petit déjeuner* together. Apparently Melinda had met Hoeltz in Paris, about a year ago, where their affair had begun. He was a frequent traveler to Europe, as it turned out. He had begged her to return to New York, and eventually, the long-distance nature of their affair too taxing, she had agreed.

Melinda Neville kept her own flat at Number 202 10th Street but spent a good deal of her time with Hoeltz, who had his own apartment behind the art gallery he owned. They had spent Sunday evening together, dined lightly the following morning, with Melinda departing to go to her studio and work. He had not seen her since. He was frantic.

The roses that had been lying upon the floor not far from Miss Conway's body had been haunting Francesca since she had first seen the murder victim Tuesday. They had not been given to Melinda Neville by her lover. "I feel certain they were a gift meant for Miss Conway," he had said tearfully. "This is not like Melinda. She would never disappear for three days without telling me where she was going and why. I fear something terrible has happened to her," he said, trembling.

Francesca had laid a comforting hand upon his shoulder. "Do you know another artist, Sarah Channing?" she had asked.

He had shaken his head no.

Now Francesca faced the young policeman guarding the door to Flat Number Seven. "Miss Cahill," the wardsman said, his eyes now as round as his blushing face. "You may go in, ma'am."

Francesca thanked him, allowed him to open the door for her, and preceded Joel inside. As she turned on a lamp, Joel said, "You think Hoeltz went and stiffed her?"

Francesca looked at him fondly. "We have simply no reason to believe such a thing, Joel." Of course, she had had to wonder the very same thing. But that was the problem of having a list of credible suspects that consisted of one— Andrew LeFarge.

"Maybe someone else gave her them roses. Maybe he was jealous and he seen red. Ye know, like in the theater."

She blinked at him with respect. "That is an admirable theory. We shall get to the bottom of this, Joel. Let us continue to hope that Miss Neville is unharmed." But Francesca did not believe it. She had a terrible feeling that the missing woman was dead.

Francesca now studied the all too familiar and gruesome room. A depiction of Miss Conway's body as she had been found was outlined in chalk upon the floor. The roses that had been scattered there were gone, gathered up, Francesca thought, as evidence. Francesca turned and gazed at the black letter *B* painted on the vandalized wall. Did B stand for Bragg? Did it stand for Bartolla Benevente, whose portrait had been mutilated by the vandal at Sarah Channing's studio? Or perhaps it stood for something or someone with which or whom she was not familiar yet.

"Nuthin' new here," Joel announced. "Don't know what you expected to find." He shifted impatiently from foot to foot, shivering.

"Probably nothing," Francesca said distractedly. She went over to the chalk outline of Miss Conway's body and paused. Had she already found a new admirer? It seemed likely, given her popularity. Was one of her ardent admirers a murderous madman?

Or had her murder been accidental?

They so needed a solid clue. Francesca thought about the connection between Melinda Neville and Sarah Channing— art. It wasn't even Bertrand Hoeltz. She thought about the connection between Grace Conway and Melinda Neville— it had been this building. The connection between Grace and Sarah had been her brother. She was at a loss.

And Sarah was alive. Grace Conway was not, and in all likelihood, neither was Melinda Neville.

Francesca paced the room, certain she was missing something and unable to determine what that something was. Finally she sat down on the sofa, having given up. There was something that she had seen or something that her mind wanted to tell her, but it simply wasn't coming to her now.

"Mebbe I had better git home an' see if my mom needs something?" Joel asked.

Francesca realized that it was getting late. She hurried to him. "I think you should go home," she said, patting his back. "I think we have done enough sleuthing for today. I have an errand to perform soon, anyway." And as she spoke, her heart lurched unpleasantly. She had delayed and procrastinated until there was simply not another excuse she could make. Evan was improving daily, and soon he would be up and about. She had to ask Hart for that loan so that Evan could pay back some of his debts.

"You sure it's OK?" Joel asked with open worry.

"I'm sure." Francesca smiled at him.

They left the apartment, pausing to thank the young officer for letting them in. Outside, Francesca halted on the sidewalk in front of the building, more disturbed than ever. *She was missing something.*

And it was right there, in front of her face; she felt certain of it.

She recalled the scene on the street two days ago when she and Joel had first arrived there. The policemen in their uniforms, the empty police wagon, the Daimler, the Mugheads. And then her gaze flew back to a stoop not far from the one she and Joel had just left.

There had been a gray-haired woman sitting there in rags, swilling her beer from a bucket. Talking madly to herself and jeering at everyone. A madwoman, a vagrant, a drunk. Just how long had she been sitting there?

Her excitement rising, Francesca reminded herself that Grace Conway had been murdered sometime on Monday, not on Tuesday night. But she could not tamp down her enthusiasm now.

She had helped feed the homeless and the poor too many Sundays to count. And the one thing she knew from her active social duties was that vagrants frequented the same locations, time and again. A city corner might be considered to be home to one, a building's stoop home to another.

"Joel, we must find that vagrant woman—the one who was loitering on the adjacent stoop on Tuesday night." She was breathless now. It was a long shot—or was it? "I am returning here after dark," she said.

And he looked at her as if she were the crazy one.

THURSDAY, FEBRUARY 20, 1902—5:00 P.M.

Calder Hart's offices were in a fine brick building on Front Street, with views of the wharves and the ships there, the bay, and the Statue of Liberty. Francesca could not appreciate his location now. She had been putting off her visit to Calder Hart long enough. She dreaded facing him after their last encounter, and even more, she dreaded begging him for a loan.

In fact, there was more than dread in her heart; there was fear. She kept telling herself that there was simply no reason for her to be afraid of a man who was such a good friend. She simply had to get that loan for Evan's sake, even if it meant spending the rest of her life paying Hart back, penny by copper penny.

Joel now gazed up at the brick building with wide eyes as several drays drawn by draft horses went by. A huge sign was hanging just below the temple pediment of its roof, and it read quite simply: HART INDUSTRIES. When Joel had learned that she was calling upon Hart, he had told her he would accompany her, as the wharf was simply too rough a place for a fine lady like herself. "How rich do you think he really is?" Joel asked breathlessly.

"I have no idea," Francesca said tersely. She reminded herself to remain calm and composed. It did not help. And looking at Joel, she wondered if the real reason he had accompanied her downtown was the ruffians lingering about the wharf or a fascination of his own for Calder Hart.

"How'd a man who was a boy like me get so rich?" Joel asked as they entered the building—and that quite answered her question.

"You might wish to ask him that, sometime."

"He'd never tell me," Joel muttered, his cheeks turning red.

"Calder is actually a kind man," Francesca whispered nervously as they passed through the lobby. It was wood-paneled, with gleaming wood floors. She knew the building was a recently constructed one, but it looked as if it had been around for decades. Several multicolored, mostly red Persian rugs covered the floors. Works of art hung on the walls. There was a pleasant sitting area. A larger than life-size sculpture of a Roman soldier on a brawny horse dominated the room.

"He's a blackguard. I heard it said. He ain't kind, Miz Cahill."

Francesca paused. "He has been kind to us," she remonstrated.

Joel looked her in the eye. "Only because you're a real pretty lady."

She decided not to argue the point. She had been to Calder's office one time before, and she and Joel set up the stairs. They were both breathless by the time they reached the fifth floor.

They entered a grand salon, where a crystal chandelier the size of a small buggy hung from the high ceiling, which was grandly embossed in gold. A large rug in shades of beige, green, and coral covered the floor; the walls were moss green, the furniture elegant and grand. The room could easily host a small ball. A Chippendale desk was at the room's far end. A young clerk stood and approached them.

Francesca gripped her reticule very tightly. It was too late to back out now—or was it? "Is Mr. Hart in?"

The clerk was disapproving. "Yes. I am afraid I do not have you scheduled to meet with him, Miss, er . . . Miss . . . ?"

"I am a personal friend," Francesca said, and the moment the words were out, she felt her cheeks heat. She knew what the young clerk assumed. He thought she was a marriage-mad young debutante hoping to ensnare Calder or, worse, a lovesick one. "Please do ask him if he has a moment to see me. Francesca Cahill," she added nervously.

The man intended to smile and grimaced instead. "He is in a very important meeting," he warned. "Please, do take a seat."

Francesca tried to do so but found it impossible to sit, and she jumped to her feet, instead removing her gloves and hanging her coat on a coatrack. Joel lounged on a settee with gilded hooves for feet, draping his wool jacket carelessly on one arm there. "Joel? After you say hello to Calder, do you mind if I have a private word with him?"

Joel blinked. "Do I *mind*?" He blinked at her in confusion. "Oh! That's a lady's way of saying I should sit out here! I'll stay here, Miz Cahill," he said, chuckling. "I don't *mind*."

She patted his head absently.

"Miss Cahill?" The clerk came running forward, looking stricken, as if he had just done something criminal and had been found out. "Mr. Hart will see you immediately. I am sorry I made you wait," he added quickly.

"Thank you." Francesca followed the clerk from the salon and down a short hall. She passed an open doorway and saw a huge conference table with perhaps two dozen chairs, the wood dark cherry, the chairs black leather, all of it bringing to mind the sound of muted whispers and the scent of Cuban cigars. Two cherrywood doors were open at the end of the corridor. A huge office faced Francesca, at its farthest end Hart's large leather-inlaid desk. He wasn't seated behind it—he was standing in the center of the room, clearly waiting for her, as always, clad in black trousers that belonged to a black suit. But he was in his white shirt and silver vest. When he saw her, he smiled.

Warmth blazed its way through her, from her head to her toes.

Today he looked like a dangerously handsome gambler, a professional one.

But perhaps that was what he really was.

"You have made my day, Francesca," he murmured, the smile in his nearly black eyes now.

"I do hope you have had a better day than that," she said tartly. It was hot in his office, but the fire in the hearth beneath the marble mantel was quite tame.

He took both of her hands in his. "It has been rather boring and quite fair," he said. He dimpled, lifted one hand, and kissed it.

Francesca inhaled and drew her hand away, acutely aware of his lips having brushed her skin. How would he react when she asked him for a loan? She would never, ever use the fact that he wished to marry her as a trump card, but she felt shameless, because it was a trump card whether she played it or not. If only their friendship hadn't changed!

Hart grinned at Joel. "Hey there, Kennedy. Are you taking good care of Miss Cahill?"

Joel nodded very seriously. "I do my best, Mr. Hart."

"Good. The way I see it, you are her bodyguard now, Kennedy. It is your duty to keep her safe and sound. And you have done quite a good job, I think, up to now."

"Yes, sir," Joel said, flushing with pleasure.

"I am present, you know," Francesca said, remaining as tense as ever. "I am an intelligent grown woman who has solved four rather difficult and dangerous cases."

"Do not pat yourself too hard on the back, as everyone in this room knows the danger you have been in. Oh— except for Mr. Edwards. Mike, Miss Cahill is never to be kept waiting. I will see her anytime that she calls."

Francesca had realized that the clerk remained in the doorway. She turned and saw him nod deferentially, his cheeks red. "Yes, sir."

"That is all. Why don't you take young Kennedy here and give him a tour of the premises?" Hart asked. "A U.S. warship has recently berthed in the harbor. Point her out to him."

"Certainly, sir. Would you and Miss Cahill like any refreshments?" Edwards asked.

Hart turned his warm gaze upon Francesca. She shook her head. "No, thank you."

"That will be all," Hart said.

Edwards backed out after Joel and closed both doors behind him.

"Alone at last," Hart said, his tone teasing.

But he had stepped closer to her, and from her perspective, he was always a tower of male strength and virility, and she jumped away, gripping her reticule so tightly that her fingers ached.

His eyes widened. "My dear, you are as nervous as a doe about to be gunned down. I am hardly a hunter with you in my sights. And you did call on me," he added, amused.

"But you are a hunter, even where I am concerned," she said tersely.

His smile faded. "Francesca, if I were preying upon you as I have other women, you'd be on that sofa right now."

She blinked, her gaze flying to the sofa against the wall—a thick plush leather couch large enough for a man and woman to make love upon. For one moment she stared, fascinated and wondering if he had made love to a woman there. But of course he had. He was, after all, the city's most notorious womanizer.

But who had been the love interest?

"Francesca?"

She looked at him. It wasn't her business. It would never be her business. "Who was it?"

"I beg your pardon?" he started.

She wet her lips. They felt numb. "Who did you make love to over there?" Graphic images seemed to be assaulting her. Calder Hart was in them all, the woman faceless.

His gaze narrowed. It was a moment before he answered, "I do not allow paramours in my place of business. Not ever."

She stared. "That's hardly believable," she finally said. But she did believe him, oddly, and she was pleased—and relieved.

"Francesca, you shall be the first lover I make love to in this room."

This was not why she had come. "I beg to differ. We both know I will never be your lover and—"

He sighed, cutting her off. He took her arm, pulled her close. Her breasts flattened against his chest, and for one moment she was stunned, thinking he meant to embrace her and claim her mouth. But he did neither; he gripped her arm, and somehow, they were impossibly close to each other. "You are so impossibly stubborn! I wasn't speaking literally. But after we are married, I feel rather certain we will christen my office in such an irreverent manner." He gave her a cocky grin. "The idea seems to appeal to you."

She flushed. "I don't think so," she said, pulling away from him, trembling. He let her go. This was becoming impossible, she thought, dismayed and rubbing her arms.

While she could fend off his marital advances—and she would, always—being around him had become the greatest challenge. He was too disturbingly attractive, too seductive, and she couldn't stop wondering what it would be like to go to bed with him. Never mind that her thoughts were illicit and shameless; never mind that she loved someone else.

*She knew it would be wild, wonderful.*

She eyed the sofa one more time.

"I can read your thoughts," he said softly.

She jumped guiltily. She must not think about *anything* now except for her mission. She must not think about how experienced he was in love affairs, or how seductive he was, or what he might murmur in her ears if she ever lay in his arms. She must not think about the hard, male body just inches away from hers. "I doubt it."

He smiled at her. "You will have to learn patience, my dear. And not because it is a virtue. And not because you are the most impatient woman I have ever met." He was thoughtful now and she would give her right arm to know exactly what was on his mind. "But because some things are simply worth anticipating—some things are so very worth waiting for." He gave her a long, unwavering look. He wasn't smiling and he wasn't amused now.

She inhaled. He had a point, one she must ignore. It was one thing to imagine making love to a man, another to actually do so. After all, she was not ever getting married and she was not the kind of woman to become Calder Hart's mistress—even if he could be persuaded to change his odd morals toward her.

She had no intention of ever breaking Rick Bragg's heart.

Then she thought about his lovely wife and felt real despair. She also recalled that just a few days ago—before she had come face-to-face with Leigh Anne—she had been determined to become Bragg's mistress. She had nearly seduced him.

She looked at Hart. Even if she ever changed her mind, she doubted she could seduce him. Not that she was contemplating it. He was simply out of her league.

"You might think to change the direction of your thoughts," he murmured.

She folded her arms tightly beneath her breasts. "So now you read minds?"

"Only yours."

"Then tell me what I am thinking."

He smiled slowly at her.

She wished she hadn't thrown such a challenge at him.

"You are wondering if you might tempt me beyond my avowed resolutions," he said.

She flushed. "I have no idea what you mean."

"Francesca!" he exclaimed. "I thought we had put all hypocrisy behind us."

"Very well!" she cried, feeling pushed to her very limit. "I am attracted to you. There, are you satisfied? I have wondered what it might be like if you made love to me. Are you happy now? And I wonder why you do not try, when you have seduced half of the women in this town!"

He was chuckling now. "You are so very frightened of the future," he said softly. "You don't have to be afraid of me, my dear."

She scowled, furious now. "You're gloating!"

"Only a little."

"Who is your latest conquest?"

"A gentleman never tells."

She glared.

He laughed again and raised his hand. "Yes, I know. We both know I am not a gentleman. Still, as we are not yet affianced, I don't think I need to share any lusty details with you—or do I?"

Since she had met him, every time she crossed his path socially he had a beautiful woman on his arm, a widow, a divorcée, or a married but unfaithful lady. It had become impossible to tolerate, really. "I am tired of this game," she finally said.

He uncoiled his lean, dangerous body and approached. She flinched but did not move back. He touched her cheek. "I am hardly surprised. But this game does have a conclusion, as I think you know. I thoroughly believe it will satisfy us both."

She was breathless, queasy, and yearning all at once. His dark eyes held hers, and the unwavering look filled her loins. She wet her lips. "If we weren't friends, would you pursue me the way you do the others?"

"Isn't it enough that I wish to marry you, and you alone?" he asked, dropping his hand but not moving away.

"No."

He stared. "But we are friends," he finally said, deadly earnest now. "You are my first friend, ever. And we have already gone over this—but you refuse to understand. I don't dabble with virgins, Francesca. In fact, I have never slept with a virgin—and while it is miraculous that you still happen to be one," and he gave her an annoyed look, "that is something I only intend to do on our wedding night."

"None of this makes any sense," she said desperately. She would never understand why a man who hated the institution of marriage had decided to marry her. She paced and sank down on the leather sofa, placed just below a huge genre painting of a barefoot woman on a beach, a basket in her arms, two naked children racing past her. If only she dared to seduce him, they would undoubtedly get their insane and fatal attraction over with, and he would no longer wish to marry her—and they could resume being friends. As it was, her body wanted to go up in flames and she could hardly breathe. She wondered what would happen if he kissed her now.

She thought she might faint—or explode.

But he was stronger than she, he was resolved, his morals made no sense, as he was a self-professedly immoral man, while she, she was perilously close to tears.

"My poor dear," he said softly, lifting her chin, his fingers long and strong. "You will not change my ambition. I have made up my mind. For better or for worse. And I do think it will be for better, not for worse, Francesca. We shall have a very enjoyable lifetime. You shall solve your cases and I shall collect my art—I intend to work less after we

are wed—and we shall travel, my dear, as much or as little
as you wish. It shall not be boring; of that I can assure you."

*He would work less. They would travel.* She wanted to
plug up her ears. She dared gaze up at him—he loomed
over her now. "If I tell you till I am blue in the face that I
am not getting married, not ever, not to anyone, will you
ever believe me?" She had to look into his eyes. He exuded
self-confidence, wealth, power. He exuded virility, and it
was more than male; it was almost beastly. She wondered
if he continued to pursue women other than his mistress,
Daisy. She wondered if he continued to sleep with as many
women as he chose. She wondered when he had last seen
Daisy. It crossed her mind that she had not seen his mistress
in a while. As they were friends, a social call was overdue.

And he hadn't mentioned what he would do with his
mistress should he really marry someone.

"No."

"So I shan't waste my breath." She looked away. She
should be relieved that he hadn't swept her into his arms
and into his bed—or onto his couch. She *was* relieved. In-
tellectually, at least. She wondered if there was medication
available to relieve the rest of herself.

"Please don't," he said firmly. "Now, is this why you
have come visiting? To discuss our current impasse once
again? I am hardly on your beaten path, being this far downtown."

She leaped up, recalling her mission, Evan's black-and-
blue countenance coming to mind. "No." Maybe she should
simply leave—she could always ask Hart for the loan another time.

"You look terrified." His gaze was searching. "Am I ter-
rifying you?"

She shook her head, dreading what she must do. "I am
terrified, Hart. I am terrified of something I must beg of
you."

He became utterly still.

Would he hate her after this? Would he lower his opinion
of her? His esteem? His respect? Would he think her to be

no different from the other ladies who wished to be in his bed for the jewels he could offer in return? She wet her lips.

He said, "You must never be afraid to ask anything of me, and you shall never beg anything of me. Ask and you shall receive."

She realized that she wasn't certain she could do this. But she had to help Evan—yet she must not alienate this man. The urge to cry choked her for a moment. "Not this time," she gasped. "You may think differently about me, rather soon, Hart."

"No. What could you possibly want from me—so desperately?" His eyes were narrow and filled with speculation—and his clever, penetrating wit. "Ah, I see. Money. You need money."

She nodded miserably, avoiding his regard. "I desperately need a loan. I swear I will pay back every single cent. It may take some time—perhaps a dozen years." She wanted to disappear into thin air, but Evan's face with his pirate patch and swollen lip haunted her now.

"How much?" he asked too quietly.

She hesitated, daring to peek at him. "Fifty thousand dollars."

"I see." He turned away, his gaze shuttering, so she could not see into his eyes—so she had not a clue as to his reaction to her request. He walked behind his desk, his back to her, remaining calm, composed. She felt ill, faint. She wondered if their friendship had just ended. She wondered if their relationship had just ended.

She should be pleased if that was the case. Because then he would not want to marry her and her terrible dilemma would be solved.

Francesca hugged herself.

She started, her arms falling to her sides. She realized he was removing a large landscape that was an odd but beautiful kaleidoscope of color from the wall, the cliffs vague, the sea patches of blue and white paint. A safe was there. She gasped as he swirled the lock and quickly opened the door. "Hart?"

He took out a bundled-up wad of dollars. Francesca's eyes widened as he removed bundle after bundle—as she realized what he was doing. When he had stacked up an amount that covered one-quarter of his desk and which Francesca could only assume was $50,000, he closed the safe and faced her. "You need only ask," he said directly.

She gasped. "Hart!"

"However, this is a large sum of money. I only ask you in return that you allow either Raoul or myself to deliver it to whomever it is going to." He faced her, his steady regard holding hers.

She sank down in a chair, not looking away, not even once. She clutched the arms, stunned. "You're loaning it to me? Such a sum? Like that?"

His face softened. "I am giving it to you, Francesca. You need not pay me back."

She could only stare, in shock. And then her heart leaped and she tried to ignore the sudden elation accompanying its wild beat. It almost felt like joy. She covered the top of her bosom with her hand. *Not only was he loaning her the money; he hadn't batted an eye, and he did not seem to hate her for her terrible request.* "Of course I will pay you back," she managed. *How could he be so generous? How?*

"Never. You are the woman I wish to marry, and this is a gift. End of subject," he added seriously.

"No." She somehow stood and did not fall down. She was trembling again. "I will pay back every penny, Hart, and I do mean it."

He shook his head, but he was amused. "How? With your dowry? I don't need this money, Francesca. I refuse to take your money as well. It is my pleasure to give it to you. Let us leave it at that. Please," he added.

She had never heard him use the word *please* before. She could only stare, and then she sat back down, at a complete loss.

She wanted to cry. With relief, and emotions she dare not identify.

*This man was handing over a lifetime's worth of savings,*

*and not even asking her what she wanted it for. He didn't even want it back.*

But of course, she would pay him back, one day. But God, Hart might have a terrible reputation, he might shock society at will, but he was the most generous man she had ever met. And her worst nightmare had not come to pass—he still felt fondly toward her.

"Don't cry," he said softly. "Not over money, my dear."

She looked up. He had come to kneel beside her chair. Now he took her hands in his, and there was so much strength there. "I am not crying over the money," she sniffed. "I was afraid you would hate me for asking."

He touched her cheek. "I could never hate you."

Their gazes locked. He did not remove his hand. Francesca stared into his nearly black eyes and thought she saw love shimmering there in those almost unfathomable depths. Instantly she leaped up—away. Hart didn't believe in love and he did not love her and she had no intention of ever fooling herself, not even for a moment! And now, as if he had been about to take her in his arms—as she longed for him to do—he jammed his hands in the pockets of his black trousers. He stared.

"Thank you, Calder."

"As I said, it was my pleasure."

"You haven't asked me why I need such a sum?" she managed.

"If you wanted me to know, you would tell me, would you not?" he asked quietly.

She nodded. "I can't tell you."

"And I am not asking." He hesitated, looking grim now, and moved behind his desk. "I feel rather certain I know what the money is for."

I can't tell you, Hart."

"I understand. But that is why either Raoul or I must deliver this sum for you. I do not want you going near the man to whom this money is owed," he said, very firmly.

She thought about how badly Evan had been beaten up. LeFarge was conscienceless. She shivered, hating him with an inner rage for what he had done—and then for mocking them all by sending his regards to her brother. Did Hart know the money was a partial payment for her brother's gambling debts? Did he know Evan's creditor was Andrew LeFarge? "Raoul can deliver it," she said slowly.

He nodded. "Fine. Have arrangements been made?"

"No." She shook her head, remaining amazed. "I hardly expected to walk out of your offices this afternoon with fifty thousand dollars in my hands."

His grin flashed, heartbreakingly white. "Darling, I doubt you could lift the satchel this money must go into." Then, seriously, "Shall I make the arrangements for you? I prefer for you to be involved as little as possible," he said.

She hesitated, searching his eyes. "You know."

"There is only one reason you could need fifty thousand dollars, Francesca," he said kindly. "Shall we cease all pretense?"

When she did not speak, he said, "Has Evan been threatened again?"

There was so much relief in sharing this burden. "No." She swallowed. "God, Calder, I am so afraid for him!"

He hurried to her and this time he took her gently into his arms. "You need not fear for him now. Let me take this to LeFarge myself. He will not dare go after your brother again; I promise you that," he added grimly, a dangerous light in his eyes.

She swallowed, trying not to think about being held by this man, against his broad, muscular chest. Oddly, along with the terrible attraction she felt for him, now she also felt safe. "You would do this for me—I mean, for Evan?" she whispered, moved almost to tears again.

"I am doing this for you," he said softly. "Let us be clear on that point."

She smiled and sniffled again.

"Come." He strode around his desk, taking her arm. "Enough maudlin humor. I have a meeting uptown. Can I give you a lift? I also wish to discuss Friday evening with you."

She nodded, smiling a little. "That would be very nice, Calder. And what is Friday evening?"

"I would like to take you to a new exhibition at the Gallery Duval, followed by dinner at my favorite restaurant. Rourke will chaperon us," he added with obvious amusement at the thought.

She stiffened as they left his huge office. And then she thought, *Why not?* The evening would be an enjoyable one, and if she did not accept, she would wind up going to someone's dinner party with her parents. And that would be, as always, uninteresting and dull. "I gladly accept," Francesca said with a real smile. In fact, she looked forward to the evening.

Mr. Edwards came rushing forward with her coat and gloves. Hart lifted a brow. "That was surprisingly easy," he said.

"You see," she flirted. "I shall always keep you on your toes."

He laughed, taking her coat from Edwards and wrapping it around her himself. "That is a part of my calculations," he murmured softly.

"I do have one small favor to ask of you," Francesca said, as Joel joined them. "May we stop briefly at Number Two-oh-two East Tenth Street? It will save me a trip downtown later tonight."

"Of course." But his gaze narrowed now as he accepted his own black wool coat from Edwards. "And whom are we calling on?"

"A vagrant, Hart. A drunken vagrant who I hope was a witness to Grace Conway's murder."

# CHAPTER
# TEN

". . . baby will fall, cradle and all, ha ha ha!"

"Francesca, this woman is too drunk to have seen anything. Not only that, she is mad!" Hart exclaimed, at once grim and exasperated.

The gray-haired woman sat on the very same stoop adjacent to Number 202 that she had occupied on Tuesday night when Grace Conway's body had first been found. She was a heavy woman of indeterminate age, with unkempt and dirty gray hair that stuck out from her filthy brown wool cap. Her overcoat had large holes, and beneath it Francesca glimpsed a thin cotton shift. Now the woman's chubby cheeks were brilliantly red, undoubtedly because the bucket of beer was already half-empty. She continued to sing "Rock a Bye Baby," frequently making up the words, and every so often breaking into laughter.

"We should go," Hart said, annoyed. He was the epitome of elegance in his black coat, fine black gloves, and highly polished French calf shoes. He did not wear a hat. Francesca had never seen him with his head covered.

"No," she said, sitting down beside the drunken woman. "Hello," she tried with a smile.

The drunk ignored her—or maybe she hadn't heard her— or, as she did not even look at her, maybe she didn't even know that someone had sat beside her. She swilled from her bucket. Quite a bit of beer sloshed down the front of her coat. She smelled sour, but it was more than beer.

"Don't sit there," Hart said, reaching for Francesca's arm. "She may be diseased, for God's sake! And the lice! She hasn't had a bath in a year, I think."

"Hart," Francesca protested. "Give me a moment."

The woman looked up suddenly. "Bugger off, asshole," she said directly to Hart.

He froze.

So did Francesca.

The woman grumbled, "Had a bath mebbe a month ago. Willits Bath House." She started singing again.

Francesca took her arm, ignoring Hart's disapproving groan. "What is your name? I am Francesca Cahill, and I do wish to speak with you!"

"Rockabye baby, rockabye baby, ha ha ha!" she crowed.

"This is a waste of time."

Francesca glared at Hart. "You have become a sulky child! Next time, I will not bring you along!"

He glared in return. "I cannot believe my brother allows you to participate in these investigations."

She sighed, ignoring him. "Miss, please! I do need your help! Please tell me your name," Francesca begged now.

The woman did not look at her. It was as if she had not heard her, but Francesca knew now that she had. She started to mumble to herself. "Why don't they help? What did I do! Oh, God, It's cold tonight! Damn leatherheads! Not fair ... Not fair at all. I want it back, I do! My good Sunday dress, that pretty blue hat ..."

"She's mad," Hart said, quietly now.

Francesca stood, hoping that was not the case. "I need to clean her up, get coffee and food into her."

His eyes popped. Hart was a master of self-control, and she had never seen him so unmasked and so stunned. "I beg your pardon?"

"Please give us a ride home."

"You . . . and her?" He was disbelieving, his eyes wide. Then, "Absolutely not!"

"What if the killer comes back for Sarah?" Francesca cried, grabbing his arm. Their gazes locked. "I know she is drunk and unclean, but I suspect she sees and knows more than she lets on. And we do not know that she is mad! I also suspect she is here frequently. Please, Hart! All I ask is that you help me get her into your coach and that you drop us at my home."

"Your mother will murder you—and never allow me in your door again," he said darkly.

"Mama adores you and you know it. She will be thrilled if you ever tell her you seek to marry me. Now do help." She turned and began to lift the old woman to her feet, slinging one arm over her shoulder and heaving her bulk up with all of her might.

The woman cried out. Then, "Help me! Help me! Agh, help me! Murders and monsters!" she screamed.

The woman sagged, resisting and almost bringing Francesca down to the ground. Francesca stared at her. "Murders and monsters?" she cried.

"Helppp!" the woman screamed.

"Oh, God," Hart snapped. He effortlessly heaved the screaming old woman over his shoulder, upside down, much to Francesca's amazement. Not looking at her, he started for the gleaming elegant barouche parked with his driver, Raoul, standing by the first of the six horses. The blacks in the traces were magnificent, the entire rig as out of place in the neighborhood as Calder Hart himself. "You can clean her up in my kitchen," he said, sounding furious. "But do not tell your mother that I have participated in this madness."

Francesca grinned. Calder was afraid of Julia, too, and she intended not to forget it. The knowledge would most definitely come in handy one day.

And then the woman who was screaming, "Help! Murder! Monsters!" as she was toted to Hart's coach on his shoulder, ceased her noise. She looked up from her contorted position, met Francesca's gaze, grinned, and winked.

Francesca blinked.

A crowd had gathered in Calder Hart's enormous kitchen.

The woman sat at the table where the servants dined, now completely bathed, her hair washed and pinned up, and wearing one of the housemaid's uniforms—a plain black dress with a starched white collar. She was drinking her third cup of coffee and eating from her second plate of beef and potatoes. She was ravenous, and now that she was clean and clothed, she looked like anyone's kindhearted, chubby-cheeked grandmother.

Francesca was the only one seated at the table, just opposite her. Grace Bragg, stepmother to Rick and foster mother to Calder, stood beside her, as did her daughter, Lucy Savage. Both women were beautiful, tall and voluptuous with slender waists and brilliant red hair. Grace was dressed for an evening out—she wore a green evening gown with diamond jewelry. Lucy wore a blue day dress. The only difference between mother and daughter other than their years and the length of their hair—as Lucy's was very long—was the fact that Grace wore a pair of wire-rimmed spectacles that kept slipping down her nose.

Rourke and his father, Grace's husband, Rathe, stood in the doorway, arms folded across their chests. Both men were dressed for an evening on the town as well. As they thoroughly resembled one another, being golden-eyed, dark blond, and very handsome, any observer would instantly realize that they were father and son.

A dozen servants observed the interloper from their respective stations in the huge kitchen, which boasted several ovens and three stoves, two fireplaces, and two long work tables.

"I would have never believed it," Lucy said. "You have done an admirable job, Francesca. She could be in Hart's employ."

Before Francesca could respond, the woman paused with fork lifted and said, "Didn't anyone ever tell you it's rude to talk about a soul when she can hear?"

Lucy flushed, coming forward. "I'm so sorry," she said.

Francesca leaned toward the woman. "Can we start over?" She smiled. "I am Francesca Cahill. The gentleman who brought us here is Calder Hart, and this is his home. Do you have a name?"

"Your gentleman friend is as rich as Hades," the woman said, "and a jackass."

Lucy tittered.

Francesca smiled and said, "He can be a thorough pain, but he has his redeeming moments. This is his family. His parents, Rathe and Grace Bragg, his sister and brother, Lucy and Rourke." There was no point in explaining that Hart wasn't actually related to any of the Braggs at all.

The woman sat up straighter. "Braggs? Braggs are in the room?"

Francesca nodded curiously. "Indeed they are. So you know of the family?"

"There was a lawyer named Bragg. In Boston. He took care of my son."

A hush fell upon the room. Francesca's heart beat hard. She heard someone enter but did not look away. "That would be Rick Bragg. He is the commissioner of police in the city here."

"My son was innocent. But everyone said he killed his wife." Tears moistened her eyes but did not fall. "Bragg believed him. He was the only one who believed him, the only one who would take his case."

Francesca's heart swelled with what felt like love and with real pride. Spending the afternoon with Hart had almost made her forget the traits she truly admired in a man—

selfless charity and the strongest sense of justice, both personal and otherwise. She smiled. "He is a good friend of mine."

"My name is Ellie," the woman said suddenly, and she gazed now coldly across the room. "An' I don't like bein' manhandled by a man, not even one as handsome as the Devil."

Francesca turned and saw that Hart had entered the room, also in his tuxedo. Her heart stopped. He was going out. That was not unusual; still, she was dismayed, when she should not care. She told herself that he was probably going out with his family. She didn't really believe it. He was going out with a beautiful woman; of that she had no doubt.

"I apologize," Hart said, coming forward to stand with his hand on the back of Francesca's chair. Her nape prickled in response to his nearness. "But I do think the bath and good meal have done wonders for you."

Ellie's eyes moistened precariously now, and she nodded, looking down. "Thank you for the hot bath and hot food," she whispered roughly. "An' the clean clothes."

Francesca could not help herself—she reached out and covered Ellie's hand. "You may keep the dress." She didn't hesitate. "I have need of a housemaid. Would you like to be employed at my home? We live a few blocks downtown." She smiled warmly.

Ellie stared.

Hart said warningly, "Do you think that is a good idea, Francesca?"

Francesca ignored him.

"You really need a maid? I could do it—I worked in a factory, but I could learn. I'm smart, I am," Ellie cried eagerly.

Francesca smiled. "You are now employed."

"God bless you," Ellie gasped. Tears rolled down her cheeks.

"Francesca? May I have a word with you . . . privately? Now," Hart said. There was nothing about his tone that indicated he was asking her a question. He was very grim.

Francesca stood and said to Ellie, "Eat up. When you're done, we will take a hansom home."

Ellie wiped her eyes, nodding. And then, "Miss Cahill?"

Francesca paused. "Yes?"

"Why did you do this? Why did you seek me out?"

Francesca hesitated. "A very popular actress lived in Number Two-oh-two, the building next door to where I found you. She was murdered this last Monday. I had wondered if you might have seen something odd or unusual."

Ellie paled. "I seen plenty," she murmured.

Francesca rushed forward. "Did you know Miss Conway? Surely you don't mean that you saw her murdered!"

"I knew her. How could I not? She was a beautiful redhead, like that lady over there." She nodded at Lucy. "She always gave me a half dollar when she saw me. She was so kind. Everyone knew she was a real stage actress."

Francesca grabbed her hands. "What did you see?"

"A monster," Ellie whispered.

For one moment Francesca did not understand. And then she was disappointed, thoroughly so. "A monster?"

Ellie nodded, her eyes wide—frightened. "A big man with no eyes and no mouth," she said.

"What?" Francesca gasped.

"I saw a monster. I saw him go into her building, I did. I don't remember when, but he was a monster, no eyes, no mouth—I ain't never seen anything like it!"

A silence fell over the room.

Francesca did not believe in monsters. She could only assume Ellie had been terribly drunk and hallucinating—or perhaps the monster she spoke of had been a result of a drunken dream.

"Francesca?" Hart grasped her elbow, his tone firm.

She met his gaze and tried to smile, so he would not know how absurdly disappointed she was, and followed him from the kitchen. In the hallway, her smile faded as she recalled that he had undoubtedly drawn her aside to chastise her for hiring Ellie. She prepared for an unpleasant battle.

But he smiled at her, a vast affection in his eyes. "I suppose I shall have to get used to you adopting stray souls," he said, his smile achingly tender.

Her heart stopped. "She isn't quite mad after all, Calder," she began. "I mean, that talk of monsters—"

"Hush." He touched her mouth with his finger. "I am not asking you to change, darling."

She did not move. She simply couldn't.

Their gazes locked.

She simply could not bear it. She breathed, her lips parting beneath his fingertip, and his smile faded and she felt the exact moment that his affection changed. Although he wasn't touching her, except with one fingertip, she felt a new tension begin to radiate from him, as warm as smoke. He leaned slowly toward her, his expression becoming strained. His eyes changed color, smoking. Francesca gazed at his mouth, inches from her own. He dropped his hand.

*Oh, God. Finally, he was going to kiss her.*

His expression changed, tightening. And Francesca saw the battle he was waging with himself as clearly as if she were standing upon an actual battlefield. Her heart lurched—he was going to walk away from her, again! And she took action.

She leaned forward purposefully, so very frightened now, brushing her mouth against his.

*Finally.* Finally she could taste and feel his lips.

He did not move.

Francesca breathed, and she had begun to brush her lips over his, repeatedly, softly, when he broke.

Hart moved. Suddenly, hard, taking over the kiss, controlling it.

Francesca sank against the wall, her heart racing impossibly, frighteningly, her sex expanding immediately, completely. His lips were firm, at once very demanding yet oddly coaxing, too, feather-light, then changing, becoming insistent, urgent. Her hands found his chest, beneath his jacket, and through the fine cotton of his shirt she felt rock-hard muscles beneath her palms, and his thickly drumming heartbeat. It was racing with alarming speed.

*She needed this man now. And clearly, he needed her, too.*

Her hands closed over his powerful shoulders and she was shocked by the power contained there. For one brief moment, he tested the pressure of her lips, not yet invasive—yet she knew there would be more. For one instant, the tip of his tongue slid slowly, deliberately teasingly along her lips—provocative and inflammatory. Francesca heard herself moan.

He seized the moment, thrusting deep. She felt him against the back of her throat. She tasted more scotch, and man. She tasted Calder Hart.

Francesca saw galaxies filled with light, shimmering around her, and she gripped his muscular neck, hanging on tight. Hart was going to take her there. . . .

He pulled away.

She gasped but could not speak—protest. Francesca collapsed against the wall, her heart exploding in her chest, her body shuddering on the brink of climax. She wanted to scream and shout and demand he continue. But she couldn't speak; she couldn't move.

He stared harshly at her face. He knew. And his eyes were smoky gray with his own smoldering lust. She had never received such a look from him before; in fact, she had never been the recipient of such an intense look before—not ever. And she knew, she simply knew, that when he strained over her, inside her, he would be looking at her this way—with purpose and resolve, all of it sexual, a warrior claiming his victory on the battlefield that would be their bed.

His hands fisted on the wall, over each of her shoulders, and he locked her there. "I am not breaking my resolution," he ground out. But his body shifted, and one touch was enough. His arousal brushed against her belly. Instantly their gazes clashed. As instantly, he shifted back, away.

"Not fair," she gasped. *"Not fair."* Briefly she thought she felt every inch of him. Throbbing heat, slick power . . .

"Life is never fair," he returned harshly.

Francesca screwed her eyes shut against tears of need.

He cursed viciously. "I am *not* corrupting you; I am *not* treating you the way that Rick has. This will *not* happen again." His eyes blazed with anger.

"No!" The word was out before she could control it. He moved away—she grabbed his lapels. She wasn't sure what she meant to do—drag him behind closed doors, rip off his clothes, or plead with him to ravish her in precisely the same way. He cut her off.

"I may be many things, Francesca, but the one thing I am is a man of my word. If I give it." He was even more furious now than before. She knew he was enraged with himself. "God damn it! We're not even engaged!"

"But you want me," she said pathetically.

His laughter was harsh. "And I shall have you—properly . . . or not at all."

She let him go. She felt tears rising and she could not stop them from falling. Because she knew he meant his every word—and she knew he would remain immovable. "But I can't marry you," she whispered, slumping against the wall.

He did not immediately reply, and she opened her eyes to find him staring. She shivered, aroused so quickly again. It took only a single look.

His mouth hardened into a line that might have been a mirthless smile. "My poor darling," he whispered roughly. "Believe me, I know exactly how you are feeling."

She shook her head, her cheeks tear-streaked and wet. "Hardly," she choked. "Because you can go to Daisy, and I have nowhere to go!"

He stared. And his expression softened—his lips started to turn upward; a twinkle appeared in his eyes.

"Don't laugh!" she shouted, striking at his chest.

He caught her fist and kissed it. "Is this a tantrum, darling? Is this what I shall have to look forward to?" His tone was teasing.

"I am not a spoiled child who has temper tantrums!" she cried.

"Hush." He pulled her close, against his solid, sexy chest, and kissed the top of her head. Unfortunately, his member remained rock-hard, without a doubt as to *his* feelings. "My entire family will hear you shouting to have sex with me."

She landed a useless blow on his chest, as one could not land a punch when pressed against one's adversary, and then she gave up. Why move? Her cheek solidly planted somewhere in the vicinity of his heart. She could hear its powerful yet ragged beat. She could feel his breath on her hair, and she loved having his arms around her. Almost as much as she loved him pressing and throbbing deeply against her belly. Francesca squeezed her eyes shut. Orgiastic images danced in her head, Hart naked and powerful; herself, naked and submissive.

"If I didn't know better," she whispered, "I would think that you are slowly but surely seducing me to your will."

Silence was his reply.

It suddenly struck her like a bolt of dazzling lightning that this was the case. That this was his plan. To torture her with what might be until she yielded to him. And oh, the plan was a good one! She jerked out of his grasp.

He wasn't smiling now. Not really. He was watching her very, very carefully, as if they were opposed to each other and he was waiting to see where and how she would now strike.

"Is that what you intend? To make me insane with wanting your lovemaking . . . until I give you what you want—marriage?" she asked furiously.

A long pause ensued. He replied very slowly, "You kissed me, Francesca."

"No! You have been teasing me mercilessly for days!"

Very carefully he said, "You make it sound reprehensible. As if marriage is the ultimate fall from grace."

"In your own way, you are pursuing me the way you have the others!" she cried. "Ruthlessly . . . seductively . . . selfishly! The only difference is that your goal with them was to bed them once or twice, and with me, it is to enslave me as your wife!"

He stiffened.

She saw the dangerous look on his face and in his eyes and knew she had gone too far.

"Enslave? I have no wish to enslave you, my dear."

"I didn't quite mean that," she retracted as quickly as possible.

"You meant it. You are a woman of passion and you always speak what is in your heart. Francesca, good night." He wheeled away.

"And you are always running away from our fights!" she shouted after him. If she'd had a dinner plate in her hand, she would have thrown it at his head—and not missed.

He whirled back. "Because you provoke me beyond all reason and I do not trust myself," he ground out, striding toward her now.

Fear assailed her—she shrank back from him, against the wall.

But he didn't stop until he was pressing her against it. "I am tempted to do as you wish—to make love to you until you can't even walk! And do you know what?" he demanded unpleasantly, furiously.

She was afraid. She was afraid of his next words, for she sensed a cruel blow.

And she was right. "I have not a single doubt that if I seduced you tonight, you would be begging me tomorrow to be my wife."

She gasped.

"And that would make my life a lot easier now, wouldn't it? But I happen to be taking the high road. The difficult road. Only you refuse to see it or believe it." He turned and walked out. "Think what you want. You always do," he said, not looking over his shoulder.

She didn't respond. There was no response she could make.

THURSDAY, FEBRUARY 20, 1902—10:00 P.M.

She heard an odd nose, almost a gasp, from the adjacent bedroom.

Catherine Holmes strained to hear, suddenly wide awake. But now silence filled her small, dark bedroom.

It didn't matter. She was terrified.

*Because she had lied to the lady investigator and the police.* She spent half of her waking moments in that rocking chair, looking wistfully out the window onto the street. Watching her neighbors and friends, watching strangers and thieves. How often had her mother chastised her for yearning for the outside world? Too late, she knew her mother was right. For she had seen what she should not see, what she must not see, she had seen a man, and she had seen his face.

For one split second, when he had torn the odd transparent mask from his face.

On Monday night, at seven o'clock.

Catherine Holmes sat up, trembling. She reminded herself that the door to the apartment was bolted from inside. The windows were locked. No one could get in. She strained to see through the shadows filling up her small bedroom. She kept her door open, in case her mother called out to her in the middle of the night, but she could not even see the threshold.

*But he had looked back and he had seen her, sitting with her nose pressed to the window glass.* She didn't simply know it. Their gazes had met, locked.

"Mother?" Catherine tried nervously. She reached for the small domed candle at her bedside. She fumbled for matches, lifted the dome. She could not light the candle. "Mother?" she called out, loudly now.

There was no answer.

She struck the match a third time, but her trembling hands refused to allow her to light the candle. *There had been dark comprehension in his eyes.*

Catherine heard a creaking, a familiar sound, from the oak floorboards in the parlor. She tensed. This time, she did not call for her mother.

*No one was in the apartment. It was a mouse.*

She slipped from the bed, wearing only a cotton night-gown, her long auburn hair in a single braid. Now she regretted not telling Miss Cahill and the commissioner what she had seen—and who it was.

*Because she had recognized him instantly.*

*Just as he had recognized her.*

And there was only one explanation for the mask he had been wearing as he came out of the building. He was Grace Conway's killer. It was too shocking for words.

She had asked herself time and again, *But why? What possible reason could there have been?* For she knew he was not mad. Or was he?

Her mouth was dry. Catherine paused to take a sip of water from the chipped mug that she kept beside her narrow bed. In doing so, she turned away from her bedroom doorway.

His hands went around her throat. "Screaming is useless," he said.

She gasped, as he was choking her, and she knew, in that instant, that he intended to strangle her as he had Miss Conway. "No," she choked.

His hand clamped over her mouth, he pushed her against the wall, somehow, with one hand, keeping an unbearable pressure on her throat. She couldn't breathe. He was choking her to death. And then she stiffened, a harsh sound escaping her, as he shoved his male hardness up against her buttocks. He started rubbing himself slowly there.

She was terrified now of rape. Rape, then death . . . Dear God, she would rather die first!

"Is it good?" he said thickly, shoving against her harder, faster now. "You like it, don't you, whore? You're all whores."

Silently, as she could not breathe, much less speak, she begged him for pity, for mercy, for life.

He began to tell her what he would like to do to her—except that she wasn't worth it. But blackness was descending like a curtain over her mind, and she could not make out his every word. She begged God now for her life.

Silk whispered around her throat.

For one instant, she thought her prayers had been answered.

# CHAPTER
# ELEVEN

THURSDAY, FEBRUARY 20, 1902—10:00 P.M.

FRANCESCA WAS TIRED. IT had been a long, even difficult day. Hart had loaned her a carriage and driver with which to whisk her and Ellie home, and Francesca had actually considered going directly to the Cahill mansion. She had quickly negated the idea. It was late, but she had been at Bragg's when it was later, and he still didn't know about her interview with Bertrand Hoeltz and that Melinda Neville was his lover. Bragg lived at Number Eleven Madison Square, just a stone's throw from Madison Park. Francesca had just asked Ellie to wait for her, telling her that she would not be very long, but the woman had fallen asleep on the seat beside her, wrapped up in a heavy cloak borrowed from Grace Bragg.

Francesca smiled a little, pleased that she could do a good deed and help someone in difficulty, and she climbed down from the carriage. The man sitting in the driver's box was awaiting her orders, and she said, "I suspect I shall be about twenty minutes."

Francesca hurried up the short brick walk to Bragg's brownstone. The building had been built several decades ago and was typically Victorian—the roof was gabled, the facade brick, the rooms within small, the stairwell narrow. Her knock was answered instantly by Peter, Bragg's man.

Francesca smiled at him. He was a huge Swede, perhaps six inches over six feet tall and quite wide with brawn and muscle. Francesca knew he was a jack-of-all-trades—at times a butler, a valet, a cook, or a housekeeper. Once Bragg had thought to foist him on her as a bodyguard.

Peter hardly ever smiled and he hardly ever spoke. He nodded. "Good evening, Miss Cahill." If he was surprised to see her at this hour, he gave no sign.

Francesca stepped inside a small, poorly lit foyer, as only one small lamp was on, sitting upon a side table against the wall, beneath a mirror. The steep, narrow staircase was just ahead and to her left, a dark runner there. Directly down the hall was the parlor, and the door was open, but the room was also dark. To its right was Bragg's office. His door, she saw, was shut.

Light, however, came from the dining room's open doorway on her right, beyond which was the kitchen.

Francesca had stopped by earlier that day. Bragg was fostering two young girls whose mother had been murdered by the Cross Killer. Francesca had arranged it, and her mother had arranged for their nanny, Mrs. Flowers. Not a day went by that Francesca did not spend an hour or two with Dot, who was two, and Katie, who was six. Permanent arrangements had yet to be made for the pair.

"Did Katie eat her supper?" she asked. Katie had been very distressed when she had first come to Bragg's, and not eating had been her way of evincing it.

Peter smiled. It was a rare sight indeed. "Every morsel."

Francesca was impressed. "And has Dot behaved herself?"

"Always," he said, with a straight face now and laughter in his eyes.

Francesca did not even try to imagine what mischief the

vivacious toddler had got into. "Is Bragg in his office?" she asked.

"I am afraid he is out for the evening," Peter said.

Francesca blinked. "Do you know when he will be back, Peter? There really is a lead I wish to discuss with him."

"He said ten or eleven, Miss Cahill."

Francesca hesitated. "Do you mind if I wait? Perhaps I can sneak upstairs and kiss the girls."

He didn't look pleased with that.

"I do promise not to wake them," she added, smiling.

He nodded. "Should I bring you a tea or a sherry or a glass of wine?"

"No. I am fine. Thank you." Francesca started for the stairs and tripped over an object upon the floor.

Peter quickly gripped her arm. Francesca saw that she had stumbled over a small valise. Now she realized a large trunk and another valise, medium-sized, were all lined up beside the stairs. Her heart skipped. "Bragg is going out of town?" she asked quickly.

"He did not say," Peter commented.

Francesca was disturbed. Every hair on her nape prickled with warning and alarm. She bent down. The small valise was a dark red, she saw, and it was definitely a woman's bag.

There was a name tag encased in leather on the trunk. She seized it. It read: MRS. RICK BRAGG.

She inhaled. Her mind scrambled for excuses. Leigh Anne was leaving town—which was why her bags were there, in Bragg's house, at the bottom of the stairs. Perhaps he was taking her to the Boston train first thing in the morning!

But why weren't her bags at the Waldorf Astoria Hotel, where she was staying?

Francesca was grim. She turned and stared at Peter. It was a moment before she could speak. "Do you know why Mrs. Bragg has her trunks here?"

"I'm afraid not," he said impassively. "The commissioner did not say."

She wet her lips. "When did these bags arrive?"

"Around six this evening, Miss Cahill."

She reached for and gripped the newel post on the smooth wooden banister of the stairs. So it had finally happened. Bragg had reconciled with his wife. She reminded herself that this had been inevitable—that it was right. She had no cause to be upset or to feel betrayed.

The front door opened. As it did, a woman's voice sounded, distinct, cultured, soft . . . pretty. There was a teasing note in her tone.

Francesca turned as Bragg's familiar slightly rough and terse voice responded, "I do not know what Mrs. Lowe intends, Leigh Anne."

Francesca held on harder to the banister. But she was upset. Because she could not turn off her feelings as simply as one did a water faucet. *Why hadn't he told her?*

"Francesca!" Bragg halted in his tracks.

She meant to smile. But she could not, so she stared instead.

They made a striking couple. He was tall and golden; she was small and dark.

"Miss Cahill!" his beautiful wife cried, hurrying forward. "Is everything all right? Are you all right, my dear?"

Francesca recovered. "I have come to discuss a new lead with . . . your husband," she said briskly. "But I can see that I have come at an inopportune time."

"Oh!" Leigh Anne had paused before her, handing off her silver chinchilla fur coat to Peter. She wore a ·silver gown beneath, one gorgeous in its design and one that revealed her perfect yet petite figure—and a great deal of surprisingly voluptuous bosom. Of course Bragg would remain attracted to her. What man wouldn't?

"Well, why don't you and Rick go into the parlor and I shall send in some refreshments?" Leigh Anne smiled pleasantly. "I don't really know what is lying about in the kitchen, as I have only just moved in, but I am certain I can come up with something. Peter? Do help."

*She had moved in.* Francesca was not surprised. She had

known it the moment she had seen those bags. It was really, truly, finally over.

Leigh Anne had started for the dining room doorway. Bragg came forward, draping his greatcoat on the chair beside the side table. "Francesca," he said urgently.

"I think this can wait until tomorrow," she managed, and she hurried past him, through the entry hall, and out the door into the night. The sorrow overwhelmed her then. What had she been thinking, to carry on even if only emotionally with a married man? But could she really let go? Did she even want to?

"Francesca!" Bragg cried, chasing her.

She turned to face him. "I am happy for you, for you both, Rick. You deserve a marriage, a family—you deserve happiness." And that noblest part of her meant it.

"It is only for six months," he said.

"What?" Hope flared. And past his shoulder, she saw Leigh Anne in the doorway of his house, watching them.

"Leigh Anne offered me an arrangement. One I am getting in writing, Francesca," he said, his tone low and urgent. "She will live with me for six months, and then I am free. Then she will give me a divorce," he said in a rush.

She was stunned. "I don't understand."

He grimaced. "I do believe she thinks that after six months, I will change my mind."

Her mind sped and raced, but uselessly, in confusion. Until she realized that Leigh Anne was probably right. "Of course you will. You still love her."

"That's not true," he said angrily. His eyes flashed. "I despise her. She is very clever, that is all. My feelings for you haven't changed," he added.

She stared. It was a long and even sadder moment before she spoke. "No, Rick, I think you should face the truth. You love her, not me. And that is as it should be."

"You dare to tell me who I carry with me in my heart, minute by minute and day after day? It is you, Francesca. You are the one I think about, yearn for, dream of. You are the one who makes me laugh and smile. You have always been the one to put a smile in my heart." He added, "And I hate it when you call me Rick!"

She finally pulled away from him. "Don't do this. Not now. Not anymore." And Hart's knowing, mocking image filled her mind. It clearly said, *I told you so.*

"I am not asking you to wait," Bragg said. "But damn it, I am not going to lie to you, either."

"You are lying to yourself. I simply do not know why," she said, but she was torn. A part of her wished to discourage his marriage—to tell him what he wanted to hear. "Hatred and love—both extreme passion . . . and, as Calder has said, the opposite sides of the same coin."

He stared, his eyes agonized. "Not in this case."

"Have you slept with her?" Francesca asked, and then could not believe the burning question had popped out. But she had to know. And terribly, she recalled the fact that just an hour or so ago, she had finally been kissed by Calder Hart.

He was clearly taken aback. "No."

Francesca shook off her sudden guilt. But what had happened at Hart's was not the issue, not now. And she would analyze that incident later. "But you will. Don't deny it. I see the way you look at her."

"Francesca, men are different from women. A man can sleep with a woman he has no feelings for."

"I am aware of that. But more important, we don't get to choose whom we fall in love with," she said sadly.

"You are being as bullheaded as ever," he snapped. "I am allowing Leigh Anne to live in my household for exactly six months. And after that, she will agree to a divorce and I shall be free. I should have told you. But we concluded this arrangement only today. For God's sake! I have been in shock myself, trying to adjust to the fact of my wife's return—and her very clever manipulations."

"I think she still harbors love for you, too." In fact, Francesca had little doubt now.

"She loves only herself." His anger vanished, his tone became pleading instead. "I don't want you leaving this way. No matter what happens, we are friends."

She realized she was hugging herself. She glanced past him and saw that his wife had left the door and it was now closed. And suddenly she wondered if she and Bragg could really remain friends. It now seemed a monumental task.

She knew he wanted reassurance from her—that she would be his friend no matter what happened—but she was not up to the task of offering comfort now. She tried a small smile instead. "I'll drop by headquarters tomorrow. There is a new development you should know about. It's late. I have to go, Bragg. If my mother sees me when I come in, I am in serious trouble."

He didn't smile. He clearly couldn't.

Francesca hesitated, kissed his cheek, felt her heart suddenly break, and walked off to Hart's waiting carriage.

FRIDAY, FEBRUARY 21, 1902—10:00 A.M.

She knocked gingerly on his closed office door. Headquarters was oddly silent that morning—no telephones were ringing, and she had heard only one telegraph. Voices were kept low, in a murmur. It was as if everyone were in mourning. Or was she the one in mourning and the atmosphere prevailing her imagination?

Bragg briskly called out. "Come in!"

She opened the frosted glass door hesitantly. She had spent most of the night tossing and turning, first thinking about him and then, against her will, considering Hart. She had gone over and over the memories she and Bragg had made. Every few moments, Hart's nearly black eyes would intrude, their message clear: *I told you so.* He had been warning her that she was headed for ruin as long as she loved Rick Bragg for some time now—ever since they had first met. Then his eyes would change, turning to gray smoke. Furious—not wanting to think about the sensual interlude of that evening—she would jerk her thoughts back where they belonged. Hart's dire predictions were wrong. She wasn't ruined, not in the traditional sense of the word, but her heart had been broken, not even once but several times over, in fact.

She had decided just last week to stand back and be Bragg's friend and support his marriage and his career. She simply hadn't known how difficult that resolution would be to keep. A night of brooding had not changed anything. She remained sad, the sense of loss insistent, but she was also confused—and afraid.

It felt as if her entire life was in upheaval once again. It felt as if nothing was ever going to be the same. It was as if she were on a terrible precipice. One step and the past would be forever out of her reach; one step and an endless fall would begin. If only she knew where she might land— and if she could survive the leap.

Now, she halted in the doorway as he looked up. Their gazes leaped together, locked. The moment of seeing him now felt terribly awkward.

He shot to his feet. "I wasn't sure you would come downtown after all."

She managed a smile. "We have a killer on the loose, Bragg. That hasn't changed."

He smiled a little, tentatively, his gaze searching. "No, that hasn't changed."

She hesitated. "I won't appear at your door again at such an ungracious hour."

He rushed around his desk. "Francesca! You may appear at my home at any time of the day or night!"

"I don't think your wife will like that."

He eyes were hard. "I don't care what she likes."

She realized he meant what he said—or he thought that he did. She almost told him that perhaps he should care about what she liked, then decided not to interfere in his marriage. That was a certain recipe for disaster.

Besides, somewhere deep down in her soul she knew he was never going to divorce Leigh Anne.

"So, are you bringing me a fresh clue?" His tone was light, as was the touch on her elbow. But the awkwardness remained.

She turned. "Bertrand Hoeltz, the owner of Gallery Hoeltz on Fourth Avenue, is Melinda Neville's paramour, Bragg."

His eyes widened. "Well," he said after a significant pause.

Francesca finally smiled. "Is that all you can say?"

He smiled back, his expression suddenly easing. "When did he last see her?"

She was relieved that they had somehow broken the tension. "Monday morning. They shared a light breakfast and then she was returning to her studio to work. He seems quite frantic." Francesca thought about Bertrand Hoeltz and added, "If he is dissembling, I cannot tell. Joel's theory is that Hoeltz might have killed Melinda because of jealousy."

"Over whom?" Bragg asked quickly.

"We do not know."

"Does he know Sarah?"

"He said he did not."

"You doubt him?"

"No. I have no reason to doubt anything that he has said, at this time," she said thoughtfully.

Suddenly Captain Shea was knocking on the door. His eyes were wide. "C'mish, sir! I think you might want to come downstairs, right now!"

Bragg rushed forward, Francesca following, more than curious. "What is it, Shea?" Bragg asked.

"Thomas Neville is at reception, shouting for his sister."

Bragg strode through the door, Francesca running to catch up with him. They exchanged glances, ignoring the elevator, as the cage was clearly on the ground floor. He took her arm as they hurried down the concrete steps, Shea on their heels. "Well, this is a positive development," Francesca said breathlessly.

They hit the ground floor landing, where they could see past the elevator cage and into the busy reception area, where policemen were booking various crooks and hoods, and where two gentlemen were filing some kind of civilian complaint. Francesca saw Neville instantly, standing alone at the front desk, pounding his fist on it, O'Malley facing him, apparently trying to calm him. "That's him!" she cried. "I saw the portrait his sister painted at Hoeltz's gallery."

They hurried forward.

Thomas Neville was close to Francesca in age. As in the portrait, he had raven black hair, dark eyes, a large nose, and thin lips. Unlike the portrait, she hadn't realized he was so tall. He was several inches taller than Bragg, and although his shoulders weren't narrow, he was as lean as a beanstalk. He was attractive in a distinguished way.

*A big man with no eyes and no mouth.*

Francesca shoved Ellie's voice out of her mind. Ellie had been drunk and hallucinating or dreaming. Besides, Thomas Neville was very tall, but big? That was not a word Francesca would ever use to describe him. He was tall, but thin and gaunt.

"Mr. Neville, may I help you?" Bragg approached, his tone calm.

Neville turned, dark eyes flashing with annoyance. "Who are you?" he snapped.

Bragg extended his hand. "I am the commissioner of police, Rick Bragg."

That took Neville aback. Then, recovering from his surprise, he said, "I have not seen my sister in days, Commissioner! I have become frantic. I think she may be missing! I had assumed she was very involved in her work—she is an artist—but now there is no possible reason for her not to have come home. I think she has disappeared!" His tone had risen into hysteria.

"Please, be calm," Bragg said quietly. "We happen to be aware of the fact that Miss Neville is missing."

Neville inhaled, and he was trembling. Then his gaze narrowed with sudden suspicion. "You are? How do you know she is missing?"

"Her apartment has been the scene of a murder," Bragg said. "Did you know her neighbor, Miss Conway, the actress?"

"A murder!" Neville stared, blanching. "Who—someone

was murdered in her apartment? But . . . that's impossible!"

"Miss Conway was found murdered there, Mr. Neville."

He stared. It was a moment before he spoke. "How—why—how was she murdered in my sister's flat?"

"We're not certain," Bragg said. "Did you know her?"

"I only knew her in passing. We nodded at one another in the hall. She was cold, not like when she was onstage. Cold and unfriendly," he added.

Francesca stiffened with interest. Cold? Every single person whom they had spoken to said Grace Conway was warm and wonderful and beloved by all.

"Let's move over to a desk," Bragg said, his smile friendly, taking Neville's elbow.

Neville nodded grimly. Then, "I simply cannot believe this," he said. "Why would anyone murder Miss Conway? And in Mellie's flat!"

They moved behind the reception counter and into a large back room filled with desks and police clerks at their typewriters. Bragg offered a seat. Neville took it. He had now lost all of his coloring. He appeared rather greenish, in fact. "Please do not tell me that Mellie is in danger," he begged. "Good God, her disappearance isn't related to the murder, is it?"

Francesca smiled reassuringly at him. "We hope not. I am Miss Cahill," she said, handing him her calling card.

His heavy black brows lifted as he read it. He looked up. "Since when do women sleuth?"

"Since I have helped the police solve four very ghastly crimes," she said, keeping her smile firmly in place.

He handed the card back to her.

"Do keep it. When did you last see your sister, Mr. Neville?"

"Sunday." He was now abrupt.

"At what time?"

He gave her a dark look. "Why are you asking me?!"

"It is important," she said softly. "Please, we want to find her as much as you do."

He sighed. "I last saw her Sunday evening."

Francesca started, as Melinda Neville had spent Sunday night with Hoeltz—or so the gallery owner claimed. Had she gone over to the gallery after a visit from her brother? Or was one of the two men lying?

Bragg was apparently on the same track. He said, "And what time was that?"

Neville looked at them both. "Does it really matter?"

"Yes, it does," Bragg said firmly.

"It was about six P.M. I had hoped we might share a light supper, but she had other plans."

Francesca exchanged glances with Bragg. "Other plans?" she asked.

Neville suddenly covered his face with his hands. "She didn't say. She had other dinner plans."

"Were Melinda and Grace Conway friends?" Francesca asked after a reflective pause. Didn't Thomas Neville know about his sister's love affair? Could he have possibly been oblivious?

"They liked one another immensely," he said instantly. "Mellie returned from Paris very recently, and somehow, they became bosom buddies. In fact, Mellie met Miss Conway the very day she was moving in. I was helping her with her trunks. They became friendly at once. I actually think they forgot my very presence." He smiled slightly then, the memory a fond one. "I suppose they had a bit in common, an actress and an artist. God knows Mellie was raised very traditionally, but at heart she was a bohemian."

"So you approved of her friendship with Miss Conway, even though you did not like the actress yourself?" Francesca asked.

"I was thrilled that she made a friend so quickly!" he exclaimed. "And I did not say I did not like Miss Conway. I did not know her at all. When I was present, she would leave. I doubt we ever exchanged more than a dozen words. But she was all laughter around Mellie."

Francesca nodded. "I see." Not that she did. "And Hoeltz? Did you approve of your sister's friendship with him?"

Neville shot to his feet, flushing now. "Hoeltz? I do not know who you are speaking of," he said.

He was lying, Francesca was certain of it.

Bragg touched his arm. "Do sit down, Mr. Neville. So you never made the acquaintance of Bertrand Hoeltz?"

Neville did not sit. His cheeks remained red. He lowered his voice to a whisper. "Mellie is a good girl. She had nothing to do with Bertrand Hoeltz!"

"So you have met him," Bragg said.

"They are friends—casually speaking. He is representing her work," Neville said, his chin up, his posture and tone defensive. "She is my only family, Commissioner. Our mother died when we were children. Our father died a year and a half ago. She is all I have and I am begging you to find her."

"We shall do our best," Bragg said, clasping his shoulder. "These questions are necessary, Thomas. Please, do bear with Miss Cahill and me. We are almost done." He smiled.

Thomas Neville sat down. Now, he looked as if he might weep.

"Do you recall where you were on Monday morning?"

Neville blinked. "Of course I do."

"And where was that?" Francesca asked quickly.

He turned his gaze upon her. "I work at the Seamen's Savings Bank on Pearl Street. I am a clerk. I start at nine and finish at five, Monday through Friday," he said.

Francesca thought about the possibility that Grace Conway could have died before nine Monday morning or after five that evening. Not that she thought Thomas Neville the murderer, but with the sheer poverty of suspects she would add him to their short list. "What time do you leave for work?" she asked.

"At a quarter past eight," he said, "I take the trolley downtown."

"Can you think of anyone who might wish to harm Miss Conway?" Bragg asked.

"I told you, I hardly knew her," Neville said.

"Do you know anyone who might wish to harm your sister?"

"Do you think someone has hurt Mellie?" Neville cried, blanching.

"We don't know what to think," Bragg returned evenly.

"Everyone loves Mellie," her brother said. "Everyone!"

Francesca leaned close. "Not everyone, Mr. Neville. For your sister is missing, and that upon the heels of the murder of her good friend. I think she may have seen something. I think she may have witnessed the killing. I think she may have run away."

And Thomas Neville's eyes bulged. "No, no," he whispered, trembling.

"Think!" Francesca cried. "Do you know of anyone who might wish to kill Miss Conway? Or someone who hated your sister enough to destroy her studio and perhaps even attack Miss Conway accidentally—thinking her to be Mellie?"

"Hoeltz," he gasped. "Hoeltz hated Mellie with all of his being."

"What?" Francesca straightened. This was clearly an outright lie.

Tears filled Neville's eyes. He shook. "She went to him last Sunday night to tell him she was leaving him," he whispered. "And I could tell how afraid she was."

# CHAPTER
# TWELVE

BARTOLLA BENEVENTE HURRIED THROUGH the Channing residence and into the salon commonly used for entertaining callers. She had just spent fifteen minutes ironing her hair and reapplying rouge to her cheeks and lips. Clad in a very fitted burgundy jacket, the matching skirt trimmed in dyed fox, a ruby necklace, and matching ear bobs, she felt she looked radiant and her best. The salon doors were wide open. She paused on the threshold for a dramatic effect. It never crossed her mind that she had made her caller wait.

Leigh Anne Bragg had been sitting on a plush velvet sofa, and when she saw Bartolla she smiled and rose gracefully to her feet. The two women had met several years ago in Rome, when Bartolla's husband had been alive and they had been on their way to their Tuscan villa. Bartolla beamed in return, swept across the room, and the two women embraced. Unfortunately, Leigh Anne was as lovely as she had been the other day when they had last seen each other. For-

tunately, Bartolla was too secure to be envious; it was
merely annoying.

"How pretty you look!" Bartolla cried, still smiling. And
she knew *pretty* was not a word that did justice to Leigh
Anne. She knew the word would grate on the tiny woman's
nerves.

But if Leigh Anne felt insulted, she did not show it. "And
you are so beautiful today," Leigh Anne replied earnestly in
her soft, breathless voice. "I love your suit, Bartolla. Please
don't tell me it was sewn in Italy? I should so love to use
your seamstress."

"I'm afraid it was," Bartolla lied. The ensemble had belonged to one of her dear departed husband's sisters, who
had given it, and many others, to Bartolla when she realized
she was too fat to ever wear them again. Bartolla had had
them all altered to fit her perfectly. She had saved a fortune
yet acquired a couturier wardrobe. And she did not have a
seamstress, because her dear departed husband had left her
poor and penniless. However, Leigh Anne could not know
that.

It was her secret.

The two women sat, arranging their skirts, as the butler
wheeled in a tray with tea and cakes. Both women helped
themselves to plates of petits fours, which they had no intention of ever eating. "So tell me, Leigh Anne, is New York
City agreeing with you?" Bartolla asked with avid curiosity.
She was simply dying to know what was happening in the
Bragg–Leigh Anne–Francesca love triangle. It was too delicious for words.

Leigh Anne beamed. A pretty flush covered her cheeks,
and her emerald-colored eyes sparkled. "I do think so. My
husband and I reconciled last night."

Bartolla almost dropped her cup and saucer. As it was,
she spilled tea upon her lap.

Leigh Anne cried out, handing her a gold linen napkin,
"Oh, I don't think it will stain!"

Bartolla wiped the spot, using the moment to recover
from her surprise. "That is wonderful news! I am so happy

for you!" She hesitated. "Have you met Francesca Cahill, dear?"

Leigh Anne's smile faded. "Yes, I did." She reached out and clasped Bartolla's hands in hers. "I cannot tell you how I appreciate your letter warning me about her. Had I not come to New York, God only knows what might have happened."

Bartolla's smile felt brittle. Yet she had deliberately stirred up the hornets' nest, never mind that she was genuinely fond of Francesca and did not really like Leigh Anne Bragg at all. But then, Francesca was not a rival. Francesca would never be a rival, and not because she wasn't beautiful, which she was. But her attention was on politics, charities, and criminal investigations. Except for Bragg—and maybe Hart—she had no interest in men.

Leigh Anne was a very dangerous rival indeed. She was too beautiful, too poised, too elegant, and Bartolla knew she could seduce any man she wished. Fortunately, Leigh Anne's interest now was her successful and handsome husband.

Bartolla hadn't been able to resist sending Leigh Anne a warning note. The idea of Leigh Anne returning to New York to rescue her husband before he fell into Francesca's clutches had been too entertaining. And now, Bartolla could not wait to be entertained.

"Darling, you are one of my best friends!" Bartolla exclaimed. "As much as I adore Francesca—and you know that I do—I simply had to let you know what was happening here in the city before everyone's curious eyes."

Leigh Anne smiled gratefully and sipped her tea.

Which annoyed Bartolla even more. "Have the two of you met yet?"

Leigh Anne set her cup down. Then, shocking Bartolla, she picked up a petit four and nibbled briefly on it. "I called on her a few days ago. I am afraid you were right." She was rueful. "She is extraordinary. At once beautiful, clever, and kind—not to mention a sleuth. It is so understandable that Rick would have feelings for such a woman—considering we have been apart for four very long years."

In a gesture of sympathy that she did not feel, Bartolla reached out and touched Leigh Anne's small, silken hand, thinking, *Well done!* "Yes, she is extraordinary. There is never a dull moment around Francesca," Bartolla said, yearning to know what had happened when Francesca and Leigh Anne met. "Perhaps the day will come when you, too, shall become her friend?"

Leigh Anne smiled. "That would be very nice."

Determined to provoke a measure of the truth from her, Bartolla prodded, "Francesca is very interesting company indeed. Perhaps the three of us should take lunch one day this week?"

Leigh Anne surprised her, proving that she was a very worthy adversary. "If you care to arrange it, I will certainly attend. Perhaps you should invite your cousin, whom I have yet to meet?"

Bartolla made an airy submissive gesture. "Sarah is always in her studio, painting. It is almost impossible to distract her from her art, but if you wish it, I will try." And as she spoke, she thought about Evan Cahill and her heart leaped.

He was so badly hurt, but he would recover, thank God. She would visit him later that day—and every afternoon while he was bedridden. She missed the time they had been spending together. Yet she needed far more than his companionship and gallantry, as she was a hot-blooded woman and he was a simply stunning young man. She knew he would be a superb lover, at once experienced and generous. She knew he would worship every inch of her lush body. Still, her plans required patience.

First he must break his engagement to Sarah, which Bartolla knew he had intended to do before he'd been in that absurd brawl. And until recently she had intended to engage in every possible sexual act with him except for an actual consummation. She had planned to withhold her ultimate favors, to tease and torment him until he dropped down on his knees and begged her to marry him. But she was growing impatient—and scared.

The way he had been looking at the haggard and dowdy seamstress the other day had really frightened her, no matter how often she told herself that there simply could not be any competition between them. Not for Evan Cahill.

But she could not talk herself out of her worries, and abruptly her plans had changed.

She must speed up the inevitable now.

And she must claim to be pregnant as soon as was possible.

They had finally calmed Thomas Neville down and had asked him several other questions. By the time they had handed him back to Captain Shea in order for him to take Neville's report, Francesca couldn't help wondering if he was their man. She and Bragg watched him, seated behind a desk, Shea now interviewing him for the official missing person report. "What do you think?"

Bragg glanced at her. "Don't leap to conclusions, Francesca."

"He clearly loves his sister. But he is odd. There is something about him that bothers me," she said reflectively.

"I think we should look into Hoeltz's alibi," Bragg said. "If Miss Neville ended their affair, I doubt she spent Sunday night with him, which means he lied to us. And that gives him motivation."

"Motivation to murder Miss Conway?" Francesca was skeptical.

"Motivation to vandalize his lover's studio in a fit of rage and or despair, and then take out his fury on Miss Conway, an innocent passerby."

"And that still leaves us with the very significant and unanswered question of where is Miss Neville—and what has happened to her? If your theory is correct, she may be hiding from her very own lover," Francesca said.

Before he could reply, Inspector Newman came barreling

through the two front doors of headquarters, huffing and puffing as he did so. He saw them instantly, veered in their direction, and halted before them, gasping for air.

"Slow down," Bragg said, clasping his shoulder. "I take it you have found something?"

Newman nodded, wheezing and incapable of speech. Hickey entered the lobby now, a tall, lean man with red hair going gray. He strolled over. "Miss Holmes has been murdered," he said.

"What?!" Francesca said, in shock.

Bragg guided Newman to a bench. "When did this happen?"

Newman breathed. "Her mother found her this morning, sir. Found her lying on the floor in her bedroom, strangled to death."

"Let's go," Bragg said.

Francesca paused in the narrow doorway of the room that had belonged, until sometime last night, to Catherine Holmes. Instantly her gaze slammed onto Catherine's lifeless form. She lay several feet from her narrow bed in her simple cotton nightgown, beside an unornamented wall. She did not lie near the doorway where Francesca stood. As Mrs. Holmes was on the couch in the parlor, sobbing in hysterics, the scene was a terrible one.

Francesca also wanted to cry.

Francesca had met Miss Conway once, and briefly. She had not met Miss Neville. Now she felt paralyzed with grief.

She felt Bragg appear at her side. Not looking at him, she said solemnly, "She lied to us about the window. I am certain she would sit there and yearn for another life, a life outside this dismal, damp apartment. She saw the killer, Bragg. And he came back for her."

Bragg touched her arm. "That is one theory, and it may be the right one." He walked over to Catherine's body and knelt down. "Her throat is turning black-and-blue," he said.

Francesca looked away. She took one last glance at the

sparsely furnished bedroom. The comforter was blue and worn, and one lacy white pillow had been used to decorate the bed. The side table was pine and poorly constructed. There was one lamp in the room upon it, as was a mug of water. A Bible was there, as well.

Several items of clothing hung on the wall pegs. Francesca turned to the broken-down armoire and opened it. She found more clothing, a pair of shoes, undergarments, and one pretty shell hair comb. She felt more saddened than before.

Miss Neville's flat had been rather unadorned, but not like this, not so starkly, so depressingly. And Miss Neville had had her art.

Francesca hoped that she was alive.

Francesca left the bedroom and was joined by Bragg in the parlor. "The door was bolted from the inside every night, and Mrs. Holmes says it was bolted when she ran into the street to shout for help this morning."

On the couch, Mrs. Holmes continued to alternately gasp for air and sob.

"I want to get this madman, Bragg," Francesca said grimly. "Before he strikes again."

"I do, too," he returned. He pointed at the window where Catherine Holmes's rocking chair sat, glaringly empty now. Francesca saw that the window had been smashed and it was wide open. "He entered and left this way."

"Why not go out the front door?"

"Perhaps he did not want to be seen in the hallway a second time," Bragg said.

"Is there any connection between Catherine Holmes and the art world?" she asked, wanting to add, *Or my brother?* But she did not.

"No."

Suddenly the chief of police came striding into the room. As he was so leonine and charismatic, he dominated the small parlor. "Commissioner, sir. Miss Cahill. I see our strangler has been at it again."

As Francesca did not like Brendan Farr—he had made it

clear he did not like her involvement in police affairs, and she found him threatening—she merely smiled and walked about the room, looking for more clues.

"Either our killer is a madman who has become fond of this building or Miss Holmes saw something she should not have seen," Bragg said. He gestured to the bedroom.

Farr went in, followed by a young officer. He also knelt beside the body, visually inspecting her without touching her. Newman and Hickey were now finishing their search of the parlor. They turned their efforts to the bedroom.

Francesca walked over to Mrs. Holmes, wishing Farr were not involving himself in the case. She sat down beside her. "I am so sorry. Has a doctor been called?"

Mrs. Holmes nodded, her face impossibly haggard now. "She was such an angel," she choked. "She was my angel of mercy! How could anyone do this?"

"We intend to find out," Francesca said grimly. Impulsively she took the woman's hands. "Did Miss Holmes know Grace Conway? Were they friends?"

"Absolutely not! Miss Conway was an *actress*, young lady, and my daughter is genteel."

"Did she know or had she ever met either Bertrand Hoeltz, Miss Neville's friend, or Thomas Neville, her brother?" Francesca stiffened, as Farr had come to stand behind her.

"She was friendly with Miss Neville, as was I. Of course we knew her brother. As for Mr. Hoeltz"—Mrs. Holmes was grim—"I told her to never even look at him should she pass him in the hallway. I told her he was dangerous."

"Did Mr. Hoeltz frequent this building? Did he visit Miss Neville here?" Francesca asked, surprised.

"Yes, he did. And he always had red roses in his arms, red roses and a bottle of French wine!" Tears returned to her eyes. She covered her face with her hands and cried again.

"Did Miss Holmes know Evan Cahill, Mrs. Holmes?" Farr asked.

Francesca stiffened, and slowly she turned to look up at him.

He stared at her, his gray eyes fathomless. "It is the one question you did not ask."

Mrs. Holmes dropped her hands. "That *friend* of Miss Conway? Absolutely not! He is as bad as Hoeltz, or even worse! Always smiling at the good girls like my Catherine. I told her not to ever smile back at him!"

"Francesca?" Bragg called quietly from the bedroom.

Francesca leaped to her feet and hurried over. Bragg was holding the Bible in his hand. "What is it?" she asked, not liking his odd expression. She had an inkling of dread.

He was so grim. He opened the Bible and Francesca realized that it was a journal, not a Bible after all. The cover of the Bible had been removed from the Good Book and attached to the journal, clearly disguising what the contents were. He had it opened randomly, and he handed it to her.

Francesca glanced at the date—it was almost a year ago—and read:

> *He came calling on Grace Conway again, and we passed in the hall. Of course, I was expecting him, as he always comes for her in the early evenings to take her out. Tonight he wore a pink carnation in his lapel. And this time, when he smiled at me, I managed to say hello! He actually said hello to me, too, then introduced himself. His name is Evan Cahill. Oh, how elegant it sounds, and how it suits him! I dared to introduce myself, and after that, he wished me a pleasant evening.*

Francesca's dread became full-blown. She skipped the rest of the page, turning to another one:

> *I heard them all night. I heard him making love to her, I heard her crying his name. Afterward, I heard him telling her how much he loves her. These walls are so thin! And later, when it was quiet upstairs, I*

*could not sleep. In my mind I keep seeing Evan Cahill
making love to Miss Conway, but eventually, she be-
comes me. Oh, God. I am so in love.*

Francesca snapped the book closed, aghast.

Farr towered in the doorway. "So she kept a journal," he
said flatly.

Francesca turned away from him, trembling. Her brother
was now the link between Sarah Channing and both dead
women.

"Are you all right?" Bragg took her hand and held it tightly.

"That journal doesn't mean anything," Francesca said as
they sat in his Daimler outside the brownstone that housed
Gallery Hoeltz.

"It means that she was infatuated with your brother. We
will need to hear his side of this, Francesca."

"If only Farr hadn't shown up!" she cried passionately.
He was trouble and she simply knew it. "He dislikes me
so!"

To her surprise, Bragg did not disagree or try to reassure
her. He got out of the motorcar and came around to open
her door. He said, "I think you should stay away from police
headquarters for a while, Francesca. Keep a low profile, if
you understand my meaning. Continue to investigate, but
with discretion."

She nodded. "I happen to agree with you," she said.

They left the roadster and soon Bertrand Hoeltz was ushering them upstairs into the art gallery. He looked terrible—
as if he had aged a decade in a day. After seating them in
his small office and offering them espresso, he said, "Please
tell me that you have good news. Please tell me you have
found Melinda!"

"I am afraid we have no news," Bragg said. "We continue to work on it."

"We need to ask you a few questions, Mr. Hoeltz," Francesca said softly.

He groaned and covered his face with his hands, then nodded grimly at them. He seemed genuinely distraught over his mistress's continuing disappearance.

"Mr. Hoeltz," Francesca said softly—nonthreateningly. "Did Miss Neville decide to end your affair?"

He straightened as if shot. His eyes were wide, shocked. "What?"

Francesca repeated the question.

He rubbed his face. "No, she did not, and I do not know where you heard such a lie," he said hoarsely. He met her eyes. "We were more than paramours, Miss Cahill. We were in love."

Francesca smiled tightly. "I am sure you were," she said, alarm bells now ringing within her mind. He was lying. He had not been able to look her in the eye when he had denied the breakup of his affair.

"Do you recall what you did Monday morning after Miss Neville left here?" Bragg asked quietly and neutrally. Francesca did not have to share a glance with him to know that he had caught the lie as well.

Hoeltz was startled. "Monday morning? What does that have to do with anything?" He seemed quite pale now.

"Please," Bragg said with an encouraging smile.

Hoeltz shook his head. "I read the *Sun*, my newspaper of choice. I then went for a walk, something I do every morning. I did some paperwork and wrote a few letters, here in my office, and then I took lunch at a small restaurant not far from here."

"Alone?" Bragg asked.

"Yes, alone. What is this about?"

"At what time did you take lunch and what is the name of the restaurant?" Francesca asked, Miss Holmes's stunning journal still preoccupying her mind.

"The restaurant is called Joe's and it is two blocks up Fourth Avenue," he said, looking upset now. He glanced back and forth between them both several times. "What is this about?"

"And after lunch?" Bragg continued, as if not hearing him.

"I had no appointments, so I began an inventory of some new work I have recently acquired. Then I went out to buy some bread and cheese for a light supper. I was expecting Melinda, but she never came," he ended hoarsely, wide-eyed with apprehension now.

Francesca looked at Bragg. For most of Monday, with the exception of his lunch at Joe's, Bertrand Hoeltz had no alibi. And his mistress had ended their affair the night before her disappearance—the night before Grace Conway's murder. "How well did you know Thomas Neville?" she asked.

"I hardly knew him at all!" He was distressed.

"Why not?" Bragg asked. "After all, he was your mistress's brother."

He flushed. "Why not? That is the exact reason why not, Commissioner. He disapproved of our affair. He disapproved of me. In fact, he was such an opinionated and difficult man that Mellie avoided him to the best of her ability. That is why she spent a year in Paris—to avoid her own brother. When she came back, we both agreed to keep him at a distance."

"But Thomas Neville visited his sister almost every day at her own flat," Francesca pointed out. That hardly seemed compatible with Melinda's wishing to avoid him.

Hoeltz was grim. "He was hard to avoid."

"I have one more question," she said. "If you loved her so much, why didn't you marry her?"

He turned red.

"Mr. Hoeltz?" Bragg prodded.

He stood. He was excessively grim. "I wanted to, of course. Desperately, in fact. But I could not."

Francesca waited.

He sighed. "I am already married, Miss Cahill. My wife lives with our children in a small town north of Paris."

# CHAPTER
# THIRTEEN

HART HAD BOUGHT HIS mistress a house on Fifth Avenue. Francesca walked slowly through a wrought-iron gate toward the stately brick mansion. She continued to worry about Catherine Holmes's infatuation with her brother and Brendan Farr's sudden involvement in the case. But as Francesca approached Daisy's front door, she was well aware that her nervousness had nothing to do with the current investigation and everything to do with the visit she was about to make. It was odd, because she was genuinely fond of Daisy, who she suspected came from a background very much like her own. But now, with Hart's intentions firmly declared toward her and the kiss they had so recently shared, she felt wary, as if calling upon the other woman was somehow an act that involved the enemy.

She also knew that Hart must never find out about this social call. For she simply had to pry—she had to know about his relationship with Daisy.

The front door was answered promptly by a servant.

Francesca was ushered into a spacious entry hall with highly polished wood floors and a wide, sweeping staircase at its end. Several paintings hung on the walls, two landscapes, a still life, and a wonderful depiction of a mother and her daughter. Francesca handed over her calling card, briefly admiring the portrait of mother and child and hoping to distract herself from her anxiety. It had been painted by someone named Mary Cassatt.

"Francesca!" Daisy cried in genuine pleasure, hurrying down the stairs.

Francesca smiled warmly in return, for one moment forgetting the man who was the common bond between them. Daisy remained the most ethereal woman Francesca had ever seen, more angelic than womanly, a vision of moonlit tones and hues. Her hair was platinum, her skin a similar shade of ivory. She was slender and delicate. Her features were flawless—huge blue eyes, startling with such a fair complexion, high cheekbones, a slim nose. If her jaw was a bit strong, one hardly noticed, as her lips were unusually full.

She was the most beautiful woman Francesca had ever seen, bar none, even Leigh Anne. Francesca had not been surprised when Hart had made Daisy his mistress. They were perfectly suited to each other physically, as he was the shadowy night, she the moonlight.

"How are you, Daisy?" Francesca said. In a way, she felt like a traitor to her new friend. She knew that Daisy was very happy with Hart and their arrangement.

"Wonderful." Daisy smiled. And to Francesca's surprise, it did not reach her eyes. Her startling blue eyes were worried. What could be amiss?

Daisy took her hand. "Come. Come into the salon. I am so pleased you have called," she said in her soft, breathy voice. The tone suited her fragile appearance.

A bit uncomfortable, Francesca followed her into an elegant salon, the walls a soft creamy gold, the furniture muted in tones of green, blue, and gold. Beautiful Persian rugs were underfoot, and three crystal chandeliers hung from the high ceiling. The room, like the house, was understated elegance. Both women settled into adjacent chairs.

Daisy was wearing a sky blue dress several shades lighter than her eyes. She held Francesca's hand warmly. "Are you on another case?" she asked eagerly. "I read all about the Cross Killer two weeks ago. My, Francesca! You have become indispensable to Rick Bragg." She was admiring.

"Yes, actually, we are working on another case, one that is rather complicated." But Francesca hadn't come to discuss the investigation. She wanted to get far more personal. "How is Rose?"

Daisy started. Rose was her best friend and her lover. Upon first realizing this, Francesca had been shocked. But in time, she had come to accept the fact that the two women loved each other. Francesca also liked Rose, who was tempestuous, dark, and sultry. "I haven't seen her in a week. You know Hart is very difficult when it comes to Rose."

Francesca could not help it. Hart was the topic she wished to broach. "He knows how strongly you feel about Rose. I am sure he is jealous."

"Jealous? Hart?" Daisy was surprised, and then she smiled in amusement. "Francesca, Hart doesn't have a jealous bone in his body. He is possessive, maddeningly so, but never jealous."

Francesca nodded, feeling grim. Here was news indeed, and it did not surprise her. He wasn't jealous, because he refused to allow himself to love, but he was possessive, which was far worse. Clearly he considered Daisy very much in the way he considered the other items he collected, a possession, personal property.

"Do not misunderstand," Daisy said quickly. "I adore Calder. I have never met a more thoughtful or generous man. I am happy with our arrangement. But he and Rose are at such odds, and it puts me in the middle, between them. They cannot stand one another. I just do not know what to do."

Francesca could not help herself. Some time ago, when she had been working on the Randall Murder, Hart had been a suspect. His alibi had been that he had been in bed with both Rose and Daisy at the time of Randall's murder. Francesca knew that he had enjoyed the favors of both women simultaneously more than once, before he had made Daisy his mistress. "He used to be fond of Rose," she commented.

Daisy said gently, "In those days, he did not know either one of us. It was strictly passion, Francesca."

She flushed. *Who would be foolish enough to marry a man who had slept with two women at the same time?*

"Are you all right?" Daisy asked, startling her. She peered closely at Francesca. "You seem . . . distracted. No, disturbed."

"I am a bit overwhelmed right now," Francesca said. She hesitated. "Bragg's wife returned to town and they have reconciled, while my brother was terribly beaten up in a bar."

Daisy gasped. "I am so sorry about your brother! And as for the commissioner, I had no idea he even had a wife! I know how you feel about him."

Francesca managed a smile. "We remain friends," she said firmly. And after all of the investigative work that they had shared that day, it now seemed possible to turn their relationship into a genuine friendship. That gladdened Francesca.

"He should have told you," Daisy flared. "And that is why I love Rose and in general do not like most men." She softened. "Calder is an extreme exception."

Francesca had to defend Bragg. "His wife abandoned him four years ago, Daisy. She took off to Europe, where she had many lovers. They hadn't even spoken in four years, much less seen one another. Her return was a surprise to us all."

"You still love him," Daisy said.

"I care deeply and I always will," Francesca agreed. She realized that her anger of the previous evening had dissipated. She simply could not remain angry with Bragg. And the sorrow—and sense of loss—had also lessened.

Suddenly Daisy glanced past Francesca. "Calder is here!" she cried in surprise and delight.

Francesca whirled in her chair to look out the window. There was no mistaking the huge gleaming barouche now parked in the street. She leaped to her feet. "He mustn't see me! He mustn't know I was here!"

Daisy gaped at her. "But . . . why?"

"I don't know how to tell you—and there is no time!" Francesca felt panicked.

Daisy stood, walking past Francesca and opening the door to a smaller salon. "I will bring your coat. Stay in here. When he comes into the salon, you can go out that door over there and through the front hall. There is a door on the far end which opens onto the gardens in the back."

"Thank you!" Francesca cried, rushing into the adjacent room and firmly closing the door. Her heart was thundering in her chest. She felt as if she were a crook caught with his hand in the safe. Hart would know she had been prying into his life if he caught her now. He would be very amused— and he would never let her forget it.

Daisy returned from the front hall, handing Francesca her coat and gloves. She smiled. "Do come again," she whispered.

Francesca nodded as Daisy backed out, quietly closing the door behind her. And before she could take a deep, reassuring breath, she heard Daisy cry out in the front hall, "Calder! It is so good to see you!"

Francesca straightened. It almost sounded as if Daisy were anxious and as if she hadn't seen her lover in some time.

But that couldn't be right. Francesca knew of Hart's sexual appetite. He would visit his mistress frequently. He would visit Daisy every night.

He replied, his drawl too low for her to make out the words. Francesca became more rigid. His tone was not the oh-so-sexy murmur that he so often used with her. It was rather barren of sensuality, in fact. How odd.

"Would you care for a scotch? Are you hungry? Or how about a hot bath?" Daisy's voice was very distinct now, and clearly she and Hart had walked into the salon Francesca had just vacated. This was her opportunity to leave.

Francesca did not move. Her heart beat hard.

"I am fine," Hart said matter-of-factly, his tone amazingly straightforward and not at all seductive, not in the least.

"Is everything all right?" Daisy asked with obvious worry.

Francesca knew she must not snoop. She walked over to the door that led to the salon and pressed her ear against it. She simply had to know more about his relationship with this woman. She could not help herself.

Hart sighed. "We must talk."

There was silence. Francesca could feel Daisy's alarm. She herself was more than surprised herself. What was going on?

"Have I done something to offend you?" Daisy then asked. "Or have you tired of me already? I haven't seen you in days, Calder." She did not whine. Her tone was soft, uncertain, but not shrewlike.

"My sweet Daisy," Hart said, but quietly. "You haven't offended me, but I have been rather preoccupied these past few days. There is something I do need to discuss with you."

"Are you ending our relationship?" she asked, her tone tremulous. "I shan't cry. I am very fond of you, but if that is what—"

"No. I am hardly ending our relationship," Hart said flatly.

Francesca could not deny the extent of her disappointment. But then, Hart was showing his true colors. He was pursuing her but keeping Daisy, and it was no surprise.

"Shall we sit down?" he now asked gently.

"I am afraid to sit down," Daisy said. And then, "Calder, I have missed you!"

"Please, let us sit." After a pause, during which Francesca imagined them sitting down together on the couch, he said, "I have decided to marry."

Daisy gasped. So did Francesca.

"What was that?" Hart asked sharply.

Francesca covered her mouth with her hand.

"I . . . I . . . Calder! This is simply stunning!" Daisy cried.

Francesca realized she had forgotten to breathe. Hart had come to discuss his marriage with her? With Daisy, his mistress? She was stunned.

"I know." His laughter was self-deprecating. "I am extremely fond of Miss Cahill, and she is the one I eventually hope to wed."

There was a stunned silence from Daisy now.

And not just from Daisy, but from Francesca as well. Calder had come to apprise his mistress of his intentions toward Francesca. In a way, it was so noble. But it did not make any sense, oh no.

"It may be some time before I gain a commitment from Miss Cahill, but when that time comes, I am afraid I will be ending our affair."

Francesca choked off another gasp and reeled as Daisy said, shocked, "I see."

Francesca leaned helplessly upon the door. Calder would jettison his mistress when they were wed? Did that mean he intended to be faithful? Was it even remotely possible?

"When she accepts your suit, you will become faithful," Daisy said rather dully.

"I see no point in marrying should I wish to carry on with other women," Hart said. "However, it may be some time before we are affianced."

"Oh, I don't think so. I rather think she might be more amenable to your suit than you think," Daisy said, sounding tearful.

"Please, do not cry. I am not good with tears. I dislike women who weep and carry on." He was firm.

Francesca realized her own eyes were flooding now. *Hart intended to be faithful to her.* It was simply too stunning to comprehend.

"Daisy," he said sharply, a command.

"I am sorry," she said. "Excuse me for one moment."

Francesca heard her walk out of the salon. She was trembling now. If she accepted Hart's suit, he would leave his mistress and give up his penchant for other women. *Oh, my God.*

*Could this really be happening?*

Daisy returned to the room. "Forgive me, Calder. It was a rather shocking moment for me."

"I understand." Francesca heard relief in his tone.

"Do you have to go?"

"I should, yes."

Daisy did not reply.

And the silence lengthened.

And when several more moments passed, Francesca became unnerved. The silence could only mean one thing. Or was she leaping to conclusions? Could Hart possibly be making love to Daisy after all he had just declared? She reached for the doorknob, trembling, and hesitated. She should not spy, and she did not dare get caught. But she *had* to know what they were doing.

Francesca turned the doorknob as gently as she could, cracked the door, and peered through.

Calder stood not far from where Francesca stood. Daisy had her arms around him and she was on her tiptoes, nibbling on his lips. For one moment, as his eyes were open, Francesca thought that he had seen her.

But his eyes drifted closed.

Francesca thanked God she hadn't been caught, was about to back quickly out, and then changed her mind. Daisy was trying to seduce him; that much was clear. Calder was hardly being responsive or encouraging. Yet he hadn't tossed her aside, either. Francesca knew that she should go, but she would be forever tortured if she didn't stay to see whether Daisy succeeded in seducing Hart or not.

She watched Daisy slip her hands beneath Hart's white shirt, and incredulous, she saw Daisy begin to sensually shift her hips back and forth, clearly rubbing herself over his loins. Francesca couldn't move or breathe; Hart's eyes opened, but he was smiling now and Francesca did not worry that he might notice her. He was becoming too involved.

Daisy reached down between them and Francesca bit her lip hard, because it was obvious that Daisy was grasping his manhood through his trousers. Stunned, she heard Daisy say, "I think you need me for a few minutes, Calder. Please, it is my pleasure. Sit down."

Francesca wanted him to tell her "No."

But another part of her wanted him to say "Yes."

Hart's jaw flexed. "You are the ultimate temptress, Daisy," he said softly. "And God, I have been celibate for several days."

"You are a man who needs a woman on a daily basis, Calder. And you are hardly married yet. Do you think to remain celibate from this day forward?" Daisy asked simply.

Francesca already knew that answer.

"Absolutely not," he said, and then his teeth flashed. "What are you wearing under that dress?" he asked.

Daisy smiled seductively. "Nothing."

"Take it off."

Francesca's heart leaped. She watched Hart help remove Daisy's dress, so adept that it slithered down her naked, flawless body and to the floor within seconds. She was mesmerized. Hart clasped his mistress's soft pale buttocks and sat down in a chair, pulling her down on top of him.

Francesca felt the fire in her own loins. She held on to the doorknob so she could remain standing up. This was, most definitely, the time to leave. But God, she could not move or breathe, and Francesca knew golden opportunity when she saw it.

Daisy laughed huskily and began licking his lips, his face.

Francesca's heart lurched; her nipples tightened; her sex swelled. And she watched Daisy toy with the seam of his lips. Francesca had just tasted him yesterday. She recalled very vividly how he tasted, how he felt, and even how he smelled. And now Hart's head had fallen back as he gave in to pure carnal pleasure, his long strong throat suddenly vulnerable and exposed, his eyes fluttering closed.

Daisy kissed his throat.

The jealousy came then. Francesca had the insane urge to run into the room, pull Daisy off Hart by her pretty platinum hair, settle herself on his lap, claim his lips with her own, and ingest all of him that she could.

Daisy unbuttoned his shirt.

Francesca's knees buckled as swathe after swathe of rock-hard chest and torso was revealed. His arms were sculpted like the statue *David*. His chest was two hard slabs of muscle. His nipples were copper-colored and very erect. Daisy latched onto one, suckling it vigorously.

Desire made her feel faint. And Hart finally groaned.

The sound was raw and so sexual, Francesca knew it was a sound she would never, ever forget. . . . Daisy was kissing him in the center of his chest. Francesca gasped, realizing her intention. She moved lower and lower, working her way down the center of his belly with her lips. Francesca gripped the door. She bit her lip to keep from crying out. Daisy unbuckled his belt, sliding off his lap to do so, on her knees, between his thighs. Francesca stared as Daisy freed Hart's manhood.

Daisy flicked her tongue over it.

Hart groaned again. His large hands clasped her head, as if to hold her down.

Daisy began laving his shaft, up and down, all around.

Then she sucked the huge head into her mouth and, a moment later, half of his length.

Francesca cried out weakly. She couldn't breathe. And she could taste him as if he were in *her* mouth and *her* throat. Somehow, she knew he would be salty yet sweet. She could feel him throbbing against the walls of her cheeks, the back of her throat. Her lips stretched taut. She wanted to suck him down even more deeply. Somehow, she could find ecstasy in doing so. She simply knew it.

Hart gasped.

Francesca blinked, clinging to the door, which was somehow more wide open now, and saw Hart on his feet, unsmiling and intense. He removed his shirt, staring down at Daisy, who now sat on the floor at his feet, her lips slick and swollen, her small breasts heaving. He removed his shoes, his socks, his trousers and drawers. Francesca bit her fist so she would not moan and attract his attention.

He was gorgeous. Man and sex.

He extended a hand, lifting Daisy to her feet. Then he swept her up and laid her on the couch. Francesca knew that if she were Daisy, she would be begging him desperately to hurry and enter her.

Hart lowered himself over her.

Francesca could not—would not—move. *Hurry*, she thought wildly, *hurry, Calder, hurry . . .*

And Hart laughed, low. It was the most sexual sound Francesca had ever heard, and then, to her shock, her amazement, her dismay, he slowly began rubbing the bulbous head of his penis over Daisy's sex. He was slick and wet. So was she. Daisy began to pant and whimper, to writhe.

Hart's rhythm increased. The tendons in his biceps and arms bulged, as did the straining muscles in his shoulders, his back, his buttocks.

"Hurry," Daisy whispered.

Or was it Francesca?

He thrust slowly, maddeningly, deep into her.

Francesca cried out.

It took a long moment to recover. Her body had exploded in sheer shameless ecstasy, her heart beat so hard it felt dangerous and life-threatening, and she had bitten her wrist to keep quiet. Sanity returned. Dear God, what had she done? And how could she have let happen what *had* happened just now?

Francesca squeezed her eyes tightly closed, disbelieving now. Dismay consumed her savagely now, and then came the equally burning, odious guilt. When suddenly she froze, recalling that the door behind her had been left wide open.

Dread overcame her.

She sat up slowly with dread, certain she would see Hart standing in the doorway, staring down at her.

She almost fainted with relief. The doorway was empty.

And then she heard the soft, rhythmic sound coming from the other room.

She quickly leaped to her feet and ran to the doorway.

Hart and Daisy remained wildly embraced. Daisy was whimpering uncontrollably—she appeared about to climax. Hart, however, appeared intent and absolutely in control. He looked capable of making love to his mistress for several hours.

Francesca shut the door, grabbed her coat, and ran out of the house.

# CHAPTER
# FOURTEEN

FRIDAY, FEBRUARY 21, 1902—5:30 P.M.

"YOU MUST HELP ME dress," Francesca shouted. "Hart will be here at any moment!" She ran past her gaping mother and sister and landed on the wide, sweeping stairs, still running.

Julia and Connie had been chatting over sherry. Now both women leaped to their feet and hurried into the hall. "Francesca?" Julia asked. "Whatever is wrong?"

"Nothing," she lied. "I am terribly late!"

Connie and Julia exchanged glances. Julia said, beginning to smile, "Now why was I not informed of this evening's affair?"

Connie shrugged, smiling. "I'll help her. And I will find out all the details, Mama," she added, lifting her silk skirts and hurrying upstairs.

In her bedroom, Francesca flung open an armoire and stared wildly at all of her gowns, many of which were new, due to the fact that she had so wanted to help Maggie Kennedy, she had hired her to make a dozen dresses that she hadn't even needed. A sea of brilliant color swam before her eyes. She had to cancel the gallery and supper tonight.

Because she simply could not face Calder Hart just yet.

"Miss Cahill? Let me help you," Bette said, entering the bedroom.

Francesca leaped around, startled, because extremely graphic images of a very naked and very aroused Calder Hart refused to leave her treacherous, stubborn, disloyal mind. Francesca muttered, "I don't know what to wear."

Connie laughed.

Francesca saw her coming up behind Bette and started, because her sister's smile seemed genuine and she hadn't seen such an expression on Connie's face in so long. "Thank God you are here!" she exclaimed.

"Having trouble deciding on a gown, Fran?" Connie teased. "And since when did you even care if your shoes came from the same pair!"

"I need help!" Francesca cried. "And I need to speak with you." She rushed to the door. "Bette, would you give my sister and myself a moment, please?"

"Just wait," Connie said, strolling over to the armoire. "Where are you and Calder off to, tonight?"

"I have decided to cancel," she said grimly. "In fact, I am positive I am ill!" In fact, the more she thought about what she had done, the sicker she became. *If Calder Hart ever learned of her spying, he would never speak to her again.*

She knew it. The act had been an unconscionable one. She had invaded his privacy and his trust. What was wrong with her!

"Dinner, I suppose? Perhaps at Sherry-Netherland's?" Connie guessed.

"He will be here at six," she snapped, frantic. "And no, we are going to supper at some place downtown where the food is excellent, but apparently it is not elegant, so no one who knows us will be there. And we shall attend an art exhibition first." She hugged herself.

"The turquoise," Connie decided. "It is new, it is the

latest, it is intriguing, and it will make your eyes appear even bluer than they are." She took the gown and handed it to Bette. "Please press this. And tell the doorman to seat Mr. Hart with Mama when he comes. Thank you."

The maid hurried out.

Francesca ran to the door and slammed it closed and looked at her sister. "I can't go."

"Fran, what has happened now?" Connie asked with real caution.

"I have done something too terrible for words."

Connie raised her pale brows. "Well, I am sure you are eloquent enough to share your latest faux pas with me, your closest friend and sister."

"I spied on Hart."

Connie crossed her arms, her gaze narrowing. "What does 'spy' mean?"

"It means I watched him make love to his mistress."

Connie finally understood and she paled. "You did what?"

"I know, I am a fool, an idiot, and terribly amoral!"

"Fran? Whatever possessed you?" Connie asked worriedly. "How *could* you?"

Francesca sank down in a chair. Glumly she said, "I was calling upon Daisy. I wanted to find out more about her relationship with Calder. When he called, I hid, because I did not want him to know that I was there, prying into his affair with his mistress." Francesca looked up. "He told Daisy he is ending it with her when we become engaged."

"That is wonderful," Connie said, at once her usual self again.

"He said he will be faithful," Francesca told her, still in some disbelief as far as that announcement went.

"Mama is right. Every rake has his day. Apparently Calder has had his," Connie said, sounding delighted.

Francesca did not smile. "Daisy was very upset. She seduced him. I should have left; I simply could not move."

Connie sat down in the adjacent chair. "Fran, I know you like Daisy, but you must be wary of her now. Her interest is in remaining Hart's mistress, even after you are wed."

Francesca was grim. "No one can tell Hart what to do, and he is too clever to be manipulated."

"All men can be led about by a woman, Fran. If you get my meaning."

Francesca thought about the way Daisy had so boldly seduced him, and she grew afraid. "What are you telling me?"

"I am telling you to make certain Daisy's bags are packed and she is out the door when you and he are finally married."

Francesca caught herself nodding; then she leaped to her feet. "Wait! We are both forgetting one important fact. I am not marrying anyone!"

Connie also stood. "Why not? Hart adores you; he is a premier catch; he is rich. Why ever not?"

Francesca gave her a disbelieving look.

Connie made a face. "Haven't you heard? Rick Bragg has reconciled with his wife. We saw them at the opera last night in a party that included the mayor and Mrs. Low."

Francesca said, "I know." And the hurt returned, slight now, but nagging. With it came so much regret.

"So?"

"I don't want to marry anyone! For God's sake, it is a lifelong commitment! If I marry Calder, it will be until I die!"

"Well, considering the fact that you are a sleuth and in constant danger, your marriage might not be as long as you think," Connie said cheerfully.

Francesca grabbed a pillow from the bed and threw it at her.

Connie laughed.

Francesca smiled, too. It was so good to hear her sister laugh again and speak like herself. Of course, her anger had been frightening—as was the fact that she blamed Fran for the state of her marriage. But anger was far better than melancholy.

There was a knock on the door. Connie opened it and

received the dress from Bette. "I will help Francesca dress." When Bette was gone, the two sisters faced each other. "You do want to spend the evening on the town with Hart, don't you?" Connie said with a knowing smile.

Francesca sighed and gave it up. "His company is very enjoyable. There is only one problem."

"That is?"

"How do I look him in the eye . . . ever again?"

Francesca felt uncharacteristically glamorous. The turquoise gown had small cap sleeves, a low-cut silk bodice, and a layered chiffon skirt in two shades, turquoise and silver. When Francesca had studied herself critically in the mirror, her every movement had caused her gown to shimmer, as if iridescent. Connie had dabbed a hint of rouge on her cheeks, then found a darker lip rouge in her handbag and insisted Francesca use that, too. Connie had taken off her small diamond cross necklace, and the glittering cross was now nestled just above Francesca's cleavage. Bette and Connie had worked like mad to tong Francesca's hair, sweeping it loosely up and carefully setting it with Mr. Randolph's Spray Elixir. Then, to Francesca's dismay, Connie had poked and prodded at the mass of hair, pulling pieces free here and there, so that tendrils caressed her cheeks and neck. In the end, the effect was disturbingly sensual.

Long white gloves completed the ensemble, and as Francesca did not have any bracelets that Connie liked or admired, her orders for the evening were for Francesca to keep her gloves on at all costs.

"You have never been more beautiful," Connie whispered. "Your eyes are sparkling with excitement, Fran." She kissed her cheek as they paused on the ground floor.

"They are not sparkling—they are glittering . . . with fear," Francesca said tartly, breathlessly. She could hear Hart's low murmur and Julia's answering tone. How happy her mother sounded.

"Silly woman," Connie chided, sounding as happy. She

poked Fran in the back and she started forward. The moment she could see into the salon where Hart and both of her parents sat, she saw him.

He appeared extremely relaxed, almost lolling upon one chair, dangerously dark and handsome in his tuxedo, and smiling at something her mother was saying. Francesca shoved every single illicit memory out of her head. For the rest of the evening she intended to have amnesia.

Hart saw her and leaped to his feet.

Francesca faltered and their eyes met.

For one moment, as he looked at her, something smug covered his features, and she thought, terrified, *He knows*. He had seen her in that first moment when Daisy had begun her seduction, and he had known she was present the entire time he made love to his mistress.

He was smiling now, but his gaze was merely warm and admiring. "Francesca, good evening."

Francesca couldn't move. Was she mistaken? Because now there was nothing on his face or in his eyes to suggest anything but the affection he felt for her and the esteem he held her in.

Francesca knew she was paranoid. She had every reason to be, and had she not been so, she would be certifiable. Now, gazing at him, she simply did not know what to think.

He chuckled, coming forward. "Why are you so pale?" he asked, his tone so low, it was doubtful that anyone could overhear him. "You look as if you are being led to the guillotine." He lifted her hand and kissed the air above it.

She inhaled. Images of him in all his glory, doing indescribable things to Daisy, filled her mind. Her body tightened with yearning and heat. *If she married him, he would do those things to her.* Aghast, Francesca turned that thought off. How would she make it through the evening? Francesca forced herself to respond. "Connie has dressed me up. I feel like a pretty doll. I do not feel like myself." The lie was a terrible one. She rather liked having become an elegant and sensuous creature of the night.

His smile broadened. His gaze was impossibly warm. "You are as beautiful in navy blue; however, I prefer the temptress who is afraid to look me in the eye tonight."

She jerked and met his gaze—his eyes were filled with laughter. *He did know! Didn't he?*

"I am almost afraid to ask why you are looking at me with such trepidation," he said, his smile fading. "Is something amiss?"

"I am very late," she said in a rush. "I have kept you waiting for half an hour."

His good humor returned. "But you are late, no doubt, because you flew in the door, having forgotten the time, involved in your case. Other women are tardy as a ploy." He didn't seem to mind that he had been kept waiting, not at all. Then, dropping his voice, he murmured, "Some things *are* worth waiting for."

Francesca was mesmerized by his stare. Did he refer to his having waited for her—or to her waiting for the moment when they made love? Was this an innocent comment, or was there an innuendo that referred to her spying upon him and Daisy that afternoon?

He turned to Connie, who stood behind her, and greeted her pleasantly. Francesca did breathe when he finally turned away. She glanced back at her sister and mouthed, *Does he know?*

Connie shook her head warningly, then placed her finger over her lips, clearly indicating that Francesca must not speak a single word on the illicit subject.

Both Julia and Andrew were on their feet. Julia looked like a cat that had lapped up all of the cream, while Andrew appeared grim and displeased. But then, Francesca knew he did not like Hart because of his womanizing ways and his frequently careless manners. "Do have a wonderful evening," Julia said, kissing Hart's cheek.

"We shall do our best," Hart returned. "Andrew." He extended his hand firmly.

Andrew took it reluctantly, without an answering smile. "And what time will you have my daughter home?"

"Before midnight," Hart suggested, looking unperturbed. But then, he was infamous for not caring what people thought and said about him. Clearly he couldn't care less that Andrew Cahill openly disliked either his courtship of his daughter or him or both.

Andrew nodded and then hugged Francesca. His eyes softening, he said, "Enjoy your evening, my dear."

Francesca nodded and hugged him. She hesitated, then whispered in his ear, "He's not as bad as you think, Papa."

Andrew grunted, refusing to give in.

Francesca settled on the velvet squabs, making certain to keep a safe distance from Hart. He seemed to know exactly what she was about, because he eyed her with amusement but did not comment, instead instructing Raoul to drive them downtown to Cooper Square. Francesca tried not to think, but it was impossible. Images of Hart and Daisy flooded her mind. And that, of course, made her distinctly uncomfortable, causing the carriage to feel small, closed, and airless. She wondered if a confession would alleviate her distress and her guilt.

"Francesca? Why are you squirming in your seat?" Hart asked.

She jerked to face him and found it exceedingly difficult not to look away from his nearly black eyes. She must remain mum. She was well aware that she had a penchant to wag her tongue too freely—this must *not* be one of those times.

"I'm hardly squirming," she said, remaining uncomfortable. She wondered if it would always be this way, now that she knew exactly how he looked beneath the elegant clothes he wore. No, it was far worse than that! She knew exactly how he looked when aroused with desire, and she knew exactly how he preferred to make love.

"I can't even begin to imagine why you are staring at me with such an expression," he murmured, amused. "I feel certain you have gotten yourself into some trouble. Do you have something you wish to tell me?"

She almost jumped off her seat. "No!" she cried.

His eyes widened. "Well, that certainly lays my suspicion to rest," he said drolly. Now his gaze became thoughtful. "Tell me about your day."

"My day?" she breathed, as if she did not understand the meaning of his words.

He was as relaxed as she was tense; he leaned back against the plush carriage seat, perplexed and amused all at once. "I know a look of sheer guilt when I see one," he said. "There is guilt written all over your face."

"You are imagining it. The day has been a trying one," she said tersely, rapidly. She told him then about Thomas Neville appearing at headquarters, and about the murder of poor Miss Holmes.

Hart was no longer amused. "First Grace Conway, and now her neighbor. Once again, you are investigating a series of murders. I do not like this," he said grimly.

"I hardly like it myself," Francesca said, relieved to be on familiar ground. "It gets worse."

"How can it possibly get worse?" he asked, one brow lifting.

"Miss Holmes left a journal. She was madly in love with Evan," Francesca said grimly.

Hart stared for a moment. "Well, this does not look good for Evan, now does it? Does he know the missing Miss Neville?"

"No, thank God," Francesca said earnestly.

"Who are your suspects? You seem quite averse to Thomas Neville."

"He's odd, but as it turns out, Miss Neville was having an affair with the owner of an art gallery," Francesca told him eagerly, glad to share her investigative work with him. "Thomas claims his sister was ending the affair, and as it also turns out, her lover, who denies the breakup, is married, with children."

"Aah," Hart murmured. "And the plot thickens. So the lover has become your prime suspect."

"It is certainly looking that way. If he was jilted on Sunday evening, I would guess that he murdered Grace Conway by accident—she found him destroying Melinda's studio. Miss Holmes was the next target, because she knew about the murder, having seen something from her rocking chair."

"And how does Sarah Channing fit in?" Hart asked.

"I have no idea," Francesca returned glumly. "That is where my theory falls apart."

Hart smiled at her. "I have no doubt you will solve the case. Who is this gallery owner? Perhaps I know him."

"His name is Bertrand Hoeltz. You know, he does seem genuinely distraught over Melinda Neville's disappearance. Do you know him, Calder?"

"Yes, I do. He is a poor connoisseur of art," Hart said. He was reflective now. "I have been to his gallery several times, but I have never liked the work he has, and I ceased going some time ago. I think I know the woman who has disappeared. I saw him with a woman once at another exhibition. They were clearly paramours."

"Were they in love? What was she like?" Francesca said, straightening.

"She was small and dark, very intense, I suspect, and rather exotic in her appearance. She is what the Europeans refer to as *jolie laide*—'pretty ugly.' That is, in spite of her severity and intensity, there was something interesting and compelling and sexual about her. I think Hoeltz was in love. I think Miss Neville was rather self-contained and self-involved." He added dryly, "Most artists are egocentric, my dear."

Very excited now, Francesca gripped his arm. The moment she did so, images of rock-hard muscles everywhere assailed her mind and she released him. "When was this, Calder?"

"Francesca"—he was gentle, his eyes smiling—"it was many months ago." But again he was studying her, and she saw that he was perplexed by her behavior.

"Oh."

"Have I done something to enervate you?"

She blinked, stiffening. "Of course not!"

"That is good. Because I have the distinct feeling that you might leap from the carriage at the next crossroads."

"We are going to supper," she managed.

"Are you certain there isn't something you wish to tell me?"

Francesca bit her lip, smiled at him, and wished that the thought of confession did not feel so appealing. She wet her lips. "Could Hoeltz be a killer? A strangler, in fact?"

Hart shook his head, amused now. "I would not know how to answer that. I hardly know the man. But given the right motivation, aren't we all capable of murder?"

She stared and he did not look away. Only a week ago, Hart had been prepared to murder the man blackmailing his foster sister, Lucy Savage. Of course, it had not come to that, thank God, and Francesca remained angry every time she thought of Lucy begging him for his help, begging him, and not another one of her brothers, to do her dirty work. "I don't know."

He smiled warmly at her. "You are so distracted tonight! I would give a small fortune to know what is really on your mind. Perhaps after supper you will relent and tell me?"

"There is nothing to tell," she said, recalling Daisy on her knees, her tongue all over his manhood. Her heart lurched, and the sensation went right through her.

"You are the worst liar," he said, but his humor remained high, happy. Then, sobering, "I took care of LeFarge today, Francesca. He has the fifty thousand dollars, and he knows beyond any doubt that if he ever assaults your brother again, he has myself to contend with." Hart's eyes were dark. "He knows I am not averse to striking back beyond the bounds set by the law."

Francesca shivered. "Thank you, Calder," she said.

Rourke had apparently picked Sarah up earlier, and when Francesca and Calder walked into the gallery, they were already there. Perhaps fifty people were present, and the mix was obvious—half of those attending were in evening gowns and tuxedos; the other half were clearly struggling artists in simple sack jackets and ill-fitting trousers, in dark and ready-made suits.

Francesca saw Sarah instantly. She and Rourke had their backs to the door and were clearly studying a huge landscape painting. Sarah was so very visible because of her fuchsia satin gown. As Francesca espied her, she saw Rourke gaze down at her, apparently listening to her every word.

"There they are," Hart said. "Let's find our host and join them."

Francesca did not move. Even from a distance, Rourke so looked like Bragg. A small amount of guilt stirred within her, as if it were disloyal and wrong to be enjoying Calder Hart's company. Then she sighed. But her and Bragg's lives had now taken separate paths, diverging for the most part. Still, there were moments, like now, when the pain of failed hopes and dreams and the sense of loss so suddenly and acutely returned.

Francesca wondered what was captivating Rourke so completely. Was it whatever Sarah was saying? Or was it Sarah herself? Francesca instantly recalled how solicitous Rourke had been when Sarah had fainted last Saturday evening at the Plaza. But he was a medical student. There hadn't been any other doctor in the house.

And Sarah was engaged to her brother. Still, it was the worst possible match, and everyone but her father seemed to know it. Evan had been packing his bags and moving out of the house the day he had been beaten to a pulp by LeFarge. He had been about to break off his engagement as well.

Francesca couldn't decide if Rourke's interest was purely compassionate and doctorly or something else. He was very attractive, and she knew for a fact that he was a ladies' man. Still, Sarah hardly fit the bill for a womanizing man.

"I can read your thoughts," Hart murmured, low, looping her arm firmly against his and pressing it to his side.

Francesca leaped. His body was hard and male. There was nothing soft or compromising about it. Their gazes locked.

It was a moment before he spoke. "Francesca, I know you are a woman of extreme passion, but you must set your thoughts aside—at least for the rest of the evening."

To her horror, she said, "I can't."

He hesitated, then slipped his arm around the small of her back, and with his other hand he cupped her cheek. Francesca felt a shockingly urgent tremor ripple through her body. She had known this evening would be an impossible one. "I fear I must distract you," he murmured in such a low and heated tone that she had images of his bed, with him looming over *her* in it, dancing through her mind.

She slipped into his arms by taking a single step closer to him, surprising them both. "Take me outside," she said, and she was shocked at how husky and urgent her own tone was.

He didn't move. Then, "No." He stepped away from her. "Hoeltz is here. I just saw him. Perhaps we can unearth a clue or two tonight?" He didn't smile.

Francesca turned away from him, trying to recover her composure. What was wrong with her? First her uncontrollable curiosity this afternoon, and now her uncontrollable desire to leap into Hart's arms and have him do everything to her that he had done to Daisy just a few hours ago.

"Francesca!" Sarah cried, from behind and approaching. "This is the most clever exhibition! Have you seen some of the portraits here? Hello, Mr. Hart. I cannot thank you enough for suggesting I be included in your party tonight." She was beaming.

Francesca faced Sarah and found her radiant with happiness. In fact, despite her awful gown, she was beautiful. Francesca had never seen her so happy or in such a glowing state—she could only stare.

"It was Rourke's idea," Hart said.

Rourke sent Hart a distinctly annoyed glance. "Who better to bring to an art exhibition than an artist?" he asked.

"There is an amazing portrait of two children by Walter Frederick Osborne!" Sarah cried excitedly. "Have you ever seen his work before?"

"Yes, but I find it too sweet for my taste," Hart said with a fond smile. "I see you have fully recovered from your illness. I am glad, Miss Channing."

"So am I!" Sarah cried, animated. "Coming out tonight was the perfect antidote for my melancholy. I am so excited by these artists—did you see the Degas? I adore his ballerinas, but this one is of Spanish dancers, and it is quite modern! Mr. Hart, with Francesca's permission, I intend to get to work upon the portrait you have commissioned immediately."

"I eagerly await the moment it is finished," Hart said.

Francesca looked from Hart to Sarah and back again. Hart had commissioned her portrait when he had seen her return from a tête-à-tête with Bragg at the Channing ball, in a disheveled state that clearly indicated what they had been up to behind closed doors. Hart had not only commissioned the portrait but had specified she should be wearing the exact same red ball gown.

Francesca had been furious, but then, so had he.

She had no time now to sit for her portrait, but she was determined to aid Sarah in her endeavor to gain recognition in the art world—something this commission would do. In fact, she had been moodily resigned to the fact that Hart intended to hang her portrait upon his wall.

Now, she found herself staring at him—and he was staring back. She was no longer dismayed by the notion. But everything had changed. Bragg's wife had come to town and Calder Hart wished to marry her.

As if reading her thoughts, Hart said to Sarah, not looking away from Francesca, "But you shall make one change. I prefer the dress Francesca is now wearing. As long as her hair is down."

Francesca could not look away from him, and her body stirred while her heart raced. The red dress held a reminder of that night for both of them, a reminder, she realized, that neither of them wanted. "My hair should be up, Hart."

Ladies posed in their ball gowns and jewels all the time for portraits, with their hair waved and tonged and swept up.

"No," he said, his smile small and answering her own. "I want it down."

Warmth filled her loins. "You won't be able to hang it publicly. It will be too suggestive."

"I intend to hang it in my bedroom," he said.

Francesca didn't know what to say. She was thrilled— and also breathless.

Rourke coughed. "I am glad we have settled upon the color of Francesca's dress and the style of her hair." There was laughter in his tone. "Shall we view the exhibition together?"

"That is a very good idea," Hart said, taking Francesca's arm and looping it firmly against his side once again. The gesture was extremely possessive, but in that moment Francesca did not mind.

She rather liked it.

"Can we start tomorrow?" Sarah asked, at Francesca's side. Rourke was beside her, a careful distance between them.

"I would love to, but I have an eight A.M. class and I am so involved in the current investigation," Francesca said. "Can't it wait for a few days?"

Sarah hesitated. "Francesca, you are always busy. There will always be an excuse. Can't you come by after your class? Give me one hour—for some preliminary sketches. But bring the dress." She beamed. "It is lovely. Not as daring as the red, but I think it suits you even more."

They paused before a landscape done by a Russian artist. The palette was very cool, the scene of a cabin in the moonlight, but it was grim and desolate. Hart released Francesca.

She glanced at him and looked again. He was riveted by the painting.

She studied him then. Not because she had the chance to enjoy his handsome profile, but because he was so engrossed in a work of art that she did not care for, finding it disturbing. In fact, she knew he had, for that moment, forgotten she was at his side.

She didn't mind.

"Isaak Levitan," he murmured, his gaze moving back and forth across the dark, desolate landscape. "The artist is spectacular." Suddenly he turned to Francesca and the intensity was gone. "I saw this artist's work at the Paris Exposition Universelle in 1900. Do you like it?"

"No," she said truthfully. "But I know why you do."

Now he grinned. "And why is that, my darling?"

She smiled back. "Because it is so evocative of the bleakness of the Russian winter. One is swept to another place and another time merely by looking at that frozen landscape and that solitary house."

He smiled. "I shall make an art critic out of you one day, Francesca."

"I doubt that," she said, flushing because of his praise.

His gaze became speculative. "Shall I buy the painting?"

She started. "That is hardly for me to decide."

"Actually, I will not buy it if you do not approve," he said.

She stared. "Calder, buy it if you must."

"Shall I buy it?" he asked again, patiently.

She knew he yearned to have it. She glanced at the frozen landscape again. In a way, as grim as the scene was, it was powerful and provocative. And shouldn't art cause one to stand and stare and think? "Yes," she decided.

He laughed and slid his arm around her and pulled her close. She tensed, all of that afternoon's images flicking rapidly through her mind, as his smile faded. His arm moved up; his hand covered her bare nape. She shivered. They were in public, and when he kissed her now, tongues would surely wag, but Francesca did not care. It felt as if she had been waiting *aeons* for his kiss.

He smiled at her and slipped away. "There is Hoeltz, Francesca."

Her libido hardly decreasing, disappointed that he hadn't kissed her, Francesca quickly turned and followed his gaze. Hoeltz was wandering through the crowd alone, a glass of red wine in his hand. He seemed grim and preoccupied— disturbed.

Her gaze narrowed. She hadn't realized it before because his presence was so unassuming, but while he was slender, he was actually tall. He stood almost a hand or so above most of the crowd. Francesca suspected he was six foot or so. And while slender, he was hardly as gaunt and thin as Thomas Neville.

Sarah said, "Hoeltz? Do you mean Mr. Hoeltz from the same gallery?" Then, "Oh, yes, that is him! I should say hello!"

Francesca whirled, grabbing her wrist. *"You know him?"*

"Yes, I do. Fran, what is wrong?"

She stared, her pulse pounding, her mind racing. "How well do you know him, Sarah?"

She shrugged, appearing worried. "I took an art class. He came to lecture once. And then recently, I brought him several portraits, to see if he would try to sell them for me. He wasn't interested, although he was very kind and quite encouraging."

Francesca could hardly breathe.

Hart took her arm. "What is it?" he asked sharply.

"We asked Hoeltz if he knew Sarah Channing, and he said no. He *lied*."

# CHAPTER
# FIFTEEN

FRIDAY, FEBRUARY 21, 1902—7:00 P.M.

NEIL MONTROSE COULD NOT help himself. He paced the salon that was adjacent to the front hall and every few moments would go to a window to peer outside. His wife had not been home all day. According to Mrs. Partridge, she had left the house just after noon with the girls, which was seven hours ago. Where could she possibly be? Were the girls all right? What had happened? Connie always had the children home by five for an early supper. He was frantic.

He did not know what he would do if anything happened to his wife or children. Had something happened? Had there been a carriage accident? The streets were icy in places. But wouldn't he have been notified?

And now, with the night dark and wintry outside, with his wife late, his children missing—or so it seemed—he wished, desperately, that he and Connie were not at odds. But he had tried everything. She was determined to punish him, and he didn't think she would ever forgive him for what he had so stupidly done. But he wasn't ever going to forgive himself, either, and it wasn't forgiveness that he wanted. He wanted her—and him—to somehow forget the past and have a real and happy future together.

If she ever gave him a second chance, he would do his best to make everything up to her. But he was losing hope. Clearly she would not accept his apologies, which were more than genuine, they were frantic, and she did not believe his vows—he would never stray again.

Suddenly he sat down, cradling his face in his hands, swamped with grief. *He loved her so.* He hadn't meant to fall in love with her when he met her—he had only wanted a proper and attractive wife, one whom he might become fond of, one who would bear his children and manage his home. He had sought Connie out because of her family's money, just as her mother had directed him toward her older daughter for his title. But when he had first looked at her, he had been more than surprised; he had been stunned, because she was simply the most beautiful woman he had ever met.

It had been so terribly easy to fall in love.

It had been love at first sight.

Now he had the most terrible thought. He wasn't sure that he even knew his own wife. She had become a stranger. But he was wondering if they had been strangers, somehow, in spite of the five years they had shared, four of which were as man and wife.

He ached to speak with her now. He ached to speak with her from the depths of his heart and soul. He did not know how. Like Connie, he had been raised in a certain manner, and serious and even embarrassing conversations with anyone, much less one's wife, had not been a part of his upbringing or behavior. He was expected to manage his estates and monetary affairs and provide handsomely for his wife and children, period. His own father had undoubtedly turned over in his grave the first time Neil climbed into bed with Charlotte in order to read her a bedtime fairy tale.

And then he heard the oh-so-welcome sound of the rumble of carriage wheels on the salted driveway outside. Neil ran to the window, shifted heavy gold velour drapes aside, and saw his wife's coach. He began to shake with stunning relief.

If anything had happened to her or the children, he might have died.

He let the draperies fall, stiffening his shoulders, recovering his composure. It was not an easy task. When he heard her musical voice in the front hall, he left the salon. Connie was handing a bundled-up and rosy-cheeked Lucinda to Mrs. Partridge, while Charlotte was jumping up and down, trying to show the nanny her new doll.

Still clad in her sable coat, Connie saw him and froze.

He forced a smile. "There you are! Thank God! I have been so worried. Where were you, dar—Connie?"

She handed her coat and gloves to the doorman. "I took the children to the park. We went skating. Then we went to Mama's." She was obviously tense and she did not smile. "The girls had supper there. I helped Fran dress for an evening out with Calder Hart."

He disliked and distrusted Calder Hart but had no wish to discuss his sister-in-law or Hart now. "I was worried, Connie. I wish you had sent word that you would be so late."

"I'm sorry. I assumed you were going out for the evening, Neil."

"I'm not. I'm staying in. In fact, I have asked Cook to prepare us an elegant supper. He is making roasted guinea hens, which I know you love." He managed a smile. Wishing she would smile back. She did not.

She simply stood there, a beautiful woman with cold eyes in a beautiful blue ensemble.

"Join me for a sherry?" he asked, feeling a familiar and chilling desperation. Still, he clasped her arm.

She looked extremely anxious now. She pulled away from him, forced a smile. "Very well." She quickly walked ahead of him into the blue room where they entertained.

Neil followed, aware of the pain in his heart. He had never had his heart broken before, but now he understood why it was called broken and not something else.

She sat down, arranging her skirts about her.

He poured them both drinks. "So Hart is pursuing your sister?"

"Yes."

"And you approve?"

"I think it is a good match."

He approached, handing her a sherry. And he could no longer contain himself. "We must speak, Connie! Our marriage has become impossible and I do not think I can live like this!" He was shocked by his own emotional outburst.

She jerked, spilling sherry. Her wide eyes found and held his. "What?"

He had taken the first terrible step. Somehow, he could not turn around and go back. "I cannot live like this anymore."

She stood up with vast dignity, but then he saw the tears filling her eyes. "I see."

"Do you?" He set his brandy down.

She lifted her chin. "First the affair. Now . . . you wish to leave me."

As this was the last wish on his mind, it was a long moment before he could comprehend her. "No! I would never leave you," he said, stunned.

The tears began to trickle down her cheeks. She fought them, her slim nostrils flaring. Her shoulders were impossibly square.

And suddenly he gripped her arms. "I cannot bear this marriage this way anymore!" he cried passionately. "I have begged you for forgiveness, and now, I beg you, give me another chance."

"Let me go," Connie whispered, trembling and crying, yet as rigid and erect as a statue.

He was a gentleman, so he was about to do as she asked—but then instinct took over. "No." He took her face in his hands. "Do not shut me out anymore, Connie. If you will not give me another chance, then say so. But tell me what you are thinking, because I cannot stand this aloofness; I simply can't."

She shook her head, the tears coming faster now, streaming down her cheeks, and she was clearly incapable of speech.

"I love you," he heard himself whisper.

She looked up—and struck him across the face.

He was so stunned that he froze, paralyzed.

She seemed to realize what she had done, because an expression of shock and disbelief covered her features. "Oh, God," she whispered, backing away.

But he was glad she had hit him, because anger was better than her ignoring him, and he seized her wrist. "No, it's all right," he managed.

She burst into tears again and covered her face with her hands, sobbing hysterically—with complete abandon.

At first, he was in shock. He had rarely seen Connie lose control, and never this way. Then he reacted. He moved close and took her into his arms, and when he felt her small body against his larger one, when he felt her softness against his strength, he began to cry, too.

He rocked her while she cried.

She sobbed like a small child for a long time.

They could not find Bertrand Hoeltz. Francesca and Hart searched the crowd in both rooms of the gallery, but he appeared to be gone. When they had rejoined Sarah and Rourke, Francesca pulled her aside. "Have you seen Mr. Hoeltz?"

"No. Francesca, what is wrong? What has happened?"

Francesca looked at her, debating whether to tell her the truth we or not. Rourke took her arm. "Is there something more that we should know about? How is your investigation progressing?"

Francesca met his concerned amber eyes. "There has been another murder," she said quietly. "The neighbor downstairs, who I believe saw something, was strangled the way that Miss Conway was, yesterday," she said.

Sarah gasped. Rourke moved to her side and steadied her. Sarah did not seem to notice. Very pale, she said, "Was she also an artist?"

"No," Francesca said firmly, hoping that would reassure her. "In fact, Sarah, even though two art studios have been vandalized, neither of the dead women was an artist."

"I don't feel reassured," Sarah whispered. She turned and glanced up at Rourke. "Do you?"

"Yes, I do," he said, taking her arm firmly in his. "In fact, the more I think about this bizarre case, the more convinced I am that you have nothing to do with it."

"How can you say that?" Sarah asked, her brown eyes wide on his.

Francesca would have asked the exact same thing.

"I think Miss Conway had an insane admirer. She was a wonderful actress, as anyone would agree. I think the admirer decided to kill her when he was rejected by her. I think it was all carefully planned—destroy your studio as a red herring, then lure Miss Conway across the hall into Miss Neville's studio to do away with her. He vandalized Miss Neville's studio merely to distract and confuse the police. The neighbor who was murdered yesterday was an unfortunate victim—as she saw something which she shouldn't have."

Sarah gazed unwaveringly at his face, then relaxed visibly. "I do hope you are right."

Francesca could not believe how well informed Rourke was—and she had not a doubt as to how he had been keeping abreast of the case, as Bragg was his older brother. "That is quite an interesting theory, Rourke." She, for one, did not buy it. But she knew what he was doing. He did not want Sarah alarmed or made ill from worry again. "Have you and Bragg been having tea?" She smiled sweetly.

"Whiskey," he returned with a smile that did not reach his eyes. His gaze was warning her to hold her silence.

Starting, Francesca realized he was protecting Sarah Channing.

"The many benefits of having a police officer in the family," Hart drawled sardonically.

"It must be very beneficial indeed," a man said from behind them all.

Francesca recognized a voice she had come to dread. She whirled and faced the nerveless reporter from the *Sun*, Arthur Kurland.

"Good evening, Hart, Miss Cahill." His smile was pleasant, his eyes eager. "You must be a Bragg," he said to Rourke. "You could be the commissioner's twin."

Francesca had stiffened unbearably. They did not need this now!

"Rourke Bragg," Rourke said, unsmiling and looking from Kurland to Francesca and back again.

"Do I know you?" Hart asked imperiously.

"No, but I do know you, Mr. Hart." Kurland extended his hand. He was a slim, dapper man, his short dark hair parted in the center. "Arthur Kurland, newsman from the *Sun*."

Francesca wanted to shout at Hart not to touch the viper in their midst. To his credit, he did not shake Kurland's hand. "Is there something you wish from us? We are late for a supper reservation."

"I was merely hoping for a comment from Miss Channing and Miss Cahill." Kurland grinned.

Dread overcame Francesca. "I fear we are late," she said, moving past him.

"Miss Channing? Did you know that Miss Conway was your fiancé's mistress? Do you think he could have murdered her?"

Sarah cried out.

"That's enough," Rourke said angrily.

Francesca whirled to see Hart step between Sarah and Kurland. "You have the manners of an oaf. I suggest you find your way out of the gallery, Kurland, before I have you thrown out—or rather," and he smiled with dangerous glee, "before I do it myself."

"I see that Miss Channing didn't know about her fiancé's

lover. But surely you did, Miss Cahill." He turned to face Francesca as Hart's hand clamped down on his shoulder.

"Hart, don't," Francesca said halfheartedly. Bragg had never been able to manhandle Kurland, as he was an officer of the law. But Hart had no such issues restraining him.

"And now Miss Holmes is dead. And she was obsessed with your brother. Any comment, Miss Cahill?" Kurland asked, eyes wide.

"My brother had nothing to do with those women being strangled," Francesca said tersely.

Hart grabbed Kurland by the arm, so forcefully that Kurland cried out. "Don't bother, Francesca." Hart dragged him from the gallery.

A silence fell. Francesca faced Sarah, who was pale with shock. "No one told me. No one told me that the actress who was murdered was Evan's mistress!" she cried, her tone hoarse and low.

Rourke still held her arm. "It's a terrible coincidence," he said firmly.

"Of course it's a terrible coincidence!" Sarah cried, ashen. "But that Kurland is an awful man and he intends to make equally terrible suggestions in his newspaper. Doesn't he, Francesca?"

"I don't know," Francesca said, and then she took her hand. Rourke released her. "But I'm afraid you're right."

Sarah straightened her shoulders. A very determined look came over her face.

"What is it?" Francesca asked.

"I've been hoping something would come up, something to end our engagement. But now I realize I must stand by your brother—no matter what."

SATURDAY, FEBRUARY 22, 1902—MIDNIGHT

"I will see Sarah in," Rourke said.

Hart lounged indolently in the squabs, his big body extremely close to Francesca. "You do that," he said amiably.

Francesca could feel his thigh burning against her own

leg. She didn't mind. If anything, she wanted him to press even closer. She had been extremely unladylike that night. She had matched Rourke and Hart almost glass for glass and they had finished two entire bottles of red wine. And the entire evening, Hart had been at her side, patient and somehow deliberate, attentive and oh-so-male, and too appealing for words.

"Good night," Sarah said. "And thank you for a wonderful evening."

Hart leaped up, no longer in the least bit indolent, getting out of the barouche with Rourke, followed by Sarah.

"Good night," Francesca said, leaning out the door. In another moment they would be alone. Throughout the evening, in spite of the wine, the conversation, and the case, she'd had flashbacks to that afternoon. And every time Hart had turned to look at her, she had melted like chocolate in a fry pan. "And don't worry about anything!" she called.

"Tomorrow right after class," Sarah returned, with a gay wave. Her eyes were bright with excitement, and as Sarah hadn't even finished a single glass of wine, Francesca knew she had enjoyed herself that evening. She watched Rourke escorting her up the path to the house, her gaze narrowing with speculation. Sarah had hardly spoken to Rourke all evening. She had spent all of her time conversing with Francesca and Hart, almost ignoring her escort.

"Is there any chance that Sarah and Rourke might be a successful match?" Francesca asked as Hart entered the carriage, closing the door behind him so that they were completely alone.

He settled down in the seat beside her. "I never make matches," he stated, as if that topic were closed.

"It is a foolish and usually hopeless endeavor," Francesca agreed, her heart tightening. Two small lamps illuminated the interior of the carriage, and she thought about what a perfect evening it had been and what the perfect ending to the evening must be.

She could open his shirt the way that Daisy had done.

Button by button, and then, if she slid onto his lap, she could truly experiment.

She jerked free of that fantasy but wondered if she dared to try to seduce him. She did not have Daisy's experience. On the other hand, she was a quick study and she had seen an inordinate amount of lovemaking that day.

He seemed to take up every available inch of space inside the compartment. He was watching her now, closely. She shuddered and sighed. If she did not try to seduce him, she might not even get a good night kiss. She could not imagine the evening ending without his lips on hers.

"I fear I have created a monster," he murmured.

She gave him a look. "No, a woman with a single cause."

He chuckled. "We could announce our engagement to-morrow," he drawled. "So I can teach you the right way to kiss a man."

She inhaled. The tone of his voice jerked her directly back to a very vivid recollection of that afternoon. "So you can teach me other things," she breathed.

"What?" He was startled. Then his gaze narrowed. "What other things?"

She had to try. The desire was killing her. She smiled at him—it felt grim—ignored his wary surprise, and, terribly afraid of his rejection, climbed onto his lap.

"What are you doing?" He seemed to choke.

It wasn't as comfortable or as sensual as she had thought it might be. Her skirts had twisted, so her legs were tied up, with one knee bent underneath her—she couldn't even sit him properly and her leg felt as if it might break. Francesca didn't answer. She met his dark eyes, saw laughter there, and quickly looked away. How dare he laugh! He would not be laughing much longer. . . . She reached for his shirt.

"What are you doing, Francesca?" he purred.

In spite of the fact that her knee felt like it was about to break off and prevented her from really having close contact with him and his intriguing anatomy—and she did wish that she knew what it was doing—she untied his tie.

He caught her wrist. "I asked you a question," he said.

She glared. "I am taking off your tie—and then I shall unbutton your shirt."

"Oh, really?" He was trying very hard not to laugh. She felt like smacking him for his silly grin. "Francesca, are you trying to seduce me?"

She glared. "Yes!"

He burst into laughter.

She lightly struck his face.

He caught her hand, the laughter dying, turned it over, seared her with a look, then pressed his mouth to the sensitive flesh between her thumb and forefinger.

Her loins warmed, swelled.

He looked up. "I am afraid you are going to break your leg," he said softly.

"So am I," she managed. "Hart, please."

He wasn't smiling now. He clasped her waist and moved her off his lap, onto the seat. Francesca quickly extended her aching leg; then, not to be stopped, she leaned forward and pressed her mouth to his throat.

He grasped her shoulders and pushed her back. "I am very, very serious about treating you as a gentleman should. Francesca, once you accept my suit—once we are officially affianced—a kiss or two would be in order. Otherwise, I am not compromising you—not in any way."

"Hart! This isn't fair! I can't become engaged—I simply do not want to get married!"

"The only way you will ever enjoy my favors is if we are wed. And that is that," he said.

She was furious. She jerked free of his grasp. It was on the tip of her tongue to capitulate and be done with it.

Both brows raised. "If looks could kill, I should now be dead."

She thought of how easily he had made love to his mistress. "I want to become your mistress, Hart."

He straightened. "Absolutely not."

"No. I am in earnest. Deadly earnest. Make me your mistress and take me to bed. Forget this insane urge to marry!"

Now he started laughing all over again. "No. Francesca,

I know how you feel—many, many years ago, I was a virgin, too. Trust me. It will all work out . . . eventually." His laughter increased. He was truly enjoying himself—at her expense.

"But you want me!"

"Yes, I do, but not in a cheap and sordid way. I have no intention of using you."

"So you use Daisy? Cheaply? Sordidly?" Francesca accused.

He regarded her carefully now. "Yes, I do. I have bought and paid for her, Francesca."

Images rushed over her, hot, wet, huge. "I saw you. I saw you make love to her this afternoon!" she cried.

It was a moment before he seemed to understand. His gaze narrowed and his expression became impossible to read. "I beg your pardon?"

"I spied. I saw her put her mouth all over you! I saw you without your clothes. . . . I saw—"

His hand closed over her arm. "You spied on me and my mistress?" He was too calm—dangerously so.

Francesca's mouth was hanging open. She closed it, wishing she had even a single clue as to what the black glitter in his eyes meant. Had he known she was watching the encounter that afternoon?

"Did Daisy know? Was she privy to your little scheme, Francesca?"

Was he angry? Or was that glitter in his gaze amusement? Still, she did not like the way he had uttered her name. "No! Daisy did not know!" How Francesca regretted her lapse of self-control. "I didn't want you to know I had called on her, and she let me hide in the adjacent room. I was supposed to sneak out, but instead, I opened the door and watched you both." He continued to stare dispassionately. She squirmed. "I mean, I meant to leave, but one thing happened after another, and I simply couldn't," she added, certain he understood her meaning.

A silence fell.

It was terrible.

Then he thrust open the carriage door. "Please come with me, Francesca," he said firmly.

Her heart raced with alarm as she obeyed. Why had she told him what she had done? Why? Was he angry? Would he end their relationship—retract his offer of marriage? She would be furious if she were him. And his grip on her arm was uncompromising.

She tried to pull away, but he would not let her do so. "I'm sorry," she finally whispered.

"You have a habit of regretting your behavior when it is simply too late," he said flatly. "Did it ever occur to you that if I wished for you to watch me make love to another woman, I might have arranged it?" He was very cold.

"It isn't the end of the world," she said. She wanted to tell him that it had been the most incredible moment of her life but decided against it.

"No, it is hardly the end of the world."

"Would you have let me watch if I had asked?" She had to know.

"No."

She winced. "Are you angry, Calder? You are so good at hiding your feelings that I cannot tell."

He hesitated, as if choosing his words carefully. "I am annoyed."

*What in God's name does that mean?* she wondered.

"Did you enjoy yourself, Francesca?"

She gaped—and began a slow burn. "Of course not!"

He began, finally, to smile. "Little liar," he said softly.

His words washed over her like a ribbon of silk, a deep, intimate, and sensual caress. "This is not the relationship I wish for us to have," he said as softly. "If I wanted you as a whore, I would take you as one."

More graphic images assailed her. "I'm sorry," she said again, breathlessly. If only she knew what he was really thinking! Would he retract his offer of marriage? The oddest pain stabbed through her chest in the vicinity of her heart. Any other man would do so, but Hart wasn't like other men. "I fear my character is a highly defective one," she said slowly. "I am always in trouble, Hart, trouble of my own making, and I know it."

"Yes, you are," he said, unsmiling and unamused.

"I take it you wish to politely inform me that you have changed your mind?"

"Changed my mind?" He was surprised. "About marrying you? No, Francesca, I am sorry, but you are not off my hook. I am angry. I don't like snoops—I don't like being spied upon. But I intend to see the day when you are wed and in my bed. Sooner," he added grimly, "rather than later, I might add."

Relief swamped her.

"Listen carefully to me."

Relief vanished—she came to attention.

"You are not a whore. You are not a woman whom I have bought and paid for. There is admiration, respect, and affection between us. I treasure those things. They are qualities I have never before shared with any woman. When we are in bed, it shall be the two of us, alone."

She began to understand. She began to genuinely regret spying upon him. It would be a long time, if ever, before she would be able to forget what she had seen.

"But now, because of your foolish, irrevocable behavior, Daisy will be in bed with us, too, won't she?"

Francesca suddenly wanted to cry. "I never thought—"

"No, you did not."

"But it will only be a memory."

"One that taints the many moments we will share."

"But what about all of your memories?" she cried. "Won't they disturb you at an inopportune time?"

He rolled his eyes. "I never think about the women I have bedded, Francesca. Each and every one has been and remains meaningless to me."

She stared, and elation crept over her, slowly but surely. "Even Daisy?"

"Even Daisy," he said. He began to smile, then wiped his expression clean, as if he refused to bend, and he took her hand and pulled her into his arms. "How can any woman, even Daisy, compare to you?" he asked, his tone finally warming.

"Quite easily, I fear," she said, but she was smiling, and their eyes met and held. "Will you forgive me?"

"Perhaps tomorrow," he said, but humor had crept into his tone. "I can see that the course of our marriage will be a rocky road indeed."

"I can accept tomorrow," she said, and she laid her cheek on his chest. Instantly his hand stroked over her coiffed hair.

Desire renewed itself. "Can we seal our bargain with a kiss?" she whispered, looking up.

He gazed down at her, tender, amused. "You saw *everything*?"

She nodded, blushing now. "I saw everything, Hart, every single thing."

He stared down at her thoughtfully. Francesca almost held her breath, wondering what to expect. It was not his next words.

"So your education begins."


In the entry hall, Rourke and Sarah paused, the doorman taking Sarah's coat. Sarah thanked him, acutely aware of Rourke behind her, and said, "You don't have to wait up for me, Henry. I will lock the front door when Rourke leaves."

"Thank you, Miss Channing, and good night," Henry said, walking out.

Leaving her alone with a stranger.

"I hope you enjoyed the evening," Rourke said rather distractedly. He was glancing out the window by the front door. Sarah wondered why, and she wondered if he would now leave. But of course he had to leave, as Hart and Francesca were outside in the carriage, waiting for him.

"The evening was very enjoyable, and I am glad Mr. Hart is buying that Levitan. It is splendid." She became excited merely recalling the Russian landscape.

Rourke stepped closer to the window, as if he had not

heard her. "Did Bragg withdraw the roundsmen? I do not see a single police officer anywhere."

Sarah tensed. "I have no idea," she said, moving to his side so she could look outside, too. Rourke was right. No police officer was in sight. And standing so close to Rourke, she felt smaller and skinnier than ever. She stepped back, away from him. "He must have dismissed them. You yourself said I am not in danger and that Miss Conway was the killer's real target."

He met her gaze, and even though he smiled, she saw how serious his eyes were. "Yes, I believe that, but until the killer has been apprehended, I think my brother should leave his men here."

"Well, your brother knows what he is about." Sarah was brisk now. It was simply too awkward being alone with Rourke at such a late hour. He was simply too much for her to manage—too charismatic, too attractive—he overwhelmed her space; he reminded her of how plain and thin she was. She was sorry she had told Henry to go off to bed, but she always hated keeping the servants up. "It is late. I must get up early and prepare for the sketches I will do when Francesca arrives." She forced a smile—it felt terribly awkward.

But he smiled back at her, a smile that brought forth both of his dimples and creased the corners of his eyes. "Are you trying to get rid of me?" It was almost as if he were teasing.

"Of course not," she said tersely, a lie.

"I am teasing, Sarah," he sighed. Then, "You don't like me, do you?"

She was stunned by his bluntness. "I hardly know you, Rourke. It would be premature for me to either like or dislike you, don't you agree?"

"No, actually, I don't. I feel that it is easy to get a sense of a stranger upon a first meeting. I feel that somehow I must have offended you, yet the more I think about it, the more certain I am that I have not." He waited, staring, his smile gone.

"You haven't offended me," she said, feeling miserable and avoiding his gaze. "You saved my life."

"You weren't dying. Sarah, do I make you uncomfortable?"

She looked at him. "Yes."

He stared, his gaze searching.

She said, "I think I should retire now."

He caught her by the arm. "Are you running away?"

"Of course not!" But she was and they both knew it.

"I think you are running away from me, but I do not know why." He was reflective. "You have no trouble talking to Hart."

Sarah bit her lower lip, suddenly desperate that she run. "Good night, Rourke." She was firm.

But his regard changed as he studied her. "Could it be that you find a single, available gentleman like myself threatening?"

"That is absurd. I am engaged, Mr. Bragg, or have you forgotten?"

He suddenly smiled ruefully. "I actually did forget. For an instant." He sighed. "I'm sorry, Sarah. I am sorry for pressing you."

She was trembling. "Good night," she said again, shaken to the core. He knew the truth. She must avoid him now at all costs.

"I do not wish to argue with you," he said softly.

"We do not know one another well enough to argue. Good night." She turned and this time hurried down the hall, as quickly as she could without actually running.

But she strained to hear him leave as she did so, and she did not hear his footsteps or the front door closing—which she would have to go back to lock. Then she decided it did not matter if he wished to stand there alone in the darkly lit foyer. Besides, he would go in another moment or so.

If only she did not feel guilty for being so terribly rude. What was wrong with her?

She shuddered. Everything was wrong, she thought, suddenly despondent. She was about to marry a man she liked but did not love; her studio had been destroyed; she had nightmares now, every night, about the intruder. And Rourke haunted her thoughts, waking and not, no matter how she told herself that he did not.

Sarah forced her thoughts to change—she had work to do. The corridor was lit at intervals by sconces. The door to her studio remained firmly closed. The police had given her permission to clean it up yesterday, and now Sarah opened the door, knowing the staff had turned the shambles back into a normal, well-kept room. She reached for the lamp on the side table by the door.

A large male hand clamped down on her mouth.

Sarah tried to scream, uselessly.

And terror overcame her. Her worst nightmare had come true—he had come back!

*He pulled her back against his hard, aroused body. He laughed and whispered obscenities in her ear. She struggled, the smell of paint suffocating, but her struggles only aroused him more. He began to tell her what he wished to do to her. He was going to fuck her, again and again, and then, when the moment was right, he would take the stocking and pull it tight. . . .*

Sarah struggled against him, the recollection of that first attack assailing her, and too late she wished she had not pretended that it hadn't happened—she wished she had told the truth.

"Little whore, did you really think I'd forget you?" he whispered, grinding his erection against her buttocks.

She couldn't breathe. His hands were large and strong on her throat, and like vises, tightening and tightening. Blackness was exploding in her brain. Fireworks followed. He removed his hand from her mouth and she gasped for air, precious air. . . . Silk whispered around her throat.

And she knew it was the end.

"Get off of her!" Rourke screamed.

The man froze, and then she was free.

Sarah fell against the wall, gasping like a fish out of

water, sinking to the floor. She held her burning neck, tears flooding her eyes in response to the pain and the aftermath of terror. Gentle arms pulled her down onto her back. She saw Rourke's golden eyes, and then he was tipping her head back, his mouth covering hers.

Fear renewed itself; for one moment she was in the throes of confusion, but then she felt and tasted the air he was pushing into her lungs and she sucked it down, again and again, until she could breathe—until she became aware of the taste of his lips, the pressure of his mouth, his hands gently clasping her head, so large, so strong, and so gentle. He ceased his ministrations. Their gazes locked. "Are you all right?" he asked.

She nodded, not trusting herself to speak.

And then she recalled the huge, hard pressure of the man's penis against her back, the sexual threats whispered in her ear, and she turned her face away, crying out.

"What is it?" Rourke asked softly.

"Get Francesca," she whispered raggedly.

# CHAPTER
# SIXTEEN

Francesca was staring at Hart, terribly curious as to just what he was thinking, his suggestive comment echoing in her brain. The front door slammed behind her. Footsteps pounded. "Francesca!" Rourke shouted.

All inappropriate thoughts vanished. Francesca whirled in real alarm as Rourke ran up to them. "There has been an attack. Sarah needs you." He looked at Hart. "Get Rick."

"Is Sarah all right?" Hart demanded.

"She seems all right, but as she has just survived an attempt at murder, I would prefer to examine her at length before swearing upon a Bible that her health is good," he said quickly, grabbing Francesca's arm.

She raced to keep up with him as they ran back to the house. "He was here? Our strangler?"

"Oh yes," Rourke said grimly, pushing open the front door. "I saw him."

She stared at him, stumbling down the corridor with him. "Did you recognize him? Was it Hoeltz? Neville? LeFarge?"

Too late, she realized Rourke did not know any of those men. "What did he look like?"

Before he could answer, Sarah appeared, staggering up the corridor. Francesca cried out, as Sarah's face was as white as an imaginary ghost and her throat was mottled with brutal red marks. Rourke broke into a run. "What do you think you are doing?" he scolded, but gently.

"I could not stay in there," she whispered, tears filling her eyes. "What if he came back?"

"He isn't coming back," Rourke said, lifting her into his arms as if she weighed no more than a baby. "Hart has gone to get the police."

Sarah was making a huge effort to be brave. "You do not have to carry me, Rourke. I can walk."

"I think that I do," he said firmly.

Francesca hurried over, clasping Sarah's shoulder as they walked into the closest room, a grand library. "Why don't you put her down on the sofa, Rourke? I shall sit with her and you can rouse the staff. We need a fire, water, tea." Her mind sped. "No, make it a nice Scotch whiskey."

"My medical bag is at Hart's," Rourke said, clearly displeased. "I'll send a servant to Doctor Finney." He placed Sarah on the oversize blue sofa as gently as if she might break. Francesca turned on the lamp beside it. "I'll be right back," he said.

Sarah looked at him, her face twisted with fear and nerves, yet oddly grim with resolution, too. "Don't wake Mother. I cannot manage her hysterics now."

Rourke hesitated.

Francesca sat down beside Sarah and put her arm around her. Sarah was as small and fragile as she looked, she thought with a pang. "Rourke? See if you can quietly rouse just one servant. A maid."

He gave her an exasperated look that said he'd rouse whomever he stumbled upon.

Sarah said, "The staff who sleep in are on the fourth floor. But the housekeeper has her room behind the kitchen."

He nodded and left, leaving the door fully open.

Francesca wished he had started the fire. "Are you all right?" she asked, getting up and turning on another lamp. The library remained huge and filled with shadows. Good God, a man could hide behind the draperies, she thought.

"No. I had hoped to start your sketches, Francesca," Sarah whispered, trailing off.

Francesca felt for her then. "You must tell me what happened."

"I know." Sarah gazed at her fearfully. "I cannot discuss this in front of Rourke or anyone else."

"All right." She took Sarah's hands and clasped them tightly. "Did you get a good look at him?"

"He assaulted me from behind. I never saw his face, Francesca." Sarah started to shake terribly. Tears filled her eyes. "The moment he pushed me to the wall, I knew. I knew it was the same man who had attacked me last week!"

"What?!" Francesca gasped. "You never said you were attacked."

"I couldn't. I couldn't speak about it. It was so horrible that I refused to think about it," she said tersely.

"I don't understand," Francesca gasped.

"I know, for neither do I." Sarah brushed angrily at a falling tear. "I was *so* afraid. I think I felt that if I pretended it hadn't happened, it would somehow be over—somehow, it would be as if it hadn't happened. I refused to think about it; it is as simple as that." Her mouth trembled and she met Francesca's gaze. "I am sorry, Francesca, sorry that I lied to you, of all people. I beg you to understand."

Francesca thought that she did. "It's all right."

"No, it isn't." She swallowed. "He has haunted my dreams, Francesca."

Francesca hugged her, hard. "You poor dear! But you must tell me what happened, Sarah—both last week and just now. You must tell me everything so we can catch this bastard!"

Sarah nodded grimly, clearly fighting tears. "I found him in my studio, painting on the wall. He saw me and I ran, but he caught me from behind, which is how I hurt my arm.

I swear to God, I don't know how I got free—I think he tripped on something. I ran to my room and hid there. The next morning I found my studio in shambles, and that is when my mother sent you her note asking for your help."

Francesca caressed Sarah's back. "Thank God Rourke was here tonight." And it was the worst twist of fate that Sarah had not gotten a look at the killer.

"He held me against the wall and I could not breathe and I was afraid he would rape me before he broke my neck!" she cried.

It took Francesca a moment to understand. "He was sexually aroused?"

Sarah nodded, her eyes huge, mostly dilated black pupils. "He said he would. He said many horrible and obscene things to me." She suddenly retched, vomiting on the floor.

Francesca held her as she retched again, several times. Her heart broke for Sarah Channing.

"I am sorry," Sarah wept now. "Look at what I have done!"

Francesca held her in her arms. "It hardly matters. I shall catch this beast, Sarah, and when we are through, he shall never ever see the light of day again!"

When Sarah had stopped crying, Francesca stood. "Let me clean this up."

"No! I'll do it!" Sarah stood unsteadily.

"Sarah—"

"I don't want to be alone here, not at night."

"All right," Francesca said, taking her arm. They started through the huge dark house. Francesca quickly became anxious. It crossed her mind that the killer could be lying in wait for them. She told herself that was absurd, but nevertheless, the house was so silent and so dark. Sarah was as tense. She started at every shadow. "It's all right," Francesca tried, not quite believing it. Their killer had an agenda now, and Sarah Channing's murder was on it.

"I just remembered something," she whispered as they entered the pitch-black dining room.

Francesca fumbled for a light on the table. When it came on she breathed in relief. "What is that?"

"He said that he hadn't forgotten me, and he called me a little whore."

Francesca stared, her mind racing. "Can you recall his exact words?"

Sarah shook her head, her nose red now, her eyes tearing again. "I'm sorry. I can't. But I will never forget the sound of his voice," she whispered.

Francesca took her hand and they left the dining room. A moment later they were in the huge vaulted kitchen, which was fully lit. Rourke stood at the stove, boiling water, for tea, Francesca supposed. He saw them and started. "What the hell are you two doing wandering around this house by yourselves?"

Francesca let Sarah sink down into a chair at the dining table used by the staff. "Sarah had an accident, and we came for rags to clean it up."

"I'll do that," the housekeeper said, appearing in her gray dress, her hair still in one long gray braid. "Miss Channing, thank God you are all right!"

Sarah nodded but did not speak.

"Mrs. Brown," Rourke said, "bring us a nice glass of port."

The housekeeper nodded and hurried off.

Rourke came over and laid his palm on Sarah's forehead. She flinched but met his gaze. "You are warm," he said.

"I am sick," she returned. "Why, Francesca? Why has this man accused me of being a whore? Why does he wish to murder me? Why?" she cried.

Francesca sat down beside her. "I simply do not know. Yet," she added.

Rourke pulled something out of his pocket. "Here," he said. "Here is some evidence for you."

Francesca realized he had handed her a lady's silk stocking. It was torn. "What is this?"

"He was using this to strangle Sarah," Rourke said. "But

considering the marks on her throat, he was using his hands, first."

Sarah closed her eyes, trembling. "Yes, he was using his hands. And when I was sure I was about to die, he tied the stocking there and tightened it." She covered her face with her hands, which were shaking uncontrollably.

Francesca quickly held her. But she looked up at Rourke. "Did you see him?" she demanded.

He was grim. "He was masked, Francesca. In fact, he was wearing a lady's stocking over his head," he said. Then, "If you do not catch this killer, I shall."

But Francesca hardly heard. *A monster, no eyes, no mouth.* Ellie had been right.


Bragg strode in, followed by Hart. Rick looked very grim; in fact, he appeared to be on the verge of anger. Francesca could guess why and knew it had nothing to do with the strangler in their midst.

Less than a half an hour had passed by; Hart must have galloped his coach through the city streets. Sarah had calmed considerably, probably due to the port Rourke had insisted she drink, sip by sip. Francesca leaped to her feet the moment Bragg entered the room.

She raced to him. "Thank God you are here," she said urgently.

His gaze skidded over her elegant turquoise evening gown and its low bodice, then shot to Sarah, still seated at the kitchen table, but now with Rourke, who had his hand clasped over one of her hands. "How is she?" Bragg asked flatly.

"She is a bit better. She has terrible bruises on her throat, Bragg," Francesca said, keeping her tone low.

"It was the same man?" he asked in a similar tone.

"Apparently so." She held his gaze. "Can we discuss the case outside?"

He nodded. Francesca left the room with him, aware of

Hart's black gaze following her. In the hall, she faced Bragg. "Look at this," she said, whispering.

She showed him the stocking. "He wore one as a mask, and used this to try to strangle Sarah. Apparently he began with his hands. She cannot recall his words, but he did call her a little whore and said something to the effect that he had not forgotten her."

Bragg's expression darkened. "I am getting a dreadful feeling, Francesca. Our madman is just that, mad, and he hates women."

"This has nothing to do with Evan, I fear," she whispered back. "It gets worse. Sarah thought he might think to rape her."

Bragg started. "Did he say something to that effect?"

Francesca shook her head. "He was aroused."

For a moment Bragg stared, and she added, "He also was profane. Sarah said he used many obscenities."

Bragg was grim. "Neither Miss Conway nor Miss Holmes was raped, Francesca."

Francesca started. "What?!"

"Both victims were thoroughly examined. Neither one was raped," Bragg said. "I did not tell you about the physical examinations because I wished to spare you."

She stared at him, remaining stunned that he had ordered such examinations on Grace Conway and Catherine Holmes.

"Our killer has very perverted appetites, Francesca."

She regrouped. "Yes, he does."

"You are Sarah's friend. You need to sit down with her and record everything that madman said."

"She doesn't remember everything. And as far as the first attack goes, she was trying to forget it completely, Bragg— almost the way a child might deny reality in order to pretend that it did not happen. That is why she did not tell us about it."

He nodded, accepting her explanation of Sarah's odd behavior. "What *did* happen?"

"She interrupted him as he was leaving her studio—they struggled briefly, he tripped, and she got away. He was obscene then, too—Sarah said she completely forgot everything until he attacked her again tonight."

Bragg absorbed this and said, "There are no police on duty outside the house."

"I assumed that, for some reason, you dismissed them."

"No such order ever came from me. If Newman issued such a directive, he had better have a good reason."

"Is he on his way?"

"I would imagine so. Where did the attack take place?"

"Her studio," Francesca said, and of the same mind, they started through the house in that direction. "Bragg, I saw Bertrand Hoeltz tonight at an art exhibition. He lied. He told me the other day that he did not know Sarah, but Sarah knows him very well."

Bragg gave her a grim look and said nothing.

"What is it?"

He pushed open the door to Sarah's studio. It had been completely cleaned up, the floors washed and waxed, the canvases stacked up, the easels set upright. Which was why the blood-red words dripping down one pristine white wall were so shocking:

## KILL THE BITCH DIES

Francesca gasped.

Bragg said grimly, "Now we know what the *B* stands for."


Francesca stood outside the studio, her mind spinning very uselessly, as Hickey and an officer began a search within for more clues. Bragg and Newman stood a few feet from her.

"Sir, I never dismissed the men! I have no idea why they left their posts! I would never do such a thing without your orders, sir!"

Bragg nodded, clasping his shoulder. "All right. Let's find out why they left their posts. If they did so out of negligence, they are both to be suspended. Why don't you put two men on it? Find them and bring them to headquarters. In the meantime, I want two men posted at the Channing house, one inside, one out, at all times, night or day."

"Yes, sir," Newman said, nearly saluting. He was flushed with anxiety and he raced down the hall to do as Bragg had demanded.

They were dealing with a madman, Francesca thought. Someone who hated women and found the act of strangulation sexually exciting. She shivered, then realized Hart stood at the corner of the corridor, regarding her closely. She straightened, hoping he hadn't seen how tired and worried she was.

He approached. "It's almost three in the morning, Francesca. By now, your mother must be hysterical."

"She's asleep. I can't leave yet, Calder." She tried a winning smile on him, but she was far too exhausted to succeed.

He brushed a wisp of hair away from her cheek. "I sent Raoul some time ago with a message, so at least they know you are safe and sound. But it is time to go. I am taking you home." His words were a statement and held no hint of compromise.

Francesca tensed. "You can't order me about as if I am a child. This is serious business, Hart. This is the business of murder!"

"I am well aware of the business you are involved in, and it is far more than murder; it is also the business of hate and sex," he said coldly.

"You do not miss a trick," she grumbled.

His gaze moved past her. "Anyone can see that writing on the wall. Besides, Rourke told me what Sarah told you. This is an ugly crime. You should leave it alone, leave it to Rick."

She felt assailed with guilt then, and she half-turned. Bragg was in the studio with his men, but he was keeping an eye on her and Hart. His face was carved in stone. She had no doubt he was also listening to their every word. She faced Hart. "I have to stay and help with the investigation. Mama will understand. As you have her twisted about your little finger, you shall be back in her good graces in no time."

"I took you out and I shall bring you back. If you need some more time, then I shall wait." His jaw was hard, his eyes black.

Bragg strode over to them. "Calder's right. There's nothing more that can be done tonight. If he took you out for the evening, he should bring you home. By now, your parents must be frantic."

Francesca looked from Bragg to Hart and grumbled, "I *despise* it when the two of you take sides against me."

"It would not be necessary if you used some common sense," Hart said.

She felt like kicking his shin. Instead, she ignored him and faced Bragg. "We need to find out why Hoeltz lied. We need to interview both Neville and LeFarge again. Someone has to crack, Bragg, before there is another murder."

"I agree. And you need to interview Sarah and get her to remember every word this madman said to her," he said grimly.

Francesca hesitated. "I can do that first thing tomorrow. I want to spend the night here, with her," she decided.

"No," both Hart and Bragg said at once.

"Why not?" She looked from Hart to Bragg again. "She needs me!"

"Rourke is staying, in case she needs laudanum," Hart said flatly. "You must get home."

Francesca met his gaze and knew he was thinking about his relationship with her parents. "Coward," she said.

He gave her a dark look and then turned to his half brother. "Is there any way I can help your investigation?" he asked, surprising Francesca.

Bragg was ice-cold. "Yes. Stay the hell away from Francesca."

Hart made a mocking sound, saluted him as sarcastically, and walked out.

"He wanted to help!" Francesca cried.

"When the hell were you going to tell me that he thinks to marry you?" Bragg demanded.

She froze.

He was furious. His golden eyes were ice. "Or were you going to tell me ever, at all?" he demanded.

She somehow found her voice. "I had hoped to spare you, Bragg."

Bragg made a sound and whirled away.

Francesca ran after him, grabbing his shoulder, but he did not stop. "Wait!"

He now froze.

She ran around to face him. "I am *not* marrying him. We are *not* engaged. I have made myself clear. It is *not* my fault that he is as stubborn as a mule!" she cried.

"Then why the hell did you spend the evening with him tonight?" he asked coldly.

"What? Why wouldn't I? I enjoy his company! And we were hardly alone—Rourke and Sarah were with us!" She began to shake with anger. "It's not as if you asked me out tonight, now is it? Oh . . . may I ask what you did tonight?" She felt certain he had escorted his wife to some damnable affair. "You have reconciled, Bragg. I am entitled to my evenings, just as you are to yours."

"I stayed at my office until eleven, Francesca," he said, "so as to avoid going home to a situation I do not wish to be in. And I told you—there is no reconciliation."

That silenced her. She was disbelieving. She finally said, "I am sorry. But as far as I am concerned, you and Leigh Anne have reconciled. Which is as it should be."

"No, it's not," he said, more angrily. "I spent half of every moment thinking about you tonight, foolishly hoping you might appear on the pretext of discussing the investigation."

Guilt pricked at her. He had been working, and she had been on the town with Hart. But she was also saddened. "If

I had appeared, that is exactly what it would have been—a pretext."

His eyes darkened, and she interrupted before he could rebut. "Let's not battle one another. Please. It's too painful. What if I tell you that first thing tomorrow I will be at your office so we can plan our strategy?" She attempted a small smile. "We must find this killer, Bragg. Immediately."

He sighed and his entire face softened, as did his eyes. "I know. I am sorry I lost my temper. I almost had heart failure when Hart told me he thinks to marry you."

"He told you," she said slowly, stunned. But of course he would do such a thing. Doing so would be entirely in character. He loved besting his half brother. He loved taunting him.

"He is using you," Bragg said quietly. "And you are falling for it, hook, line, and sinker. I am afraid for you, Francesca."

She stiffened with dread. "No. We really are friends and—"

"How can you be so fooled! He threw his plans in my face! He was gloating at stealing you away from me—especially as he knows my hands are tied for the next six months! There is nothing he enjoys more than to see me squirm in discomfort—or worse. It has always been that way. He is my worst rival and you know it, as you have seen it for yourself."

She hugged herself. She knew Hart was fond of her—and she also knew how jealous he was of Bragg, and vice versa. She knew they had fought bitterly their entire lives. Yet she knew Hart wanted her. She also knew he would never steal the woman Bragg loved away from him.

She closed her eyes, shaken. *But did she really know that?* And so what if Hart wanted to take her to bed? His passion meant nothing. He had been with hundreds of other women. She wasn't half as beautiful as Daisy, to mention one. Yet she was the one he so suddenly wished to marry.

"Francesca," Bragg said urgently, pulling her close. "I

am not trying to hurt you—I am trying to protect you from a very ruthless man."

She smiled bravely at him. "First of all," she choked, "Hart knows I am not marrying anyone. So you need not worry about me so."

He brushed hair away from her eyes, her cheek. "I will always worry about you. It's like breathing the air. It is something I simply must do."

She hesitated, because the one thing she had with Bragg—that she did not have with Hart—was trust. Then she thought about the fact that it had taken Bragg some time to mention the fact that he had a wife whom he was separated from. Oddly, she did trust him, in spite of that, because trusting him was as natural to her as breathing the air he had spoken of. She relented. She closed her eyes and let him pull her even closer. There was more than comfort in the circle of his embrace, there was also safety, and it was huge.

*If only there was a way to know how Hart really felt, and if he was such a bastard as to be using her.*

Francesca was appalled with her thoughts. She was an optimist by nature. She believed in Hart's goodness. She had never thought, for a moment, that Hart might be using her to get back at his brother.

Until now.

"You should go home," Bragg said roughly, releasing her. His gaze had warmed and she knew what the look meant.

But she was too shaken to have more than a vague longing for the man whose arms she had just been in. She did not look away. At least with Bragg she knew where she stood—and she felt as if she always would.

His wife might remain in his home forever, but he would always care about her, and if there was ever danger, he would be the first to rush to her side.

"Let's go, Francesca," Hart drawled from behind her.

She flinched and turned and saw him regarding them with cool, dark eyes, his arms folded across his chest. He looked very annoyed. His jaw was flexing repeatedly.

Her heart lurched hard, painfully.

"I'll see you in the morning, then," Bragg said softly.

Francesca nodded, but not happily. She was acutely aware of the man standing before her—of the fact that he had a wife waiting for him at his home, no matter how he dreaded going there—and the man glowering at her from behind, and the fact that he was the most complicated person she had ever met. "I'll try to speak with Sarah first," she said.

Bragg nodded and walked back into Sarah's studio.

Francesca turned.

"Shall we?" Hart asked, not pleasantly. He reached for her arm.

Francesca dodged him, wondering then if she was a complete fool, the same kind of fool that hundreds of other women had been where Calder Hart was concerned. Her mind had never become more set. She would *never* marry him, no matter how much she might wish to leap into his bed.

"Sometimes," Hart remarked unpleasantly, "I wish I were a strangler—and then I would strangle my brother and it would truly be good riddance, once and for all."

# CHAPTER
# SEVENTEEN

THE NIGHT WAS BLACK and still around them.

Hart thumped his fist on the roof of the carriage compartment, and a moment later the carriage rumbled forward. Francesca stared warily at him. One small lamp illuminated the spacious passenger compartment, causing shadows to play across Hart's disturbingly handsome face. He remained in a foul mood, she saw, glowering at her, but she had been far happier earlier in the evening, too. She had taken a seat at the farthest possible corner from him. Tension filled the air.

"I wonder if it will always be this way," Hart remarked in the cool, mocking tone she had come to hate, "a perfect evening spoiled by the mere appearance of my half brother." He turned the full force of his dark, unblinking gaze upon her.

Hart had gloated over his wish to marry her. Francesca knew Bragg would never lie. "Why? Why tell Bragg that you have oh-so-suddenly decided you must take a wife and that wife is to be me?" she cried.

He stared for another moment and said tersely, "I am not someone to hide my intentions."

"Really?" As tense as she was, she was also aware of an odd hurt coming over her. "Are you certain it was not mentioned deliberately—with the intention to wound and to win?"

"Oh, is that what you think?" he demanded, the one hand that lay between them on the royal blue velvet seat clenched in a fist.

"I don't know what to think," she said almost bitterly. But of course she did. She was a fool, for she was only one of the many women he had chased. She was not special and she did not hold a unique place in his affections.

"I think the time has come to smash some sense into my brother. It is time he minded his affairs and stayed out of my business—especially where you are concerned," Hart ground out.

"Oh, that will truly help matters, to come to blows! I don't understand you, Hart, and I fear I never will," she said harshly.

"I am not asking you to ever understand me," he snapped. "I am only asking that you do not judge me unfairly."

His words were a blow. She sat utterly still. She knew how misjudged he was, how slandered and maligned, but this was the first time he had ever indicated that it truly bothered him. And she felt terrible, for she prided herself on her fairness. He did not deserve to be held guilty without a trial.

He was silent, looking away, as if he knew he had spoken foolishly.

"Why?"

He faced her. "Why what?"

"Why are you doing this?" she asked quietly. "Am I to be a prize in your war with Bragg, Calder?"

His eyes widened, remaining dangerously hard. "So he

has convinced you of my utter immorality, my complete depravity, at last."

"He has done no such thing!" she cried.

"No? You are the one person who has always believed in me, Francesca."

She squirmed. He was right. She knew he had a good side—she had seen it too many times. "But you threw your intentions in his face."

"Yes, I did. But only after he had aggravated me beyond all self-control! He is always telling me to stay away from you—ordering me, as if I were still a small and pitiful orphan crying for his mama. I do not take orders from him. And he has no rights where you are concerned, not any more. *Not* since his wife moved back in."

She wanted to believe that Hart had mistakenly told Bragg of his plans, and that it had not been a deliberate part of his war. But Hart's version of events and Bragg's were seriously at odds.

"I fear we shall always fight over you, Francesca," he added suddenly, darkly.

"No, because I shall not allow it. I simply shall not."

Hart suddenly began to smile. "If anyone can end our bitter rivalry, maybe, in a way, it could be you."

She almost smiled. Instead, she sobered. Somehow she had had the courage to ask him if he was using her to hurt Bragg, but she did not know whether to believe him or not. Suddenly it occurred to her that she would never know the truth. He was the ultimate player in all kinds of games of power and morals. If he wished to bluff, she would not be able to ever reveal his hand—not unless he wished her to.

She stirred. There was simply too much that was unknown and enigmatic and dangerous about Calder Hart.

"I don't want to argue with you," he said softly, taking her hand. "But when I see how quickly you melt for my brother, it infuriates me," he said.

She had been about to draw her hand away, not because she remained angry, but because the night was still and close, and her pulse had quickened erratically in response to all that she did not know about the man sitting beside her. She hesitated, not wanting to annoy him further. "I have always been honest with you. I am not going to start to dissemble now. There will always be strong feelings between Rick and me. We will always be the best of friends and you cannot change that."

He was unmoving. "Of course. As the two of you are the perfect match. Never mind that he has reconciled with his wife."

"Please don't lash out at me," she said quietly, but his truthful words hurt.

"I am sorry. But I am not the one who failed to reveal his marital status until it was too late. I am not the one who has already broken your heart and disappointed you, several times, I might add. I am not the one who stands deliberately between us, while taking a very beautiful wife to bed, day and night."

She recoiled. "He isn't sleeping with her!"

"Francesca, there is much I do not know about this world, but one thing I do know, beyond a doubt, is that Rick is insanely attracted to his wife, and if he has yet to sleep with her, more fool he. It is only a matter of time. You may take my word on that."

Had she been a small child, she would have clapped her hands over her ears. "I refuse to discuss him and his wife."

"Then let's discuss him. He is going to do his best to poison you against me," Hart said intensely. "You have to know that."

"He isn't trying to poison me against you, Calder. He is trying to protect me from being used and hurt." But she had graphic images dancing in her head now, of Bragg and Leigh Anne.

He was incredulous. "My marrying you uses you? My intentions are noble ones! And may I ask *who* hurt you, Francesca? I have not broken your heart! In fact, barring my reputation, I have given you no cause to doubt me or my intentions, now have I?"

He was right. She shivered then, uneasy. "But you admit

you do not love me," she finally said. "So you must agree, there is reason for my confusion."

"The only reason for your confusion, my dear, is my half brother and the fact that you have decided to keep him in your heart no matter the cost—and in spite of how he feels about his wife, he will now do the same, although for a very different reason."

"What does that mean?" she asked, stiff with dread.

"Oh, it means that as much as I think that Rick loves you—that he admires you, respects you, is attracted to you, that for him you are the Ideal Woman—I know he has never gotten over his wife. And in his case, given the fact that she is a whore and a bitch, the attraction shall certainly be fatal. He should have kept her in Europe for his own peace of mind. But now she is back. Within a month she will have him where she wants him. But he will not let you go, and it is me you accuse of nefarious motives. It isn't I, Francesca, oh no. My oh-so-noble brother will cling to you even as he beds his wife—merely to prevent me from attaining any happiness at all."

"You are wrong," she gasped, shocked by the scenario he had just painted. "You are very, very wrong!"

"And you are naive," he said harshly. "But it is one of the reasons I am so fond of you. Perhaps, one day, the blinders will come off."

She could not take it anymore. She was shaking. And the worst part was, once again Hart had brutally told her what he thought, and it was an honesty that caused real pain. But he was wrong! He had to be. "Hart, the two of you must end this absurd rift!"

He laughed without mirth. "It will end the day one of us dies."

She became still. She was furious now, and all she could think of were two things—Bragg in bed with his wife and Hart marrying her to hurt Bragg. Her anger escalated dangerously. "I have had enough," she said coldly.

He started, leveling his black eyes upon her just as the

coach rolled out of Central Park and onto Fifth Avenue. "Really?"

"Really. I suggest you mend this particular fence, Hart, if you want a chance at having my hand."

He stared. "Is that a threat?" he asked too calmly.

"Yes, it is."


The moment he got home, Bragg walked into his study at the end of the ground floor hall. The fire in the hearth was almost but not quite dead—a few heated coals glowed amid the ashes there. He turned on the lamp behind his desk, removing his jacket and rolling up his sleeves. A glance at the grandfather clock in the corner of the room showed him that it was four in the morning. He went to the decanter on the credenza and poured himself a scotch, adding melting ice from the brass bucket beside it.

Images of Francesca, lovelier than ever in her turquoise gown, vied for his attention with images of his half brother, sardonic, mocking, triumphant. He trembled with anger and envy. He had spent the evening consumed with the investigation, but they had, apparently, been out on the town.

Hart could seduce any woman he set his sights upon. It was only a matter of time until he seduced Francesca. Bragg cursed.

He knew Hart would never marry her. It was a ploy, a dastardly one. He would court her to destroy Bragg's sanity, seduce her to pour salt on the wound, then walk away, scot-free and laughing.

"Rick?"

He jerked at the sound of Leigh Anne's soft, feminine voice. He did not need this now, oh no.

She paused in the doorway, clad only in an ivory satin peignoir trimmed with lace. She might as well have been naked. The satin wasn't sheer, but it clung to her figure like a second skin, revealing her outstanding breasts, her tiny waist, and the plump, intriguing vee between her thighs. He stared and the way she had once spread her legs for him, laughing and wanton, filled his mind.

"Is everything all right?" she asked quietly. "It is four in the morning, Rick."

If she dared to ask him where he had been all night he might throw her down on the rug and take what she so wanted to give. He was that wound-up, that angry. He jerked his gaze up to her face, past large, erect nipples. "I have been working," he ground out. He drained the scotch, set the glass down.

"I was worried," she said as softly, her gaze searching— as if she cared. "I heard you come in at half past eleven— only to go out shortly after again."

"There is nothing to worry about," he said, rather rudely. "My work sometimes requires my attention in the odd hours of the night." He was careful to avoid looking down her peignoir again. But he was explosive, and half of it, he knew, had to do with the state of celibacy he'd been in since arriving in New York for his appointment. The other half had to do with the fact that he imagined that Francesca was, at this very moment, in Hart's arms.

"But you are not a detective. You are the commissioner," she said, stepping into the room.

He finally met her emerald green eyes. They held a sensual promise—as always. And her hair was down. It was as straight as a sheet of paper fresh off the press, a thick, long mane of raven hair that gleamed like the satin she wore. "I am going up to bed," he said firmly. He started past her.

She caught his arm. "For how long do you think to avoid taking me to bed?"

"I am tired, Leigh Anne," he warned. But her lips were parted and moist, her nipples were inches from his chest, and he was physically aroused. If he took her, he would hurt her, savagely and deliberately, because ever since he had left the Channing residence, he had ceased to be a gentleman.

"Our agreement is to be man and wife for six months." She wet her lips. A sheen appeared there. "I know you want

me. It's fairly obvious. And I haven't forgotten how wonderful it is to be with you." She smiled a little then.

It wasn't as seductive as her eyes. She was acting like a
virgin or a schoolgirl, tentative and uncertain. He knew there
was nothing uncertain about her in bed. In fact, in bed, his
little wife was the perfect whore. What he did not want to
remember now was how fond Leigh Anne was of a particu-
ular act, one most gently bred women abhorred. It had been
very easy to teach her to get on her knees and take his
manhood and suck it down her throat. He stiffened impossibly more. He would never forget what her mouth felt like
as it closed around his shaft.

"Why do you resist me? Because of Miss Cahill?" she
asked almost earnestly.

"Yes." He shoved past her, cursing her, and cursing himself and his damned inconvenient memory.

She did not follow him. "You are a fool. Do you think
to remain faithful to her?" She was incredulous.

"Yes," he said, refusing to glance back at her.

"But that is not a part of our agreement!" she cried.

"To hell with the agreement," he said, and he pounded
up the stairs—alone.

SATURDAY, FEBRUARY 22, 1902—9:00 A.M.

Bragg was at his desk, in his shirtsleeves, looking as if
he hadn't slept at all that last night. Francesca studied Bragg
for one moment, feeling a pang of compassion for him, too
well knowing what he must be going through. He suddenly
looked up and saw her. Instantly he smiled.

It changed his expression, lighting his face, his eyes. She
smiled in return, refusing to think about his accusations toward Hart or their bitter rivalry now. She hurried in, clutching the *Sun* and the *Times* in one hand. "Good morning."

He leaned back in his cane-backed chair. "Now why do
you look as if you have had eight hours of good sleep, while
I appear as haggard as a vagrant this morning?" The light
in his eyes was warm and affectionate.

She had to smile again. "I hate to say this, but in spite of the evening's terrible events, I passed out like a drunk when I got home."

His smile faded, but he continued to study her.

She guessed his concerns. "Hart was a perfect gentleman—even if we did argue terribly."

Bragg looked away. Then, "You will go out with him again, won't you?"

She put the newspapers on his desk, refusing to engage in the subject of Calder Hart. Especially as she did not know what she should do now. Besides, they had serious business at hand that morning. "Kurland has struck again," she said softly. She was resigned. In a way, she had known it was only a matter of time. Kurland seemed to have become fascinated with her sleuthing, which meant he was always in the shadows, waiting for a scoop.

"I've seen the papers," he said. The headlines glared up at them both. The *Sun* read:

### STAGE ACTRESS FOUND STRANGLED— CAHILL MISTRESS UNTIL RECENTLY

The *Times* was a bit better. It read:

### CITY STRANGLER CLAIMS TWO WOMEN, THIRD MISSING

"We ran into Kurland last night at an art gallery," Francesca said, taking a seat. "I refused to speak with him and he leaped on Sarah. Sarah hadn't known about Evan's relationship with Grace Conway. She was very upset to realize that Evan's mistress had been strangled and that she was not an anonymous actress."

"I feel very badly for Sarah, especially in light of last night."

"So do I," Francesca said somewhat glumly. "I haven't stopped by yet to ask her what the strangler said. I suspect she will sleep rather late today."

"I agree. The two policemen who were posted at the

Channing residence said they received orders from Sergeant Henley that their assignment was over." His golden eyes held hers.

"And?" She stiffened.

"Sergeant Henley said he never issued any such orders. The two roundsmen swear another officer gave them. An officer they did not know. An officer we cannot seem to locate. His apparent name was Kelly." Bragg stared significantly now.

Francesca stared back, her mind whirling. "What are you suggesting? That there is no officer named Kelly? That someone posed as a police officer, dismissing the guards so our killer could make an attempt on Sarah's life?"

"That is exactly what seems to have happened," Bragg said grimly.

"That means our strangler is very clever!" Francesca cried.

"Worse, it means he is very bold and highly motivated. I fear he is fearless."

She stared at Bragg with growing horror and he stared back.

"Have Andrew and Julia seen these papers?" Bragg asked, returning to the original topic.

"No. I stole the two newspapers, but Mama and Papa will learn of the accusations Kurland has made against Evan within hours. It will be the talk of society today." She felt terrible for her entire family now. While Evan was better with each and every passing day, he was still grieving for Grace Conway and he hardly needed to be accused of her murder. Julia and Andrew remained extremely distraught over Evan's injuries. They would be horrified by Kurland's news article.

"He makes suggestions, not accusations. He doesn't accuse Evan of murder," Bragg said calmly.

"No, but he points out very succinctly that Evan Cahill is the link between Sarah, Miss Conway, and Miss Holmes. He suggests that Evan is the worst of womanizers, ruthless and callous, going through women the way I might drink water. Only the most foolish reader would not wonder if Evan did not get rid of his unwanted mistress, attempt to do so to an unwanted fiancée, and then rid himself of an unwanted and insane admirer."

"I am sorry it has come to this. The article in the *Times* was fair. In any case, I will issue an official announcement as to the state of the investigation. The press has been scheduled for one this afternoon." He smiled at her. "In it, I shall state unequivocally that, while we are following all leads to their conclusions, your brother is not a suspect."

"Thank you," she said gratefully. "But I am afraid the harm has already been done." She sighed heavily.

Bragg stood. "Only to Evan's reputation, and that will be resolved when we bring our killer to justice, Francesca. Are you up to another interview with Hoeltz? I think it is time we find out why he lied about knowing Sarah."

She shot to her feet. "I am more than ready, Bragg."

He smiled at her and, with his hand on the small of her back, guided her out.


Bertrand Hoeltz did not look happy to see them. Upon answering the doorbell, he merely opened the door an inch or so and stared out at Francesca and Bragg. Joel, who as always had refused to come up to Bragg's office, was with them. He remained by Bragg's roadster.

"Mr. Hoeltz, it is I, Miss Cahill. I need to speak with you again."

"I'm afraid I am occupied," he said, beginning to close the door.

Bragg stuck his foot there so the door could not close. "Mr. Hoeltz, we have not met. Rick Bragg. Commissioner of police."

Hoeltz sounded as if he moaned. But he opened the front door to the building, allowing them in.

Francesca exchanged a glance with Bragg. "I saw you at the Gallery Duval last night," she said.

"Really?" Hoeltz appeared confused. "I was only there

for a moment or two; going out was a mistake."

"And why is that?" Bragg asked.

"Why? Surely you know that my dear friend Miss Neville is missing. I am desperate for word on her whereabouts!" he cried.

Francesca again exchanged a look with Bragg. "Mr. Hoeltz, Sarah Channing was in my party last night. She was eager to say hello to you."

Hoeltz paled.

"Did you not tell Miss Cahill that you did not know Sarah Channing?" Bragg asked.

Hoeltz choked. "I lied! I have been caught! I lied because I am so afraid!"

"Afraid of what?" Bragg asked calmly.

"Afraid of what?" Hoeltz gasped. "Mellie has vanished! Mellie is gone! I am afraid of being accused of her murder!" he cried.

"No one is accusing you of anything," Bragg said.

"I didn't kill her!" Hoeltz was near tears. "I adored her! I didn't kill anyone!"

"Mr. Hoeltz," Francesca said firmly. "No one has insisted that Melinda is dead."

He blinked. "But that is what you think."

"I don't know what to think," Francesca said, and it was hardly true. By now, Melinda Neville was dead. It was merely a matter of time before they found her body. "But perhaps that is what you think?"

He paled. "If she isn't dead, then why hasn't she come home?"

Bragg took his arm. "Mr. Hoeltz, I'd like to continue this conversation downtown."

"Downtown?"

"At police headquarters." Bragg was firm. "So, please, if you will?" And it was not a question.

Hoeltz seemed excessively nervous as Bragg led him outside. As they paused in the bright winter sunlight, Inspector Newman came hurrying toward them. "Sir! Sir!" he cried, flushed with exertion.

Keeping a firm hold on Hoeltz, Bragg asked, "What is it?"

Newman paused, gulping air. "Found . . . witness," he said.

"You've found a witness?" Francesca asked quickly, with a rush of excitement.

Newman nodded, not yet capable of full speech.

"Who is it?" Bragg asked as quickly.

Newman nodded eagerly. Then, "That lady . . . the portrait . . . Miss Neville did!" he cried.

Comprehension came. "Mrs. Louise Greeley? She is your witness?" Francesca asked.

"Yes!" Newman cried, finally finding his voice. "She was a friend of Miss Neville's—ever since she sat for the portrait. They had brunch on Sunday last. And Miss Neville was distraught. You see, she had decided to end it with Hoeltz, and planned on telling him that night."

Hoeltz chose that moment to jerk free of Bragg's grasp. He started to run.

But Bragg had the reflexes of an athlete. He set chase—and an instant later had smashed Bertrand Hoeltz up against the building wall. "You are most definitely coming downtown, Mr. Hoeltz," he said.

SATURDAY, FEBRUARY 22, 1902—4:00 P.M.

It was no longer impossible to see in the room. Days ago, her eyes had adjusted to the lack of light, although her lungs had not adjusted to the stale air, and her wrists and ankles had not adjusted to the shackles placed there. She knew the small room she was imprisoned in was a cellar. The floor was earth, dank and damp; she could smell it. But she did not know where it was. She had been brought there unconscious and blindfolded, after being viciously assaulted in her flat. Her dear friend and neighbor Grace Conway had heard her cries and had tried to help—and in the end, she was the one who had been murdered. Every time Mellie recalled the sight of her friend choking to death, she wept.

Attempting to escape her bonds was useless. She had tried that when he had first tied her up, and had only succeeded in rubbing her wrists raw. He had found her bleeding, and that had amused him. It had made him laugh.

She tensed with dread. Soon he would return, because he returned twice every day, and she could not bear it. Why hadn't someone found her? Surely her neighbors had noticed that she was missing. Dear God, why hadn't help come? Would she ever be rescued? She was not ready to die!

She had screamed until she had no voice left, but wherever she was, it was far removed from society.

Outside the locked door, footsteps sounded on wooden planks.

She began to cry.

The bolt was lifted, the padlock unlocked. Her breathing became shallow and rapid.

The door opened, and briefly his tall silhouette appeared in the doorway.

She began to pant in panic.

He closed the door and slowly walked over to her, reminding her of all that he would like to do to her, that he had thought about doing to her, but that he wouldn't do because she was a whore. He hated whores. Why did she have to be like all the others? Were there no decent women, no ladies, left? How could she do this to him! He bent and gripped her face in his large hand and she whimpered.

"Don't worry," he said. "I am not killing you yet."

She tried to breathe; she tried to speak. "Please, let me go. I won't tell."

He laughed, seizing a hank of her hair now and twisting her head back. "I'm never letting you go, but I think you already know that, don't you?"

She managed to meet his gaze. He had the eyes of a sadist and a madman, burning with lust and genius. And the worst part was, she knew him, and somewhere deep inside herself she had always, secretly, been afraid of him. Now she had to admit her darkest fears—that he would never let her live to tell the world who he was . . . and what he was.

"They'll never know it was me!" he crowed, and he let her go.

He untied her so she could use the chamber pot, tossed her bread and cheese, retied her hands and feet, and then he was gone.

Melinda Neville wept.

# CHAPTER
# EIGHTEEN

SATURDAY, FEBRUARY 22, 1902—5:00 P.M.

"HAVE YOU SEEN THIS, Andrew?" Julia asked the moment her husband walked in the door.

Andrew handed his bowler hat, his ivory-tipped walking stick, his coat and gloves to the doorman. Julia dangled the *Sun* at him, her expression set and severe. "Yes, I have seen it. How could I not?" Worry rushed over him yet again, for perhaps the hundredth time that day.

Julia stared grimly. "Please come into the parlor," she said, and it was hardly a request.

He sighed, preparing himself for battle and wishing it weren't so. He followed her into a small salon, mostly used for entertaining family and close friends. He knew she remained angry with him for the terrible argument he'd had with Evan, the result of which had been Evan's decision to move out of his house, attached and adjacent to their own, and the terrible assault on last Monday. She didn't have to tell him she was angry; he simply knew it. But he was angry, too. "I do not control the newsmen of this city," he said.

Julia shut the door behind him. "Why not? You have enough money to control whomever you choose."

"Are you now blaming me for this news article?" He was incredulous.

"We both knew Miss Conway was Evan's mistress. I blame myself for turning my gaze the other way and pretending I did not know of the very improper affair. But I blame you for not doing something to prevent these kinds of insinuations from getting into the newspapers!" she cried. "We have enough to worry about, do we not? Connie is melancholy, Evan is gravely hurt, there have been two murders and he is connected to both women, and Francesca is chasing after a married man! Our family is falling apart and I cannot manage it, not another moment." She sat down on the sofa and seemed close to tears. But Julia rarely cried and she did not do so now. "How have we come to this, Andrew?"

He sighed. His wife was a woman of steel. He truly adored her, and he had from the first moment they had met. And he knew that, in the case of Sarah Channing, he had done the right thing in forcing Evan to become engaged, in forcing a marriage upon him. Evan had no spine, no ambition. He was as different from both of his parents as night from day. He was the gravest disappointment Andrew had ever had. He wondered what he had done to deserve a lackluster son whose only interest was in gaming and tainted women. A son who seemed to despise him, a son who had shown no respect. For only absolute disrespect could cause Evan to disown his own father and his own birthright, all so he wouldn't have to marry a proper woman like Miss Channing.

Andrew sat down next to Julia. "Our family is going through a difficult time, but we will prevail, Julia. I shall see to it."

She looked at him out of moist eyes, but he saw hope there. And then she took his hand. "Thank you, Andrew," she said.

He started but squeezed her hand, not wanting to relinquish it, thrilled with the contact. "For what?"

"For being my Rock of Gibraltar, once again."

He smiled then. "I cannot let this family fall apart, Julia."

"Nor can I." She hesitated. "I am sorry we have been arguing so. But Evan's sudden determination to disown himself from us has terrified me. I should die if I ever lost my son."

Andrew took her into his arms. "I know." And he did know how his wife adored her only son, how she saw only the good in him, and never the wastrel, the rogue.

"Please, please, let him end his engagement to Sarah," Julia begged. "Please let him win this single time, so he stays with us."

"This is not about winning!" Andrew cried, releasing her. "I only tried to do what was best for Evan! And now it doesn't matter what I do, because he has decided to end the engagement himself—just as he has decided to leave his house and the business."

"But if you spoke with him, if you apologized, if you said you had been wrong, I know he would stay."

Andrew stiffened. "But I was not wrong."

She also stiffened. "I know. I know why you wanted Sarah to be his wife, and I agreed with you at the time. But now, everything has changed. I am asking you to go to him and tell him he was right and that you are wrong. To mend the fence, Andrew. Please. I do not want to lose my son!"

He got to his feet, heavily. He loved Julia and would do anything for her, but he also loved his son. And to give in now served only Julia in the short run. It was time that Evan became a man. Spoiling him would accomplish nothing. "It is time that Evan grew up," Andrew said quietly. "Please try to understand. He needs a path in life; he needs goals; he needs ambition. My coddling him will only make him more of what he is—a very spoiled young man."

"I can't believe you will let him quit the company and move out of his house!" Julia gasped.

"I have thought about it. I think it might be the best thing to ever happen to him—better even than marriage to Miss Channing," he said.

Julia cried out.

He reached for her. "Don't run away from me, too. I am doing this for Evan. Julia, you have trusted me for twenty-five years. You must trust me now." He hesitated and added, "Please. I need you."

She stared. "I don't know if I can, Andrew."

"You are the strongest woman I know. You can let him go. Trust me, Julia, it is for the best."

"You never loved him," she whispered.

"No, you are wrong. I love him so much that it hurts."


Maggie was surprised to find Evan not in bed but standing before the marble mantel of the hearth, leaning upon a cane. He seemed to be deep in thought, and she had little doubt why. Her heart ached for him.

And for a moment she had to stare, because he was as gallant and as handsome in appearance as a prince.

He suddenly turned his head as if he had sensed her presence. He saw her and slowly smiled.

She could not help smiling back. *You are such a sweet fool, Mrs. Kennedy, and too kind for your own good.*

Maggie refused to listen to Joe now. "Mr. Cahill, I just thought that I would call—I was told to come directly upstairs," she said nervously.

"Do come in," he said, continuing to smile as if he was very pleased to see her. He limped toward her.

Maggie rushed forward. "Should you be up and about?" she asked with worry. She noticed that the bruises were fading from his face, although he still wore the eye patch. That only gave him a dangerous air and, somehow, made him impossibly attractive.

"Finney approves," Evan said. "And I cannot stand to be in bed another moment. Besides, I have some tasks I must do." He gestured toward the open armoire then.

Maggie blinked, for the first time seeing a large valise

on the floor. "Are . . . are you going somewhere?"

"Yes, I am. I am moving into the Fifth Avenue Hotel," he said.

She was stunned. "But . . . but why?"

He smiled gently at her. "It is a story that makes no sense."

She simply could not believe that he was leaving his wonderful family. But she had been in the Cahill home for almost two weeks, and she had both eyes and ears. She knew there had been a terrible time between him and his father. "I should love to hear it," she said gently.

He leaned on his cane and took her arm. She trembled and quickly avoided his eyes.

*Ye had to come back and get burned, now didn't you, Maggie girl? What do ye think ye are doin'?!*

"You are the kindest woman I think I have ever met," Evan said softly, forcing her somehow to meet his vivid blue eyes. "But I refuse to burden you with the unpleasantries of my life. How are the children?" he asked then, eagerly.

"They are fine," she lied. They were complaining roundly about being home, except, of course, for Joel, who truly understood that their brief stay in the world of the rich had been illusory in every way. "They have asked for you, too."

He seemed pleased. "Would you bring them to see me? At the hotel? I plan to check in there tomorrow."

She nodded, her heart leaping, because she would have another excuse to see him. But she quickly pulled away from him now. Her arm felt naked where he had been holding it. Joe was right. This was foolish and, worse, dangerous. She was on the verge of falling in love with a man she could never have, a man from the highest levels of society, a man engaged to another woman—even if unhappily—a man who only thought of her as a friend. Not to mention the fact that he was clearly in love with another woman. His feelings for the Countess Benevente were obvious.

"What's wrong?" he asked, reaching for her and turning her to face him. "You appear so sad!"

She forced a smile. "Actually, I came because I wished to offer my condolences, Mr. Cahill. I am so sorry about Miss Conway."

His smile vanished.

She had seen the *Sun*. Rather, a co-worker who knew she had just spent ten days recuperating with the Cahills had told her that the dead actress was Evan Cahill's mistress and that the story was in the newspaper. Maggie had rushed to six newsstands upon leaving the Moe Levy Factory that evening, looking for a remaining copy of the *Sun*. She had finally found one.

She hadn't been aware that Evan had a mistress, but she simply knew that he had cared about her, because she knew he would only be with a woman he felt affection for. And she was simply appalled that the newsman had seemed to make Evan Cahill out into a reprehensible and immoral rogue, one who might have murdered his unwanted mistress and then the crime's only witness. Evan was hardly a rogue. He was a gentleman with a good and noble heart.

"You saw the newspaper?" he asked, limping over to the sofa facing the fireplace.

Maggie nodded, then realized he couldn't see her as he sat down. She rushed to follow him. "Yes. I am so sorry."

He stared at his lap. "She was a wonderful woman and I fell in love with her at first sight. But all men did. I loved her very much, once upon a time." He looked at Maggie grimly. "She was as kind and caring as she was beautiful." He suddenly smiled at her and she saw tears in his eyes. "When she came into a room, it was like sunlight pouring inside. She lit up every room she entered."

Impulsively she sat beside him, wanting to embrace him but not daring to. "I saw her at the theater once. She was very beautiful and very talented, too." But she wondered when he had fallen out of love. Perhaps it had been when he had met the bold and beautiful Countess Benevente. Had he not been engaged to Miss Channing, Maggie felt that the countess would be his perfect match.

"We fought, Mrs. Kennedy, and it is a regret I shall bear

for the rest of my life. The time had come for us to part ways. God, I so wish now that I had stayed with her just a bit longer!"

She had to touch him, she had to comfort him, and she gingerly touched his broad, hard back. He didn't seem to notice, as he had covered his face with his hands. "I am quite certain she loved you, Mr. Cahill. Please, do not feel such guilt. You are not to blame for her death. And Miss Conway surely knew that your relationship would end someday. She would not want you to blame yourself—not if she really loved you."

Evan met her gaze and smiled slightly then. He cleared his throat. "Thank you, Mrs. Kennedy. So that is why you came?"

She nodded, clasping her hands tightly in her lap, suddenly aware of her knee touching his thigh. But she felt as if she would betray her feelings should she reposition herself. Worse, she was incapable of looking away.

He didn't speak again. A long odd moment passed, one that became stranger with every beat of her heart—one that became more tense. His gaze suddenly dropped from her eyes, moving slowly over her face, darkening. And then he turned and stared at the fire, no longer smiling.

"I should go." She leaped to her feet, shaken. Had he stared at her mouth? Or was it her imagination—and wishful thinking?

He got up with some effort, leaning upon the silver-knobbed cane.

"You don't have to get up!" she cried, more nervous now, oddly, than she had been before.

"Of course I must stand up," he said, and his expression had relaxed somewhat. "A gentleman always stands when a lady does."

It was on the tip of her tongue to point out that she was not a lady. She wasn't gentry or upper-class and she never would be—she didn't count in his equation for respect and manners toward the fair sex. But she simply nodded.

"Are you all right?" he asked, hobbling around the sofa

and walking with her to the door. "Mrs. Kennedy, is anything wrong?"

She stared at him, her heart thundering in her breast.

*Oh yes, everything is wrong! I finally find myself yearning to be in a man's arms, and it is a man I can never have—at least, not in any proper way!* Maggie did not delude herself. She knew that the best she could ever hope for was a shameful affair. And it was simply not in her character to carry on in such a way. "Everything is fine," she breathed.

He looked skeptical. Then, "I think not. I wish you would confide in me. And I wish you had stayed here," he added.

"It was time to go home. My side is completely healed."

He was staring at her.

"Are you all right?" she asked in confusion.

"There is one thing I must ask of you, but I do not want you to be insulted," he said.

She stiffened. For one moment, a moment that was half-dread and half-hope, she thought he had read her mind and that he would suggest she become his mistress.

"Is it safe where you and the children live?"

"You think this is a good idea, Miss Cahill?" Joel asked warily.

They were standing on Broadway in the crush of rush hour. The avenue was lined with hansoms, carriages, and several backed-up electric trolleys. Crowds whirled around them, the passersby on their eager way home. It had begun to snow.

It was also growing dark. And as they were standing below the bold sign for the Royal, LeFarge's main saloon and gambling hall, the sounds of male conversation and laughter drifted out to them from within.

Bragg had returned to his office and Francesca had decided there was one last stone to turn over, never mind that Bertrand Hoeltz had the strongest motivation of all their suspects to harm Melinda Neville. The portrait of LeFarge, painted as Napoleon, remained engraved upon her mind. If Miss Neville had painted LeFarge, the waters were growing murkier indeed. It could be a coincidence, but it had to be explained.

"This is not a good place fer a lady to be," Joel remarked. "It's even worse than that saloon where we found Gordino, or the one where we found Craddock."

He was simply too astute for a small boy. No one had ever learned of her forays into those sordid saloons downtown, except for Bragg's family, but here there was every chance she would run into a family friend or acquaintance. Francesca sighed. "I fear I have no choice."

"Yer fly gentleman won't like this," Joel grumbled. "I heard him say yer not to go to the Royal, Miz Cahill."

"I shall not tell Bragg if you won't." She smiled briskly at him. "Let's get this over with. After last night, I am exhausted, and I am more than ready to get home." She wanted a hot bath, a Scotch whiskey (which she had already debated stealing from the library), and her supper on a tray in her room. Oh, how Hart would be laughing at her shameless ways now!

She smiled to herself.

Joel now sighed, looking more than worried. He gestured in a way that Hart had so often done, asking her to precede him in. Surprised and amused by the imitation, Francesca stepped up the limestone steps of the square building, took a breath, and pushed open one iron door.

Instantly a big man who was standing just inside the door barred her way. But not before she saw a beautiful room that looked like a men's cigar club. The walls were paneled in wood, Persian carpets covered the floor, and the chairs and sofas were heavy and plush. Two groups of gentlemen were seated separately, with drinks, cigars, and newspapers. This was not what Francesca had expected. For a gaming hall, this was staid and elegant. "Members only, unless you got permission from the boss to come in," the big man said in a Scots accent.

Francesca hardly heard him. To her dismay, Richard Wiley was sitting with two gentlemen in a far corner, sipping scotches while engaged in what appeared to be an earnest conversation. Once, her mother had thought to force Wiley upon her as a suitor. He had seemed very fond of her, in fact. Now, Bragg's admonishment that she was not to go to the Royal rang in her ears. She shifted so the Scot was hiding her from Wiley's view, should he look toward the door.

"It is very important that I speak with Mr. LeFarge," Francesca said, handing the Scot her calling card. "I am afraid my business is urgent and simply cannot wait."

"You stay there," the Scot said, not even looking at her card. A vast staircase was at the far end of the salon, but the Scot instead disappeared behind a pair of solid, gleaming mahogany doors. Francesca faced Joel, putting her back to the present company.

"So this is where Mr. Cahill plays his cards most nights," Joel muttered. "Fanciest saloon I ever did see. Where is the bar? Where are the poker tables?"

"I think the lobby serves as a lounge," she murmured. "I suspect the gaming part of the establishment is up those stairs."

"Miss Cahill? Is that . . . is that you?"

Upon hearing Richard Wiley's voice, Francesca winced. Well, her reputation had hardly been that bright to begin with. Now, of course, it was close to shreds. She turned with a bright smile. "How are you, Mr. Wiley?"

He seemed taken aback to see her inside the Royal. "Why, I am fine, thank you." And then he began blushing madly. He was extremely tall, perhaps six-foot-four, and lanky, and now he towered over her. "I, er, I am conducting some business here with some friends," he said lamely.

She realized he was far more horrified to be caught at the Royal than she was. Francesca warmed up. "Are you a member?" she asked.

"No!" he gasped. "I am truly here upon the invitation of Messrs. Braddock and Crane!" he cried. "But . . . what are you doing here?"

"I am on a case," she said brightly. "And I must speak to Mr. LeFarge."

He hesitated. "I have read all about you, Miss Cahill, and I must say, I had no clue a few weeks ago that you were so . . . so . . . intrepid!"

She didn't think he meant it as a compliment, but she took it as one. "Why, thank you."

He swallowed. "Well, in any case, this is no place for a gentlewoman." He was disapproving now. "I would quickly conduct my business with Mr. LeFarge if I were you," he said.

Thank God she had never once looked twice at Richard Wiley. "I intend to do just that." She remained cheerful. "And, Mr. Wiley?"

He paused, about to return to his associates.

"If you do not mention that you have seen me here, then I shall not mention that you do business here, either."

His eyes widened. "I . . . that is blackmail!"

"Not really." She smiled, and just beyond him she saw the Scot leaving LeFarge's office, coming toward her and Joel. Her heart skipped.

"He'll see you," the big man said.


Andrew LeFarge's office was decorated in the same style as the huge salon she had just left. He offered her a sherry, which she declined. He did not offer Joel anything. Then, the doors solidly closed behind them, LeFarge sat behind his large oak desk, with Francesca and Joel seated in the two facing bergeres. "This is quite the surprise. And what may I do for you today, Miss Cahill?" He smiled benevolently at her.

She did not smile back. Every time she came face-to-face with this man she could only recall what he had done to her brother, and it infuriated her. "I have come to ask you about the portrait in your front hall."

He was surprised. "My portrait?"

"Yes, the one where you are in a French military uniform, posed like Napoleon."

"So you have admired it?" He was pleased.

"Hardly." She remained as stiff as a board.

He stood. "It is obvious you dislike me, but I fail to see why."

"I think we both know the reason," she said, gripping her hands tightly together. "But I must know who painted that portrait."

"An unknown artist," he said, his gaze speculative. "She was highly recommended to me by a patron here."

Francesca stared, her mind racing. And there was dread, as for one moment she feared that somehow that patron was her brother. If so, he would become a connection between each and every woman involved in the case, dead, alive, or missing. "Was the artist Melinda Neville?" she asked stiffly.

"Yes. How did you know that?" He appeared surprised.

She refused to tell him anything. "And how did you learn of her, Mr. LeFarge, if you please?"

He studied her. "Easily enough. Her brother is a patron here, and he had mentioned that his sister was an artist recently returned from Paris." He shrugged.

She stood. "Thomas Neville is a patron of this club?!"

"Yes. He is here almost every night."

She stared, her mind racing. The puzzle had become endless. Where did this piece fit in? "Does he know my brother, Evan?"

"I should think so. They both frequent my establishment on an almost nightly basis."

She did not know what to think. Evan did not know Melinda Neville—or he didn't think he did. But he knew Thomas. Meaning that Evan remained the only solid connection between each of the four women. And then Francesca realized that was not so—Hoeltz was as connected. He had known Sarah, and through Melinda he had surely been acquainted with both Grace Conway and Catherine Holmes. And what about Thomas Neville? Francesca quickly realized he was only linked to three of the four women—he did not know Sarah Channing.

And while LeFarge could never be mistaken for a big or

tall man, Francesca did not rule him out as a suspect. He was the kind of man to hire thugs to do his dirty work. In his case, he could have struck at Sarah and Grace Conway to threaten Evan—the murder of Catherine Holmes and the disappearance of Melinda Neville would then be incidental.

Francesca sighed. It seemed as if they were no closer to solving the case than they had been four days ago. "Do you know where Miss Neville is?"

"Hardly. Why?"

"She has vanished. It would be very helpful to locate her as soon as possible."

"Miss Cahill, the woman painted my portrait well over a year ago—before she ever left for Paris. We did not even speak, except when she asked me to turn my head or body. She was rather cold, very severe, and very involved in her commission. Why would I know where she is? Isn't that a question you should ask Thomas?" His black eyes were hard now, very hard, reminding her of all that he was capable of.

"I should love to ask Thomas again," she decided.

"Then why don't you?" LeFarge smiled.

Francesca stiffened. "I beg your pardon?"

"Why don't you ask Thomas Neville? After all, he is upstairs," LeFarge said.

# CHAPTER
# NINETEEN

CONNIE GULPED DOWN A breath of air for courage. It did not enhance her courage—as she had none. She knew Neil despised her now. No lady ever behaved as she had done. She was terrified, now, that her marriage was over.

The door to his study was open. He was hunched over his vast desk, engrossed in his papers. For one moment, she studied him, aware of her heart pounding with such force that she felt ill and faint.

What he had done was wrong. But in a way, it had been her fault, for denying such a virile man his pleasure. Should they manage to go forward now, she would never deny him again. And at the thought of being in his arms, her heart skipped and skidded wildly.

*It had been so long.*

She felt a tear on her cheek. But she was never going to be in his arms again. She felt certain. Oddly, she loved him even more now than she had before his affair, and it had taken this moment for her to realize it. If only he would forgive her for her terrible behavior the other day.

He suddenly looked up, and the moment he saw her, he paled.

Connie could not smile. "Neil?" she whispered. It was so hard to speak. "Can we speak?"

He stood instantly. "Of course." He did not smile, either. He was grim, more dark and grim than she had ever seen him. There was no laughter, no light, in his brilliant turquoise eyes.

He moved out from behind his desk slowly as she entered the room and they paused before each other. Her heart pounded like a drum. It was deafening. How could she tell this hard, angry man that she loved him still? Did she dare? The idea of his final and absolute rejection terrified her.

"Yes?" he asked.

She wet her lips. "I am so sorry," she managed. "I have never been more sorry than I am for my terrible, reprehensible, inexcusable behavior the other day."

He stiffened with surprise. "What in God's name are you speaking about?"

Surely she had misheard. "My hysteria, Neil."

He was motionless. "You are entitled to hysteria, Connie—and to anger and any other emotion you feel. There is nothing to apologize for. In fact, everything is my fault." He looked down grimly, toying with the papers on his desk.

She was stunned. "No," she heard herself whisper.

He started, looking up and into her eyes. "I beg your pardon?"

*She could not let him go.* Connie blurted, "Neil! Surely you . . . want nothing more to do with me . . . don't you?"

He went still, his eyes wide, disbelieving. "What? How could you think such a thing?"

"My behavior—"

"To hell with improper behavior!" he cried. "I adore you, Connie. I always have and I always will!" he cried.

She remained in disbelief, but only for an instant, when she realized that she was going to have her life back. "Neil, I still love you. I don't want to lose you!" she cried.

He stunned her then. He rushed out from behind his desk and crushed her in his embrace, against his big, solid body.

She had forgotten how perfect it was to be in the circle of his arms, with his powerful heart thudding beneath her cheek. She began to cry. Her own arms tightened around him. *What had she been doing, thinking? She loved him so.*

His hand cradled the back of her head. "You don't hate me?" he asked roughly. "Connie, you don't hate me for breaking your heart and being the worst cad imaginable?"

She shook her head and then whispered, "No. I wanted to. . . . I was so hurt, Neil—so terribly hurt—but my heart won't allow me to hate you. I miss you!"

He seized her face in both hands and kissed her, hard.

She stiffened; then, as his kiss gentled and as he urged her lips to part, as warmth rapidly spread through her limbs and torso, beginning, finally, to build in every forbidden part of her, she relaxed, dazed, thinking that she had forgotten how much she loved his taste, his tongue. Tentatively she allowed her tongue to finally meet his thrusting one. Neil moaned without breaking the kiss and somehow, impossibly, deepened it, until Connie felt as if they were making love, just with their mouths, while the rest of her body was aflame.

His large strong hands slid up and down her small back. And finally he tore his mouth from hers, panting hard, and he rained kisses all over her face, her cheeks. Connie kept her eyes closed, and his kisses gentled, becoming feathery caresses on her skin. When he ceased, she opened her eyes and their gazes met. He was, she saw, as breathless as she.

He finally cupped her face in his hands, no longer kissing her. "Connie. I love you. I will never, ever stray again. I will live like a monk, if that is what you wish for me to do."

"Neil." Tears filled her eyes. She had almost lost him. She had almost lost everything, she thought. "Let's go upstairs."

His eyes widened in surprise. "The staff—the children . . ." he began.

"Take me upstairs, Neil," she said. And Connie smiled at him.

He smiled back, took her hand, and obeyed.


Leigh Anne sat at the dressing table in her small, drab bedroom, staring at her reflection in the mirror, a hairbrush in hand. She was wearing a satin wrapper over a corset, lacy drawers, and her gartered stockings. The wrapper was very loosely belted, exposing a vast amount of bosom, as the corset barely covered her breasts. It made her tiny twenty-inch waist even smaller. She wore slippers with low heels, so she was an inch taller. She hadn't bothered with any rouge, as she truly did not need makeup, but she had dabbed French perfume behind her ears and between her breasts. Rick had sent a terse note home earlier that afternoon, explaining that he would be back at seven. She was expecting him at any moment. Expectation made her breathless.

*Why in God's name had she stayed away for four years?*

She had been very angry with him when he had refused a position in one of Washington, D.C.'s most prestigious law firms, and that anger had grown day by day as the harder and longer he worked, the poorer and less socially acceptable they had become. Leigh Anne decided she had been a fool. She should have believed in him. Look at what he had become, and not just politically.

She shivered.

The note had said he would be working in his study all evening. He had advised her to make her own plans. Leigh Anne stared at herself. Her emerald green eyes sparkled with excitement, with desire. She had been doing nothing but making plans ever since receiving Bartolla Benevente's note in Boston, the one insinuating that her husband was carrying on with, if not in love with, another woman.

This was Leigh Anne's third day in residence with her husband, but they remained strangers—it was as if she was a houseguest. She hadn't lost confidence in her powers of seduction and persuasion, but Rick had changed. Four years of anger and bitterness had hardened him, and he was no longer simple to manage and easy to control. He had become a set and determined man. She found the changes fascinating and even frightening. There were moments when he truly intimidated her. And she had forgotten, truly, how gorgeous he was—how looking into his golden eyes and at his lean, muscular body made her mouth water and her body tighten.

She was fiercely glad that he hadn't slept with Francesca Cahill. Not because the other woman was more beautiful than she, as she was not. But because she knew her own husband, to a point, and she understood why he was so attracted to the pretty sleuth. Miss Cahill was exactly like Rick—fervently reformist by nature, highly ethical, indifferent to the material world, and intrigued by any mental challenge. They were, Leigh Anne sighed, two peas in a pod. But that was very boring, was it not?

Vinegar enhanced oil.

Oil added to oil was tasteless and bland.

Leigh Anne finished brushing her long raven-hued hair, then realized she was being watched with some fascination in the mirror. She smiled at the angelic toddler drooling as she sucked her thumb in the doorway. "Hello, Dot," she said softly.

"Pa . . . pa?" Dot shouted, ambling forward and falling on her face. She began to scream.

Leigh Anne leaped up and rushed to her. She had many faults, all of which she was aware of, but an indifference to children was not one of them. In fact, once she had hoped for two children of her own, a boy and a girl. Newly wed at the time, Rick had hoped to negotiate with her—he had wanted four. Laughing, she had refused. Then he had pushed her down onto the sofa and pushed up her skirts and they had made love. . . .

"Dot, come here; it's Mrs. Bragg. It's all right, sweetheart," she murmured, lifting the child into her arms.

Dot clung, whimpering. "Pa. . . . pa!" she demanded.

Leigh Anne shifted, realized that she could not get up,

and sat down on the floor. "Pretty girl," she said softly, meeting the child's huge blue eyes. She had been stricken to find out that not only was Rick fostering two homeless children, but the little one called him Papa. Now it didn't seem that terrible, just sad. She had learned from Mrs. Flowers, their recently employed nanny, that the girls had been raised fatherless and that only two weeks ago they had lost their mother to a crazed murderer. "Poor baby," she whispered.

"Pa . . . pa!" Dot cried, on her feet now and grabbing hanks of Leigh Anne's hair.

"Ow," Leigh Anne said, but with a smile. The child was adorable, if rather demanding. "Do not pull my hair, Dot. And Mr. Bragg will be home shortly." She stroked the child's golden curls and wondered if Rick still wanted children. She continued to debate the strategy of becoming pregnant with his child.

And she thought of how it would be when he finally caved in and took her to bed. Images filled her mind, so tactile that, for one moment, she could feel him inside her. He was huge and strong and she would never forget what being together with him was like.

"Papa!" Dot exclaimed, pushing Leigh Anne away, then falling in her haste to turn and race away.

Leigh Anne jerked and found Rick standing in the doorway, staring at her, as Dot now staggered awkwardly toward him. Instantly, as his eyes slipped lower, she was aware that her wrapper was almost completely open, allowing him a generous glimpse of her breasts, her waist, and even her inner thighs. Anticipation had been swelling within her for the past hour or so, and now it heightened considerably.

His jaw flexed, his eyes darkened, and he looked away. "Dot, sweetie! Come here," he said, ignoring Leigh Anne now.

Leigh Anne slowly got up, triumph searing her, and she pulled the wrapper slightly closed. She watched Rick lift Dot and twirl her high while she squealed. "Where's Katie?" he asked, settling her in his arms.

"Kitten." Dot beamed. "Kitten."

"I think that means the kitchen," Leigh Anne said quietly.

His gaze jerked to hers. "I know what it means," he said. Then, recovering his manners, he said grimly, "Good evening."

"How was your day?"

He stared down her wrapper again, but just for an instant. "Hellish. I hope you've made plans for the evening?"

She smiled. "Of course I have," she lied. "I'm having a late supper with a friend."

For one moment she thought he started, and she sensed his suspicion. He wondered if her friend was a lover. She said gently, "We have an agreement, Rick. I am hardly going out on the town with a gentleman."

"I hardly care," he returned, walking out with Dot in his arms.

Leigh Anne waited ten minutes. In those ten minutes she sat back down at her dressing table, staring at her reflection, but thinking about the way Rick had looked at her. How long did he think to hold out? And why? For God's sake, they were married, never mind if he was in love with someone else. But then, she had never understood him completely; in fact, his sense of morals and duty had bewildered her more often than not. Virtue was, more often than not, an inconvenience to be ignored. Unless one was born Rick Bragg.

They were nothing alike. But that was, she knew, the real reason for their undying attraction to each other.

Ten minutes later, her wrapper firmly belted and completely closed—up to her neck—her hair pinned up, as if she truly intended to go out that evening, Leigh Anne went downstairs and to his closed study door. She knocked.

"Come in."

She entered and paused. He was at his desk, having taken his jacket off, his shirtsleeves rolled up, revealing his hard forearms. His tie was gone, his shirt unbuttoned, exposing his strong throat and the interesting space between his collarbones. How many times had she run her tongue over the hollow there? And other, far more fascinating, hollows? She quivered. He was standing at the window, a scotch in hand, staring out at the small, snowy backyard and the patch of snow belonging to his neighbor. Beyond that, curtains were drawn in the windows of the facing brick house. The view was an uninteresting one.

He turned and stared at her, unsmiling and grim.

She smiled at him and closed the door behind her. "You're welcome to join us, Rick. I think you might like Harold Weatherspoon and his wife."

His jaw tightened. "How do you know Weatherspoon? He is one of Low's biggest supporters."

"I met the Weatherspoons in the south of France, a year or so ago." She smiled at him.

He didn't look happy. "I have work to do, Leigh Anne."

"It is very commendable, how seriously you take your job," she said. And in truth, she meant it. In a way, he had become very much like his father and grandfather, two very powerful, wealthy men.

He did not reply. He turned his back on her and stared out the window instead.

"Well, if you change your mind, we shall be at the Mirage," she said softly.

His back was very rigid now.

Her loins were soaking wet.

She reached for the doorknob but other than that did not move.

He downed the entire glass of whiskey in a single gulp.

She didn't move, because she sensed that an explosion was imminent, that his restraint was—finally—gone.

She could hardly wait.

Not turning, he ground out, "Did you really come down here to invite me to dinner?"

She wet her lips and did not answer. She waited, careful and on fire.

He turned. "Did you?" he shouted.

She backed up against the door, breathing harder now. Their gazes locked.

He cursed and threw the glass at her. She didn't duck, she didn't even flinch, and the glass broke somewhere to the left of her shoulder. Shards of glass cut her cheek. Then he started violently toward her.

He was enraged. It was hard not to cringe, but this was what she wanted, desperately, so desperately that she thought that one touch might be enough to send her into the best orgasm she had ever had. He caught her hands and slammed them high above her head. "This is what you want, isn't it?" he demanded, thrusting his stiff groin against her.

She looked into eyes as hot as her own. The difference was, he was livid, livid because he was losing to his lust while she was winning, and the fear made it almost impossible to speak. And she felt every inch of him throbbing and wanting against her. "Yes."

He let her go, ripped open her wrapper, and tore her corset down to her waist. Leigh Anne had expected anger, but not so much. And as he grabbed her breasts, forcing them upward, mauling her, hurting her, exultation swept over her. Her sex swelled impossibly. She pressed it hard against him. She whimpered as he took an engorged nipple between his teeth, grinding his rigid arousal against her abdomen. She cried out again and again, in pleasure and pain, but she did not move, while he thrust against her.

He paused, shaking and panting. She opened her mouth to beg him not to stop, then somehow thought the better of it. She had forgotten how much she wanted this man. She was going to die if he did not impale her, and soon.

But he did not. His expression twisting, he met her gaze and he shoved his hand between her thighs and seized her sex, hard, grunting harshly as he did so. Her drawers were soaking wet, and the moment he had her in his grasp he became still, their gazes locking again.

And she couldn't stand it—she shoved her sex against his hand, trembling wildly, barely able to stand, finally gasping his name. "Rick. Rick!"

"Damn," he said savagely. *"Damn."*

His face was strained with lust, his eyes livid with rage.

Then he looked down, tearing her pretty French drawers apart, in two. Leigh Anne cried out, exulting again, aching to grab his head, his hair, *him*, but knowing to remain utterly passive, utterly submissive, and utterly docile.

He slid to his knees, pinning her lips wide apart with his thumbs. It hurt. And then his face was there, his mouth and tongue everywhere, and she began to come, sobbing her release, vaguely aware that she had forgotten how this man made love, how he worshiped her sex, like he was worshiping every inch of it now. His tongue refused to stop, and he was using his teeth, until pain replaced the pleasure. She knew he wanted to hurt her just as she knew he needed her, this way, now and always, and she began to sob in another mad climax again.

She was boneless as he dragged her to the floor. *Why did I ever walk away from this, from him? No one else made love like this, no one* . . . she managed to think, dazed. And then he grabbed her by a hank of her hair, jerking her head back.

Her gaze flew open and the first thing she saw was his manhood, huge and distended, over her face; then she looked past it, trembling in fresh excitement, and she met his eyes. He smiled dangerously at her. "Show me what you've learned," he said.

She shivered, because he had changed unthinkably. She had married a gentleman, and he had become ruthless and savage somehow.

"Come closer," she whispered.

His mouth turned up. He pressed against her lips. Leigh Anne sighed and he took instant advantage, swiftly penetrating. She began to use her tongue and her throat muscles. She heard him groan in real pleasure, no longer able to deny it or her.

His thrusts took him deeper. Her mouth hurt, but she loved the pain, because every taste was better than chocolate, better than champagne, and his face was glazed now, glazed with pure pleasure, and she thought, *He will never be able to walk away from me now,* and her loins began to drip again as she sucked and watched him fighting to delay his climax.

His gaze flew open; he gasped, appearing stunned.

*Hurry,* she mouthed.

He inhaled hard, eyes wide, intent on one single act, and he pulled back, away, thrust between her legs, as hard as he could, and he drove her across the floor, into the wall, thrusting again and again. Leigh Anne could not wait. She felt her body explode abruptly, and then she felt him filling her with his hot seed, gasping out, mindless and hers and hers alone, and even aloft in the black, star-spangled universe, she smiled, knowing she had won.

"Have you found her?" Thomas Neville cried, hurrying down the wide, sweeping staircase.

Francesca regarded the tall, gaunt man with severe features. His dark eyes were not severe, however; they were wide, desperate. "I'm afraid not, Mr. Neville. I am sorry," she added.

He paused before her, clearly dismayed. "But haven't you interrogated Hoeltz? He is the key to her disappearance, Miss Cahill, I know it! He has certainly done something terrible to her," he added grimly.

Francesca thought that he was probably right. "He is being interrogated downtown at police headquarters, even as we speak," she said, hoping to be reassuring.

Neville's eyes flickered, with satisfaction, Francesca thought. "Good."

"How well do you know my brother, Mr. Neville?" There was no point in wasting an interview.

"We have known one another for years. We have had dinner together upon occasion, although not recently, I fear. Why?" He finally smiled, appearing puzzled by her question. "Melinda asked him several times if she could do his portrait. He declined."

The world became dangerously still. *"What?"*

He smiled at her. "He said he did not have the time to sit for a portrait."

*Evan knew Melinda Neville. He had lied. But why?*

Suddenly Thomas Neville took her arm. "Do sit down, Miss Cahill. You are very pale. Will you faint?"

She jerked free. Her brother had lied to *her*. "I am fine," she managed. She swallowed hard. "Thank you for your time, Mr. Neville, and I am sorry I had to ask you such unpleasant questions. Joel?" She turned, and as she did so, she caught sight of the big Scot standing beside the front door, watching her and Thomas Neville. Instantly he looked away, at the ceiling, as if bored.

"Let us go." She managed a breathless smile. But her ears had begun to ring. Could Evan have possibly forgotten meeting Melinda Neville—a woman who was not at all his type? She prayed so.

"Please find Mellie!" Thomas Neville called after her. "Please."

Francesca did not look back, her feet carrying her as swiftly as possible without running to the front door. She took Joel's hand as the Scot opened the door, and somehow she managed to thank him. But her nape prickled and she had to glance back over her shoulder one last time.

She was being watched again. This time, it was Andrew LeFarge, who had come to stand upon the threshold of his study. Then her gaze moved and she realized that Richard Wiley was also staring after her from where he sat with his entourage across the spacious lobby.

A moment later she was standing on Broadway, cloaked in the darkness of the recently fallen night. Francesca moved into the halo of a gas lamp with Joel.

"Miz Cahill, you don't look too good," Joel said, peering anxiously up at her.

Evan had lied directly to her. There was no other possible conclusion to draw. When had he ever done such a thing? And why? "I am a bit shaken." She took a deep calming breath and clasped his small shoulder. "Joel, it is late. You should go home. Let's find a cab and I will drop you before I go home."

"I'll walk. It ain't far from here an' it will be faster."

He was perhaps ten or twelve blocks away on foot. Less if he cut through alleys. Francesca nodded. "But go directly home. Maggie must be worrying about you by now."

He started backing away. "I'll be home in ten minutes," he boasted.

She did smile. "And be careful," she advised.

He grinned and turned and broke into a run. She winced as he began dodging through the coaches and carriages on the avenue, before dashing right in front of an overcrowded electric trolley. Then, as he disappeared into the crowd across the street, she sobered. It briefly crossed her mind not to ever tell Bragg that Evan had lied about his acquaintance with Melinda Neville.

But Evan was not their killer, and he had had some terrible reason for lying. Besides, she trusted Bragg. He was not about to accuse Evan of murder.

A hand seized her shoulder, hard.

Before fear could assault her brain, she was thrust rapidly across the sidewalk and into a dark alley. And as her assailant shoved her face-first against a brick wall, Francesca opened her mouth to scream. But a hand clamped down there, so that only a muffled gasp sounded, as another large hand closed around her throat.

The stunning knowledge clicked. *The strangler had found her . . .*

# CHAPTER
# TWENTY

SATURDAY, FEBRUARY 22, 1902—8:00 P.M.

PANIC ASSAILED HER — HIS hand was brutally squeezing her throat, choking her, and his body was pressed against hers now. There was no mistaking his grossly huge sexual arousal. A man she did not know, a murderer, was thrusting his sex against her buttocks. Francesca choked, writhing to get away, but her efforts were useless, and he laughed in her ear.

"You're all whores, now aren't you, Miss Cahill?" he sneered, his tone a rasp.

Her heart thundering wildly in her breast, Francesca became motionless, determined to identify him from his voice. Yet she could not. It was obviously muffled.

His hand tightened on her throat. She cried out, panting in raw fear now, hard and fast. "But you're the biggest whore of them all, aren't you?"

She tried to speak. Her mind said, *Let me go*. But no words escaped.

He jammed her harder against the wall, and she was

caught between brick and his stiff sex. Terror consumed her. Would he rape her? Sarah's frightened whispers echoed, increasing her panic to the point where she could not breathe at all. She was on the verge of suffocation. *He wanted to rape me, Francesca.*

"Afraid?" He laughed. "Is the city's most notorious little sleuth afraid? Where's Bragg? Oh! He's not here to save you!" He laughed again.

She wondered if her arm might break, jammed as it was between them. There was no air now. The night had become darker somehow. She was about to faint.

"You I might fuck. I will fuck you while you die. Because you're so pretty," he said roughly. "Ever take it in your mouth? I'm going to push it down your throat while your heart stops, Miss Cahill. I heard dying in ecstasy is the ultimate climax. What? Are you shaking?" He laughed, finally removing his hand from her mouth.

*She knew this was her chance to scream.* But instead, she sucked down the precious life-giving air desperately while he lifted her skirts from behind. *She knew she had to break free now.* But her mind was blackness and shadows, and her body refused to obey; there was only sweet, sweet oxygen searing her burning lungs.

"Oh, God, bitch," he said, grasping her buttocks.

*It was going to happen if she did not react now.*

"Ow!" he cried, his grip on her easing as an object hit the ground beside them.

Francesca thought, *Joel!* She somehow jammed her elbow backward, but even before the bone connected with her attacker's rock-hard torso, he grunted in more pain. Francesca realized that he was being pelted with stones.

"Git off of her!" Joel screamed, enraged.

The man cursed, releasing her.

Francesca fell to the ground, instinctively clutching her throat, which throbbed terribly. She heard more rocks hit the ground, the wall. She turned on her hands and knees, saw a tall, broad-shouldered form and the grotesquely disguised stocking-clad face. Joel dived at his ankles.

He went down.

Francesca reached for the rock not far from her hand.

He cursed and threw Joel away, looked at her once, a monster with no eyes and no mouth, then launched himself to his feet and disappeared into the night at the far end of the alleyway.

Francesca collapsed in the dirty snow and began to cry.

"Miz Cahill! Miz Cahill!" Joel scrambled over on his knees. His small hands covered her back. "Did he hurt you? You all right?"

She could still feel the man's erection against her body, his breath in her ear, his hand on her mouth, on her throat. She choked the sobs down. She was too strong to cry. She wasn't dead. She wasn't dead and she hadn't been raped and damn it, she wasn't going to weep.

Joel stroked her back. "Please don't cry. C'mon, Miz Cahill. We gotta get outta here. Please get up."

She managed to stop sobbing, aware of the tears drying on her face, burning her with cold. She breathed deeply, harshly, again and again. *Thank God for Joel Kennedy,* she thought.

"Let's go to Hart. He can help. He'll help you, Miz Cahill. Please get up!" Joel pleaded.

Hart. She would rush into his arms and be safe.

"Git up!" Joel begged.

Francesca pushed herself up into a sitting position. Hart? She had to see Bragg. She had to see him immediately, tell him everything, and he would hold her and tell her that everything was all right. Why was Joel telling her to go to Calder Hart? And why did she, oddly, almost wish to do so? She wiped her eyes with her gloved fingertips. "Joel." Finally she could speak. Her voice was hoarse. Each uttered word burned her throat. "Did you see who it was?"

"No." Joel was grim and anxious all at once. "He was tall. Real tall. But with that mask, I couldn't see nothing."

Francesca no longer knew what to think. She was still breathing hard, she was in shock. "How . . ." She clutched her neck and winced. Touching the flesh there hurt. "How did you know to come back?"

"I turned to wave on the other side of the street. As soon as a dray passed, I saw this man dragging you into the alley," Joel said, his face pinched and pale. "How badly are you hurt?"

"I'm fine," she lied, praying it was true. But she did not feel fine. Every time she thought of her assailant, she felt him pressing against her with a savage and unsatisfied lust, she recalled his horribly obscene words, and she thought she might retch. She began to get to her feet, trembling. Joel jumped up and assisted her, then began looking around them warily—as if afraid that the strangler would return.

Francesca was equally afraid. Together they rushed to the safety of the crowded sidewalk and began to hail a cab. And as they waited for an unoccupied hansom to pass by, Francesca felt his eyes upon her and knew he lurked nearby.

Joel stood behind her as she rang the doorbell of Bragg's town home. While she waited for Peter to answer, she felt the tears rising up within her again. She refused to cry. She was hardly any worse for wear. She had survived the strangler's attack. Now her biggest regret was that she hadn't been able to hear his voice clearly or get a look at his face without his mask.

She recalled Ellie's description now, *a monster, no eyes, no mouth.* God, the old woman had been right.

Peter opened the door. He took one look at her face and coat, and his eyes went wide. "Miss Cahill?"

She managed a tight smile. "Is Bragg in?" She hadn't seen his motorcar in the street, but he had a carriage house behind his home, where it was parked overnight.

Peter seemed to hesitate, which was odd. "Do come in," he said quietly, his impassive and characteristic expression returning.

Francesca stepped into the foyer.

"Would you like to wait in the salon? May I bring you tea?" Peter asked.

Francesca saw worry in his blue eyes and realized she must look wretched. "No, thank you. It is urgent, Peter," she stressed.

He nodded and ascended the stairs, which meant that Bragg was not at work in his study. It became impossible not to pace, wring her hands, and fret. A moment or two passed by and Bragg did not appear. Francesca became still. What was taking so long? Now a quiet kind of dread began as more time dragged by. He was obviously at home. He was upstairs. What could be taking him so long?

She did not want to even consider the answer to the question.

Footsteps sounded on the stairs, at last.

Dread overcame her, as the footsteps were not Bragg's— they belonged to a woman.

Francesca looked up and saw Leigh Anne coming down the staircase, clad in a dark green satin wrapper. She froze.

Her stomach protested and lurched wildly again.

Leigh Anne paused on the second-to-last step, which made her taller than Francesca. "Good evening," she said, smiling.

Francesca could not speak. Nausea overcame her now. Leigh Anne's long hair had been braided into one sleeping braid, but it was only half past nine or so. The wrapper was tightly belted around her small body, but Francesca felt certain that she was naked underneath—her nipples were erect and clearly visible against the fabric of her gown. Her face was flushed. Her eyes glowed. Her mouth was terribly swollen.

An image of Bragg and Leigh Anne passionately entwined and then a recollection of the feel of that man's hard, stiff body against Francesca's own assailed her almost at once. She turned quickly away, afraid of retching now.

"Are you all right, Miss Cahill? Would you like to sit down?"

They had been making love, Francesca managed to think.

Leigh Anne had clearly just been in the throes of passion; she had clearly just gotten out of Bragg's bed. As usual, Calder Hart had been right.

Francesca met her soft, sated eyes, vaguely saw the surprise and concern mingling there, and turned hastily away. She simply could not bear to look at the other woman. "I can . . . I can see I have come at an inconvenient time," she said hoarsely.

"He is sleeping, Miss Cahill. As I am sure you know, he has been working extremely long hours this week. If it is urgent, I will wake him," Leigh Anne said.

Francesca had to get away from her, him, the house. "No." She rushed across the foyer. "No, it is hardly urgent!" she cried. As she opened the front door herself, she saw them again, making love, Bragg and his wife. Then she heard that lewd, rasping whisper in her ear. *Ever take it in your mouth? I'm going to push it down your throat while your heart stops.*

Francesca fled into the night.

The hansom rolled away, down Hart's large paved driveway, through the tall, imposing wrought-iron gates, and onto Fifth Avenue. Francesca stood in the driveway where she had climbed out of the cab, shivering uncontrollably and gazing at the imposing facade of his house. Tears blurred her gaze, but she fought them, staring up at the huge sculpture of the stag on top of his roof. Why was she so upset? Bragg and Leigh Anne had reconciled, and he had every right to bed his wife.

But it was more than that. *She had been assaulted and almost raped while he was making love to the other woman. He insisted that he despised her, but clearly, he did not.*

"Miz Cahill? It's darned cold. Let's go in."

Francesca knew she could not enter Hart's house. Not now, not like this. "I'm going home," she whispered, Hart's dark, sardonic image superimposing itself on top of Bragg and Leigh Anne. She turned away and heard the strangler's crude sexual threats again. Her stomach turned over, hard. Her stride quickened.

She felt dampness on her cheek and brushed it away. She realized she was not wearing her gloves. She had lost them somewhere that day.

Francesca hurried up the driveway, trying desperately to block out the events of the entire evening. It was simply impossible, and Joel was right: it was so cold, too cold to be outside. Then she heard Joel rushing up behind her, his footsteps crunching on the snow as he set chase.

"What in God's name are you doing?" Hart demanded, catching up to her and seizing her arm.

He turned her to face him and she looked up into his handsome face and shook her head, suddenly incapable of all speech.

"Joel said you were attacked!" he exclaimed.

She wet her lips to tell him that she was fine. Not a single word came out. Instead, she began to tremble uncontrollably, and images assailed her all at once: Leigh Anne flushed and glowing in her wrapper, Leigh Anne in Bragg's bed with Bragg, the strangler running away into the night.

They stood some distance from the house and Hart remained a shadowy figure, even this close. "You're not all right," he said flatly then, putting his arm around her and pulling her against his side. He was in his shirtsleeves. "Come inside. You're frozen! You're shaking like a leaf."

She had to get words out. "Thank you," she whispered.

His arm around her, he carried her along with him up the driveway. "I am afraid to ask what happened to your voice," he said very grimly.

She closed her eyes, and it hardly mattered, as his strength propelled her up the steps and inside. When had this man become a safe haven? She tried to remind herself that he was danger, pure and simple, but she could no longer convince herself.

He stiffened as they paused in the front hall. Francesca opened her eyes and saw him staring at her. She tried a smile and knew it failed. "I'm . . . fine."

His jaw flexed. His eyes were black. "Take Miss Cahill's coat," he snapped. "Get Rourke in here, Alfred." Hart's tone was so dire that Francesca glanced at Alfred to see if he might fear for his life, should he not obey.

But Alfred seemed incredibly distressed as he took her coat off her shoulders.

"And bring a scotch," Hart said in the same furious and strangled tone. "Two glasses—one bottle," he added.

"I'm fine," Francesca said, pleased that the ability to speak was returning, that her voice sounded less hoarse—although speaking still burned her throat.

"Your face is scratched. Your neck is turning black-and-blue. You are not fine," he said, leading her into a small salon that she had never before been in. "You were attacked by the City Strangler?"

She nodded as he guided her to a sofa. "Joel saved my life," she said grimly, and then she felt that revolting pressure against her body again, heard his obscene threats, and saw Leigh Anne in her wrapper on the stairs. She folded over, hugging herself.

Two warm, strong hands gently took her face, forcing her to look up. Hart was on his knees in front of her. "I am going to kill this man," he said.

She started and could not look away from his quietly furious and extremely determined eyes. "Please, I have enough to worry about. Let the police handle this now. Please, Calder."

He softened. "You came to me. You came to me, Francesca," he said intensely.

And his meaning was clear—she had come to him, not Bragg. She looked away. Tears rose up, hard and fast. She squeezed her eyes tightly closed against them. *Don't tell him,* she thought. He did not need to know that she had not come to him first.

He did not release her face. Then she felt his lips brushing her mouth, softly, sweetly, again and again.

Her heart stopped, then began to beat, hard and fast, urgently.

She felt the moment his need to comfort changed—it was simultaneous with the rise of her own need, her own desire. *She could lose herself in this man's arms, in his body, his bed, and forget everything. . . .*

Francesca clasped his shoulders, her mouth opening beneath the more insistent pressure of his now questing lips. His tongue quickly penetrated, and heat flamed in her loins; their mouths met again and again, fast and hard now, urgently, teeth touching, tongues deep, entwining, and she simply could not get enough of his taste, his tongue, his mouth, and as his kisses became more urgent, passion became frenzy. For the first time since she had known Hart, she felt the ruthless, raw, unfettered passion in him—she felt him going over the brink of his self-control—she felt certain that this time, now, in moments, he would be surging hot and hard and sleek within her.

And he pulled away. But did not leap to his feet; he remained kneeling. Their gazes locked, Francesca stunned that she had been wrong. How did he have such willpower?

"I desperately need to make love to you," he said hoarsely. One hand moved from her cheek to her hair and over the back of her head. She realized that her hair had come down. *"What happened?"*

She could think of only one thing now: Losing herself in this man's arms. Having his powerful body inside her own fragile bruised one; having him fill her, complete her, save her. "Make love to me," she begged, tears suddenly falling. "Please, Calder. Make love to me now."

His eyes widened and then he pulled her close and to her feet, holding her tightly against his own body. She gasped when she realized he was as feverishly aroused as she. There was no mistaking the heated, throbbing arousal against her belly. In that moment, the realization was stunning. *I love this man,* she thought, bewildered and dazed.

"You're crying," he said roughly—and it sounded as if he might be crying, too. "Your face, Francesca, how did your face get so scratched?" His embrace tightened so she could not look up to see if he was really tearful or not.

"I . . . He shoved me against the wall," she whispered. "He was strangling me, Calder. I know now how poor Miss Conway felt, and poor Miss Holmes! And the things he said . . ." She didn't want to cry and thought she was in control of her fear and the rest of her emotions, but she felt the wetness tracking her face, burning her raw skin, and she was surprised by it.

"Who was it?" He didn't release her. He kept her cheek buried against his chest, her body enfolded in his, pressed securely against him. He remained hard and erect. He kissed a soft, throbbing spot on her neck.

"I don't know," she gasped as he lifted his head and looked down at her. Their gazes met. She saw anguish in his dark eyes, anguish and suspicious moisture, and she could not move. *He was crying for her.*

"Calder?"

"What is it, darling?" He cupped the base of her skull gently.

"I thought he was going to rape me."

His eyes widened. There was no mistaking the shock, the disbelief, and then the raw fury rising there. Their gazes held. They stared. Then he cradled her face in his hands and kissed her tenderly on the mouth. "But he did not," he whispered roughly.

Francesca felt the tension within her—as emotional as it was physical—melting away, cell by cell and inch by inch. Then her body began to melt too—far differently.

He lowered his face and began kissing her bruises, one by one. The kisses were feather-light.

Desire came in a flood tide. Her knees buckled and she moaned, clinging. His mouth moved from the side of her neck to her throat. He gently opened the top button of her collar, pressed his lips gently there, opened another button, kissed the exposed flesh, and another. The last kiss was precariously close to where her cleavage began. Gently pressing his firm, damp lips there, he did not move, and Francesca held his strong body in her arms, faint with need now. She murmured, "Oh, Calder," and heard a tone she had never before heard, in her own voice, stunned with desire, faint and weak with need, raw with passion.

Hart stiffened, but just as he began rubbing his face lower over her breasts, Rourke demanded, "How is she?"

Hart straightened instantly and their gazes met. "Calder, stand back," Rourke said briskly.

Their gazes remained locked. An aeon seemed to pass. So much had happened and so quickly that now Francesca was aware of one stunning comprehension—that Calder Hart truly cared about her. She smiled through her tears. He would always take care of her, she thought. It was a stunning and wonderfully profound comprehension, a revelation that filled her with pleasure and joy.

Hart stepped back.

Rourke came forward. "Please sit down," he said firmly but kindly.

Francesca obeyed, but she could not look away from Hart. He continued to stare, Alfred behind him, a tray with a decanter of Scotch whiskey and two glasses in his hands. Rourke was inspecting her face, and then he tilted her head up and back, looking at her throat and neck. He smiled reassuringly at her. "Is there anything else I should know about?"

She realized for the first time that her palms were also scraped. She turned them over and showed them to him.

"How is she?" Hart asked, not having looked away, not even to blink.

"So far, so good. She has some cuts and scrapes on her face, but I doubt there will be any scars. Is your throat sore?" he asked gently.

"Terribly," Francesca whispered. She could hardly focus on Rourke. Hart now ran his hand through his short, thick, curly hair, appearing at once grim and explosive. Now his passions were bent on apprehending the strangler. Francesca thought about how she had begged Hart to make love. She wondered if they might have actually done so if Rourke had not appeared. She felt certain that Hart had not had any self-control left then.

Hart suddenly turned and accepted a scotch from Alfred, came over, and handed it to Francesca, who took a sip immediately. The whiskey burned her throat, but she knew that in a moment she would feel soft and warm and pleasant, and she took another sip, feeling that man again, thrusting against her and telling her what he was going to do. She quickly opened her eyes and realized she had downed most of the glass. That day had turned into a nightmare.

Hart was staring grimly at her. Not turning, he said, "Alfred. Send Raoul to fetch my half brother."

Francesca froze.

"Then ready a guest bedroom. Miss Cahill will spend the night under Rourke's care." He faced her. "I will bring your parents, Francesca. They must be told."

She clutched the empty glass. "No."

"Francesca." He softened. "Darling, you are only slightly the worse for wear, and I will wait until Rourke has made you presentable, but your mother and father will be frantic when you do not come home. I must go over and gently explain to them . . . something." He darkened as he uttered that last word.

"I might twist the truth a bit," Rourke said quietly.

"No," Francesca said again, barely able to breathe. "Do not get Bragg, Calder."

He started, his eyes widening in surprise.

"Please," she added.

And he stared, his gaze narrowing now with speculation.

Francesca remained on the sofa. She was sipping her second scotch, having finished giving Inspector Newman a detailed report of the attack. Hart stood protectively a few feet from her, where he had positioned himself well over a half an hour ago. He didn't drink or speak, but he had listened to her every word. There were no secrets between them now.

The doors to the small salon were solidly closed. Francesca knew, though, that most of the Bragg family had gathered in the hall outside. When Newman had been escorted inside, she had glimpsed Rathe and Grace, Nick D'Archand, their handsome nephew, and Lucy and her husband, Shoz, all huddled in whispered conversation. She could imagine the train of their thoughts. And the absence of the city's police commissioner was now glaring.

Francesca refused to think about Bragg now. Hart had deferred to her wishes not to summon him, and Chief Farr had been called instead. The city's chief of police stood beside Newman. Farr had arrived within minutes of the inspector but had allowed the detective to do all of the questioning.

"Well, I think we have it covered, Miss Cahill," Newman said. His brown eyes were gentle and kind. "I'm sorry you had to go through such an ordeal."

"Thank you. Will you pick up LeFarge and Neville for further questioning?" Francesca looked at Brendan Farr as she spoke, tensing instinctively as she did so. She knew he did not like her, as he never had, not from the moment they had first met. But then, he was a part of the old guard of the Department and would not care for any civilian's interference in police affairs, much less that of a woman.

"Why don't you let us worry about the details of this investigation, Miss Cahill?" Farr replied with a smile that did not reach his eyes. "I think this evening's events have proven that criminal investigations are best left to my men."

Francesca smiled stiffly at him. It was reasonable now to conclude that LeFarge or Neville had been the assailant. Unless Hoeltz had been released earlier—and he had followed her to the Royal. But the time of his release would be easy enough to discover.

Farr continued to smile at her. "I must request that you stay out of police affairs from this point on." He faced Hart. "Mr. Hart, it is best for everyone involved if Miss Cahill gives up her sleuthing until the strangler is found."

Francesca wished Farr would disappear off the face of the planet. She smiled, felt that it was more a bristling, and said, demure, "Whatever you wish, Chief."

"He is right," Hart said, giving her a look that said that

he knew she was lying to Farr's face. "This case is beyond your scope, Francesca."

Francesca smiled at Hart in a similar manner and finished her second glass of scotch. She was more than ready to throw in the towel—for that evening. But tomorrow, why, tomorrow was another day, and she had had enough. If Farr did not make an arrest, she must take matters into her own hands. But how?

Suddenly an intriguing notion struck her.

The strangler had meant to murder her and he had failed. What if she set a trap for the killer?

He clearly wished for her to be his next victim. What if a trap was set with her as the *bait*?

She stood, excited now, and came face-to-face with Hart and Farr. And in that instant, she realized she had been expecting Bragg to be there, so she could eagerly share her new idea, so they could debate it, so they could begin to formulate a plan to entice the strangler into a foolproof trap.

"What is it, Francesca?" Hart said, too sharply.

She looked at him and hesitated. Would Hart agree to her idea? She doubted it. Bragg would be hard enough to persuade, yet she knew she could do so. With Hart, she knew no such thing. She decided to remain mute. Nothing could be done that evening anyway. She smiled. "Nothing. I've had too much to drink, I fear. I had a notion, but it's absurd." She smiled again, brightly.

Hart stared, filled with suspicion now.

"We may have more questions for you tomorrow," Farr said. "Newman, let's go." He nodded at Hart. "Thank you for your help. And, Miss Cahill? It is a fortunate instance, indeed, that you were not seriously hurt tonight, or worse."

Francesca kept her smile plastered on her face until he left.

"Just what are you up to, Francesca?" Hart asked, reaching for her.

She was surprised to be pulled against his side. A delicious warmth unfurled within her. "I am not up to anything, as you put it."

"Somehow, I doubt that," he said. But his face softened and he smiled at her as they stepped into the hall.

Instantly the Bragg family descended upon them. From the corner of her eye, Francesca watched Farr and Newman speaking in the foyer, waiting for their coats.

"Are you all right, Francesca?" Grace Bragg asked. She was the foster mother of both Hart and Bragg, and now her blue eyes were filled with concern.

Francesca smiled at the red-haired woman, who, although middle-aged, remained beautiful, even with the spectacles she wore. "I have certainly had better days," she said.

"Calder says you are spending the night here," Grace returned as Lucy, her equally red-haired daughter, paused beside them. "How would you feel if I saw you up to your rooms?" She smiled warmly then.

Francesca had so wanted to be liked by this woman. She smiled back. "Female company is just what the doctor ordered," she said. Looking past both women, she saw that Farr and Newman had their coats on and were about to leave. But Brendan Farr had paused in front of a sculpture of a reclining nude and he was staring at it. Francesca had seen the somewhat sensational nude before. Now, however, something tugged at her. She stared.

Farr turned away, his expression impossible to read.

"Excuse me," Francesca said quickly to Grace and Lucy, and she started through the front hall toward the two police officers.

"Never saw anything like that," Newman was saying to his superior, his cheeks beet red. "Rich gents are odd, aren't they, Chief?"

"Everyone knows Calder Hart enjoys his whores," Farr returned evenly.

Francesca stopped short, a dozen feet from the front door.

Alfred ran up to the policemen, murmuring, "Good night," as the doorman opened the door.

Newman stepped outside, but Farr suddenly glanced over his shoulder and instantly his iron gray gaze met Francesca's.

Her stomach heaved.

He nodded politely and walked out.

Francesca could not move. Her heart was thundering explosively in her breast. She could feel his hardness against her buttocks, brick against her cheek, hear the rasped obscenities in her ears. *Ever take it in your mouth? . . . I heard dying in ecstasy is the ultimate climax.*

Francesca cried out, clinging to the wall.

"Francesca!" Hart reached her in a stride. He seized her arms, turning her to face him. "What is it?"

*Everyone knows Calder Hart enjoys his whores.*

"Oh, God." She trembled violently, knew she was about to become ill. "It's Farr."

Hart stared at her.

Francesca wrenched free and ran for the closest water closet.

# CHAPTER
# TWENTY-ONE

FRANCESCA CAME OUT OF the bathing room in a peignoir borrowed from Lucy. The redhead, who was just a few years older than she, had settled herself on the foot of the canopied bed in Hart's guest room. Grace had disappeared, declaring she would have Cook arrange some refreshments for Francesca. Hart had also left, to impart the news of Francesca's whereabouts to Julia and Andrew. Now Francesca walked barefoot across the huge bedroom suite, the Aubusson rug underfoot exquisite. A fire crackled in the hearth beneath a white marble mantel veined with gold. The walls were painted the softest shade of pastel green, and the ceiling above had been scalloped with pink and gold. Several beautiful paintings adorned the walls—a mother serenely bathing her child, a brooding seascape, fisherwomen on the beach with baskets on their heads. The room was as dramatic as the rest of Hart's home. Yet it was also elegant, sublimely so.

Francesca settled down in the bed, and the moment her

shoulders and back touched the six down pillows stacked at its head, she realized how exhausted she was. Briefly she closed her eyes.

But she did not want to think about Brendan Farr now—and his image assailed her strongly. But was she right? Francesca knew she was extremely distraught—and she knew she had no proof that Farr was the City Strangler. But God, for one instant, when their eyes had met in Hart's front hall, she had felt certain it was he. Now she did not know what to think—and she was filled with doubt. He might be a crooked police officer and he might hate her, but that hardly made him a killer. And now, with actual physical distance and some time placed between them, she felt that she had been too quick to accuse him. Hart had told her she was too distressed to be able to think clearly. He had told her to get some rest. She shivered, deciding she was, in all likelihood, wrong, and then felt Lucy take her hand.

"You are so brave," Lucy said quietly. "When your parents come, you had better button the collar of the wrapper, Fran."

Francesca smiled at her and buttoned up the collar. Her mother would have apoplexy if she ever saw the darkening bruises on Francesca's neck. "I wasn't brave tonight. I was terrified, Lucy. In fact, I have never been so afraid." She thought about Brendan Farr again. Why would he vandalize Sarah's studio and then kill Grace Conway? It made no sense, none!

Lucy leaned forward to hug her. "This time, Hart is right. This case is too dangerous!"

Francesca hated to admit that Hart might be right.

Lucy settled back on the foot of the bed, studying her. Then she said, "Where is Rick?"

Francesca flushed.

"I mean, the two of you work together solving crimes. I don't understand why he isn't here."

Francesca looked away, recalling how lovely and sensual Leigh Anne was. "He reconciled with his wife," she began. She wanted to tell Lucy that she hadn't wanted to disturb him, but she did not want to lie to her new friend.

"I know!" Lucy cried, at once angry and upset. "He has always had a fatal weakness for that horrid tramp! I cannot even begin to tell you how I wish she would vanish into thin air! But no, she has come back, to wreck his life once again!"

Francesca drew her knees to her chest and hugged them. "But they are married, and I think his fatal weakness has something to do with love."

Lucy blinked. "You defend their reconciliation?"

Francesca shrugged. The sadness remained, but it wasn't as overwhelming as it had once been. In fact, it was more of a faint ache that she could ignore. "There is no one I admire more than your brother, Lucy. And while I believe he is terribly fond of me, I think a bond remains between him and his wife, a very strong bond, one that will never go away."

"So you blithely support his marriage?" Lucy was aghast.

"I am hardly blithe about your brother. But as my sister Connie pointed out, I have no rights, none, and Leigh Anne has every right, Lucy, to be with him now."

"I thought you loved him."

She smiled and knew it was sad. "I do." Then she closed her eyes and thought, *I did.*

Her heart tightened as Hart intruded upon her thoughts. Then it sped wildly. Surely she was not falling in love with him! That would be more than dangerous—it would be fatal. She might as well crawl out on a shaky tree limb—while a saw was going through it! No, she wasn't in love with Calder Hart. That brief moment of insanity had been due to the trauma of the attack. She was terribly fond of him and terribly attracted—that was all.

"So it is Calder now—instead of Rick?"

She stiffened. Did she dare tell Lucy about Hart's proposal? She hesitated.

"What is it?" Lucy asked quickly.

Francesca shook her head. "Nothing," she said.

"If Calder and Rick were not brothers, I would approve.

Because Rick is married and because Calder isn't what he claims to be—not at all. He deserves love—they both do." She was thoughtful now. "Calder is different. He seems happier than I have ever seen him. He will always be a rude cynic, but he is not half as bad as he once was. I think it is because of you." She smiled a little. "I have never seen him so undone as he has been this evening."

Francesca's toes curled. A thrill chased up and down her spine. "Well, there is certainly an attraction between us, but only a very foolish woman would think it to be anything more." She did not want to recall how he had seemed to care so deeply about her just an hour or so ago. She had been very vulnerable then, still raw from the attack of the City Strangler, and she had not been thinking at all clearly where Calder was concerned, oh no.

"Calder is a hard and difficult man," Lucy mused. "But so was my husband when I first met him." She smiled then, to herself. "Even hard men can soften—given the right woman."

"I am not the right woman for Hart," Francesca said sharply, while a treacherous little voice inside her head answered, *Why ever not?*

Lucy studied her and then shrugged. "Well, I doubt Calder will ever think to settle down and marry, so this conversation is moot. Besides, he knows how you feel about Rick—and how Rick feels about you."

Francesca leaned forward. "What does that mean?"

Lucy started. "I don't understand."

She wet her lips, careful now. "Bragg thinks Hart wishes to strike at him through me, Lucy."

Lucy's eyes widened. "They have been rivals ever since I can remember!" she exclaimed. "When my father brought them home, Rick was eleven, Calder nine. Rick was always trying to look after Calder, and Calder was always defying him. If Rick told him to be inside the house by dark, he would come back an hour later. They first came to blows when Calder was twelve. I remember it because I was right there. Rick was looking after Calder, as always. I don't remember what the argument was about, but Calder turned around and punched him in the nose. Rick was in shock—and Calder was furious. He hit him again—and then Rick struck back. It was horrible—bloody—Father had to break them up. And from that day, they frequently fought that way. Calder hated Rick telling him what he could and could not do—what he should do. He hated the fact that Rick was responsible, while he was always in trouble. But what he really hated was that Rathe was Rick's father and not his."

Francesca's heart turned over with stunning sympathy now. "What he really hated was that Rathe came for Rick, but his own father did not come for him when their mother died," she said softly.

"Yes, I think you are right."

Francesca wondered if that was still the basis for Hart's jealousy of his half brother.

Lucy said, "But they are grown men now. I know them both so well. Calder would never pursue you to hurt Rick. Never! That was a silly, immature game played when they were adolescents. They have both outgrown such rivalry now."

Francesca stiffened with dread. "*What?* Are you saying that Calder has trespassed upon Rick's affections *before*?"

Lucy looked upset to have spoken so baldly. It was a moment before she replied. "Francesca, those games were played when they were boys. It was a long time ago!"

Francesca struggled to sit upright, filled with alarm and dread. "What games?" she cried. "Are you saying that Hart has pursued women Bragg was fond of?"

"I shouldn't have said a thing," Lucy said, her expression turning stubborn. "That was a decade ago, Francesca. Really. They have long since gone their separate ways."

Francesca realized that she was hugging a fluffy pillow now. She couldn't force a smile; she could only stare and recall Bragg's furious insistence that Hart was using her to strike a fatal blow at him. And Bragg believed it.

Francesca refused to believe it, but she was afraid.

And suddenly her mother and father rushed into the

room, Grace and Hart pausing behind them in the doorway. "Francesca!" Julia cried. "Calder says you slipped on some ice and fell from a hansom! Are you all right? Oh, dear! Your face!"

As Julia embraced her, Francesca looked past her mother's shoulder at Calder Hart. His eyes were warm as they met hers, but they held a cautioning note.

Francesca looked away. She was not reassured—she did not know what to think.

SUNDAY, FEBRUARY 23, 1902—10:00 A.M.

Somehow she had overslept. Francesca paused on the threshold of Hart's breakfast room, a room the size of most people's formal dining rooms. She was not surprised to find the long, dark, polished oak table empty, with a single setting left there. As she had come downstairs, the mansion had been extremely quiet—clearly, none of the Braggs slept in, and she suspected everyone was out, the house deserted except for the staff.

Francesca walked over to the sideboard, chasing away all of her memories of the night before. One covered platter contained scrambled eggs and sausage, another pancakes. She helped herself to the former, and despite her resolve, images of Hart, Bragg, and Brendan Farr assailed her mind. Thinking of Farr, she lost her entire appetite.

Was she right about him? Could he possibly be the City Strangler? In the light of day, it seemed absurd.

But last night, when he had looked at her, she had been certain.

"So you are up," Hart said softly, behind her.

She whirled, almost spilling the contents of her plate. "Yes." Faced with Hart now, completely dressed in a black suit, so devastatingly seductive, her heart began to thunder. "Good morning. Thank you for all that you did for me last night, Calder." She avoided his dark eyes.

He studied her. "Something happened last night, didn't it? When I returned with your parents you refused to look me in the eye, and now you are as nervous as a schoolgirl on her first date."

Francesca meant to smile. She grimaced instead and hurried to the table. She had hoped he would be downtown at his offices when she awoke.

Hart followed. "And I don't think this is about Farr."

She sat down and attacked her eggs, moving them about her plate.

"Francesca." He sat down beside her and laid his palm over her hand.

She faced him, trembling. "I could be wrong about Brendan Farr. I realize that."

"You are probably wrong. All of the evidence points to Neville. But I do not want to discuss the case now. Have I offended you?" His black gaze held hers.

And she simply could not look away. She reminded herself that he had been nothing but a good and honorable friend since they had met. Then she reminded herself of his terrible reputation and the rivalry with his brother she herself had witnessed firsthand. She recalled the sheen of tears in his eyes last night. Or had she been seeing what she wanted to see?

This man had openly professed his absolute disinterest in marriage when they had first met as near strangers. Now, months later, he had reversed himself. Why?

Francesca was hardly a fool. She knew she had some charm, but she wasn't half as beautiful as the women she had seen him with.

Still, she knew with her entire heart that he was genuinely fond of her. Of that she was certain.

But a man like Calder Hart didn't marry a woman because he was fond of her. What should she do?

The solution was simple: *Carry on as they were and do nothing.*

She trembled and turned away from him, closing her eyes tightly, stunned at the disappointment surging within her. And a terrible image of her in a wedding dress and veil, walking down the aisle of a church with Calder Hart waiting for her at its end, assailed her then.

"Francesca? You are clearly upset with me. I am beginning to think my sweet sister Lucy has said something to you. She is the worst gossip." He spoke very quietly, and no matter how she tried to tug her hand free of his, he would not let it go.

"I am fine. I am not upset with you. You have been nothing but kind," Francesca said, not looking at him.

"Sir?" Alfred entered the room. "Commissioner Bragg is here and he insists upon seeing Miss Cahill."

Francesca jerked, her heart lurching, facing the doorway. Bragg strode in, past Alfred, looking very grim. No, he was more than grim; he was angry.

Hart shoved back his chair and slowly stood. "I wondered how long it would take you to come," he said mockingly. "I take it your wife sleeps in?"

Bragg did not look away from Francesca, although she saw his eyes darken even more. "Get out, Calder," he said.

"I beg your pardon," Hart said smoothly. "This is my home. If anyone is to leave, it is you."

Bragg whirled.

Francesca sensed he was about to strike his half brother in earnest and she leaped to her feet. "Not now!" she cried nervously.

Hart smiled unpleasantly at Bragg, clearly waiting for a blow and relishing the opportunity to strike back.

"Calder, would you leave us for a moment?" she pleaded, walking over to him and touching his hand.

He started and met her eyes. Then, with real disgust, he nodded and strode out.

He had left both doors wide open. Francesca walked to them and closed them solidly. Then she paused to take a deep breath before facing Rick Bragg.

"You were attacked last night! And I learn of that this morning at headquarters?" He was as disbelieving as he was angry.

She remained standing with the doors at her back, her

hands behind her on the brass handles. She didn't know how to respond, but the one thing that had always been there between them was honesty and truth. "I went to you first," she said, and heard how rough her own tone sounded.

He stared—and his eyes widened with stark comprehension.

"Leigh Anne said you were asleep." Francesca held his gaze. She fought not to tremble. She fought to smile. "I had clearly come at an inopportune time. I left." She squared her shoulders with all the dignity she could muster.

He was turning red.

Francesca raised her hand, sensing an explanation—one she did not want to hear. "I made a huge mistake. I should have never called at such an hour. You are married— rightfully so. Do not explain. Please, do not."

"Damn it!" he cried. "You don't understand—I don't even understand! How badly were you hurt? Newman made light of the attack." He came forward but paused before her and did not move to touch her.

How odd that was. Because once, not so long ago, he would have swept her into his arms, held her, comforted her, loved her. Once upon a time, he had been her safest harbor. But all of that had changed in one fell swoop last evening. Or had it been changing for some time? She opened her mouth to tell him that she was fine, thinking that it was better this way, not to discuss his private life, his intimate affairs.

Yet once, they had been able to share everything. Now his wife stood between them as solidly as a brick wall. It was impossible to speak.

He cursed again, savagely, turned away, ran his hand through his dusty golden hair. It was shaking. Then he faced her, shoving his hands abruptly in the pockets of his wool suit jacket, as if to restrain them there. "Are you all right? You look terrible. Your face is scratched and bruised. Your neck . . ." He could no longer speak, either.

She had to turn away from him. Because in spite of the evening he had shared last night with his wife, it was so evident that he still cared. *When did life become so terribly complex? So incomprehensible?* she wondered.

"Francesca, please."

She finally met his frantic gaze. "I survived. I am a bit bruised and I was frightened, I admit, but it is not as terrible as it looks." She hesitated as he stared, then added, "We lied to Mama. It does no good to tell her I was attacked. She thinks I fell on a patch of ice."

"You had better change your shirtwaist," he said grimly.

Francesca nodded. The collar of her white shirt was too low to hide the bruising on her neck and throat.

"I want you to tell me everything that happened. Do not omit a single detail."

Francesca walked away from the door and realized she was putting more space between them. But the need was instinctive now. Not turning, her hands idle on the dining table, she told him about her conversation with LeFarge and finding Thomas Neville at the Royal. She then revealed that Evan and Thomas were well acquainted and that Melinda Neville had wished to paint Evan's portrait—that he had lied about not knowing her. And when she had walked out of the saloon, she had been attacked just a moment later.

Francesca tensed, remembering being seized without warning from behind. The memory was so vivid and acute that it felt real. As if the assault were happening all over again. "I never even heard him come up behind me, Bragg," she whispered. "He was so swift that I never got a look at him. He dragged me into the alley and shoved me against the wall and . . ." She stopped. "You know the rest."

He cursed. "Hoeltz has confessed nothing, Francesca. And we kept him overnight—so he is *not* our man."

Francesca stared at him. She was sweating, she realized, and a knot of fear curdled her insides and stiffened her spine. "It's not Hoeltz, Bragg."

He started. "Newman said you could not identify the assailant."

She swallowed. "It's Brendan Farr."

Bragg gasped. *"What?"*

"I thought it was Hoeltz. Every clue, every indication, pointed to the jilted lover who loved too much. Obviously he could have been attacking Melinda's studio in a rage for her rejection, and perhaps even Melinda herself, when he was interrupted and seen by Grace Conway. How simple it would be to say that Hoeltz murdered her to hide the deed—and did the same to Miss Holmes. I might even speculate that he struck out at Sarah first because she was a substitute for his mistress—but that act was simply not enough. And then he struck out at me, because I was getting too close to uncovering the truth." She smiled grimly at Bragg. "I have even suspected Thomas Neville of being our strangler, of having a love-hate relationship with his sister, of attacking Sarah and then Melinda just as I have described Hoeltz doing. But it's not Thomas Neville."

"You have just accused my chief of police of being the strangler, Francesca. Do you realize how serious that accusation is?" His eyes remained hard, wide. His expression was extremely grim. "What evidence do you have?"

She had to sit down. She grasped the table now, revolted by every memory of the attack that she had. She swallowed. "Before Farr left this house last night, I overheard him making a comment about Calder. He said, *'Everyone knows Calder Hart enjoys his whores.'* And then he looked at me over his shoulder—and then he left."

Bragg walked over to her. "That is the evidence you have?" He was incredulous.

"I know." She looked down at her hands, realized they were trembling, and hid them on her lap. "In the light of day, it sounds foolish, absurd." She knew she wasn't wrong.

"You must be wrong," Bragg said firmly. "You have no evidence, not a single clue!"

"The only evidence I have is the feeling in my heart," she said, meeting his gaze and aware of how foolish and unprofessional she sounded. She added, "I am terrified of him now."

Bragg seemed an instant away from reaching for her. Francesca sensed that he fought himself, and in the end his self-discipline won. "In the past, you have had excellent instincts," he said slowly.

Francesca nodded. "Yes, I have."

Bragg sat down at the table beside her, finally taking both of her hands in his. "Give me his motivation, Francesca," he said.

She inhaled and realized that she was trembling. "He hates me."

Bragg stared, trying not to appear incredulous, but she saw that he was.

She wet her lips. "He hates me, and all women, I think. The strangler hates all women, Bragg."

"We do not know that Farr hates women. I understand he has a mistress."

"He's not married, is he?"

"He has never been married," Bragg said slowly.

"How odd," Francesca said tersely. Then, "When this investigation started, my brother was the single link between Sarah and Miss Conway."

He searched her gaze with his own eyes. "Are you suggesting that my chief of police wished to strike at you through your brother?" Again, he tried to keep his expression impassive, but Francesca saw the disbelief in his eyes.

"Yes," she whispered. "And Melinda and Miss Holmes got in his way."

A long moment passed. Bragg stared. "So what does he wish to gain? Has he attacked Sarah and Miss Conway merely to cause trouble for your brother? To make him and your family suffer? To see you suffer?"

"Someone leaked the news of my brother's involvement to the press," Francesca said.

"That could have been anyone," Bragg said, omewhat angrily.

"Someone impersonated a police officer, dismissing the guards at the Channing residence."

He stared.

"Our killer is a madman," she added, their gazes locked as if with a padlock and key.

Bragg was grim, understanding. No one need understand the motivation of an insane killer perfectly. Reflectively he said, "He also despises me."

"The strangler has been enjoying himself, Bragg, and not just sexually." She shuddered, but it was true. "He is fearless."

Bragg stood abruptly. "I think you're wrong. But I am not going to dismiss your theory completely. I want this kept extremely quiet," he said. "I will have Peter keep a very discreet eye upon him."

Francesca swallowed. "That is a good idea." She understood that he could not have a police officer shadowing his own chief of police. "I also have an idea," she said hesitantly, her heart accelerating with sudden fear. *Could she really do this?*

He waited, his expression set and severe.

"I think we should set a trap for the strangler, Bragg. He wants me. He failed. He will surely—"

"No!" Bragg exclaimed in horror.

She stood up. "We can meet with Farr and Newman in your office. Bring Neville in, as we know it's not Hoeltz. Start to question him. Then I will make it clear I am dissatisfied with the investigation, that I feel we have missed a clue at Melinda Neville's flat. I will go there, alone. I suspect that Farr, if he is the killer, will come after me there."

"Absolutely not," Bragg ground out.

"But you will be hiding there with your men." Her heart was pounding in fear and dread. "How else will we ever catch him?"

"You shall not be the bait in a trap, Francesca," Bragg said flatly. "And that is that."

Francesca simply stared. Her pulse had become deafening now. She had never been more afraid.

Alarm filled his features. "What are you going to do?" he cried.

"I can set a trap by myself, Bragg—or we can set one together," she said.

# CHAPTER
# TWENTY-TWO

SUNDAY, FEBRUARY 23, 1902—11:30 A.M.

FRANCESCA STIFFENED WHEN THERE was a knock on Bragg's office door. They were in his office at police headquarters. Because it was Sunday, the five-story brownstone was eerily quiet—no typewriters sounded, nor were any telegraphs transmitting or telephones ringing. Even Mulberry Street was sleepy on the Sabbath day—when they had arrived earlier there had been one single soul in sight: a beggar asleep on the police building's front stoop. Now Francesca reminded herself to remain calm and composed as Bragg gave her a reassuring smile before calling out for Brendan Farr to enter.

The chief of police walked in. He was a big man with broad shoulders, and Francesca had to work hard to keep her breathing even when he saw her and halted. If he was displeased, she could not tell. His expression was impossible to read. He did not even blink. He was solidly built. He had, she saw now, large hands. Her heart drummed wildly in her chest, making her feel faint and ill.

God, was she the mad one to think that one of Gotham's finest was the City Strangler? Her pulse continued to drum thickly, sickly.

"Commissioner." Farr nodded. He smiled politely at Francesca. "Do you need to see me?"

"I should have been apprised of Miss Cahill's attack last night," Bragg said calmly, walking up to the other man. Rick Bragg was six feet tall, broad-shouldered, lean yet muscular. Next to Farr, he seemed short and slender. Francesca guessed that Farr topped him by a good four inches. Her heart beat even faster now. It was hard to breathe. She felt trapped. She wanted to escape the room. She needed air—it was as if she might actually choke.

*Could she really go through with this?* Could she bait the trap herself? Extremely reluctant, Bragg had gone along with her plan, but only as she had threatened to do so on her own, with only Joel for protection, if he did not. Now she knew she would have never been able to bait the trap without Bragg's help. Farr terrified her.

"I'm sorry," Farr said, seeming genuinely contrite. "It was late, Saturday night. I thought we had the situation under control. I decided not to disturb you, as your wife had just returned to the city." He gave Francesca an impersonal glance. His eyes, she saw, were cold. Or was she imagining it?

"Next time anything similar ever occurs, you disturb me, no matter the time of day or night, even if it is Christmas Eve. Newman is bringing Neville back. He should be here at any moment."

Farr's expression was hard to read. "It was too late last night to see if he had an alibi regarding the attack upon Miss Cahill. I was going to go down to the Royal myself tonight to see what I can learn."

"Good," Bragg said. "Meanwhile, we need to thoroughly interrogate Neville now."

"You want to leave that to me?" Farr asked.

"I'd be happy to," Bragg replied.

Francesca watched the two men. Both would be unbeatable poker players, she thought. It was simply impossible to guess what either man might be thinking.

Newman walked in, a bleary-eyed Thomas Neville with him. In fact, Neville was so disheveled that it appeared he had slept in his suit and tie.

"Do sit down," Bragg said, pulling a stiff wood chair forward and before his desk.

Neville glared. "I sleep late on Sundays, Commissioner. I resent being dragged out of bed by your leatherheads on a Sunday morning."

"We only wish to confirm your whereabouts last evening," Bragg said. "Do sit." It was an order.

Neville dropped down in the uncomfortable armless chair and then sighed. He glanced at Francesca. "I already know that you have not found my sister," he said.

"How is that?" Bragg asked.

"I asked Inspector Newman," was Neville's droll reply.

A silence fell. Francesca stared at Neville, but stare as she might, she could not get a violent physical reaction from him as she did from Farr. Her senses refused to warn her against him, however odd he might be.

Farr said, "I'd like to ask you some questions, Mr. Neville."

"Feel free." Neville sighed again. "But could I possibly have a cup of coffee?"

Before Farr could begin, Francesca interrupted. "I am going to go and leave the two of you to police affairs," she said to the chief and Bragg. Her smile felt sickly. She felt herself flush. "Bragg?" She gestured at the door.

He walked with her the few steps to it, where they paused, well within earshot of Farr and Neville. "We are missing something, Bragg," Francesca said quietly, but not too quietly to be overheard. "I can feel it. I am going to go back to Miss Neville's apartment and see what I can find."

Bragg sighed. "I think you're wrong, but go ahead. I would join you, but I am afraid I have a luncheon to attend." His gaze held hers, the light there dark with concern.

"I'll be fine." Francesca smiled at him, but her heart was

racing with alarming speed. She didn't dare look back at
Brendan Farr. Instead, she gave Bragg one last look and
hurried from the room.

Her fear made her feel faint.


Francesca waited.

No police officer had been outside Melinda Neville's flat
and Francesca had been given the key before leaving police
headquarters. Bragg had hidden a half a dozen roundsmen
in Louis Bennett's flat, just across the hall. By now, Bragg
himself would be somewhere outside the brownstone, with
more men, awaiting her signal from the window—or her
scream. Francesca's cheeks were aflame. She had been waiting in Melinda Neville's apartment for an hour. By now,
Farr would have finished his interrogation of Thomas Neville. If her presumptions were right, he would be appearing
at any time. She was so frightened that her breathing was
fast and shallow.

Francesca shifted restlessly. She was sitting on the sofa
in the salon, the chalk outline of Grace Conway's body not
far from her feet. It was a very graphic reminder of what
the killer could—and meant to—do. The room was lost in
shadows in spite of the small table lamp she had turned on;
she had also turned on a light in the bedroom, leaving that
door open. It was time, she thought with rising panic, to
pretend to be searching the flat for another clue.

Francesca got up, trying to compose her breathing and
failing. It was hard not to glance at the front door, which
she had closed but left unlocked, the better to abet the strangler's entry into the apartment—and her trap.

But she had to walk around and give the strangler a
chance to enter the apartment and steal up on her. And just
as Francesca was about to force herself to walk into the
bedroom, a movement behind her made her whirl.

A mouse dashed across the wood floors, disappearing
beneath the sofa.

She laughed in relief, turned, and screamed.

Thomas Neville stood in the bedroom doorway, staring down at her.

Her dazed mind swung into action. *Neville was the one.* Francesca whirled, but he seized her from behind, and just as she opened her mouth to scream, she realized that he was not wearing a stocking over his face. She turned— and saw that he was crying.

But silently. Tears were streaming down his face.

"She's dead, isn't she? That's why no one can find her. Is she dead?" he cried, dropping his hand.

Francesca's heart surged wildly in her chest. She backed away carefully, never removing her eyes from him. "I think so. I am sorry."

Neville walked over to the sofa and collapsed there, weeping.

Francesca stared. Thomas Neville was not their killer. She walked over to him, then sat down beside him. "You didn't do it, did you?"

He sobbed into his hands. "No. I loved her. She didn't love me, but I loved her. She was the mother I never had." He sobbed more loudly, then said, "I lied. I lied to you and the police, Miss Cahill. She loved Hoeltz. And he loved her. God, I hate him!"

Francesca patted his back, pitying him. She got up and went to the window. She pulled the draperies wide, pushed open the window, and was blasted with icy air. She waved, but she was grim, because her clever idea of trapping the killer had failed.

Neville sprawled on the sofa now, no longer crying but despondent. Francesca whispered, "I am so sorry. We will find her killer, Mr. Neville."

He looked at her. "I admire you, Miss Cahill. Melinda was like you, you know. Brave and determined, and so very intelligent." His face crumbled. "She didn't love me. Not at all. I'm her *brother*!" he cried.

"I'm sure she loved you," Francesca said gently.

He looked at her sadly, clearly not at all persuaded by her words.

Bragg walked into the room with Newman and Hickey. He took one look at the scenario in front of him and said, "So we've cleared Neville."

"Yes, we have," Francesca said. She rubbed her temples. If the killer was Farr, why hadn't he taken the bait? Either he was too clever or the killer wasn't Farr, and their only other suspect was Andrew LeFarge.

*Just as the only other targeted victim was Sarah Channing. She, like Francesca, had survived the City Strangler's attack.*

"Bragg!" Francesca cried. "Sarah—we must get to Sarah—before the strangler strikes again!"

Their gazes met. His eyes widened with comprehension, and they turned and rushed out of Melinda Neville's flat.

Bragg pounded on the door. It was opened immediately by a servant. Francesca cried, "Where is Sarah?"

Taken aback, the doorman blinked and said, "I believe she has gone out."

Francesca stared at Bragg, dismayed. He seemed equally grim. He faced the doorman. "Where has she gone?"

"I have no idea, sir."

Francesca began to shake. Sarah had gone out, and, if Francesca's theory was right, was making herself extremely vulnerable to another attack.

"Commissioner! Miss Cahill! I thought I had heard the door." Abigail Channing beamed, coming into the front hall.

"I am afraid we are here on police business," Bragg said. "We must locate Sarah, Mrs. Channing. Do you have any idea where she is?"

Mrs. Channing started. "She said something about a second chance, and then she simply raced out. You see, she received a note this morning."

Francesca's heart lurched. *Sarah was walking into a trap.* "Please, Mrs. Channing, you have to think! We have to know where Sarah went—and whom she was meeting."

Mrs. Channing was dismayed. "I have no idea. She was

so excited and in such a rush. But wait! Perhaps we can find that note—unless she took it with her."

Five minutes later Sarah Channing's pretty pink-and-white bedroom was being turned upside down, with Francesca growing more frightened by the moment. There was nothing on the secretaire or the bureau, nothing in the dressing room. "Let's try her studio," she whispered dryly.

"Oh! You know, she did leave with one of her paintings in hand. Wrapped in brown parcel paper," Mrs. Channing said.

For one moment Francesca stared, and the comprehension seized her. *A painting, a note, a second chance...* "Hoeltz!"

The front door of the brownstone building where Hoeltz had his gallery was unlocked. Confused, Sarah pushed it open, as her repetitive use of the door knocker had not produced any results. No lights were on in the hall or stairwell, and as there was only one window by the front door, it was exceedingly dark inside. Sarah hesitated, alarmed.

But there was no reason for alarm, she told herself. This was the most amazing opportunity, and she could only conclude that Hoeltz had glimpsed her at the exhibition Friday night and had decided to give her work another chance. Sarah picked up her wrapped canvas, and as it was large she needed to carry it with both hands. Her coach and driver waited on the street.

She entered, used her knee to close the heavy front door, and, when it clicked closed, grew more nervous. A terrible memory of the attack Friday night overcame her. She found it hard to breathe.

Oddly, she thought about Rourke's timely rescue, and his handsome face seemed to calm her shattered nerves a bit. She hadn't ever thanked him. She knew she was being disgracefully rude in not doing so, but for some reason, she simply could not be herself around that man. *He* set her on edge.

She sighed and smiled ruefully. It was time to admit the truth. He was fascinatingly handsome, she had never met a man like him before, and that was why his mere presence turned her into a tart shrew. Thank God he would be returning to Philadelphia next week.

She started up the stairs.

By the time she reached the second floor landing, she was breathless. To her surprise, the door to the art gallery was also ajar. Warnings went off inside her mind, as explosive and sudden as fireworks. Was something wrong? "Mr. Hoeltz?" she called out, pausing on the threshold of the first exhibition room.

There was no answer. Sarah laid her painting down carefully, leaning it against the wall. "Mr. Hoeltz?" she called out again, more nervously now.

There was no answer. The huge room with its dozens of paintings and its several sculptures seemed empty.

But Sarah knew she was not alone.

In that instant, she felt eyes upon her, and she froze.

She tried to tell herself that it was her imagination, while her brain began screaming at her that she must run, leave, now. Her heart beat with such power and speed that her chest ached. Sweat began to gather on her brow, in her armpits, between her breasts. But surely the attack Friday night had made her paranoid, when nothing was amiss.

Sarah scanned the room. Other than two very large busts on solid three-foot pedestals, there was nowhere to hide. She was alone. But that in itself made no sense. Where was Mr. Hoeltz?

Her gaze moved back to each pedestal, but only a child could hide behind one.

The eyes remained, boring holes into her, but were they on her back?

Sarah turned quickly, but no one stood behind her in the hall.

She turned as quickly, but no one faced her, either.

Then she saw the hand.

Lying on the floor, peeping out from the next room.

Sarah gasped, realizing now where Hoeltz was—in the next room, unconscious, hurt, or dead. Shaking like a leaf, she had begun to back away when she smacked into a hard, big body.

*It was her worst nightmare come true.*

"Hello, Sarah," a terribly rough and familiar rasping voice said.

It was a voice she would never forget: the voice of her assailant—the voice of the man who had tried to kill her.

Sarah screamed.

The hansom had just halted in front of the brownstone housing Hoeltz's gallery. Bragg was about to pay the fare when a scream filled the morning.

Francesca and Bragg leaped outside, the cabbie shouting at them, demanding his money. As they raced across the sidewalk, Francesca fumbled in her purse for her gun. From the corner of her eye she saw that Bragg had already withdrawn his own revolver.

The front door of the building was locked.

"Damn it!" Francesca shouted, sweating madly now.

Bragg didn't hesitate. With his elbow, he bashed in the glass window next to the door. "Wait here," he said, using his arm to sweep the window clean of glass shards.

As if she would stay behind. Francesca waited for him to climb through; then she did the same. She lifted her skirts and ran up the stairs on his heels.

"Damn it, I don't want you in here!" he shouted, not looking back.

She didn't answer, using all of her breath to run. They burst into the front room of the gallery and saw a huge man with a stocking over his head strangling Sarah Channing.

She wasn't against the wall. She was facing them, and her face was turning blue.

"Release her!" Bragg shouted, aiming the gun.

The strangler saw him and pulled Sarah in front of him,

using her as a shield now, no longer strangling her to death. She began to cough and choke, but the blue hue faded from her face, leaving it starkly white instead. The killer did not answer for the obvious reason of not wanting to give his identity away.

He started backing up, with Sarah in his arms.

"Release her," Bragg commanded. "It's over. You will not get away. My men have surrounded the building."

That, Francesca knew, was a lie. And Brendan Farr was clever enough to know it, too.

The killer seemed to smile at them as he dragged Sarah around the corner and into the next exhibit hall.

Francesca and Bragg raced after him. When they reached the threshold there, they paused, exchanging glances, pressing against the wall. "Stay here. Don't move," Bragg said.

She had no intention of staying safely behind the wall while a killer had her friend in his power.

Bragg looked around the corner, as did Francesca.

The strangler had Sarah in one arm, but he had already pushed open the window at the exhibition hall's far end. An iron fire escape was there. Francesca suddenly glanced down and gasped. Bertrand Hoeltz lay at their feet, dead. His head had been blown away, a revolver lay in his hand, and a note was on the floor beside him. It quickly crossed her mind that the strangler had set up Hoeltz to take the fall for him.

The strangler began pushing Sarah out onto the fire escape.

"He's going to take her with him," Francesca shouted.

Bragg aimed his gun. "No, he's not," he said grimly, and he fired.

Francesca had no idea how good a marksman Bragg was, and when the strangler jerked, apparently hit in the shoulder, she cried out in relief. But he shoved Sarah face-first onto the iron stairs, then turned, withdrawing a gun, and he fired back at them.

Acting purely upon reflex, Francesca dived to the floor.

"Get down!" Bragg shouted simultaneously. He knelt and fired back, around the wall and into the other hall.

Francesca scrambled to her knees and crept up to the corner.

"Get back!" Bragg shouted, sweat pouring down his face. But Francesca dared to peek, and she saw the killer standing there, still and erect, holding his gun, aiming it at them. Then blood blossomed on his chest and he slowly keeled over, finally crumbling to the floor.

Francesca began to rise.

Bragg pushed her down. "Stay down!" he hissed.

A gunshot sounded, striking the edge of the wall where Francesca and Bragg huddled. Francesca ducked, holding her head, and heard Bragg grunt beside her as an odd thick *plop* sounded. She turned, afraid he had been hit, but she saw nothing—there was no blood on his tan greatcoat. "Stay back," he said tersely, his golden eyes wide with determination, his face drawn into savage lines.

"Don't do anything foolish," she whispered. "I don't want to bury a hero."

He grunted and she realized he had been shot and that he was in pain. Very carefully, aiming his gun, he started slowly forward toward the prone killer now.

The strangler lay on his back. He did not move. But his gun rested loosely in his hand.

"It's a trap," Francesca gasped, terrified that Bragg would be shot again—this time fatally.

And just as she spoke the killer kicked at Bragg, causing him to lose his balance and go down in a heap. Bragg's revolver skidded across the floor. The killer got to his knees, raising his gun as Francesca screamed in warning. Bragg rolled over, kicking out and tripping the other man, who fell. And suddenly both men were in each other's grip, wrestling back and forth on the floor. Francesca quickly realized that the strangler had not released his gun—and that he and Bragg were fighting over it.

Francesca ran forward. Bragg had the killer's wrist and the gun was aimed at the ceiling—it went off. Francesca did not hesitate. She seized Bragg's revolver and tried to avoid being tripped by the flailing men. Bragg had been flipped onto his back, and now, his coat open, she saw the blossoming blood on his chest.

She jammed the barrel of the gun hard in the back of the strangler's head.

"Freeze!" she shouted. "Freeze, Farr, or I will kill you!" And she meant it, too.

He froze.

But Bragg had taken matters into his own hands. He jammed his knee into the other man's groin, and as the strangler collapsed, Bragg got out from under him and up to his feet. Instantly he knelt on the killer's back, one knee grinding into his kidney, jerked the man's wrists behind him, extracted handcuffs from his belt, and snapped them on. Then he tossed the killer's arms down, looking up at Francesca. "Thanks." Sweat was pouring down his face. Blood was pouring down his white shirt.

Fear blinded her now. "You're hurt!"

"It's not as bad as it must look." As he rose, he pulled the stocking from the man's head and turned his face to one side.

Francesca gasped.

It wasn't Brendan Farr.

It was Thomas Neville.

# CHAPTER
# TWENTY-THREE

SHE HAD BEEN SO cleverly duped at the eleventh hour. Francesca simply stared, recalling how Neville had been weeping on his sister's sofa not too long ago and how she had tried to comfort him.

"So it was you after all," Bragg said, pulling Neville to his feet. He was bleeding profusely from a third wound in his chest.

But Neville's eyes burned now, and hatred was etched all over his face—he didn't seem to know that he had been shot three times. "She loved *him*! She hated *me*! I was waiting and waiting for her to return from Paris, and when she does, it was to be with Hoeltz! Mellie was a good girl until she met him. Don't you see?" His tone turned pleading, and tears filled his eyes.

Francesca's stomach heaved precariously. But Neville seemed to be in a talkative mood, and she seized the opportunity. "There is only one thing I truly do not understand. Why did you vandalize Sarah Channing's studio?"

His eyes turned black. He staggered, but Bragg held him up. "Mellie had promised me supper—yet she did not show up. I went to the Royal, and the moment I saw your brother, I recalled the fact that he despised his fiancée and that she was also an artist. As the night progressed, I became intrigued with the idea of meeting Miss Channing. Of meeting her and punishing her for all that she had done to your brother. And the more I thought about it, the angrier I became. I didn't plan to vandalize her studio, Miss Cahill. But when I found an open window and let myself in, when I saw her portraits, her portraits of *whores,* it just seemed so right. She, too, was clearly a whore! Mellie was a good girl until she met Hoeltz! She was a decent woman, a lady! He turned her into a whore! He lured her away from me, from our genteel life, from the family that we were, into his world, a world of art and sex. He took Mellie away from me." He spat blood at her feet.

"Wreaking havoc upon Sarah Channing wasn't enough, was it?" Francesca asked quietly, but with some worry now. This man needed a doctor, but then, so did Bragg. His shirt, beneath his sack jacket and coat, was covered with blood. She did not know how much was his and how much belonged to Thomas Neville.

Neville stared, and for a moment she thought he would not answer—or that he could not. "No, it wasn't enough," he finally said, suddenly subdued. He seemed to gasp then in pain and he almost collapsed, except for Bragg. "I tasted what revenge could do. I *yearned* for more. I *yearned* to do to Mellie what I did to Miss Channing." His eyes glittered with lust and insanity.

"So you went back to Mellie's flat," Francesca said flatly. "You broke in. She caught you in the act. You killed her—and Miss Conway happened by. Then you killed Miss Conway, as she was a witness, and Miss Holmes, too. And I assume you went back to murder Sarah, as you had acquired quite a lust for murder, Mr. Neville."

"How clever you are," he said, smiling now, but the expression was twisted with pain. "And yes, I did enjoy killing

those whores—and every single woman deserved to die! I
went back to get Sarah because she deserved to die, too.
But you are wrong about one thing. I did not kill Mellie. I
would *never* kill her. I *love* her. How could you think for a
moment that I would kill her?" he cried.

Francesca exchanged a startled glance with Bragg. Then
she saw Sarah climbing back inside through the window
from the fire escape. She was as white as a sheet, her brown
eyes huge in her small face. "Francesca? Are you all right?"
she cried.

Francesca ran to Sarah, putting her arm around her. "Are
you all right?" she demanded in return.

Sarah nodded, but she was trembling. "Mr. Hoeltz is
dead. He murdered Hoeltz," she gasped.

"Did you see it?" Bragg asked sharply.

Sarah shook her head negatively. "No, I did not. He was
lying there dead when I arrived." She shivered violently.

"He ruined my sister," Neville said furiously. But he was
beginning to sway precariously upon his feet from loss of
blood. "He got what he deserved! They all did! Only you,
Miss Cahill, escaped your just deserts."

Bragg kicked him in the knee. Francesca was stunned as
Neville collapsed in a heap, his face turning white, gasping
for breath. Bragg crouched over him. "I intend to see to it
that you get the electric chair," he said, low. "You are finished, Neville. Finished."

Everyone stared at Thomas Neville, who lay bleeding and
handcuffed on the floor. Francesca was aghast.

"She'll get hers. Whores always do," he spat. Blood was
in his spittle.

"Don't!" Francesca cried, afraid Bragg would strike him
again. His brutality stunned her—but she had seen it once
before, on another case, when he had almost killed a thug
named Gordino. But then, the life of a small boy had been
at stake.

She rushed over to them both. "Tell me one thing," she
asked, kneeling over Neville, who seemed close to passing
out. "How did you think to frame Hoeltz for it all?"

"I made him write a confession and a suicide note," Neville choked. He was choking on his own blood. He was dying.

"But he was in jail when I was attacked," Francesca said.

Neville met her gaze. ". . . didn't. . . . know."

Francesca straightened. "He needs medical attention."

Bragg simply looked at her.

"He's dying!" she cried.

"Do you care?" he asked.

"Where is Melinda?" Francesca whispered to Neville, not moving any closer, and shocked at Bragg's hard and cruel response.

Neville's gaze shuttered.

"Where is Melinda?!" Francesca cried.

Bragg dragged him to his knees by his coat collar. "Is she alive? Where is she, you sonuvabitch!"

"In the basement," he gasped. "I've been keeping her in the basement here, all this time, right under Hoeltz's nose."

Francesca did not wait to hear any more. She ran across the room and through the first exhibition hall. As she left the gallery, she saw Inspector Newman and Brendan Farr coming up the stairs. Her gaze locked with Farr's. His gaze was ice-cold.

"It's Neville. He's in cuffs, but he is dying," she said. "He needs a doctor."

She rushed past the two men and down to the basement level. The door there was padlocked. She rattled it wildly. "Melinda? Miss Neville? Can you hear me? Are you in there?"

"Yes! Oh, God, help me! I am a prisoner here!" the other woman cried frantically.

Suddenly Bragg was at her side. "Stand back," he said.

She stepped aside instantly and he jammed his body shoulder-first into the door. The door snapped open, the chain of the padlock instantly breaking. Francesca rushed past him and in the shadows of the cellar saw the small dark-haired woman tied to a chair.

Melinda began to cry.

Francesca rushed to her and held her while Bragg untied her bonds.

SUNDAY, FEBRUARY 23, 1902—6:00 P.M.

Francesca walked into Bragg's office, followed by Bragg. She hung her coat on a wall peg, tossed her gloves on his desk, and turned anxiously to study him. He was hanging up his own tan greatcoat.

"Let me do that!" she cried, rushing to him.

He smiled weakly—pained—at her. "Thank you," he said hoarsely.

She took his coat and hung it up. He had finally been treated at the St. Francis Hospital, and now his right arm was in a sling, his shoulder bandaged beneath his bloody shirt. The bullet had lodged itself in a fleshy area just beneath his collarbone, and it had taken almost an hour to remove it and sew the wound up. Bragg looked terrible and not simply exhausted. His face remained garishly white, he had stubble of growth on his jaw, and deep lines of pain were etched about his mouth and eyes. The wound might not have been a life-threatening one, but the procedure had been a surgical one, he had lost some blood, and he had been advised to go home and rest for several days to prevent the onset of infection.

Neville had also gone to St. Francis, but he had died shortly after arriving there.

Francesca took Bragg's arm. "You should go home. Why don't I drop you off in a cab?"

He shook his head. "I want to make a preliminary report while today's incident remains fresh in my mind."

"Oh, Rick. It can wait," she said, wanting nothing more than to see him home and resting in his bed.

He smiled a little at her, went to his desk, opened a drawer, and produced a bottle of Scotch whiskey and a glass. He poured, his hand unsteady. "Thank God Melinda Neville is alive. Traumatized, but alive."

Francesca wished he would offer her a scotch. "I feel so

terribly for her," she said. Melinda had broken down in grief upon learning of Hoeltz's murder. Francesca had tried to comfort her the best that she could, but it had been impossible. A police officer had taken Melinda to a friend's after she had given her statement. Apparently, other than to terrorize her, her brother had not harmed her. Melinda, however, was convinced that he had ultimately intended to murder her.

Bragg sank down into his chair, looking on the verge of collapse.

Francesca quickly moved behind his desk, beside him. "A report can wait," she said urgently. "You are in pain! You lost blood! They had trouble finding the bullet; you were in surgery for almost an hour! Please, Rick."

He stared up at her. "Why are you calling me Rick now?"

She hesitated. "Because we have both made our choices."

He was silent, staring.

His door flew open. Francesca was expecting an officer, but Leigh Anne rushed in, her face devoid of all color, her eyes wide with fear. "A newsman told me! Rick, are you all right?"

He straightened, his eyes on his wife. "I am fine."

Francesca's heart turned over, hard, with sudden anguish. As Leigh Anne rushed over to Bragg, apparently stunned by his bloody shirt, Francesca stepped away from him. She could not look away from the domestic scene she was witnessing.

"You are coming home this instant!" Leigh Anne exclaimed in a burst of anger.

"I have work to do." But he did not look away from her.

"You always have work to do! You can do it in the morning! You're hurt and you're coming home." She was so upset that two bright spots of pink colored her cheeks—and tears welled in her eyes.

Francesca sighed, surprised by how sad she suddenly felt and reminding herself that this was as it should be. Rick Bragg needed to give his wife another chance. That much was so very clear. A real chance. A chance to win his heart one more time.

"Why didn't you send for me when you were on the way to the hospital?" Leigh Anne suddenly cried. "I'm your wife! I should have been at your side!"

"You haven't been at my side for four years," Bragg said dryly.

Francesca turned away just as Peter appeared in the doorway. She smiled at the big Swede. "I think Bragg might need some help getting home," she said softly.

Peter nodded.

"Peter! Help Rick with his coat. He is going home and that is that," Leigh Anne said, and finally she looked at Francesca.

Francesca could not smile. "The wound was not a serious one," she said. "He will be fine in a few days."

Leigh Anne stared at her, and then, as Peter retrieved Bragg's coat as Bragg gulped down his scotch, she started toward Francesca. Francesca tensed. Leigh Anne faced her grimly. "Thank you for all that you did today on my husband's behalf," she said, her emerald green gaze holding Francesca's. It did not waver. It was earnest.

Francesca somehow twisted her lips into a smile. "He is my friend," she said.

Leigh Anne studied her closely. "I am beginning to see that."

Francesca could not speak.

Leigh Anne turned and raced back to Bragg, who was now on his feet, his coat draped around his shoulders, and instructing Peter to take several files from his desk. She did not look pleased to see that he was taking his work home. "God, we have to get that bloody shirt off of you!" she cried.

"It looks worse than it is, really," Bragg said. His gaze moved past his wife and to Francesca. His regard was also sad, and it was searching.

Francesca turned away and walked out.

MONDAY, FEBRUARY 24, 1902—9:00 A.M.

"Thank you, Ellie," Francesca said as the beaming woman placed a tray of hot chocolate and still-steaming pastries on the table before the window.

"My pleasure, madam," Ellie said.

"Please, 'Miss Cahill' is fine," Francesca returned, still in a simple cotton nightgown and a pretty floral wrapper. Bette had finished drawing open every single drapery in the room, and now the young maid began fussing over the table Ellie had just set, placing the single rose in its bud vase first in the center, then to the side.

"Thank you, Bette," Francesca said, clasping her shoulder. "You needn't fuss so."

Bette said, "She forgot your orange juice, Miss Cahill. I will bring it right away!" She glared at Ellie and rushed from the room.

Ellie's happy face fell. She looked aghast.

Francesca went to her. "Actually, I do not need any juice today. You have done a wonderful job, Ellie. One would think you had been employed in this house your entire adult life."

"Really?" Ellie was hopeful, her eyes uncertain but shining.

Francesca nodded and escorted Ellie out. Then she leaned against her bedroom door, extremely thoughtful.

She had not slept at all last night.

Last night, with the Case of the City Strangler solved, she had spent every restless moment thinking the unthinkable, fighting the urge to do the unthinkable.

She quickly walked over to the breakfast table so prettily set up in her bedroom and sat down, sipping her hot chocolate and staring out across the white, frozen lawns that swept away to Fifth Avenue. The snow was beginning to melt. The avenue had become slushy, ice turning to mud and water, and the passing carriages and coaches sent up sprays of slush. *What if?*

She was so scared. Hart's handsome image with his sardonic eyes haunted her mind. Other images followed, a tormenting and teasing kaleidoscope—Hart and Daisy, Hart in his office, Hart on his knees, cradling her face in his hands.

She set her cup down and hugged herself. She was fatally attracted to him; there was no more denying that. Call her a fool then, as were hundreds of other women, but she had spent most of last night recalling his taste, his touch, and wishing desperately to be in his arms. How she had wanted to unburden herself and tell him all that had happened and how they had solved the case. And they were friends. They were good friends, even if they did not have very much in common.

Friendship and passion were not the worst basis for a marriage.

She shivered, amazed that she had been contemplating doing what she had promised herself she would never do with any man.

She reminded herself that she did not love him.

The man she loved—the man she would always love—belonged to another woman, and rightfully so. In fact, Francesca was certain now that Leigh Anne really loved Rick Bragg. Her fear for him yesterday had proven that. And Francesca so wanted him to be happy, and she wondered if, given time, he and Leigh Anne might not find happiness together. He deserved happiness. No one deserved it more. And the more Francesca thought about it, the more she felt that she must intrude and encourage him to give his wife a second chance at his love.

But for him to have that chance at genuine happiness, she must stay far away from him. As sad as that thought was, she knew too much affection remained between them, and it would hurt his chances for a real reconciliation. They would remain friends, but even their platonic relationship had already changed. After all, she was a woman and he was a man, and now Leigh Anne had turned a relationship of two into a far more complicated affair.

If she married Hart, it would be so much easier to attain

a more casual and less threatening friendship with Bragg.

Her cheeks heated. So did every inch of her body. Hoping to disengage oneself from a former love interest was a terrible reason to marry.

But Connie was right. Hart would, eventually, marry. Francesca didn't even have to think about it to know that she would be terribly jealous and furious when he did.

*Would it really be so bad to become Hart's wife?*

Hart wasn't a reformer, he did not give a whit about politics, and Francesca knew all of his donations went to museums and libraries. She felt quite confident that he would donate as she asked him to, and while there was nothing wrong with charities involving the arts, she felt strongly that the poor should be taken care of first. Still, there would be no political debates, no political fund-raisers, and he would never share her burning desire to change the world.

Perhaps it was a terrible match, she mused, her heart sinking. Because it was a match that would be made for a lifetime.

And what about the day that must eventually come, when his eye wandered to another younger, prettier woman? If they had the bonds of love there between them, that day would not be threatening. Without those bonds, Francesca knew she would be terribly hurt by any disloyalty or worse on his part.

Of course, she did not have to make a decision now or at any time in the near future.

But she was trembling with fear and anticipation, with trepidation and excitement.

"Fran? Thank God you are up!" Connie cried, racing into the room.

Francesca had been reaching for her hot chocolate, which she almost spilled. "Con? What a wonderful surprise!" She could hardly believe her sister was up and fully dressed and it was only nine in the morning. Not only that; she was wreathed in smiles. In fact, she was flushed, her eyes sparkling—and Francesca instantly became suspicious.

Connie closed the bedroom door and grinned. "I thought you should be the first to know. Neil and I are taking a holiday."

Francesca prayed that what she was thinking was true. "What?"

Connie laughed, the sound happy. "We have decided to go up to Newport for a long weekend. But we shall go to Paris in the spring."

Francesca began to smile. "Connie, it's frigidly cold out. No one goes to Newport in the winter."

"We are. We shall bring fur throws and knit socks and our skis and we will drink hot cider and roast marshmallows and do other things." She laughed.

"You have reconciled!" Francesca cried, rushing to her.

Connie nodded and they embraced, clinging and rocking. "I am so in love," she whispered when they drew apart.

Francesca put her arm around her. "I can see that. I am so happy for you. Connie, Neil adores you. He always has. He always will."

"I think so, too." She was beaming. "Anyway, we will leave town on Wednesday. Can you help me shop? I think I need some wool breeches and some very heavy sweaters."

Francesca raised her eyebrows at her. "That's all?"

Connie turned a delicate shade of pink. "Well, I was also thinking of something French and lacy and sheer."

"I will definitely help you shop," Francesca laughed.

When he awoke, he was surprised to find himself in a nightshirt in his bed, his entire right shoulder and side, almost down to his waist, throbbing in pain. The curtains were slightly parted and he could see that it was late in the day. And as he struggled to sit up, the events of the previous day flashed through his mind. He had been shot, but the City Strangler was dead and the case was finally officially closed.

Leigh Anne suddenly came into the room, an angelic vision in a rose gown, impossibly gorgeous, somehow appearing innocent and demure. He stiffened. She was carrying a tray with a covered bowl, and the savory aroma of chicken soup drifted to him. She smiled at him. "You're finally awake."

He panted with the effort of sitting, every small movement burning his shoulder, his arm. *What new act was this?* "What time is it? Why didn't you wake me!" He was dismayed; he had work to do—more than a single man's share—for it was Monday.

Her smile faded as she set the tray down on the small nightstand by his bed. "Rick, it's almost four o'clock. Finney wanted you kept on laudanum for the pain. He wanted you to rest. I want you to rest."

He turned to stare at her, angry and incredulous, both at once. "I have work to do," he gritted. "How dare you interfere with my duties?"

She stiffened. "That is not fair."

"Very little in life is fair," he snapped, wishing she might disappear from his room, his home, his life. She thought to coddle and care for him now? It was a bit late. Four years too late, in fact. "I am going to work," he said, managing to stand. He gritted against the stabbing pain in his shoulder and upper chest. It felt like a knife, and a hundred times worse than yesterday. Then, he supposed, he had been in shock and oblivious to the extent of his wound.

"No," she said firmly. "You are not going to the office today."

He had misheard. He turned and faced her. "Excuse me?"

"You are staying in bed," she said firmly but breathlessly, her eyes wide and locked with his. She appeared vulnerable now. He hoped she was frightened of him—as she well should be. For he felt like bodily ejecting her from his room.

"You dare to tell me what to do?" he asked very softly—dangerously.

She nodded. "Yes, I do. Finney says you are to stay home and in bed for three days—at least."

"Like hell," he snarled.

"You're hurt!" she cried.

"Not that hurt. I have work to do. Or have you forgotten

the extent of my responsibilities?" He stalked past her, flinging open the armoire.

She was silent, behind him.

He removed a pressed shirt, a tie. He turned.

Her eyes spat fire. "I had forgotten. Nothing has changed. You wake up—and go to work. You come home at some ungodly hour—work some more—and go to bed. Nothing has changed."

"That's right," he said, pleased with her assessment. "You don't have to be here, remember? It was your idea, not mine. You can agree to a divorce this very instant—and not be tortured by my schedule."

She placed her small fists on her tiny waist. Her bosom heaved, indicating her own distress and temper. "We have an agreement. We have signed contracts. Six months together as man and wife, Rick. I am not leaving you."

"Well, that's certainly refreshing, considering that is what you are best at." He was suddenly overcome with the pain of the discovery he had made four years ago, that his wife had left him. In that instant, the precise moment, which had once haunted him, returned to assail him full force. He had come home late, as usual, and found his house empty of all her things, a single note left behind—the tattered remnant of their love and their marriage. The letter, four years ago, had read:

Dear Rick,

I have decided to take a holiday in France. I meant to discuss it with you, but every time I tried to talk to you, you were either going out the door, involved in work, or falling in exhaustion into bed. I simply cannot live like this anymore. As we never see one another anyway, what difference does it make if I take an extended holiday? Maybe we both need this time apart. I certainly do.

By the time you receive this letter, I suspect I shall have been at sea for some five or six hours. I shall stay at the Excelsior Hotel in Paris for the next month, and I will inform you of my whereabouts after.

Your loving wife,
Leigh Anne

He hadn't thought about that exact moment in many years and was stunned to recall every single line of her sordid letter.

"That was an ugly thing to say," she said with surprising dignity, a wounded look in her eyes.

"I believe it was the truth," he snapped, on the brink of losing his self-control.

"You are such a coward!" she cried. "I, at least, can admit my part in the failure of our marriage. But I have not heard you say, not even once, that you were even partly to blame. I married a man, not a lawyer. And what I wound up with was even less than that!"

"I shared every single dream I had while we were courting," he snarled, feeling very vicious now. "I never hid the fact that I wished to reform society. You married me knowing I was a hardworking man."

"I married you thinking you were going to take a normal job with normal hours! I married you thinking we would have a decent life—not one of poverty! I never dreamed I would be married to a ghost! As a lawyer, you must know you misrepresented yourself."

"You know," he began unbuttoning his nightshirt, furious, "other women do not leave their husbands. Marriage is until death. It became inconvenient for you and you left. You didn't even think to work through a difficult time."

"You don't know what I thought—or what I think. You never have, Rick." Tears filled her lovely eyes and her full lips quivered.

"I don't care what you think anymore, Leigh Anne. And I certainly don't mind our little agreement." He smiled coldly at her and stepped out of the shirt. Her gaze instantly moved over his chest to his manhood. He ignored her and stepped into his long underwear. "I find our arrangement rather convenient. Obviously."

It was a moment before she spoke. "Yes. That is obvious. You will always want me. You always have. That will never change."

"In bed—yes, I rather think I will always want you. And why not?" He began buttoning up his dress shirt. "No one is better in bed, Leigh Anne, but I think you know that."

"I enjoy sex and I am not ashamed to admit it. I enjoy it more with you than with anyone else, especially now," she said, not even blinking. He could tell by her dilated pupils that she would not protest if he dragged her into his bed now.

And because he was tempted to do so, he hated himself and lashed out yet again at her. "Someone taught you well."

"You taught me well, you fool!" she cried, trembling.

He stared, refusing to believe her, never mind the swarm of erotic memories. "You know, I have no trouble bedding you every night, but in six months I am getting my divorce. Nothing will change my mind."

"Right now, I hate you," she panted.

"Then leave." He stared.

"Oh no. I am staying. I am staying, Rick, and no matter how cruel you think to be, how sordid, ugly, and mean, there is nothing you can do to change my mind."

He stared.

She stared back. "Because I think I love you," she said.

Instantly he flung out his arm and knocked an expensive crystal vase and two books from the bureau to the floor.

She flinched.

"Liar," he said.


Francesca stood in the huge entry hall of Hart's home, wringing her hands and telling herself over and over again that she did not have to make any decision now, especially not one that involved her entire future. Her internal protestations fell on her own deaf ears. It was as if the tiny seed of possibility had somehow taken root and become an unmovable and fully grown oak tree. It was as if she had become some kind of puppet on a string, the puppeteer the Devil himself—Hart.

She shivered. If she really married him, could their friendship survive the trials and tribulations of marriage? She now realized how dear to her he had become. She never wanted to jeopardize their friendship.

He came striding into the front hall, clad in a tuxedo, the most handsome man she had ever seen—and would ever see. He was going out, she thought, dismayed. And jealousy overcame her. Which beauty would he be escorting on his arm? Would he bring her back here to his home, or would they go to hers or to some discreet hotel room?

"Francesca!" he cried, smiling broadly.

Instantly she found herself smiling back. He was so obviously thrilled to see her, and her heart turned over, hard. "Hello, Calder."

He grasped both her hands, studied her face, and murmured, "Oh ho. You are as nervous as a hare. I am instantly suspicious, when you appear on my doorstep in such a state of anxiety. What's wrong?"

She wet her lips, tugging her hands free of his. "Nothing. Not really. Well, I have been thinking. But I can see that you are on your way out."

He stared. "I shall be late." He took her arm and looped it in his, held it firmly against his side, and walked her into the same small salon they had been in the other day. Shutting both doors, he faced her. "You are usually the most coherent woman I know."

She tried to smile, failed, and began trembling. "I have been thinking quite a bit."

He smiled briefly in amusement. "Darling, no one thinks more than you. I doubt you ever give that clever brain of yours a rest. I am almost afraid to ask what the subject of your brooding is."

"You."

Now he folded both arms across his broad chest. His smile was gone. "Ah, I see."

She was also hugging herself. "I have been considering your proposal, Hart."

He dropped his arms, staring. He had become still.

She couldn't smile. Her lips felt stiff, like brittle toffee. "It has become tempting," she whispered hoarsely.

He didn't move and he didn't speak.

She wished he would say something. "I . . ." It was hard to speak. She saw herself standing in a church aisle in her wedding gown. She saw Hart at the aisle's end, in his tuxedo, smiling, waiting for her, a minister before him. *What was she doing?*

"Good," he said tersely.

Her gaze flew to his. Their gazes locked. She couldn't look away, she couldn't breathe, and briefly, she could not speak.

He stared. "Are you telling me that you have come to your senses? That you accept my suit?"

She nodded breathlessly.

His set face did not change. Not for a long, breathless moment. And then he began to smile, slowly, a smile that covered his face and reached his eyes. But it wasn't broad. Speculation remained. "I am not going to ask why. I am afraid to know what mental gyrations have brought you to this point in time." But his gaze was filled with a single question now: *Why?*

She wet her lips. "I mean, we hardly have any interests in common and—"

He approached her in a stride, pressed his fingertip to her mouth, silencing her. "Stop. Do not speak and do not move."

She blinked, but he turned and left the room.

Her heart was overpowering her now with its speed. *Oh, dear God, she had done it!* She laid her hand upon her breast but could not calm it. *Oh, God.* She felt as if she were on a runaway locomotive, and even though the choice was hers, she simply did not understand herself. Yet she could not get off the train. Instinct told her to leap and run. For it would crash, she was certain—but she was glued aboard it, for better or for worse.

Suddenly Hart returned, smiling slightly, devilishly. He did not bother to close the doors, pausing before her. "You know, darling, I never did propose."

"What?" She was taken aback until she saw a tiny velvet box in his hand. *Was that what she thought it was? Impossible!* "What's that?" she cried.

He laughed, the sound warm and rich, engulfing her. He put the small jeweler's box down on the side table next to them and clasped both of her hands, bringing them to his mouth. His kiss stirred her completely. "Will you do me the great honor of becoming my wife?" he asked.

Her eyes widened and met his. *And the train picked up speed, dangerously, impossibly, its destination unknown.* "Yes," she heard herself whisper, trembling now with fear and what felt suspiciously like joy.

He smiled, releasing her hands. A moment later he was holding the little box up for her to see, and it was now open. A magnificent pear-shaped diamond engagement ring was there, flanked by three more diamonds on each end.

She stared, wide-eyed. "What's that?"

"Silly woman," he said affectionately, slipping the ring onto her fourth finger.

Her heart stopped. She had a single moment of paralyzing fear, in which Rick Bragg's handsome face assailed her mind, his gaze wounded and accusing. It was instantly followed by his wife's lovely image, and then the unwelcome moment was gone.

She stared at the gorgeous ring—and then up at the gorgeous man looking so intently at her. "Calder, it's beautiful. I don't understand. When did you purchase this?"

"The morning after I realized you were the one," he said.

She stared into his nearly black eyes. Now the navy blue flecks there were highly visible. "I . . . I don't know what to say. How brashly confident you were!"

He laughed. "I never give up when I am on a quest, Francesca," he said, the laughter dying abruptly. He lifted both of her hands again and kissed them. "I will speak to your parents immediately."

"But you are on your way out," she managed, made breathless once more by the feel of his firm lips on her skin.

"My plans for the evening have changed," he murmured, giving her a suddenly intent and very direct and meaningful look.

Her loins filled. She did not move.

He smiled slowly, knowingly. "You may think that we have little in common, but there is something we do have in common, Francesca," he said.

"Yes," she murmured weakly.

He slowly pulled her close. "Does six months meet with your satisfaction?" he asked seductively, taking the lobe of her ear between his teeth and tugging on it gently.

She gasped. And an image of him straining over her, with a very tactile sensation of him filling her, hot and huge and wet, overcame her. Her knees gave way.

He laughed softly and slowly drew his tongue around the inner curves of her ear. "Shall we plan a wedding for six months from now?" he asked huskily.

He was holding her upright. She could not think. She clung to his broad shoulders. "Hart," she gasped.

"Calder, darling, it's Calder."

Of course she knew his name. She closed her eyes, turning her face toward his, awaiting his kiss. But no kiss came. Instead, he nuzzled her throat very gently. She felt his tongue slide over a bruise. She gasped. And somehow her hand slid down, over his rock-hard chest, to grip the waistband of his trousers.

"I hate what he did to you," he suddenly said, against her neck.

"I know," she managed, thinking about what might happen if she dared to move her hand even an inch lower. She was fully aware of what was there. "I'm fine, now," she said.

He kissed her throat, the underside of her jaw, its edge.

She slipped her hand into his trousers and touched the huge, throbbing, bulbous tip of him.

Hart inhaled hard.

"Oh," Francesca whispered, her eyes flying open. She had to explore. "Oh," she said again.

He suddenly lifted her into his arms, used one foot to kick the door closed, and carried her to the sofa. "I can see this will be a very difficult engagement," he said, and in spite of his thick tone, he was laughing.

Six months. He wanted a six-month engagement. Francesca found herself on her back on the sofa, with Hart looming over her. Six months? She might be able to wait six minutes. "Six minutes," she countered, her face feeling as if it were on fire.

His eyes widened. "I beg your pardon?"

She fought for clear and coherent thought. "I mean, six days—er, weeks. Why don't we have a six-week engagement?" Her mind sped as he began to laugh. "I mean, two weeks?"

"Darling, is it that bad?" He stroked his hand over her breasts. Her nipples leaped to attention and her body became rigid. "No one has a two- or even six-week engagement. Your mother would shoot me should I suggest it."

He was rubbing his third finger over one nipple very slowly now, as if he didn't even know what he was doing— which she doubted. She somehow swallowed. "Mama loves you. You may do whatever you wish and she will still adore you."

Now his thumb continued the torture. He continued to smile at her. "Even a wedding six months from now will raise many eyebrows. People will assume I have gotten you pregnant, darling." He suddenly bent, and through the layers of silk and wool, he plucked her nipple with his teeth.

She slipped her hands into his hair and held him there. "Don't stop," she begged, meaning it. "Whatever you do, Calder, don't stop."

He lifted his head and looked her in the eye and said,

"Then it is settled. Six months. That takes us to mid-August. The perfect time for a wedding."

She grabbed his hand and replaced it on her breast. "Fine," she gasped.

He grinned at her.

"Do you enjoy tormenting me?" she cried.

"It is all a part of lovemaking," he whispered.

"Really?" She feigned innocence, touching his strong neck and, for one moment, stroking him there.

He stilled, watchful and waiting now.

She felt a sudden vast power. She slid her hand lower, beneath his tuxedo coat but over his shirt, using the tips of her fingers only. She stroked down his chest, his flat, hard belly, and she paused.

He didn't move. He only watched her face.

She smiled a little, excitement making her faint, and she dared to go lower, until, over his trousers, she traced the outline of his arousal, again and again.

"Somehow, I thought you might be an adept student, Francesca," he murmured.

"You can teach me anything," she whispered, meaning it.

His jaw flexed. His temples throbbed. His eyes had turned coal gray. "And I will," he said. He moved over her then, coming down on top of her, taking her into his embrace, their mouths finally, frantically, fusing.

And when, a long time later, Hart broke away from her, getting up and pacing away in an attempt to compose himself, Francesca smiled. Slowly, her hair rioting down her back, her lips deliciously swollen, her body vibrantly alive, she sat up.

Hart stood facing the empty fireplace, his back to her, his broad shoulders stiff with unrequited and raging desire. He had removed his tuxedo jacket some time ago, and when he finally faced her, his dress shirt perilously wrinkled and unbuttoned to his waist, the hard slabs of his chest completely revealed, he looked more than disheveled. He appeared every inch the notorious womanizer, at once disreputable and oh-so-dangerous to any woman's foolish heart. He did not smile. He looked at her the way no man had ever looked at her before, bar none.

Francesca shivered.

She was marrying Calder Hart. For better or for worse, in six months' time.

Francesca realized that she was smiling.

*AS THE STORY OPENS, Claire Hayden is giving a magnificent party for her husband, but things aren't going well between them. Her marriage is on shaky ground, her husband is mysteriously distracted, and their finances are in trouble. And Claire suspects these problems may go even deeper . . .*

The first guests were just arriving, and everything was as it should be. The decorations were fabulous—a combination of peach-hued rose petals strewn everywhere, even on the furniture, and hundreds of natural-colored candles in various shapes and sizes and clusters on every conceivable surface, all burning softly and giving her entire house a warm, ethereal glow. The bar had been set up in the closest corner of the living area to the entryway, and it looked perfect with flower petals strewn over the table, amongst the bottles and glasses, and over the floor. A waiter in a tuxedo stood at the door with a tray of champagne flutes, and another waiter stood beside him to take wraps, just in case any of the ladies had worn them. The deejay had set up in the back of the living room, and soulful jazz was softly filling the house.

Claire began greeting guests. Her home quickly filled with some of San Francisco's most renowned and wealthy residents; there was also a scattering of Los Angeles media moguls and New York businessmen, mostly high finance types. Claire knew almost everybody, either through David's business or because of the charities she worked so hard for. Her real friends she could count on one hand; still, she socialized frequently, and she genuinely liked many of the people she constantly dealt with.

Claire saw her father as he entered the house. A mental image of the Courbet hanging on her bedroom wall flashed through her mind.

Jean-Leon Ducasse was a tall man with a thick head of white hair. He was a Frenchman who had fought in the Resistance during the Second World War, and although he had immigrated to the States in 1948, he did not, to this day, consider himself an American. Everything about him was very European and Old World. He smiled as he came to Claire and kissed her cheek. "You look wonderful," he said. He had no accent. His nose was large and hooked, but he remained a handsome man, young-looking for his age, his hair iron-gray. No one would guess that he was in his late seventies; he looked sixty, if a day. It never ceased to amaze Claire that so many women still found him attractive. Tonight he was alone. His current girlfriend was an attractive, wealthy widow in her late fifties.

Claire hoped that her worries were not reflected in her eyes. She smiled brightly. "You look great, too, Dad. Where is Elaine?"

"She's in Paris. Shopping, I believe. I was invited to join her, but I did not want to miss David's birthday party." He smiled at her.

Claire thought he was being sardonic. She was almost certain he would not care if he had missed David's birthday. But it was always hard to tell exactly what her father was thinking, or what he meant. Jean-Leon had raised Claire alone; Claire's mother had died when Claire was ten, a victim of breast cancer. He had been preoccupied with teaching and later, after his retirement, with his gallery. And even when he was not teaching at Berkeley, he was either traveling around the world in the pursuit of another masterpiece or new talent, or lecturing at foreign institutions. Claire had been raised by a succession of nannies. They could have been close after her mother had died, but they were not. As a child Claire had never sat on his lap or been told stories at bedtime. "Well, I'm glad you could be here, Dad," she said, still distracted. What kind of trouble could David be in? Surely it wasn't serious.

She prayed it wasn't something illegal.

Jean-Leon was glancing around, taking in her every guest and the decorations. "You have done a very nice job, Claire. As always."

"Thanks, Dad," Claire said softly.

An elderly couple came up to Claire, smiling widely. The woman, Elizabeth Duke, was tall and thin and quite regal in appearance, clad in a red Armani jersey dress, while her husband, who was in his early eighties and about her height, was somewhat stooped. William Duke embraced her first, followed by his wife. "Claire, the decorations are fabulous," Elizabeth cried, smiling. "And that dress suits you to a tee, dear." She wore a large Cartier necklace, set with diamonds. Somehow, she carried the ostentatious piece well.

They were an English couple, with homes in Montecito, Sun Valley, New York and Southampton, as well as San Francisco. Claire had known the Dukes her entire life, or so it seemed. They were avid art collectors, and close friends of her father. Elizabeth had adored Claire's mother.

"Where is that handsome husband of yours?" William Duke asked jovially. He was retired, but the company he and Elizabeth had built from scratch in the fifties and sixties was a private one, with financial holdings and properties all over the world. He was fond of David, and at one time had hoped to have him join his firm. The deal hadn't worked out, but Claire had never known why.

"He'll be down in a minute," Claire said, hiding her concern. Where was he? What was taking so long? She already had a headache. She fervently hoped that David would have changed his mood by the time he came downstairs—and that he would not drink too much that night. I'm in trouble, Claire. "He's running a bit late." She flashed what felt like a brittle smile.

Elizabeth Duke stared. "Is anything wrong, Claire?"

Claire tensed, aware of her father and William regarding her. "It's been a long day," she said, giving what was quickly becoming the party line, but she took Elizabeth's hand and they slipped away.

"I do know that," Elizabeth said kindly. "But don't worry, you know how to plan an event, Claire, as everyone who is anyone knows. I can already see that this evening will be a huge success." She smiled and leaned close. Whispering, she said, "William and I thought long and hard about what to give David for his birthday. We decided that the two of you have been working far too hard. So we are offering you the house in East Hampton for a month over the summer, Claire."

It was a magnificent, fully staffed home with a swimming pool and tennis court on Georgica Pond. Claire grasped Elizabeth's hands, about to thank her. But she never got the two simple words out. Somehow, she knew that she and David were not going to spend a month together in the Dukes' Hampton home. Neither one of them would want to. It would be a month of bickering and arguments. Their marriage was over.

It was suddenly so clear to her that neither one of them had any interest in salvaging it. It had been over for years.

*Oh, God*, was her next single thought. She smiled at Elizabeth but did not even see her.

"Claire? I know you and David are struggling right now," Elizabeth said kindly. "This might be good for you both."

Claire was an expert at keeping her emotions reined in. She worked hard to keep a sunny façade in place. Perhaps she had learned to do so when her mother had died so suddenly, leaving her, for all intents and purposes, alone. She had certainly felt alone when Cynthia passed away, because her father had felt like such a stranger. Or maybe her father had taught her by example how to remain calm and composed no matter what. How to shove any feelings of a personal or emotional nature far, far away. Now, Claire felt a sudden lump of grief rising up, hard and fast, impossibly potent. It was accompanied by a real and terrible fear.

"I'm sure it will," Claire said automatically, not even aware of what she was saying.

"Everything will work out," Elizabeth said softly. "I am sure of it."

Claire knew she was wrong. "Yes, it will." She had to hold it together, she had to keep it all in. *Divorce*. The word loomed now in her mind. It was engraved there.

Elizabeth squeezed her hand. Claire watched her rejoin William, and found herself facing her father. Claire felt uncomfortable, hoping he hadn't overheard them, and then he said, "I heard you are short a few VIPs for Summer Rescue Kids."

This was a welcome subject. "I am."

"I think I can help. I have a client who's new in town. I'll feel him out for you."

"Thank you, Dad," Claire said, far too fervently.

He seemed to be looking right through her. No, he was looking past her. "And here's your errant husband," Jean-Leon added softly.

Claire's gaze whipped to David, who was approaching, and then back to her father. What had that comment meant? But Jean-Leon only smiled at her and Claire turned her attention back to David.

He was more than handsome and self-assured in his dark gray suit, and the pale blue shirt and yellow tie did amazing things for his leading-man good looks. More than a few women were craning their necks to glimpse him more fully. As David paused to shake hands and accept congratulations, Claire stared. He was beaming as he accepted hearty back slaps from his male friends and soft kisses from their wives and girlfriends. Finally, he seemed to be genuinely enjoying himself.

David reached her father. His smile never faltered, but Claire knew it was a pretense. She watched them shake hands. "Happy Birthday, David," Jean-Leon said smoothly.

"Thank you."

"I hope you like your birthday gift."

David extracted his hand. "What can I say? That was so generous of you."

"So you do like it?" Jean-Leon's tone never changed, but he seemed to be pressing—and Claire suddenly tensed.

"It's a masterpiece. Who wouldn't like it?" David returned, his smile frozen.

Claire stepped to his side, glancing anxiously from one man to the other. Clearly there was a subtext to their exchange, but just what was it?

"Then I am very pleased. Where did you hang it?"

"In the bedroom," David said.

"Hmm," was Jean-Leon's response. "A shame. A painting like that should be on public display." He turned his stare on Claire. "You should hang it in the living room, Claire."

Claire had the feeling that if she agreed with her father she would be disagreeing with David. And that was the last thing she wished to do just then. "How about a drink, Dad?"

"Fine." Jean-Leon ambled away, moving into the crowd, greeting those he knew. David stared after him. So did Claire.

"Sometimes he really bugs me," David said.

Claire jerked. "What is going on? How could you argue with him now?"

David just looked at her. "He can be a pompous ass."

"That's not fair," she began.

"Oh, cut it out, Claire. You know that because he's brilliant in the world of art, he thinks he's smarter than everyone else—including you and me. But you know what? If it weren't for your mother, he wouldn't be where he is today.

Her money bought him his success. Her money made him what he is today."

"David!" Claire was aghast. "He's my father! How can you say such things?"

He gave her a look. "Let's do what we have to do. Smile, Claire. This was *your* idea." He walked away.

She stared after him, his last nasty comment making her as angry as she had been earlier in their bedroom upstairs. She did not deserve such barbs. And he had no right to talk about her father the way that he had. His accusations were hurting her now, even though they were partially true. It was no secret that Jean-Leon had started both his gallery and his art collection with her mother's generous support. But wasn't that what spouses did for one another?

Claire watched David greeting the Dukes. He seemed a bit curt with them, she thought, and then she turned away. The night had only just begun, but she needed a moment to herself. She had a massive headache, and she was beginning to feel ill in the pit of her stomach. She hurried down the hall and into the sanctuary of the den.

The doors were open. It was a big room with the same smooth, pale oak floors as the rest of the house, but unlike the rest of the house, most of the room was done entirely in soft, natural earth tones. Claire plopped down on a rust-colored leather ottoman, cradling her face in her hands. Her marriage was a charade. There was just no point in it anymore. It was really over.

And David wouldn't care if she raised the subject of a divorce. Claire was certain. She refused to abandon him if he was in the kind of trouble he claimed to be, but they could separate until the crisis—whatever it was—passed.

Claire began to tremble. She stared down at her shaking knees and realized she was finally losing it.

"I'm sorry. I didn't realize anyone was in here," a man's voice said.

Claire leapt to her feet in surprise. A man had walked into the middle of the room and he was regarding her curiously.

Immediately Claire smiled, wishing he would turn around and leave. She vaguely recalled greeting him at the front door, but did not have a clue as to who he was. Somehow she managed to walk over as if nothing were wrong, hand outstretched. To her horror, her hand was shaking. She slid it into his anyway, praying he would not notice. "I'm certain we met. I'm your hostess, Claire Hayden."

He shook her hand, the contact briefly and vaguely surprising her. But his gaze dipped to her trembling hand. "Yes, we did, Mrs. Hayden," he said, no longer smiling. He was grave. "Ian Marshall. I'm a friend of your husband's."

Claire pulled her hand free, aware of flushing. But it was too warm in the den. "Claire." She smiled automatically.

"I hope I'm not interrupting, Claire?" His gaze was searching.

Claire had the unwelcome notion that he knew she was crumbling bit by bit beneath her immaculate exterior. "I was going to make a phone call. I'm with the Humane Society, and I wanted to check on a stray we picked up that had been hit by a car," Claire said lightly, hoping that he would take the hint and leave.

He did not.

In fact, he just stood there, regarding her. He was a tall man, six-foot or so, with dark hair that was neither too short nor too long. He was clad in an impeccable suit, as were most of the guests that evening. His shoulders were very broad and Claire knew the suit had to be custom-made. Claire realized she was staring, but then, so was he. She also realized that the room was too quiet. "Can I help you?" she tried.

"I think you don't like parties, Claire," he said.

Claire felt her eyes widen as their gazes locked. His kind tone was like a hair trigger, and she turned away, even more shaken. "Of course I like parties." But he was right. Parties were a part of her work. Rarely were they social events, and a time to eat, drink, or be merry. Parties were an opportunity to raise badly needed funds for important causes, or to pay back or laud those who had helped her in the past. Claire would never let anyone hold a party for her. Her last official birthday party had been when she was sixteen.

"Just not this one?" he prodded.

She whirled. "It's my husband's birthday," she stressed. "It's a wonderful evening for us both." To her horror, her tone cracked on the last syllable.

"It's okay. I know how tough these things can be." His tone was kind, his gaze unwavering.

Claire felt her control disintegrate. Just like that, in an instant. To her horror, tears filled her eyes. She turned away before he could see.

"Hey. Don't cry," he said softly, from behind her.

Claire couldn't answer. How could this be happening now? She fought to hold back a flood of tears. *If she divorced David, she would be alone again.*

But their marriage was over. She had seen it in his eyes, and she felt it, too.

*She had been alone her entire life. When she had married, she had never wanted to be alone again.*

But she was different now. She was a strong and successful woman. She was not a frightened, bereaved child.

"Here."

Claire saw a tissue being dangled over her right shoulder. She accepted it gratefully and while she was dabbing at her eyes, she heard him wander past her. He was giving her some space with which to compose herself, but he was not leaving her, either. Claire peeked at him out of the corner of her eye and saw him studying the seascape above the mantel. Her heart seemed to kick her in the chest.

It was the most shocking sensation.

Claire stared at him, stunned.

He faced her with a smile. "That's better. Beautiful women crying make me all nervous and jittery. I have a whole bunch of sisters, and every single one of them loves to cry."

She had to smile. "How many sisters do you have?"

"Four. All younger than me." He grinned. His dimples

were charming—they made him look as if he smiled all the time.

"Growing up must have been chaotic."

"It was hell. Pure and simple hell." He smiled at her and winked. Then seriously, he said, "I've got big, broad shoulders. Feel free to use them any time."

She felt herself beginning to blush. Worse, he seemed to mean it. "I'm fine now, Mr. Marshall. Truly, I am. I don't know what happened. I never get so emotional." She could not look away from his eyes. They were green.

"Ian, please. And all women are emotional. Trust me, I know."

She smiled. "I'm not emotional." She was firm.

"I doubt that." He wasn't smiling now. "Any woman who dedicates her life to bettering the worlds of kids and dogs has a huge and bleeding heart."

She stared. "How do you know what I do?"

"I'm a friend of David's," he said. "Remember?"

Something had changed, and Claire didn't know how or when it had happened. The room was still. Everything felt silent and unreal. Claire was very aware of the man standing just a few feet away from her; his presence seemed to charge the air around her.

"Is there anything I can do?" he asked seriously. "Can I somehow make this a better evening?"

She was amazed. He really meant it. "No." Her smile became wide and genuine. "Not unless you can make the clock strike midnight?"

He smiled in return. "Well, I could sneak around the house and change all the clocks."

"But all the men are wearing wristwatches."

"We could tell the bartender to pour triples."

Her eyes widened. "Souse them all!" she cried.

"And no cake," he added, dimples deepening.

"No cake. To hell with the birthday," Claire agreed fervently.

"There's always that yacht my friend has moored in the

Marina—we can probably see the Lady Anne from your terrace." His gaze was penetrating.

Claire's smile froze. Her heart lurched with an awareness she should not have. An image of her and this stranger jumping into a car, driving down the hill, and sneaking aboard his friend's yacht, hand in hand and barefoot, filled her mind. She stared at him.

"I'm sorry." His gaze was searching. "I was only joking."

Had it been a joke? She hesitated. "I hate to say it, but the idea is tempting."

He didn't speak. He waited.

Claire realized that if she said, "Let's go," he would take her hand, and they would. *It was so tempting.*

They stared at one another. Claire could hear her own heart beating. She was actually considering leaving her own party and doing the unthinkable.

He looked past her, towards the door.

Claire didn't have to look to know who was there, and she stiffened. Reality hit her like cold water splashing in her face. She turned.

David stood on the threshold of the room. "Claire!"

Claire's shoulders stiffened as if someone had placed a heavy yoke on them; she faced her husband. "Yes?" She was going to ask for a divorce. Soon—not that night, because it was his birthday, but tomorrow, or the next day.

"Everyone's asking for you," David returned, glancing from her to Marshall and back again. The glance seemed hostile if not suspicious.

Claire hesitated, surprised. She looked from David to Ian again. Her husband hadn't spoken to Ian, but he was regarding him coolly, and Claire knew jealousy had nothing to do with his coldness. David had never been jealous of her when it came to other men. He knew she would never betray him that way.

Ian smiled. "Hello, David," he said. "Happy birthday. I brought you a little something I think you will appreciate. I left it in the hall."

David's nod was curt, his words tight and cut off. "Marshall. Thank you. Let's go, Claire."

Claire was bewildered. Clearly David did not like Ian Marshall. Had a deal gone bad? It wasn't like him to be so rude. She walked over to her husband, but smiled at Ian Marshall. "Shall we join the others?" But what she really wanted to say was, thank you.

"Of course," he said, with an answering smile. But his eyes were on David and they were filled with wariness.

Claire didn't like it at all. The tension between the two men was unmistakable, and the only question was why.


Guests were finally leaving; the party had been a huge success. Claire judged it to be such because most of her guests were smiling and happy and pleasantly inebriated. After the buffet dinner, many of them had even danced to seventies rock 'n' roll on the terrace beneath the glowing full moon. Most important, no one had seemed to notice her dismal mood or the fact that she and David hardly spoke to one another.

About thirty people remained. It had gotten cold outside, which was usually the case in the Bay Area, and everyone had clustered in the living area, mostly seated on the various couches, chairs and ottomans, after-dinner drinks in hand. David was playing a jazz tune on the grand piano. He was a gifted pianist, but he had never pursued his talent. Even having had more than his fair share of wine and vodka, he was playing splendidly.

Claire wished he hadn't gotten drunk. Recently—or not so recently?—he had started to slur a little when he was drinking, and to stagger just a bit. Claire studied him as he switched to an Elton John tune and began to sing. Two women were standing beside him, the blonde clearly mesmerized by him. They started to sing, too.

Claire turned and saw Jean-Leon watching her. He glanced at David and then back at her, shaking his head with disgust.

Claire tensed. She gave her father a reassuring smile and turned away. She left the party, and at the stairs, she slid off her sandals. Her feet were hurting her.

The night seemed to have become endless; she was exhausted, yet eager for a new day. And with the eagerness was anxiety and fear. She was really going to ask for a divorce. She was going to leave David, and somehow, be alone.

It was frightening and it was thrilling.

Slowly, she went upstairs, gold sandals dangling from one hand. At least she could stop smiling now.

On the upstairs landing Claire came face to face with Ian Marshall. "Good God!" She cried, her hand on her palpitating heart.

"I'm sorry," he said quickly, clearly as stunned to meet her as she was. "I didn't mean to scare you—you surprised me, too."

Claire's pulse slowed, returning to normal, as their gazes met and held. He smiled at her. "Tough night, huh?" He glanced at the sandals with their precarious heels and tiny straps dangling from her fingertips, but then his gaze sharpened, moving quickly back to her face.

Claire could only stare at him, recovering some of her surprise. What was he doing upstairs? The party was downstairs. Claire smiled a little. "It's insanity, isn't it? What a woman does for glamour."

"Not really. That dress is a knockout."

Claire's heart leapt at his words.

"But I'd bet anything you look great in a pair of jeans and a T-shirt," he said, and his smile faded. "What's wrong, Claire?"

She did not move. "What are you doing upstairs?"

His gaze moved over her features slowly. His smile faded a bit as he understood. "I'm not snooping, Claire. Someone was in the powder room downstairs and the staff directed me to the bathroom in the guest room up here."

Claire shook her head. "There's another bathroom in the den."

"It was also occupied."

She met his gaze. "I see." She was relieved—but of course, what had she been thinking? He was too nice to have been snooping around her home. "What do you do, Ian?" she asked curiously, leaning against the wall.

"I'm a consultant. Generally for firms who do business in Europe or the Middle East. In fact, I just got back from Tel Aviv a few days ago."

Claire nodded; that hardly gave her a clue as to what his profession was.

He touched her bare arm briefly. "You seem tired. Are you calling it a night?"

Claire shivered and looked up at him. The urge to ask him to drive down to his friend's yacht suddenly overcame her. The evening had been a hard one. She hadn't had a single chance to relax, and it *would* be relaxing, even fun, to sit with this man and sip champagne in peace and quiet. Of course, it was also an impossible and forbidden notion. "I wish I could. There's still a good two dozen guests downstairs."

"They're pretty happy down there. I don't think anyone would know if you slipped off to bed." His smile faded.

Claire knew he hadn't been making an innuendo, but the word "bed" made her flush, and she thought—but wasn't sure—he was thinking about that word, too. Claire knew when men were attracted to her. She was aware of being a pretty woman, and she knew Ian found her attractive. With her marriage in its death throes, she felt vulnerable and even afraid of herself.

But she would never cross any inappropriate lines until she was divorced.

She swallowed. "Did you have a good time tonight?"

"Yes, I did. And thank you for asking." His gaze found and held hers.

"I'm glad you enjoyed yourself," she said fiercely, meaning it. Their gazes caught again.

This time, he didn't speak. He just smiled at her, as if he liked her a lot and did not want to end the moment.

Claire felt herself flushing. It was time to go and there were no ifs, ands, or buts about it.

His gaze wandered over her, lingering on her dangling sandals. "David is a very lucky man."

"Are you flirting with me?" She smiled because he was and she needed it.

"Is it a crime? You're blushing, Claire. It's nice."

"It's nice to have a nice man flirting with me," she said truthfully.

His eyes widened. "It must happen all the time!" he exclaimed.

"Not really," she said.

He shook his head. "Go figure."

Claire laughed. It was her first real laugh of the evening.

He smiled. "You even have a nice laugh." His smile vanished. "I had better go." And he gave her a long look.

Claire tensed, certain she knew what that look meant. Just as she was being swept away by a flirtation with him, he was being swept away, too. And he did not trust himself either.

As they stood there, sounds were drifting up from outside, coming around from the front of the house. Good-byes. Car doors slamming. Engines revving.

"Good night," he said quickly, and turned and was gone.

"Good night," Claire murmured as he disappeared down the hall. She leaned against the wall, feeling as if she had been run over by a truck. Would their paths cross again? She very much hoped they would.

It was a long moment before she moved. Instead, she replayed their two encounters over and over again in her mind, as if she were a teenage girl with a very severe crush. When she realized what she was doing, she laughed at herself, because she was thirty-two, not twelve. Claire went into her bedroom for another pair of shoes.

A moment later, Claire paused on the threshold of the living room. A dozen guests remained, but all were in the process of leaving.

She sighed. Jean-Leon was chatting with the Dukes in

the foyer. The turquoise-clad blonde who had been hanging all over David for most of the night was slipping on a wrap. Claire suddenly realized that David was nowhere to be seen. Puzzled, she walked to the foyer and said good night to the blonde.

Her name was Sherry. "I had a wonderful time," she gushed.

"I'm glad," Claire said, wondering if she were sleeping with David. It would not surprise her.

Sherry thanked her, glancing past Claire as if looking for someone—and Claire knew she was looking for David. A moment later she left.

"It was a great party," Elizabeth said to her. "And it's so late! We have to go. Claire, we will talk tomorrow."

Claire nodded as William hugged her. "Dear, once again, you have outdone yourself. The food, the wines, everything was superb. More important, you are superb." He smiled at her. "Have brunch with us on Sunday?"

"I'll try." Too late, Claire realized she had said "I," instead of "we." The Dukes stepped out to their waiting car and driver.

Claire said another series of good-byes, then turned to her father. "Have you seen David?" One more couple was putting on their coats, and the bartender was finishing breaking down the bar.

"No, I haven't. He's drunk, Claire," Jean-Leon said with disapproval.

Claire sighed. "I know. Maybe he went up the back stairs and to bed."

Her father kissed her cheek. "I hope David knows how fortunate he is to have you as his wife. The party went well, Claire. No thanks to him."

Claire smiled, refusing to buy into the subject, and said good-bye. Finally, all of her guests were gone.

Promptly Claire kicked off her lower sandals as the last two waiters left the house with the last of their equipment. The caterer came up to her. "Everything's done," she said. "The leftovers are put away, dishes and glasses ready for party rentals to pick up first thing tomorrow, and the kitchen as clean as a whistle." She smiled at Claire.

Claire thanked the slim, middle-aged woman, whom she used often for various events. "Thank you so much, Mrs. Lewis. Once again, everything was just perfect."

Mrs. Lewis beamed. Then she said, "Do try to relax a bit, Mrs. Hayden. I can see you're not yourself these past few days."

Claire stared after her. Could everyone tell that her marriage was over? Could she no longer hide her true feelings? Disturbed, Claire went to the front door and locked it.

She sighed. The party was over. Everyone had enjoyed himself, even David. The night had been a success.

She thought about Ian Marshall and smiled a little.

Don't go there, she told herself sternly. It was only a harmless flirtation.

But somehow, she knew it was more.

Claire turned off all the downstairs lights except for one in the hall. The house was so quiet and still after the party, when just moments ago it had been filled with conversation and music and so many people. She walked upstairs quietly, not wanting to wake David, but certain that he wouldn't wake up even if she did make noise. The quiet engulfed her. It should have been peaceful. Instead, unease prickled at her.

She flicked on the light in the bedroom.

The king-sized bed was empty.

It wasn't even slept on.

Claire stared at it, for a moment unable to comprehend that David wasn't there, asleep. *Where was he?*

Claire was concerned. This was so odd. Her nape seemed to prickle again. Claire went back into the hallway, turning on the lights to chase the last of the upstairs shadows away. Now she was acutely aware of the house being too silent around her. The dogs were kenneled in the yard out back. She was alone in the house—but no, that wasn't true. David was in the house. Except—the house *felt* empty.

That was impossible. David had passed out somewhere,

she decided with a flash of anger. Gripping the railing, she hurried downstairs.

It was so dark, and there were shadows everywhere.

"David?" Claire called, turning on lights one by one as she entered the living room. She did not expect him to be there, and he was not.

She turned on the last hall light and walked down to the den. Claire pushed open the door, which was slightly ajar, and hit the wall switch, flooding the room with light. "David?" But he wasn't there, either.

On impulse, she checked that bathroom—it was empty. Her heart began to thud in her chest. Where could he be?

He's only passed out somewhere, she told herself, trying not to become frightened.

Claire hesitated before the home office they shared. What if he had fallen and hurt himself?

Then she pushed open the door, quickly fumbling for the light, praying that he would be asleep on the couch inside. It came on and she looked around, but the office was empty.

She felt unbearably alone. Worse than ever before.

Claire hugged herself. Somehow, she knew that she really was alone in the house. It was a sickening feeling. Panic assailed her, making her dizzy.

*She needed to get the dogs.* But to get to the kennels she had to cross the back yard, and she was afraid to step out of the house and into the looming night.

Claire thought she felt movement behind her. She whirled. The threshold was vacant. It had been her imagination, nothing more.

*Where was David? Where could he be?*

*Was she really alone in the house?*

Claire now ran through the entire house, to the kitchen and dining room on the other side. As the caterer had said, her kitchen was as clean as a whistle—no one would ever know that she'd had a party that night. And it, too, was empty.

Panicked, Claire stepped into the dining room. This time she didn't bother to turn on the light; the illumination from the kitchen showed that it was empty. *What was happening?*

She rushed to the phone and called her father, but there was no answer. He lived in the city—he should be home at any minute. She decided not to worry him and did not leave a message. But she would kill David when she found him, she decided.

Claire hesitated, then unlocked the kitchen door, telling herself that there was nothing to be afraid of. She turned on the outside lights. The back yard brightened, and across it, she could see the wire kennels. The dogs had awoken and they began to bark.

Claire left the kitchen door wide open and ran across the yard to the kennels. She let out the dogs, hugging them all. She was shaking. "Where's David? Hey, Jill? Help me find David," she cried.

The dogs seemed very happy, oblivious to her worries, and they raced ahead of her and into the kitchen, all except for her beautiful purebred poodle.

Jilly paused, sniffing the air, and she began to growl.

Claire didn't know what to think. Jilly was a very intelligent dog, and a great watchdog as well. "What is it?" she asked hoarsely.

Jilly growled again—and she took off.

Not into the kitchen, but behind the house, disappearing toward the terrace. The terrace where, just an hour ago, her guests had been dancing beneath the moon and the stars.

Frantic, territorial barking sounded from the terrace where Jilly had just disappeared. Claire needed a flashlight. She didn't have one and she couldn't think where one was. Filled with fear, Claire headed after her dog. She reminded herself as she turned the corner of the house that her neighborhood was absolutely safe. But she knew something had happened, otherwise her dog would not be so upset. It crossed her mind to call the police, but what would she say? She reached the terrace behind the house and fortunately, the lights she had turned on inside the living room shone directly upon it. Relief filled her.

David was passed out in a chair at the terrace's farthest end.

Damn him! Claire thought furiously, not knowing whether to cry or shout.

Jilly had halted a dozen feet from him, and she continued to bark wildly. Now the other dogs came barreling over to him, and they began to bark as well, causing pandemonium. *They were barking at David.*

Claire stiffened. Why were the dogs so upset? "David?" Claire hesitated as the barking escalated in urgency. David did not move, and granted, he'd had a lot to drink, but shouldn't the noise awaken him now? She broke into a run.

Claire reached David and had a flashing premonition, but she grabbed him anyway and his head fell back—and that was when she saw the blood.

His throat was sliced open. *Bloody and sliced open.*

Blood covered his neck, his shirt, his chest.

*He was lifeless.*

She screamed.

———

BRENDA LOVES TO HEAR FROM HER READERS. YOU CAN E-MAIL BRENDA AT WWW.BRENDAJOYCE.COM, AS WELL AS ENTER HER LATEST CONTEST. DON'T MISS IT!

DON'T MISS

# DOUBLE TAKE

BY

## BRENDA JOYCE

**AVAILABLE IN HARDCOVER
IN JULY 2003
FROM ST. MARTIN'S PRESS**